Stormy Leigh

Stormy Leigh

by
Sharon Foster

Virtue BOOKS

A Division of Harrison House Publishers
Tulsa, Oklahoma

Stormy Leigh
ISBN 0-89274-535-5
Copyright © 1988 by Sharon Foster
Route 2, Box 363
West Plains, Missouri 65775

Published by Virtue Books
A Division of Harrison House Publishers
P. O. Box 35035
Tulsa, Oklahoma 74153

Contents

1	An Icy Encounter	7
2	Home for the Holidays	21
3	The Prodigal	31
4	A Visit to Westmoor Heights	43
5	An Unwelcome Guest	59
6	The Christmas Gift	69
7	How Stormy Got Her Name	79
8	The Ways of the World	89
9	A Matter of Forgiveness	99
10	The Valley of Decision	111
11	Two Worlds in Collision	121
12	A Birthday That Holds Many Surprises	141
13	The Best Laid Plans	159
14	A Truce Is Declared	175
15	A Working Vacation	193
16	A Need for Perfect Peace	209
17	The Truth Is Exposed	223
18	Some Hopes Go Up in Smoke	237
19	Love Your Neighbor	249
20	Days of Trouble	265
21	The Course of True Love	285
22	Burning Some Bridges	297

23 An Old-Fashioned Hayride   303
24   Foreclosure Threatened   313
25 Loss of a Good Friend   319
26 Plain Talk From Mother   325
27 Making Peace With God   339
28 An Answer to Prayer   351
29 A Double Wedding   363
30 Living Happily Ever After   369

Stormy Leigh

1
An Icy Encounter

Without taking her eyes from the icy road, Leigh switched the radio to a different station. The soft, mellow strains of a nostalgic Christmas song drifted about her. She relaxed against the back of the seat with a deep sigh. The song made her feel sad in a way and suited her mood exactly. Slipping long fingers through the soft red curls that clung to her forehead, she swept them back impatiently. There were more miles behind than ahead of her, and she was tired and irritable.

The road stretched before her like a silver ribbon, winding and twisting through lonely, snow-whitened hills. It seemed hours since she had seen another motorist. She felt like a snow goose starting south too late, winging her way alone, weary and forsaken. If she had not thought it childish, she would have expressed her frustration to the cold world around her by honking loudly.

A quick glance at her watch showed her she was running a little behind schedule. Her foot pressed harder on the accelerator. She had planned to make an early start, but just as she was leaving, the telephone rang. She had been tempted to ignore it, and now she wished she had as the bitter memory of the call returned. She recalled the conversation with tears.

* * *

"Hello?"

"Leigh?"

"Yes."

"This is Cliff," he said. "Do you have a few minutes?"

"No, Cliff, I don't," she answered coolly, conveying by her tone that the harsh words spoken the last time they talked had not been forgotten.

"Please, Leigh! I need to talk to you. Couldn't I come over? Just for a few minutes?"

His soft, persuasive voice held a hint of impatience, and she hardened her heart.

"I'm leaving in a minute, Cliff. We can talk when I get back," she said, making her voice unfriendly.

However, the longing to see him and be with him caused the words to catch in her throat. Determining not to give in, she forced herself to remember the incident that had precipitated their last argument. While she was remembering, Cliff continued to remonstrate with her over the phone.

"But, Leigh! You *know* how much I want you to go home with me this weekend. Please, can't we just let bygones be bygones?"

He sounded sincere, and she had waited for this invitation so long that she almost relented. But the memory of Denise in a skimpy, blue evening gown, walking into the restaurant on Cliff's arm made her see red again.

"Do you really think I would accept your invitation now?" she had cried scornfully. "Why don't you ask Denise? I'm sure she would be more than happy to go."

As she thought about the phone call, she was glad that he had not been able to see the shimmering tears she had dashed away with a shaking hand or the sudden quiver of her soft, full lips.

"I told you Denise doesn't mean a thing to me. What more can I say?" he retorted, angry at not immediately getting his own way.

Heedless of his rising temper, she gritted her teeth and said coldly, "Then I'd like to know why you took her out and lied about it!"

"I took her out because she has been hounding me for months. You know she has! You've seen her hanging around me. You even commented on it. I didn't tell you because I thought you would make a scene — and I was right!"

His words bit into her, piercing her heart. She closed her eyes in pain, refusing to voice the accusations that came hurtling to her lips.

"But, Leigh," he began to wheedle, as if suddenly aware that his harsh tone had revealed a trait he wished to keep hidden, "you shouldn't let one friendly dinner with another girl bother you. You know you mean the world to me. Come on! Say you'll go home with me. We'll have lots of fun. I promise."

Leigh kept silent on her end of the phone realizing that he had lied to her. Also, he did not seem to think she should care if he dated another girl on the sly. She had considered them to be practically engaged, but evidently that did not mean as much to him. Suddenly, she saw his weekend proposal in a different light. It was a casual invitation offered in the hope of soothing her hurt feelings. Her brown eyes flashed dangerously. She was not going to be soft-soaped that easily!

"Come on, Leigh. What do you say?"

"I say no, Cliff. I'm going home. I'll see you when I get back." Her voice was firm, but she felt sick inside as if something she held dear and precious suddenly had become cheap and common.

He threatened sullenly, "I wouldn't be too sure of that. If you can't take a little competition now and then..."

"Competition!" she sputtered furiously. "Is that what you call it? I call it cheating! The least you could have done was be honest with me."

"Well, I would have, if you weren't an old-fashioned prude," he had snarled.

She laughed bitterly, "There was a time when you called those 'old-fashioned virtues' a part of my charm."

That remark silenced him. Apparently fearing he had said too much, he once again changed tactics.

"I'm sorry I said that, Honey. Please don't be mad."

She said nothing, waiting as he plowed on uncertainly, not knowing quite how to win her back.

"Forgive me, Leigh. I just got mad and lost control. I'm really sorry."

"Goodbye, Cliff," she said softly, and hung up the receiver.

* * *

A scalding tear splashed in her lap, recalling her to the present. She had no idea how much time had elapsed or how far she had traveled during her painful memories of Cliff's inexcusable behavior.

Through blinding tears, she saw a school bus approaching. Suddenly the bus slipped sideways on a patch of ice, and she panicked. All the experience and confidence gained in the years of driving on this kind of road deserted her. Her reflexes took over as her tired brain reacted automatically to exaggerated danger signals caused by blurred vision. She whipped the wheel toward the ditch, slammed the brake to the floorboard — and knew immediately she had made a mistake. The school bus straightened out as her car left the road. She jerked her foot off the brake, but it was too late.

Too scared to do anything except hang on, she watched helplessly as her little car leaped a ditch and headed for a fence. Frantically, she tried to steer toward an open gate she saw on her left, and the car spun in a complete circle before shooting through the small opening. Bumping across the rough field, her car careened toward a big pond. Her foot hit the brake again, and the car slid to the edge of the pond with its wheels locked in silent protest.

"Well, of all the stupid things to do!" she fumed in utter disgust.

"I know better than that," and she stared in frustration at the icy pond now splintered by a long crack running from beneath the car's front wheels.

"It'll be dark by the time I get home, and Mother and Dad will be worried sick. It's all your fault, Clifford Callahan," she stormed, determined to place the blame on the man who had betrayed her trust.

"If you had not upset me so much before I left, I would've had my mind on my driving!"

A soft sound outside the window startled her, and she turned to see a pair of big, soft eyes looking in at her. A thick, moist tongue curiously licked the car, goading her into action.

"Move out of the way, you stupid beast," she grunted, trying to open her door. "Don't you know your tongue is liable to stick to the car if you don't stop that? And I don't need any wet slobbers to freeze on my windows. Now, move it!"

The brown cow lumbered awkwardly backwards as the tall young woman stepped out of the car. Her hair caught the fire of the sun, as she placed her hands on shapely hips. She scowled at the big gentle creature as if it somehow was to blame for the whole unfortunate incident. Then her shoulders relaxed.

She reached out wanting to stroke the velvety nose and crooned in a low, husky voice, "It's not your fault, Brownie. It's all mine. You can't help it if I did a dumb thing, can you?"

The girl, the cow, and the little red car looking like a feather in the cap of the pond presented an odd-looking combination to the big man at the crest of the road. He was traveling behind her when the car skidded out of control and left the road. Some farmer must have forgotten to close the gate when he finished feeding his cattle, but good had come of his oversight.

Uttering a quick prayer for the driver's safety, he parked his truck and ran to look down the embankment. Frowning as his eyes traced the car's path through the snow, he breathed a sigh of relief when he saw the tableau in the snow-covered meadow.

He began to wade across the pasture toward the girl. She did not seem to be hurt, neither was her car nor the cow! He smiled faintly. She probably was upset about her plight, although as he had been in a position to see, her drastic action had been totally unnecessary. His concern gave way to amusement.

"That was quite a ride you took, Miss," he said as he neared her, his smile widening into a mischievous grin.

Leigh's head shot up as she whirled to face the big man approaching her with long strides. Her own height had given her a sense of equality with all of the men in her world. But this man was larger than any man she knew, and his size put her on guard. Thoroughly irritated by the whole situation, she did not take kindly to the laughter she heard in his voice.

"It was unavoidable," she snapped defensively, unwilling to admit even to a stranger that she had made an error in judgment. She glared at him, daring him to disagree with her.

"Oh, really!" he drawled, his bushy, black brows raised skeptically. "Pardon me, Miss, but it's ladies like you who lend truth to the term, 'women drivers'."

"Wh-why! How dare you!" she spat out, stamping a booted foot. "Who do you think you are to be talking to me like that? I didn't ask for any help from you, and I'll thank you to leave me alone!" Her blood was boiling, and her cheeks blazed with color.

"Well, Miss," he shoved his cowboy hat back on his head, "maybe you *should* ask for my help, seeing as you've gotten yourself in quite a fix."

His smile flashed again as he folded his arms and studied her furious face. But she was blind to his attractiveness. She took his teasing smile as mockery and his folded arms as male egotism, and she itched to knock him down. However, the temptation quickly dissolved under his bold eyes and the uncomfortable idea that she would have more success knocking down a granite mountain. She looked at him speculatively and determined to put him in his place with feminine coldness and scorn, which only seemed to further amuse him.

"Thank you, Sir, but I can *manage* on my own."

"All right, let's see you," he chuckled as she rammed doubled fists into the pockets of her jacket.

He continued to stand and watch as she studied the situation. She drew in a deep breath of frigid air and wished he would go away.

Finally, she whirled on him, yelling in frustration, "Are you just going to stand there and watch? I told you I don't need any help. Now, please *go away*," and she shot a vicious look at him, but he refused to budge.

"Am I making you nervous?" he asked softly.

He knew there was no way she could back the car out of the pond. Its front tires were too deeply mired in icy mud. But far be it from him to try to stop her determined efforts. She would reach the same conclusion soon enough. Besides, she did not look as if she would take his word for it *without* checking it out for herself.

"Are you kidding? *You* make *me* nervous?"

Her glare was a withering laser that would have reduced a smaller man into a puddle at her feet, but it seemed to bounce off him like the soft stare of a doe. She stamped her feet briskly to rid them of snow. Then with another angry look at the grinning spectator, she jerked open the car door and slid inside. At a sharp twist of her wrist, the sturdy little engine roared into life. She slammed the gearshift into reverse. Her foot connected solidly with the accelerator, and she rammed it to the floorboard.

But the car was no match for the mud. Instead of moving out of the morass, when she revved the engine, the tires plowed steadily downward until the front bumper rested on the ice. The car sank deeper as Leigh revved the engine. As she rolled down the window and leaned out to see the wheels, a shadow fell across her face. Placing one big, calloused hand on her door, he bent over to look her in the eye. His other hand reached past her to turn off the key.

"This sure is a little car for such a big girl," he teased, with a glint in his dark blue eyes.

"I'll have you know this car is perfect for me," she sputtered indignantly, outraged that he would comment

14

on her size as if she were too big. He probably was one of those men who, great hulk though *he* was, preferred petite blondes.

"Just teasing," he said smoothly, the faint twist of his lips letting her know he was aware he had scored again. He backed away from the door and stooped down to assess the situation better. The late afternoon sun glistened on his black curls as he swept his hat from his head. The sound of her deep, long-suffering sigh struck his ear, and he rose to his great height with a smothered grin tugging at his mouth.

"Looks as if I'll have to go get the truck and pull you out," he said cheerfully. "Unless, of course," he leaned toward her to catch another dark look as she scanned his innocent-appearing features suspiciously, "you would prefer to wait for someone else to help you."

"And that could be quite a wait," he added dryly. "The man who owns this land would not be coming back tonight, the vehicles that travel this road are few and far between, the nearest towns are twenty miles south or thirty miles north, and night will be upon us in a matter of minutes."

He straightened up, folded his arms, and waited. When she did not immediately answer, he prompted her impatiently, casting an eye toward the setting sun.

"Well, Miss. What'll it be?"

"All right! All right," she ground out ungraciously. "You can pull me out."

"Say please," he said, watching her expressive face with narrowed eyes.

A shadow of stubbornness settled between her sullen brown eyes. She glared at him in silence.

"Say please," he repeated, "or we'll be here all night. And by my calculations, we are in for a blizzard."

"Please," she suddenly shouted at him, angry tears of defeat welling up uncontrollably. Oh! If she were a man, she would show him a thing or two.

An odd expression lit his eyes as he said sternly, "Every child should be taught good manners."

Turning on his heel, he stalked back up the hill, leaving her to stare after him in speechless rage. What a horrible creature he was! He should be ashamed to treat a woman in such a way. He was a big, overgrown bully! She raked her fingers through her hair. Why on earth did she have to have trouble in this deserted place with this awful man as her only means of help?

Catching a glimpse of her wild-looking eyes in the rear view mirror, she laughed hollowly. She looked rather strange herself. The tired eyes looking back at her had a lost-child look. They were shadowed by short, thick lashes and underlined with dusky circles of unrest. She stared blankly past their beauty, seeing only the unhappiness and uncertainty that she felt.

Then, into her view came a big, red, 4-wheel drive truck plowing effortlessly through the snow, completely swallowing the tracks made by her own vehicle. She felt a strange kinship with her little car as she realized it was to be manipulated by this big, snorting beast much the same way she had been by its owner. Thrusting the thought away as being too fanciful, she rolled down her window as he got out of the truck and walked up to her door.

"Just follow my instructions," he said quietly. "I'll have you back on your way in no time."

She nodded meekly, fighting the urge to tell him she knew what to do. She bit her tongue hard and lowered her rebellious gaze to the last button on his heavy, ranch-style coat. He studied her face, making sure she was paying attention to his instructions, then moved quickly back to his own truck. He could see her profile as she turned in the seat waiting his signal. He frowned, wondering what had caused the pain haunting her big, beautiful eyes.

She was a very pretty and a very spirited young woman. But there was something sad and sort of pitiful about her. He suddenly wanted to see her eyes sparkle with joy, to see her face glow with happiness. But she was like a wild, young filly, stubborn and rebellious. He felt sorry for her and wanted to spank her at the same time. She intrigued him in a way he could not understand — but he did understand the danger involved in pursuing stray thoughts about pretty girls. It would take more than beauty and brains to entice him. He had been a bachelor too long not to be wise to the ways of women.

A sharp toot of her horn brought him back to the task at hand with a jolt. Her eyes were flashing fire as she jerked her head in exaggerated signals to let him know she was tired of waiting. He laughed under his breath. The girl could barely tolerate him. And to him, she was insufferable. There was no way he would want to tackle the job of changing her ways! That was better left to someone who had more patience and tact than he. Yet he admired her beauty and spunkiness. Maybe she was just a prodigal angel. He smiled at her stormy face. An angel? The thought triggered an old painful memory from his childhood that he dismissed quickly.

Guiding her back through the narrow opening of the gate, he pulled the car back up onto the road. Its wheels spun willingly, but without the traction of the big truck, it would have been helpless. He jumped out to unfasten the chains between them, then tipped his hat gallantly as she rolled down her window.

"There you are, Miss, all safe and sound without a scratch on your pretty little car."

"I guess I should thank you," she said grudgingly.

He threw back his head and laughed loud and long. The sound rang through the snow-covered valley as she stared at him resentfully.

"Only if you want to, Miss," he said at last, slapping his hat back on his head. "Only if you want to."

She watched him disdainfully, wondering what could possible be so funny. He leaned over again to look at her, his eyes sparkling with interest in spite of himself.

"Although we've been like ships that crash in the night rather than ships that pass in the night, I'd still like to know your name."

"Leigh," she said stiffly. Her abrupt manner left him in no doubt that she considered the exchange of names unnecessary. "S. Leigh," she said, knowing he would think she meant "S. Lee" and that she did not want to give him her first name.

"Adrian McAllister." He bowed low, sweeping a trail through the snow with his hat, "At your service any time."

She drove away with no intention of looking back, but she could not resist the temptation. She glanced in the rear view mirror. He was standing by the edge of the road looking after her. Then he turned as she topped the hill, and she knew he was going back to close the gate. She put the episode behind her and set her face toward the evening sun.

When she reached the next town, she stopped to buy gas and call her parents, explaining that she had been delayed and would be later getting home than she had planned. As she continued on toward home, the roads became more treacherous. A swirling fog began to freeze on the windshield as the wet road froze into a sheet of ice.

Several times, she slowed to a crawl, straining to see the outline of the road.

Occasionally a blaze of headlights would leap out of the darkness and just as suddenly disappear. She would not allow herself now to think about anything but driving. When she finally crossed the city limits of Shelton, she breathed more freely.

Fifteen more miles to go!

2

Home for the Holidays

As she neared home, she approached an old house, still respectfully called Westmoor Heights by the residents of the Shelton area. The secret castle of her childhood, it had decayed through the years. Still, the thought of it brought a smile to her lips. The owner had been dead for a number of years, and an heir had not been located, so it had remained vacant.

When she was a child, the huge house had provided the perfect playhouse. Often she had run through the meadow, climbed over the boundary fence of her father's property, crossed a brook, and climbed through a broken window to while away the hours in childish fantasies, dreaming of her "Prince Charming." All sorts of sweet memories were stored within its big, stone walls, and she took her attention off the road long enough to glance sentimentally toward the house as she passed.

The fog had lifted, and the sight that met her eyes was unbelievable. Unable to resist seeing it closer, she pulled into the driveway and stopped. She spent several minutes staring in wonder. It was as if a dream had come true. As nearly as she could tell as she pressed her nose hard against the car window, the grand old house had been completely restored.

Several of the large windows were aglow with light, and lights lined the paved drive. The shrubbery had lost its ragged look, and each evergreen was trimmed with tiny, blinking lights. The house itself was outlined with a flowing stream of twinkling lights that framed each window and door before running up the sides of the house. More lights lined the roof and criss-crossed each of the four chimneys like winking stars.

It was not enough to say that the scene was outstanding. It was spectacular! Sensational! Leigh rolled down her window gulping in the frosty air.

Her attention was caught by the life-sized nativity scene placed between two giant spruce trees on the front lawn. As she leaned out into the falling snow, she heard a soft melody floating in the air. She wanted to stay longer, but as another car moved slowly past, she remembered that her parents were waiting.

Half a mile farther, she turned into the drive of an old, two-story farmhouse. Home! And it felt so good to be there! She had not been home in two years.

"I'll have a lot of catching up to do," she thought, with tears in her eyes and a lump in her throat, "but it doesn't look as if much has changed."

Before she could get out of the car, the front door of the house flew open, and a stream of young people came pouring out to meet her. She was swept into a flood of excited arms and greetings. The car quickly was emptied of its luggage and gifts as everyone pitched in to carry her things inside.

She cried happily as she was hugged and kissed and made over as a long, lost sister should be. Until at last, she insisted they stand back so that she could look at them. With shining eyes, she studied each of her brothers and sisters. In turn, they watched her shyly. She was amazed at the change in only two years.

Her brothers, Keith and Kyle, stood shoulder-to-shoulder, husky in build and nearly as tall as she. They shared their father's golden brown hair and sparkling blue eyes. Their identical faces were wreathed in smiles. Keith had the same impulsive nature that so often had motivated her and could usually be found at the bottom of any mischievous pranks that occurred. His twin was quieter and more serious-minded, often providing an excellent scapegoat for his more outgoing brother. However, their love for each other was very special and touching to see.

Her sister Barbara stood beside Keith, and Leigh could hardly believe how pretty she had become. She was eighteen, two years older than her twin brothers and seven years younger than Leigh. She had developed into a strikingly beautiful young lady. Her hair was more golden than the twins', and her eyes were larger and a deeper blue. She had been blessed with flawless skin and a very feminine shape. Petite in size, she was everything Leigh had always wanted to be. Her small, pretty hands rested lightly on the shoulders of a young child. It was the little girl who stole Leigh's heart and breath.

She had been a mere baby of three when Leigh left home for the city. Now she was a very serious, intelligent young lady. Huge, brown eyes stared solemnly from beneath long bangs. A little rosebud mouth puckered thoughtfully as she eyed the tall woman she had been told was her other sister. Her heart-shaped little face was framed by rippling waves of hair. Her nose was slender and delicately flared, a smaller edition of Barbara's. Her dusky cheeks were plump and rosy. Leigh could remember that with her smile came a set of adorable dimples — the only ones in the family, as a matter of fact. Her hands were clasped in front of her, resting lightly against an old, faded pink, print dress. Leigh instantly recognized it as one of her favorite dresses when she was Amy's size.

"Amy?" she said softly, dropping to her knees and holding out her arms.

A pair of dimples flashed spontaneously as the child moved shyly toward her. Leigh hugged her gently, feeling as if she were embracing a porcelain doll. Round little arms were wrapped briefly around her neck, and a wet, little kiss was planted firmly on her cheek. Then Amy turned and ran back to Barbara, peeking out from behind her to check on Leigh's reaction.

"Where are Mother and Dad?" Leigh asked as silence enveloped them.

"They're still out at the barn finishing the milking," Keith volunteered.

"They sent us in to get cleaned up," Kyle finished his brother's explanation.

There was a rattle at the back door, and Amy sprinted down the hall shouting as she went, "Mommy! Daddy! Stormy's here. And she's got red hair. Really red! You oughta see it. It's red as Daddy's barn!"

Barbara and the twins looked anxiously at Leigh, wondering how she would take Amy's odd announcement of her arrival. When she burst into laughter, they joined her in relief. The twins laughed until tears streamed down their cheeks as they held their aching sides.

"She's a real case," Keith croaked, groping for his handkerchief.

Barbara smiled apologetically, "She really is unpredictable."

"She's adorable!" Leigh exclaimed. "I can't believe how much she's changed. And as far as that goes," she looked fondly at her sister, "I can't believe the change in all of you."

She motioned toward the boys who were disappearing down the hall.

"They must have grown a foot taller — not to speak of all those muscles. And you, Barbara," she studied her sister's face. "You are absolutely beautiful."

"Oh, Stormy," Barbara disclaimed, but her fair cheeks bloomed with color. Her eyes sparkled at the compliment.

"It's true," Stormy insisted. "You are!"

"Stormy?"

Hearing her mother's voice, Leigh whirled and met her coming from the kitchen.

"Mother," she cried, her voice ending in a choked sob as she flew into warm, welcoming arms.

"It is so good to have you home again, Stormy," her mother said shakily, stroking the red head burying itself in her shoulder. She pushed the girl away gently, and all the love she felt for her firstborn shone in her face.

"Let me look at you. I've got to get a good look at you."

Her hungry eyes searched the tired, young face, noting the dark shadows of disillusionment beneath the huge eyes, the sad droop of the full lips. Her heart responded to the unhappiness she saw, and she knew her daughter needed love and rest. She hugged her again, patting her comfortingly on the back, until the sound of a deep voice from the kitchen separated them.

"Stormy Leigh? Is my little girl home again?"

"Daddy! Oh, Daddy!" Leigh left the sweetness of her mother's arms and ran to the kitchen into the strength of her father's arms. Hiding her tears in his rough, flannel shirt, she closed her eyes and relaxed in his arms. She felt like a little girl again as she breathed deeply of the familiar small of dairy feed, milk, and hay, and heard the old familiar name, "Stormy Leigh."

"You've been a long time coming home, little girl," her father said huskily, tears shimmering in his vivid blue eyes, "a long time."

25

"I know, Daddy," she whispered, "too long."

"A-hem," a discreet cough sounded behind them. "Charles, I think I'll be going. I'll see you first thing in the morning."

But Charles Winters stopped the man as he opened the back door.

"No, wait, Adrian. I want you to meet my oldest daughter."

The big man slowly closed the door and turned around. Leigh froze in horrified recognition. The man was Adrian McAllister! Oh, no! It couldn't be. Not *him*, of all people. But it was.

"How in the world did he beat me home?" she thought frantically, then remembered that she had stopped for fuel and spent several minutes on the phone.

In three long strides, he stood in front of her. His face was solemn but there was an undeniable twinkle in his eyes.

"Stormy, this is Adrian McAllister. He has been a very good friend to us during the past year and a half," her father said, eyeing her stiff, unfriendly face in perplexity.

Then he turned and clasped the younger man's shoulder with an affectionate grip.

"And, Adrian, this is Stormy Leigh."

"Aha," Adrian chuckled, and for no explainable reason Leigh felt her cheeks flare with heated color.

"I beg your pardon?" Leigh's father looked from one to the other in confusion. "You act as if you already know one another."

"Slightly," Adrian's voice was smooth. "I just, ah, know her by a different name."

"I don't understand." Now Charles was really confused, and Leigh glared at Adrian, who smiled faintly.

"I understood her last name to be Lee," Adrian softly explained, "S. Lee ... *Miss* Lee."

She squirmed in embarrassment under his mocking smile, as he added, "I knew your oldest daughter was named Stormy Leigh, but I did not get the connection with this young lady until now. However," he looked at Leigh challengingly, "I think '*Stormy*' suits her better."

Leigh's temper flared. She began a cutting reply, but her father intervened.

"Oh, I see," he grinned, "Maybe I had better tell you the story behind her unusual name."

"Dad!" Leigh protested, fearing Adrian would only laugh and further humiliate her.

"All right, Honey," he hugged her hard. "I won't tell it tonight." He looked at Adrian and smiled a little sadly. "Stormy Leigh has never liked her name. Someday I hope that will change."

"Is that you, Adrian?" Anna Winters called, entering the kitchen with Amy at her heels. "Oh, good. I'm glad you're still here."

"Adrian," Amy shrieked, darting around her mother and jumping into his arms. She flung her arms around his neck, kissing his lean cheek as he lifted her off the floor. Stormy's heart throbbed jealously as she saw the sweet closeness between the man and the child.

"How's my little girl?" he asked, tugging at a long, brown curl.

"I'm all right," she wrinkled her nose at him. "But you smell like cows."

"Amy!" her mother scolded.

"It's all right, Anna," Adrian laughed. "She's just telling the truth. He playfully tweaked Amy's nose. "And if I don't put you down, you're going to smell like cows, too."

He set the child down, and she ran to grab her father's hand, swinging it vigorously back and forth as she gazed at Adrian with round, adoring eyes.

Barbara slipped quietly into the room, tied a ruffled apron around her trim waist, and began to empty the pans simmering on the stove. Adrian spoke to her and was rewarded with a lovely smile and a flutter of golden lashes. Seeing the innocent flush of color on her sister's cheeks made Leigh wonder if Barbara considered the handsome man to be more than a friend.

"Will you eat supper with us?" Anna asked hopefully, looking around for a potholder.

Adrian took one look at Leigh's mutinous face and decided to refuse.

"No, Anna, not tonight," he sounded regretful. "Maybe some other time."

Leigh felt a sharp, guilty twinge, but she promptly ignored it.

"Are you doing anything special for Christmas?" Anna asked him.

"No, not really," he said quietly.

But she was quick to catch the wistfulness in his voice. She could picture him sitting in his house all alone, and it was a bleak picture. Christmas was not Christmas if there was no one else with whom to share it. He had joined them last year, and in spite of Leigh's odd behavior toward him, she knew he felt they were almost his family.

"We would love to have you spend it with us," she said warmly with a motherly smile.

"In fact," her husband said, slapping Adrian heartily on the back, "We won't take no for an answer."

Amy tugged on Adrian's hand until she got his attention.

"Yes, Amy?" he patiently squatted down to her level.

"Please say you will," she begged with glowing eyes. "I've got a present for you."

"Well, in that case, I guess I'll just have to say yes, won't I?"

She began to dance excitedly around the table chanting loudly, "Adrian's coming for Christmas! Adrian's coming for Christmas!"

"I'm glad you're coming, too," Barbara said softly as she passed him on her way to the pantry.

"And you, Stormy. Are you glad I'm coming?" Adrian asked softly.

She could not answer him. The hard pounding of her heart stifled her words. She wanted to run away like a child and cry. All the joy of coming home for Christmas vanished at the thought of him being there. Her day would be ruined! What did her family see in him? As far as she was concerned, he had ruined her whole weekend.

She kept her eyes on the floor until she could bear his dark, piercing eyes no longer. Then she spun on her heel and walked away, calling back over her shoulder to her mother.

"I'll be back in a few minutes. I'm just going to run upstairs and freshen up."

"All right, Dear." Her mother bent down to peer into the oven, poking expertly at the roast of beef.

"Take your time. It'll be a few minutes before supper is ready."

Leigh met the twins halfway up the stairs. Promising to join them as soon as she changed clothes, she hurried on toward her old bedroom. She wanted to be alone for a few minutes.

3
The Prodigal

Memories flooded her mind, and quick tears stung her eyes as she looked around her old bedroom. It looked so dear, so familiar, so unchanged. The same old quilt covered her bed, and she reached out to touch its faded softness. The tiny, yellow flowers that had once danced in bright patterns across its plump, hand-stitched top had paled into mere pastel shadows. She patted the quilt gently like an old friend.

It had never bothered her that her bedroom suite was old and scarred, nor that as a child she had slept under sheets made of bleached feed sacks. She had been a teenager before she realized her family rode the high side of poverty. There had been hard times, but they always had been happy and healthy. They had been knit together with the bond of God's Word. Constant communication with Him had strengthened their communication with each other. Stormy knew of no one with as much faith and trust in God as her father.

Charles Winters' favorite antidote for life's problems was, "Trust in God, completely. Have faith in Him. He already knows about the problems and is in control of every situation. God's Word in Psalm 37:25 says, 'Yet have I not seen the righteous forsaken, nor his seed begging bread.' God will provide."

Leigh moved restlessly to the window seat and sat down. Somewhere, somehow, during her time away from home, she had lost contact with God. The Heavenly Father she had once asked about so eagerly at her father's knee

31

now seemed far away. Thinking about spiritual things made her uncomfortable. She was not too sure what she believed anymore. Perhaps there was a God who lovingly watched over His children. Then again, maybe it was all just tradition, an old-fashioned belief that played no real part in society, other than cultural, or form and ritual.

Shrugging her shoulders, she dismissed the troublesome thoughts and opened the curtains. As a child, she always had looked toward her "mansion on the hilltop" before going to sleep. Tonight, she became entranced with the sight of its Christmas splendor and fell to dreaming about the man who might have restored it.

However, when his face materialized as Adrian McAllister, she angrily got up and moved over to her suitcase. Horrible man! He was even ruining her daydreams. She rummaged through her clothes in search of a warm sweater. Oh, how she wished she could expose him for the wolf she suspected him to be.

"Stormy," Barbara called softly, "supper's almost ready."

"Be right down," she answered, slipping her feet into soft moccasins.

Pausing in the doorway of the kitchen, she looked around at the sight of her family working together. Her mother was making a skillet of gravy, and her father was carving the roast. Barbara was busy mashing potatoes, while the twins filled the drinking glasses. And Amy, well Amy was cheerfully digging big dollops of butter out of a large container and plopping them into two small bowls.

Leigh grinned at the pert little tongue caught between tiny, white teeth as the little girl concentrated on getting the butter out of the big spoon. Looking cautiously at her mother, Amy took a chubby finger and pushed the butter into the bowl. She jumped and looked up guiltily as her finger was suddenly captured in a towel. Her bottom lip quivered apprehensively as she eyed her newly found big sister. But she only received a reassuring smile and a hug as Leigh turned to offer her help to her mother.

Inquisitive brown eyes studied the back of the red-haired stranger, and Amy cocked her head to one side. Maybe this other sister would be all right. In fact, Amy suddenly saw her playing a major role in the constant need to have an ally when one got caught doing things one should not be doing. Then the butter provided a more interesting subject, and she began to make fanciful swirls in it with the edge of her spoon. The butter became an icy floor, and the swirls became the cut of her skates, as she glided to the tune running through her imagination.

"Stormy, can you take the biscuits out of the oven?" her mother asked, glancing up from the heavy iron skillet.

"Surely," Leigh answered, her heart responding with a sweet pang to the old familiar name, "Stormy," which fell so lovingly from her mother's lips. She grabbed a potholder and headed for the oven, feeling as if she had never been away.

The family took their places at the table with the parents at opposite ends, the twins on their father's right, and the three girls on his left. They all bowed their heads as he began to ask a blessing upon the food.

"Our Heavenly Father, we thank You for this day and for the blessings it has brought our way. We thank You for health, peace, and love, and for meeting our every need. I especially thank You for bringing Stormy Leigh home safely, for protecting her as she traveled dangerous roads. It is good to have her home, Lord.

"I ask that Your hand of love rest upon each member of my precious family, and that each day they might know and experience Your closeness, that they might daily grow to love and trust You more. And now, Lord, I thank You for this food You have so graciously supplied. We ask Your blessing upon it. Amen."

Immediately the family began to talk, sharing the happenings of the day. But Stormy kept silent, fighting back the tears. It had been so long since she had heard someone talking to God. Her heart was touched. A sharp hunger rose in her spirit. How long had it been since she had felt His presence?

But then the enemy of her soul came to whisper convincing words in her ear.

"That's just sentimentalism you're feeling. There's something about coming home after you have been away a long time that would make anyone feel teary-eyed. You think it's God's presence you feel? Huh! Think again. You know better than that. Haven't you learned anything about reality since you left home?"

Because her young heart was bewildered and confused, Stormy unwisely listened to the voice whispering in her ear. With cool rejection, she turned away. All desire left her to regain the heavenly crown she had laid aside in search of materialistic things.

She joined in the laughter and conversation, wearing a bright smile to hide her aching heart. Soon she decided that her "depression" was due to tiredness. After all, it was no easy thing to make a five-hundred-mile trip in a day, especially in bad weather. Thoughts of her trip brought back the unpleasant memory of the man who had determinedly rescued her. Glaring viciously at her slice of beef, she stabbed at it spitefully. Unconsciously, she gritted her teeth and grimaced.

"Stormy?" Her mother's soft voice erased the image of Adrian, and she glanced up startled. "Are you all right? You're looking pale and making faces at your plate. Does something not taste right?"

"Oh, no, Mother. I'm all right. Just a little tired," she laughed lightly, a carefree note carefully expressed in her voice. "As far as the food is concerned — it's fantastic! I've not had a meal like this in months."

Then, casting around for conversational topics to draw the attention away from herself, she asked casually, "Say, who fixed up the old Westmoor place? I saw it on my way home, and I couldn't believe my eyes!"

"Yeah! It's really something, ain't it?" Keith's voice rang with enthusiasm.

"Isn't it," Barbara corrected.

"Yeah, that too," he said mischievously, a wide grin splitting his handsome face, as he wrinkled up his nose at her.

"That's Adrian's place," Kyle said quietly, a certain amount of pride in his voice.

All the color drained from Stormy's face. Her fork fell from shocked fingers to clatter loudly against her plate.

"You've got to be kidding!" she exploded, her feelings rushing out in a torrent. "How on earth could it be *his* place," she wailed, looking wildly around at them.

There was immediate silence as six astonished faces turned toward her.

"Honey," her mother shook her head in bewilderment. "What's wrong?"

Stormy stared blindly at her food. Every inch of her tired body screamed a rejection of Adrian's ownership of her beloved Westmoor Heights. She shoved back her chair, intent on escaping the curious faces swimming in a blur of hot tears. But just as she started to get up, a loving hand descended heavily on her shoulder. She turned a haunted face toward her father.

"Stormy, wait a minute."

Unwillingly obedient, she sank back into her chair, ignoring the scalding tears that splashed on her limp hands. Her stricken eyes sought her father's face, looking for the comfort and understanding that always had been there for her.

"After you went upstairs, Adrian told us about your accident, but he didn't seem to think you were hurt — just a little upset and aggravated at being delayed."

Charles looked at her with concern in his eyes, "Did something else happen that we should know about? Were you hurt, little girl?"

But now that the chance had come to fire judgment against Adrian McAllister, she found she could not say a word.

"Uh, no, Daddy," she reluctantly muttered, dropping her eyes. "I wasn't hurt — except maybe my pride."

Looking up with a shaky grin on her face, she continued, "It was kind of a shock to find myself barreling toward the ditch and doing everything I knew *not* to do." She shrugged her shoulders helplessly, "Guess I wasn't keeping my mind on my business."

"Probably had it on your city beau," Keith scoffed playfully, accidentally stumbling on the truth. He immediately received a sharp kick on his shin from the long leg of his sister.

In response to his yelp, she made a ferocious face at him. The rest of the family broke into laughter as the tension ebbed away. Then Amy boldly announced her intentions of growing up and marrying her other sister's beau, Ray Carlton, if Barbara did not hurry up and do it.

"Ray Carlton? Really?" Stormy looked at the sweet, bashful blue eyes and the blush that tinted Barbara's cheeks the color of wild roses. "He always was a nice guy. Terrific guy, in fact. I used to have a terrible crush on him before he went away to veterinary college."

"I know. I can remember," Barbara said painfully. "He was stuck on you too. He didn't even know I was alive until after you left."

"Just another case of 'older sister leaves home, younger sister steals her man,'" Keith sighed dramatically.

"Yeah," his twin echoed, his soft gaze resting with pretended concern on Stormy's smiling face. "But what I want to know is what we are going to do about this city dude of Stormy's?" He shook his blond head worriedly. "I just know he'll never fit in with us farmers."

Keith laughed, "Boy, can we have some fun teaching him to slop hogs and milk cows — but first we'll have to teach him which is which!"

Stormy felt a wave of laughter bubble up from deep inside at the sight of her brothers' comically alarmed faces. The idea of them trying to coach Cliff in the finer points of farm life was hilarious. At last, she gave in to a fit of giggles that erased the last traces of dejection and irritation and made her feel like a teenager again. The sound of her laughter, in turn, brought gladness to the eyes of her parents. Their eyes met, and the message was clear and understood: Stormy Leigh had come home.

After the last dish had been dried and put away, they all gathered in the long family room. They found places to sit and waited in expectation as Charles Winters lifted the heavy family Bible down from the mantle. As he seated himself in a well-used armchair, he looked up to smile at his eldest child.

"Looks as if we're in for a blizzard tonight. Sure am glad you're home safe and sound, Stormy."

"Me, too, Daddy," she snuggled farther into the corner of the couch and drew a colorful handknit comforter around her bare feet. Faintly, in the back of her mind, another such comment surfaced, one made by another man in another place.

"Mr. McAllister thought we'd be getting a blizzard tonight, too," she said impulsively, then bit her tongue in vexation. Why on earth was that man constantly on her mind?

Her father looked up from the open Bible and nodded knowingly.

"Adrian's the best weatherman we have in the district. He has a special talent for forecasting weather changes. We all respect his judgment."

"Yeah," joked the witty Keith, "he's got a built-in radar. Wonder if it works on women?"

Barbara playfully twisted his ear. "One thing's for sure, Brother, *you* don't have a built-in radar for women, or you wouldn't have placed yourself within reach of this one!"

Keith squirmed beneath her ruthless grip, and Kyle laughed.

"Stormy?" Amy left her mother's side and went to the couch. "Why do you call him Mister McAllister? That sounds funny. We all call him Adrian. I want you to call him Adrian too. He'll think you don't like him if you call him 'Mister.'"

Stormy felt her heart skip a beat. How could she answer the child? She could not stand the man! The idea of calling him by his first name as if he were a friend was repulsive.

"Amy, Honey," Anna Winters came to her oldest daughter's rescue. "You have to realize that we've known

Adrian for a long time. To Stormy, he is practically a stranger. She's just being polite. And he is older than she is."

Amy pursed her lips and cocked her head like a little robin as she listened. Then she turned to regard Stormy with a satisfied gleam in her big, dark eyes.

"Well," she said smugly. "he won't be a stranger long. When he comes Christmas, I'll remind you to call him Adrian." She patted her sister comfortingly on the arm. "Then you won't ever have to call him Mister again. Okay?"

Stormy could not resist the impulse to gather her in her arms and kiss her soft cheek. "You're precious," she murmured, "why don't you curl up here beside me while Daddy reads us a story?"

As he began to read, a hush fell over the family. Even little Amy sat in fascinated silence as his voice brought the Words of God to life. Stormy listened to an old story that she had heard many times as a child. This time, however, her conscience was pricked, and she began to fidget.

Amy shifted restlessly. Realizing that her little sister was being disturbed by her squirming, Stormy tried to sit still. But her mind was still actively drawing vivid pictures of the story unraveling from her father's lips.

"The Prodigal Son of Luke 15:11-31 ... " somehow she identified with him tonight. She understood the eagerness with which he left home to seek his fortune, understood the drawing appeal of a world offering numerous pleasures, and yes, she understood the jaded, lost feeling he had experienced on his way back home.

But, oh, such a soft warmth enveloped her lonely spirit as her father recounted the great joy of the boy's father over his return. Her heart yearned over the joy of reconcilement with the father and the wonderful feeling of being home. What a beautiful sight it must have been to see the father in all his luxurious robes run toward his dirty, ragged son and clasp him to his heart!

When the story had been read and the Book reverently placed back on the mantle, Charles looked around at his family and began to talk.

"I want to make two very important points about the story we have just read," he said. "First, the young man didn't think about going home until he was on the verge of starvation. It was not until he 'came to himself' that he saw and recognized a need for his father. When he realized his father's mercy was the only way of escape from his poverty and wretchedness, his eyes were opened. Then he looked back on the treasures he had left behind and made up his mind to go home. He would go home to his father and to all the protection and blessings his father's home would give him."

Charles shook his head sadly. "So many people in the world are searching for something. Many of them never come to the point of recognizing their need for their heavenly Father. It's Him they are really desiring. Their spirits are crying out for a personal relationship with their Creator. But so often they're afraid that if they do make such a decision to seek Him, He won't want them because of all the bad things they've done.

"And that brings me to my second point," he smiled at the serious young faces. "I want you to know that God is always ready to welcome you. He desires that you be His children and that you want to stay in His care and keeping. If for some reason, you choose to leave His presence or to stray away, He still loves you. It would sadden Him greatly, but He would still love you.

"Then when you came to the realization that you can't make it without Him — and you can't — He is waiting at the door, longing for you to come home. He is kind and forgiving, and always will welcome you home with open arms."

"But Daddy," Amy protested, tears of loyalty shining in her eyes, "I love Jesus! I never want to make Him sad."

"I hope and pray you never will, child," her father said softly.

But he could see the numerous traps and snares that lay in wait for his little ones. They would never know the countless hours he spent praying for them as he drove the tractor, milked the cows, and carried out all the other endless tasks of farming. His clear, wise eyes sought the bent head of his eldest daughter, and he knew in his heart that all was not well with her.

Stormy once again was miserable. She kept seeing herself in the shoes of the young man in the story. She wondered if she too had walked away from her Father's care. A part of her longed to re-establish her relationship with Him, but her heart longed to keep traveling the exciting path she had chosen. She was not sure she wanted to give up the world. Yet the word "compromise" always had an evil ring to her. She needed to choose one way and stick with it. It was ridiculous to keep being torn into emotional shreds by her inability to make a mature decision.

Unconsciously, however, the heat of Satan once again applied itself to her soul through the memory of worldly attractions, searing the feeble attempts of her conscience to alert her to the weak spiritual state into which she was slipping. She lifted her head and smiled at her father, determined to free herself from the gentle wooing of God's Spirit — which she threw off as nostalgia — by forgetting the scriptures that tugged at her heart.

After she was ready for bed, she wandered over to her window and pushed aside the curtains. The howling wind and swirling snow obscured all sight of Westmoor. She shivered and crawled into bed. There was no denying she was glad to be home. But the man living in her dream-house had put a damper on her visit.

She was beginning to wish she had relented and gone with Cliff to his parents' home for the holidays. In spite of their disagreements, she loved him. She wanted to meet his parents. A forlorn tear trickled down her cheek and plopped onto her pillow. It was fortunate she could not see into the future — or even as far away as his parents' house, for they were entertaining a female guest, one with silky, blond hair and beguiling, baby-blue eyes, one who spent the evening openly flirting with Cliff.

4
A Visit to Westmoor Heights

At 4:30 a.m., the Winters household began to stir. With a groan, Stormy rolled over onto her stomach, burying her head under the pillow. Her usual rising time in the city was at least 7 a.m., and after staying up half the night entertaining miserable thoughts about Cliff, she felt like greeting the morning with a frown and a grumble.

"Stormy?"

Before long, little bare feet padded softly to her bed. The springs creaked as the slight figure climbed up beside her. Persistent hands tugged at the pillow held tightly over her head.

"Stormy? Aren't you ever going to get up?" Amy complained.

"Breakfast is ready. Come on, Stormy! Get up." The little girl gave up on removing the pillow from her sister's tousled head and began to pull off the covers.

"Amy! You little monster. You're freezing me," Stormy scolded grumpily as the cool air went through her thin gown.

She reached to pull the covers back up, but the child was too quick for her. Amy scampered off the end of the bed taking the covers with her. Her childish shrieks of laughter rang in the cold room like tinkling chimes. She ran toward the door as Stormy scrambled after her.

"Oooh! This floor is cold," Stormy squeaked as her bare feet made contact with the wood floor.

Recoiling from the shock, she rose to her tiptoes. The door closed with a bang as she grabbed up her robe and flung it on. Grumbling about not unpacking her clothes the night before and doing something worthwhile during her sleepless hours, she scouted around for an old pair of blue jeans. She found a bulky, green sweater and a green-and-white pin-striped shirt to wear under it. Flinging them over one arm, she hastily grabbed clean undies and headed for the door.

Amy was nowhere in sight as Stormy dashed down the hall to the bathroom. But as she turned to close the door, she saw her scooting back into her bedroom.

"Little rascal! I wonder what she's up to now?" she muttered as she turned to draw her bath.

After bathing and dressing, she decided not to make up her face. She did not wear much makeup anyway, and she would just be around the family all day. She straightened up the bathroom, gathered up her robe and gown, and went back to her bedroom. She quietly opened the door and peeked around it.

Amy was bent over her suitcase. As Stormy stepped into the room, she whirled around, clutching a silk nightgown in her chubby hands. Her plump, little cheeks flamed brilliantly, but she tried to look innocent.

"Caught you snooping, didn't I?" Stormy said.

"Uh ... uh ... not really," Amy stammered. "It was sticking out of the suitcase. I was just gonna put it back. Honest," her lashes fluttered with sincerity.

"Oh?" Stormy nodded her head knowingly. "Do you like that gown, Amy?"

"Oh, yes," the little girl breathed, her face glowing with pleasure. "I like to feel it," she stroked the gown with admiring fingers. "But I 'specially like the one with little pink ribbons an' bows on it," she bubbled, then stopped and caught her tongue between her teeth, aware that she had given herself away. She looked up, her brow wrinkling with apprehension.

"That's all right, Amy," Stormy spoke kindly. "You're welcome to look at everything I brought with me. But it isn't nice to snoop. You should always ask to see people's things. Do you understand?"

"Yes," Amy hung her head with shame, "Are you mad at me?" She peeked at her sister through her lashes.

"No, Honey, of course not!" Stormy hugged her, gave her a swat on her bottom and pointed her toward the door. "Now, go tell Mother I'll be right down. And Amy," the little girl looked back with a grin, "don't eat all the biscuits. Okay?"

"Okay," Like sunshine through rain, a smile beamed across her face as she skipped merrily down the hall singing her favorite Christmas carol in a very high key.

The blizzard seemed to have blown itself out, and dawn promised blue skies and sunshine. However, before long the day turned dark and cloudy again, and the wind chill factor dropped several degrees in a matter of hours. The night's storm had added another foot of soft, white snow, much to Amy's delight and the adults' dismay. It would be harder to get to the fields and tend the livestock.

Stormy found herself working hard at chores she had not done in years as the family tried to complete the day's work before dusk. Shortly after dawn, she helped the twins milk, then helped feed the hogs and fed the dogs and cats, pausing only briefly to pet them. She helped Barbara and Amy gather the eggs and scouted around the outbuildings noting various changes. Later, she helped her father load hay onto the truck for the next morning's feeding, then returned with him to the house for lunch.

The family met briefly around the long, oak table for a quick, hot meal of soup and sandwiches. They talked about the work done that morning and the work still to do that day. Then they separated, each to his own task, inspired by the promise of an evening of fun.

Darkness fell quickly, and Stormy and her father walked back to the house with the moon glimmering occasionally through the dark clouds. They had spent the afternoon in the woods cutting firewood. Their breath fogged in the clear, cold air as their feet crunched through the new crust of ice. Stormy felt a sudden rush of pride and a prickle of tears as her father placed his arm around her shoulder. Her pain and tiredness lifted as he complimented her.

"Well, little girl, I see the soft city life hasn't ruined you," he teased gently. "You've still got the stamina to work hard outdoors all day." He smiled warmly as she looked up at him.

He continued, "As a matter of fact, I don't know what I'd have done without you. We got enough wood cut today to last for a while. Now I can enjoy Christmas without worrying about the house getting cold."

Stormy straightened her tired shoulders, thinking she would gladly cut wood all night if it would lift some of the load off her father. Impulsively, she flung her arms around him, overwhelmed by gratitude for all he had done for them.

"I love you so much, Daddy!" she cried, her voice muffled in his heavy coat. Then she turned and ran into the house.

The phone rang while they were eating supper. Kyle got up from the table to answer it, and when he returned, his face glowed with excitement.

"Adrian's on the phone. He wants to know if we can come over for a while tonight."

"Oh, can we, Daddy? Can we?" Amy bounced up and down in her chair.

"What do you say, Anna?" Charles asked his wife. "Would you like to go? Or do you have too much to do?"

"No, I think I've done about everything I had planned, and the rest can wait. I'd love to see his house decorated for the holidays." She smiled at Kyle, "Tell him we'll be over about eight."

Stormy's heart sank. She had envisioned a quiet evening spent with her family. An evening of soft Christmas music, a cosy, warm fire, and enjoyment of the huge, evergreen heavily laden with homemade goodies. She was tired, and she didn't feel up to being in the company of Adrian McAllister! The festering thorn that had pricked her all day finally worked itself out into the open as she helped her mother put away the dishes.

Her father and the boys had gone to clean the snow off the family's old station wagon, and Barbara had taken Amy upstairs to change clothes. Unable to hold her frustration any longer, Stormy turned to her mother.

"Mother, why did you invite Adrian here for Christmas?" she burst out, and to her horror, she started to cry.

Anna looked at her daughter in astonishment.

"Why, Stormy, I had no idea it would upset you this much, or I wouldn't have." A troubled line settled between her fine brows. "Adrian's like family to us. He doesn't have anyone else. I couldn't bear to think of him being alone on Christmas. We all love him and enjoy being around him."

"You wouldn't say that, Mother, if you knew him like I do," Stormy cried bitterly, not caring how irrational she sounded.

"And you wouldn't treat him the way you do, if you knew him the way we do," her mother said steadily. "Adrian is a good man and a Christian. As far as I'm concerned, there is no better man, besides your father, in the whole community."

"But why would a man with all his money — and he must have a lot to be able to fix up the old Westmoor place the way he has — care about socializing with us if he didn't have an ulterior motive?" Stormy argued, her brown eyes snapping determinedly.

"We don't have anything that amounts to anything, except Dad's land that adjoins his," she continued, "and he is not a fool, Mother! He knows you and Dad own the richest bottom land in the valley!"

She had hoped to plant a seed of suspicion in her mother's mind, but Anna laughed.

"Adrian's a good friend, Stormy," she said firmly, "and he could be a friend of yours if you would let him." She shook her head, "He's not the kind of man to let money or power determine his friends."

"But, Mother. He's so rude. And he always wears that mocking smile. I'd just like to slap it off his face!"

Stormy felt her temper begin to rise as she recalled Adrian's attitude when her car ran off the road. But her mother's next words hit her like a bucket of ice water, and her anger sizzled away to nothing.

"Stormy, my girl, I think you had best examine your own actions before you throw the first stone."

Stormy felt her heart surge painfully as the words cut her to the quick.

"I was hoping not to have to say anything to you. I hoped you had matured enough to change your own behavior so that I wouldn't have to say anything. But since you've brought up the subject, I must tell you that *you* were *extremely* rude to Adrian last night. To be honest, your father and I are really disturbed about your attitude toward him. I don't know what happened between the two of you, but I do know you've been taught not to judge others. And you're bordering on the edge of that, my dear.

"He was a guest in our home," her mother continued, "but you couldn't have made it any plainer that you wished he would leave. Stormy, you were brought up with good manners, yet you were positively rude to him. He would have stayed for supper if you hadn't made your dislike so obvious."

"Did he tell you that?" Stormy asked incredulously.

"He didn't have to," her mother answered quietly. "It was in your face for all to see."

Stormy could not say another word. Everything her mother had said was true, and it hurt terribly. But she was not surprised at the stern admonishment. Her mother was frank and honest with her children. If she saw something in them that should be corrected, she did not hesitate to do it. Stormy felt thoroughly chastened.

"Stormy ... Stormy," her mother repeated until she raised her eyes reluctantly. "We *are* going to Adrian's house tonight, and we're going to have a lot of fun. It's up to you whether you want to go or not, but I'd really like for you to come with us."

With a warm and loving smile, she soothed her daughter's hurt feelings. "I know you will enjoy seeing the house. It's stunning on the inside," she added, as she placed the last clean glass in the cabinet, gave her daughter a hug, and left the room.

Stormy went up to her bedroom and paced the floor. She wanted to go — and yet she did not want to go. She still suspected Adrian was just being nice to her family in order to get his hands on the farm somehow. But it was hard to pass up a chance to see the interior of the old manor. She wanted so much to see the restored house.

A soft knock on the door brought her to a halt, and Barbara said, "Stormy? Can I come in?"

"Of course," Stormy welcomed the interruption. "Come on in."

Barbara stepped into the room and eyed her sister anxiously.

"Aren't you dressed yet?"

She looked very pretty and sweet in a soft, powder-blue sweater with a matching plaid skirt. A blue ribbon was threaded through a braid wound around her shapely head. Her cheeks were flushed with excitement, and she glowed with a natural beauty, making her sister feel old and slightly envious.

"We're about ready to leave. We told Adrian we'd be there around eight," she reminded Stormy.

Stormy suddenly made up her mind. She was not going to Westmoor Heights to see Adrian, but she was going to see his house.

"Why don't you pick out something for me to wear," she waved a hand toward the closet, where she had found time during the day to hang up her clothes.

"Oh, Stormy," Barbara said wistfully, "You have such beautiful clothes. But then you have a perfect figure. These clothes wouldn't look half as good on me. I'm too short and shapeless."

Stormy laughed, "And I always thought *you* were the one with the perfect shape."

She eyed herself disdainfully in the mirror, glancing without interest at her shapely figure, discrediting her long, slender legs and narrow waist.

"I'm much too tall to be considered beautiful, and this red mop of mine would never win a beauty contest!"

She tugged an unruly curl into place with an impatient hand, not seeing the finger of gold woven by the overhead light through the curls until they became a halo of molten fire.

"You could wear this," Barbara exclaimed with delight, as she pulled out an old favorite of her sister's

It was a deceptively simple dress, but expensive and cleverly cut. An elegant wool dress of forest green, it was designed to fit any occasion. Barbara's keen eye for design alerted her that the dress was a real jewel.

"All right," Stormy agreed as she applied a light coat of mascara to her short lashes.

She had decided not to go to any extra pains with her looks, but somehow, the green dress deserved better. Besides, she could not deny a growing excitement that prompted her to look her best. Never for a second would she have admitted setting out to impress Adrian. But a secret little smile danced on her lips as she ran downstairs with Barbara to join the others.

The night was frosty. Their breaths rose in the air like puffs of smoke from miniature locomotives as they hurried to the car. Everyone was in high spirits. Stormy breathed in the intoxicating air and atmosphere of merriment and felt exhilarated. Her tiredness and irritation dissolved with each breath she took. Tonight was going to be special, after all. She could feel it in her bones.

Charles Winters drove slowly up the driveway to the huge stone house as they admired the fairyland of twinkling lights. Stormy exclaimed aloud as she saw again the large, hand-carved nativity scene. She felt a gripping emotion rise up within her as she gazed at the lovely face of Mary whose features were highlighted with a soft, white spotlight. She longed to get out and walk among the statues, touching them, and admiring the workmanship.

"I've never seen anything like them," she said. "Who made them? They're so lifelike."

"Adrian did," Kyle answered, his voice ringing with pride and respect. "He can do just about anything with his hands."

Stormy was shocked. Somehow the idea of Adrian putting so much time and effort into creating something so beautiful, something that had represented Christianity through the years, did not fit with her image of him. She was silent the rest of the way up to the house.

When they stopped in front of the mansion on the wide, paved drive, Stormy stared at the house in rapture. An enormous full moon had banished the clouds finally and smiled down as if warming the charming, gray stone face of her old friend. The light picked out the delightful little turrets that peeked above the roof like stiff, wiry curls. The house was an impressive and gracious country manor.

Its unique architectural design — shaped into a square with a swimming pool and paved courtyard as its centerpiece — was only part of its charm. Long, elegant windows had replaced the tiny ones that had once made the house resemble a stone fortress, and the huge chimneys now breathed out the welcoming scent of wood smoke.

As the rest of the family trooped inside, Stormy paused to run a hand over the cold, hard surface of the wall. Lost in youthful memories, she did not see the man who patiently held the door open for her, nor the way he watched as she stroked the smooth stones.

"Stormy Leigh," his voice was soft and warm, very masculine and compelling.

Her eyes lifted to the shadowed ones that kindled an immediate response in her. Unconsciously she swayed toward him, totally unaware of how enchanting and angelic she appeared in that instant of innocence. With the sweet, trusting attitude of a child and the rising emotions of a woman, she lifted her lovely, captivating face to him. Huge, dreamy brown eyes drew him closer as her soft, full lips parted. She sighed deeply, lost in her own reveries of past fantasies about this place and about her "Prince Charming."

A deep shudder shook the large frame of the man who stood in the shadows. For a long, unguarded moment, his eyes blazed with the light of a new fire as passion raged through his soul. A tiny muscle in his cheek twitched. He whispered her name again and moved toward her as one totally helpless against her call. He was lost to all except the lure of her eyes and the promise of her lips.

The moonlight bathed her fair skin with a fine, creamy glow and cast shadows around her wide innocent eyes. Dewy lips glistened, parted in anticipation, and tiny curls of air vanished into the night with each soft, quick breath she took. Soft, silky curls lost their brilliance to the moon, lying in dark, subdued tendrils around her alluring face.

The man looked at her face with the eye of a sculptor and saw the finely chiseled bones that outlined it so sweetly and marveled at the depths of her eyes. She was utterly captivating, and he could not resist the temptation to take her in his arms. Their eyes locked in moonlit fascination. As his dark head bowed slowly toward her, she closed her eyes in submission.

Her hands doubled into fists as she clung to his dinner jacket to keep from swooning at his feet. The touch of his warm, hard lips made her heart leap with excitement, and a slow, delicious warmth spread throughout her body until she melted weakly into his arms. Her mouth, like a budding rose, parted to meet his in sweet, hungry desire, even as her legs trembled and threatened to buckle. Suddenly, everything seemed so right and so good.

She was prepared to give her heart to the dark stranger who held her, willing to surrender herself to him. Words of love rose from her heart to her lips but were never uttered, for harsh reality shattered her illusion as he suddenly spoke.

"Child, you're dreaming. I'm not whoever you're pretending I am."

She heard the note of amusement in his voice, and came abruptly to her senses, spurning the fantasy that had made her weak and caused her to act like a fool. But there was no way she could act composed and sophisticated. She was too shaken. Her lips tingled from the pressure of his, and her insides quivered like jelly.

He put a casual arm around her to steer her toward the door, but she jerked away. The word "child" burned in her brain. She knew he thought she was immature and naive, and that hurt. Her face was pale. Her eyes mirrored her own shock at her actions and feelings.

When Adrian reached around her to open the door, he saw her face. Quickly, he stopped and bent to look her in the eye.

"Stormy Leigh? Are you all right? You look as if you might be sick."

"I am sick," she stormed, her eyes beginning to flash and fresh color spilling into her cheeks. Her quick temper came to her rescue. "I'm sick of you! I ... I!" she sputtered with antagonism, her only defense against humiliation.

"Hate me?" he questioned softly. "I hope not, little girl."

"Don't call me that!" she exploded childishly, hating the sound of her favorite pet name on his lips.

He laid a restraining hand on her arm as she started to jerk the door open.

"There's no need to get upset over what happened. I'm sure it isn't the first time you've been kissed. And I enjoyed it. A pretty girl and moonlight are made for romance."

"Oh ... " she sputtered again, enraged that he would casually admit enjoying something she now regretted deeply. "You'd enjoy kissing any girl, moonlight or not."

She tried to scorch him with a withering expression, but failed miserably and was forced to enter the house with his deep chuckle ringing in her ears.

"Where have you been?" Amy demanded, casting a suspicious eye on them.

Stormy's cheeks flamed crimson as Adrian laughed.

Anna, who had just returned to the hall in search of her youngest, saw the look on Stormy's face and smiled. It was the look of a very confused young woman who has just been thoroughly kissed. Ah, yes, she knew the look. She remembered the feeling well. She smiled again, and wondered and hoped.

Later, Stormy rolled and tossed on her bed, trying to find a comfortable spot, as she replayed the evening in her mind. Her mother had taken pity on her, rescuing her from Adrian's teasing remarks by providing a long, interesting tour of the house that allowed her daughter time to regain most of her composure. The interior of the grand old house had been restored with painstaking care. Heavy satin draperies veiled the long windows, and the sheen of highly polished floors created mirrors of perfection for priceless heirlooms placed in each room.

Stormy had gazed to her heart's content, trying to paint a picture of each beautiful thing in her mind so she could remember it later. Then, like a tall, slender rose swaying in the breeze, she had descended the wide, curved staircase in the front hall. With unconscious elegance, her head carried proudly, she had again fallen into living out her fantasy of stepping down the stately steps as mistress of Westmoor Heights. Regal as a queen within her castle, she had stepped daintily, long fingers lightly caressing the dark, stained bannister.

Flinching in the darkness of her bedroom, she recalled the instant her eyes had rested on the dark, guarded face of Adrian McAllister as he stood at the foot of the stairs with her father. She had nearly lost her footing, as confusion between dreams and reality jolted her. Flustered, she had managed to escape his presence by insisting on seeing the Great Room again.

During the rest of the evening, she had found herself constantly aflutter. The icy fruit punch was delicious, as were the rich delicacies placed before her that she had not been too upset to munch greedily. Much to her disgust, however, she had found her eyes frequently straying to her host. Even the lovely, old-fashioned charm of the house had not diverted her attention for long. Yet he had paid her scant attention, and she had not received the same warmth from him as did the rest of her family.

"Not that I wanted his attention anyway," she muttered, flouncing over to the other side of the bed. Yet she had suffered a distinct pang when he had flashed a smile at Barbara and told her how lovely she looked. His compliment that "blue was certainly a color made for Barbara" was true enough, but he was out to hoodwink her family. She just knew he was!

However, even her strong feelings of hostility could not explain away the simple fact that if he had told *her* how stunning she looked and that green must have been created for her, her treacherous heart would have gone wild. In revenge for hurt feelings, she determined somehow to expose his deceitfulness. She would make him pay dearly for that hateful kiss!

She tried to block his face from her mind but could not. It was too easy to remember the way his hair curled around his ears and teased the collar of his shirt. It was too easy to remember the way he had impatiently brushed it off his high forehead with a long, lean hand, a hand that was hard and strong, yet sensitive and talented, a hand that curled possessively around her neck holding her still as he kissed her.

She shivered at the memory and buried her head under the pillow. But even there his eyes sought her out. Her mind dwelt on their dark beauty. They were an unusual blue that magnetized one, yet revealed nothing of their owner's secret thoughts, deep-set about a well-shaped, masculine nose.

Yet it was the thought of his lips that made her mouth grow dry and her heart beat faster. His lips were beautifully shaped, and the flash of strong, white teeth against his dark skin was enough to make any girl's pulse race.

She was honest enough to admit she was peeved because he had not paid her any attention the rest of the evening. But why she cared, she did not know. Why had she tried to impress him in the first place? She did not even like him! She decided to have nothing more to do with him.

The light grew pale as the moon moved across the sky, and finally she closed her eyes in troubled thought. Soon the breaking of the dawn would dispel all the shadows of the night. She would open her eyes to a new day — but *he* would still be there.

5
An Unwelcome Guest

She was awakened early Christmas morning by a rowdy little girl who barreled into her bed like a wayward cannon ball.

"Stormy! Stormy!" she cried, bouncing up and down on the bed. "It's Christmas! It's Christmas!" Her voice rose in feverish excitement, "Hurry. Get up."

Stormy pulled her down next to her and began to mock-tickle her until she subsided in giggles.

"Aha," Stormy growled, "thought you could sneak in here and wake me up and get away with it, did you? Now what are you going to do?"

Amy pretended to surrender, but as her sister relaxed her hold, she pulled away and rolled off the bed. Stormy laughed as she watched her dash away to wake up the others. The little girl's excitement was contagious. She felt wide awake.

Shivering with excitement, she scrambled out of bed and dressed for comfort in a favorite old skirt of coffee-and-cream tweed with a soft, cream-colored blouse. Forgetting for the moment that an unwelcome guest would be there that morning, she decided to skip putting on makeup. She then hurried to the top of the stairs to join Barbara and Amy. In spite of her almost sleepless night, her eyes were bright and clear. She felt happy and care-free.

Breakfast was a festive occasion with everyone rushing around to help get it on the table and making sure no one else had sneaked off to peek at the presents under the tree. When they were all seated, Charles Winters gravely bowed his head. He offered up a very special, very beautiful prayer of thanksgiving for the Christ Child. Unashamed tears rose in the eyes of more than one family member before he finished, and little Amy echoed his fervent, "Amen."

Later, as they finished straightening the kitchen, a knock sounded at the front door. Kyle ran to open it and returned a moment later, his arms laden down with gifts, followed closely by Adrian. The visitor's hair was frosted with snow flakes, and his long arms were stretched around another pile of packages.

Stormy started guiltily. How could she have forgotten that he was coming? She found herself wondering if she could sneak back upstairs and put on some makeup and a prettier dress.

"Stormy?"

She blankly stared at her mother.

"Honey, would you take Adrian's coat and hang it in the closet?"

She panicked, but her mother already had turned to greet the guest and help unburden him. She moved toward him reluctantly.

"May I take your coat?" she mumbled, keeping her eyes on the toes of his western boots.

A long, lean finger suddenly lifted her chin. She gaped at him in astonishment, her lips parted in surprise.

"So," he examined her nose carefully, "you do have freckles. I thought so. Most redheads do."

She gasped in indignation. Her eyes blazed as she rebelled against his comment. She hated with a passion the freckles that peppered her nose, although they had paled as she grew older.

"Careful!" he warned laughingly. "No temper tantrums on Christmas, or you won't get any presents. Besides," he bent and effectively closed her mouth with a quick, hard kiss, "they're cute. Merry Christmas, angel."

Her lips burned with the fire of his touch. Her legs threatened to buckle as shimmering waves of excitement flowed over her. But she was left holding his jacket as he turned away to hug her mother and plant a respectful kiss on her still youthful-looking cheek.

"Anna, you look perfectly stunning."

As she gazed around at her brood all together again, Anna was radiant with happiness, and her beautiful eyes glowed happily.

"And you're a tease as always," she laughed gayly and tucked her hand under his arm to lead him into the living room. "But I'm so glad you came. We're just getting ready to read the Christmas story."

"Oh, great!" he exclaimed with delight. "I was afraid I'd missed it."

"You can sit over here by me," Amy called, patting her chair with one hand and beckoning imperatively with the other.

After affectionately greeting the others, he agreed with her wishes and seated himself beside her.

"Who's reading this year?" he asked, gazing around at his adopted family.

"I thought perhaps Stormy might like to read it," Charles said, looking questioningly at his tall daughter who was trying to stay in the background.

"We've missed having her home the last two Christmases, and we'd like for her to have the honor. Would you like to read, Stormy Leigh?"

"I ... I," Stormy felt her color rising as Adrian's dark eyes intently watched her. She tilted her chin, squared her shoulders, and stepped gracefully across the long room.

"Sure, Daddy," she said as she picked up the treasured Bible and seated herself on a low stool at her father's feet.

But as she began to read the age-old story of the birth of Jesus, the dear, familiar words caught at her heart, blinding her eyes with tears and making her voice quaver. The same feeling also gripped the hearts of her listeners until there was not a dry eye in the room.

Stormy once again felt the reality of His presence, and she struggled to understand the message His Word was communicating to her. It was a message of love that she ached to know in depth. When she finished reading, she sat with bent head, hands gently smoothing the worn pages of the old Book.

"That was beautiful, Stormy," Anna's sweet voice rang out with pleasure, and Barbara chimed in, "It certainly was."

"But when are we gonna open the presents?" Amy asked with such a longsuffering sigh that everyone burst into laughter.

"Right now," her father assured her. He motioned toward the great pile of presents beneath the fat fir tree. "Go ahead, Amykins. You can hand out the gifts."

Stormy covertly watched Adrian's face as Amy headed excitedly toward the tree. She was not sure what she was expecting to find. Skepticism? A touch of scorn for the gifts the family had wrapped in paper salvaged from last Christmas, for the bows made from scraps and imagination, and the ornaments cut from colored construction paper? They had nothing that could in any way compare to the lovely decorations at his home.

But all she saw was a boyish light of joy in his eyes and a sense of eager anticipation as he waited beside the twins for whatever bounty might come his way. In time, she forgot to watch him and compare his expensively wrapped presents to theirs. She too became engrossed with the impressive pile of gifts rising beside the low stool on which she still sat.

A warm, woolen, plaid skirt in lovely shades of turquoise and a matching hand-crocheted silky-feeling sweater that shimmered in the light brought an ecstatic sigh from her parted lips.

"Oooh, Mother! This is gorgeous! Absolutely gorgeous. But," she shook her head in mystification, "when did you find time to make it?"

"In the wee hours of the night," Charles said dryly.

"Now, Charles," Anna twinkled up at him like a new bride, leaning over to kiss him. "You know you didn't mind."

"I don't mind anything," he whispered for her ears only, "when you look at me like that."

Stormy barely heard the whispered intimacy, but uncontrollably her eyes darted to Adrian. She knew intuitively that he had overheard also, and she flushed.

She collected a wooden stationery box from Keith, a leather billfold from Kyle, a set of embroidered bureau scarves from Barbara, and a lumpy, little, fringed pillow with a hand-painted scene of their home from Amy.

"Amy," she smiled at the proudly beaming child, "did you make this all by yourself?"

"Yes," the dark head nodded shyly. "Mama showed me how."

"Well, I think you did a marvelous job," Stormy declared, hugging the misshapen little pillow to her heart. "I'll treasure it forever. All of these gifts are *so* nice. They are things I can certainly use. You are all so creative."

She in turn was showered with an excited chorus of appreciation for her gifts.

"Stormy Leigh," her father spoke quietly, "This is from me." He handed her a flat, white box. "I thought you might be needing a new one."

Stormy lifted the box lid carefully, parted the tissue paper, then stared with mixed feelings at the white leather Bible. Guiltily she remember the old one lying on the top shelf of her closet collecting dust. She opened to the inscription and read, "To our daughter and God's, from Mom and Dad."

"Thanks, Daddy," she said huskily, her eyes brimming with tears.

"I've taken the liberty of underlining some verses in it. Maybe they'll be helpful to you sometime."

"Daddy! Oh, Daddy! Come see what Adrian got me," Amy's shrill voice broke into the tender seclusion that enveloped Stormy and her dad. Grabbing her father by the hand, Amy urged him to his feet and over to a large rocking horse.

A magnificent creature, it had a flowing glossy mane and tail, and its muscles rippled in the light as it moved on curved rockers.

"Adrian! It's beautiful. A superb piece of work," Anna said in awe, as she stroked the polished nose of the wooden pony. "It must have taken months to make it."

"It was well worth it," Adrian's dark face glowed with pleasure as he lifted Amy onto its back. "Besides, I knew you always exchanged homemade Christmas gifts. To me, they are special because you put a little of yourself in each of them. So I decided to do the same thing."

His smile was almost shy as he looked to them for acceptance. "It makes me feel more like family."

"Oh, Adrian. I love you," Amy threw her arms around his legs and hugged him as hard as she could. Lifting her shining eyes to his face, she said boldly, "And when I grow up, I'm gonna marry you."

Laughter rocked the room as Adrian bent to kiss her soundly on the top of her head.

"It's good to know I won't die an old bachelor," he declared, as he gave her pony a push. "And now that I know you'll be happily entertained for a little while, my love, I'll hand out the rest of my presents."

But Amy never heard the end of his sentence. She already was riding into a favorite playtime fantasy of cowboys and Indians — one in which she always had the part of the heroine, whether cowgirl or Indian maiden.

"Keith, Kyle. Can you help me carry in some more things?" he asked.

"Sure," they chorused instantly.

"But, Adrian," Anna protested. "You've already given us so much." She waved a hand toward the expensively wrapped gifts beneath the tree, lending an air of elegance to its homey look.

The big man only smiled. "Those are just extras that I picked up sometime back in case there was not time to finish my real projects."

He started out the door, "Be back in a minute."

The open door let in a gust of raw, biting air, and Adrian stepped hastily outside, closing the door firmly behind him.

Stormy turned anxiously toward her mother. She had gotten so caught up in the atmosphere of love and giving that she had temporarily laid aside her hostility toward the unwanted guest. At the moment, he seemed more important than the man she had left behind in Kingston.

"Mama, do you think he might have gotten me a gift?" she asked worriedly.

A thoughtful, pleased expression highlighted her mother's face, as if she could glimpse some hidden thing of which her daughter was unaware.

"I mean, he really doesn't know me," Stormy babbled on as the satisfied look on her mother's face deepened. "It's just that I'd hate not to give him something if he gave me something." Wide-eyed and flustered, she looked anxiously at her mother for advice.

"Well, knowing Adrian, I'm sure there's a gift for you somewhere in that beautiful pile. He isn't one to leave anyone out."

Anna fully expected her daughter to take offense at the thought, but the eyes that met hers were almost childish in their eagerness.

"I'll be back in a minute. I've got something upstairs I can give him."

As she ran upstairs, her feet felt light, and her heart pounded with a fresh excitement. She threw open the door to her bedroom, ran to her suitcase, and flung it upon the bed. Hectically scattering things in every direction, she came to the object of her search. She had bought it impulsively, loving it the instant she saw it. She had wrapped it lovingly, weaving dreams into its ribbons and pinning hopes into its big fancy bow, all the while planning how she would present it to Cliff.

But her hopes and dreams had come rapidly undone when she had seen Denise on Cliff's arm. She had gone home that evening with tears streaming down her cheeks, grabbed up the package and crammed it into the back of her suitcase. When she packed to go home for the holidays, she had smothered it with clothes, uncaring that its pretty wrappings were crushed.

Now she uncovered it with a sigh of relief. At least, it was something she would be proud to give. She did not have to feel ashamed that she had nothing of value to give Adrian McAllister. But her brows puckered and her lips pursed as she viewed the flattened state of the poor bow. Giving it a jerk and a twist, she poked her fingers inside the loops and tried to raise it to its former height. It was hopeless. So she smoothed the pretty, crumpled paper as best she could. Then with a characteristic shrug of her shoulders, she hugged the package to her and hurried downstairs.

6
The Christmas Gift

The sound of excited voices drew her swiftly back to the living room in time to see her mother and Barbara opening a large box apiece. All of them were struck speechless, in awe at the craftsmanship that had transformed wood into objects of marvelous beauty. His presents for Anna and Barbara were pieces of furniture dating back to earlier eras in design.

For Anna, there was an elegant, lady's writing desk with curved legs. Its hinged top was engraved with laughing children whose faces and clothes had been painstakingly handpainted. It had tiny, useful drawers that opened with rounded knobs.

For Barbara, there was a heavy cedar chest. This was not the modern rectangular box, but an old-fashioned chest made much like today's dressers. A scrollwork of vines and flowers had been embossed upon its lid and trailed down its spacious drawers. With many "oohs" and "ahs," the women touched the gleaming wood and explored the drawers with natural curiosity before flying back to Adrian to smother him with thanks and hugs.

The twins were just as excited about the work tables Adrian had made for them. They were extremely gifted in working with wood, metal, and leather, and were overjoyed by their gifts.

Charles had received a gift from Adrian too large to bring in the house! It was a new trailer on which to haul hay. He satisfied himself with a quick run outside to look it over and then came back inside to view it again through the window.

Unashamedly, he embraced Adrian, his voice suspiciously muffled, "Thank you, Son. I've needed one of those for a long time and haven't your skill at building things — although the twins are developing in that direction. It looked as if it would be a long time before I could afford to buy one! I wish I could tell you how much this means to me."

"It was a privilege to make it for you, Charles," Adrian said with respect as the father stepped back and wiped away a stray tear with the back of a big, rough hand. "You're the best friend I've had in my entire life. I'll never be able to thank *you* enough for opening your home to me and sharing your family with me."

Having tired of her fanciful daydreams on the rocking horse, Amy appeared at Adrian's side. She had investigated each of her family's gifts as she crossed the room, and now she had a question for her friend.

"Where's Stormy's present?" she asked loudly, hopping first on one foot and then the other, looking for all the world like a bright-eyed robin.

"Amy, child!" her father admonished, a heavy hand descending sternly in rebuke on his youngest's shoulder.

"It's all right, Charles," Adrian was amused and not in the least embarrassed. "I would rather the child be forward, than shy and backward. It'll stand her in good stead when she has to face the world. I'm glad you're training her in manners, but today is Christmas. I love to see a happy, curious child, so please don't scold her on my account."

Amy, not sure exactly what he had meant but correctly interpreting his gentle tone, stared up at him unrepentantly, one dainty foot tapping impatiently as she awaited his answer. Adrian lifted his dark head and stared intently at Stormy, trying to gauge what her reaction would be to his next statement.

"Well, Amy, Stormy Leigh and I don't know each other very well, and I wasn't sure what she might like. But I brought one of my favorite pieces in the hope that she will enjoy it as much as I have."

He moved over to the tree and bent to pick up a large, flat package wrapped in plain, white paper, bound with a brown, satin bow. Then he walked slowly toward the tall girl who had resumed her seat on the low, wooden stool, sitting with her long legs tucked neatly under her. Stormy had been fighting embarrassment ever since Amy had spoken. But when Adrian turned toward her, she pulled a fake cloak of calm around her nervous limbs and masked her misgivings with a bright, artificial smile. Lifting guileless brown eyes to him, she unconsciously challenged him by her very attitude.

"Fire and ice," he said softly, although no expression showed on his handsome features. "Strange and delightful combination. Fire maiden or ice lady, I never know which it will be. Utterly fascinating."

Stormy could hold his gaze no longer. She knew his words had reached only *her* ears, but they rang loudly in her head. She suddenly felt as if she were suffocating. Her whole body was suffused with heat. She saw his feet stop in front of her, but she did not lift her head.

An unexpected shudder shook her from head to toe, and some strange emotion like childish distress flooded her, keeping her lashes quivering on her smooth cheeks in uncertainty. Her lips grew dry, and she gasped aloud when a long, blunt finger lifted a stray lock of hair from her shoulder and caressed it gently with his thumb. She watched helplessly as the wisp of hair curled itself tightly around his finger. Something melted inside her, and she was as helpless as the fiery curl that wound so meekly around that uncompromising forefinger. Her heart beat erratically, making her breath come unevenly.

He withdrew his finger from the clinging curl and laid the package in her lap without another word. She was so intent on grasping the package with shaking hands to keep it from slipping to the floor that she was not even aware he had walked away. Really! He had the most peculiar effect on her. She never knew what he was going to do or say next!

"Stormy! Are you going to open your present?" Amy was thoroughly disgusted with the slow pace of things. Walking over to her sister, her fingers stole out to pull at the ribbon.

"Amy," her mother admonished, "let Stormy open her own present."

"That's all right, Mother," Stormy smiled at the child whose face had fallen at her mother's rebuke. "I think I could use the help of some nimble fingers."

Amy needed no second invitation. After darting a cautious look at her mother to make sure she was staying within her good graces, she proceeded to help her sister rid the package of its wrappings.

"It's a picture! A wood picture," Amy squealed, wrinkling up her delightful little nose in pleasure. She touched the plaque with inquisitive little fingers.

Stormy felt a large lump rise up in her throat. She frantically wondered if she was going to disgrace herself by bursting into tears. She sniffed hard and examined the plaque with devouring eyes. She sought out all the little details that had been duplicated with realistic exactness.

There in her lap in raised detail, carved into a single piece of solid wood, was the likeness of Westmoor

Heights. Its creator had caught the excellent profile of the grand old house, the little stream that flowed through the low meadow on the west side, and the fence with its overshadowing trees that separated Westmoor from her father's land.

"Oh, look, Stormy!" Amy shrieked, grabbing her sister's unsteady arm and trying to direct her gaze.

"Look at the deers! Look at the deers! There's three of them — a daddy deer, a mama deer, and a baby deer. Come look," she commanded the rest of the family, motioning wildly with one arm. "Come look at the deers!"

While her family admired the lovely piece of art, Stormy closed her eyes, letting an old memory float over her.

It had been a sunny day in June when she had seen in reality the very scene depicted on the plaque. She twitched her nose, recalling the scent of freshly mown hay, wild honeysuckle, and fresh spring water. The little stream had splashed merrily against the small rocks that studded its length, gurgling happily at the froth it created. It had provided restful music for the tall, lanky, red-haired girl who dangled bare feet in its cool shallows and tried to build underwater castles with her toes. She had frozen in place as a large, antlered buck strode proudly into her view, closely followed by his graceful, timid mate, and two spirited fawns dancing on tiny hoofs. She had watched them for what seemed an age, thrilled to see their beauty and innocence.

She aroused herself from her memory with difficulty and found everyone staring at her expectantly. Uh, oh! Her color began to rise. Had she missed something? Was she supposed to answer someone? She turned anxious eyes toward Amy, knowing the child would probably repeat whatever had been said.

"Aren't you gonna thank him?" the child obliged in a loud whisper, making exaggerated signs with her big eyes.

"Oh, uh ... yes. Of course," Stormy gulped, bracing herself for the forbidding task that loomed before her. It should not be all that hard to do. After all, she loved the plaque in her lap. Yet it was hard to thank the man who had been inspired by a love as great as hers for the great, gray house.

"Uh ... uh ... thank you, Mr. McAllister," she stuttered, wanting to say it with all the warmth she could. But to her dismay, her voice sounded stiff and cool.

"Adrian," Amy prompted.

"What?" she asked in confusion, staring distractedly at the little girl who had firmly wedged herself between her mother and her sister.

"Adrian." Amy was persistent, nodding her head decidedly. "'Member? You were gonna start calling him Adrian today. 'Member?" She looked at Stormy, her dark head cocked to one side. "I said I'd help you. 'Member?"

"Amy," Stormy shook her head doubtfully, unwilling to use a more familiar term of address with a man she wanted to keep at a safe distance. "I don't think...."

"Sounds like a great idea to me!" Adrian interrupted, forcefully pulling the conversation into his own arena.

"What do *you* say, folks?" and he looked around at the smiling faces. Stormy knew she had lost.

"Want to try it again?" he asked mischievously, watching the sparks begin to illuminate her soft eyes.

"Not really," she wanted to retort. But for the sake of her family and the holiday spirit, she put on her most gracious air and said sweetly, "Thank you, Adrian."

Her tone and words were perfectly acceptable to her unsuspecting family, but she saw Adrian's eyes narrow and his lips thin slightly. He had clearly read the scorn behind her thanks. She shivered at the warning in the sharp jerk of his dark head. Instinctively, she knew if she did not heed that warning, he would not hesitate to administer discipline. She shivered again. There was a certain thrill in the thought that made her lip quiver and her legs feel weak. A fleeting thought that he would make an excellent father startled her, and she moved away from the idea at full speed. There was no way she wanted to consider that he might have any good traits!

Just because he could create beautiful things and had given her a lovely gift did not mean that he was on the up-and-up in his relationship with her family. She clucked her tongue in decision. She would keep a close watch on him and see if she could figure out the reason for his friendliness. Maybe her family was naive, but she certainly was not.

Two years out in the world had opened her eyes to a lot of fake people. She was not going to have her precious family hurt by this shyster. Rich people did not associate with poor people for no reason at all. There was something odd about the whole situation. Adrian McAllister had something up his sleeve. Her hand slipped down beside the stool, following the path of her thoughts. She had decided not to give him the present she had laid down on the floor at her feet.

But it was too late. Amy's quick eyes had followed her movement. She pounced on the gift.

"Oh, Adrian," she squealed, snatching the box from Stormy's reluctant hands, "Here's another present for you. Isn't it, Stormy? Isn't this Adrian's present?"

Wretchedly, Stormy nodded, and watched in dismay as her little sister ran to Adrian. No one but her mother saw the look on Stormy's face. The others were gathered around Adrian, watching his nimble fingers undo the squashed bow. Anna studied her daughter's face, reading the vivid emotions with accuracy. She sighed softly and rose to her feet.

"Stormy," she held out a hand, and after a second of hesitancy, it was grasped. She then led the girl over to Adrian's chair and leaned over to view the gift he was holding with such great care. Stormy held back a little, wondering if he would find her gift silly. She wished she had kept it for herself. But when he raised his head, his eyes held a look of delight.

"Stormy Leigh," his voice was warm and vibrant. A light shiver, like the touch of a feather, ran all the way down her spine. "This is stunning. Absolutely beautiful." He touched it with a light, admiring finger.

"It's uh ... just a paperweight," she mumbled, unable to stop the sweet, glad feeling that was sweeping away her better judgment.

He held it up high enough for everyone to see, and the light from the window caught hold and brought it to life. It was a lovely full-blown rose captured in a large, round, crystal globe. Resting on one of its velvety, crimson petals was a large butterfly. From wing tip to wing tip, it was splashed with every vivid hue of the rainbow, colors that vibrated with life upon a black, silken underskirt. It was poised serenely on the petal with its head uplifted as if giving thanks to its Creator before drinking the sweet nectar of the rose.

Adrian shook his head slowly. "No, Stormy Leigh, it is not just a paperweight to me. It's a picture of God's handiwork in all its perfection. A creation like this puts man's efforts to shame. God truly is the Master of every form of art."

He looked toward Stormy just as the light caught her also within its grasp and touched the enchanting profile of her face with a rosy glow.

"Man can never take an object and make it more beautiful and more perfect than the One who first created it. Thank you, Stormy Leigh. I really like it. I'm going to put it where I can see it often. It'll help remind me of how big and wonderful God is."

This time, when Anna Winters looked at her eldest child, she smiled. This girl looked more like the one who had left home two years ago. Gone was the cynical air, suspicious manner, and haughty eyes. She had the look of a child who has just been rewarded for doing something worthwhile.

The watching mother wished she could have the guarantee that her daughter would stay happy. But she knew that only a change of heart could change a way of life. So she lifted the girl up to the Lord in silent prayer, asking that He would guide her steps and protect her from the ways of the world. She was fully satisfied that He was able to keep those whom she committed into His keeping, and with a smile, she left Stormy in His care.

7

How Stormy Got Her Name

Christmas dinner turned out to be a happy affair after all. Stormy felt like a new person. She laughed a lot, and no thought of Clifford Callahan disturbed her. Her job, her friends, and her other lifestyle seemed far away as she joined whole-heartedly in the celebration. She felt happier than she had in months, and her joy sparkled in her smile.

Adrian was surprised to see the difference in her. Right before his eyes, she had changed from a very pretty girl to one of amazing loveliness. In fact, his eyes developed an alarming habit of following her around as she helped set the table and prepare the meal. He wondered what had happened, but thought it best not to ask, contenting himself with the hope that it would be permanent.

Stormy was not sure what had happened either, but she was not going to waste time trying to figure it out. She had a sneaky feeling it had something to do with receiving a few words of appreciation from a man who she thought disliked her as much as she disliked him.

"Chalk that explanation up to female reasoning," she thought, and grinned. It did not make sense, but it was true.

They seated themselves noisily around the table, and a sweet, warm feeling stole over Stormy as she looked around at each member of her family. They were so precious. Each of them was so special and dear. Why had she not come home more often? Why had she not realized how much she was missing? Her mother had written faithfully each week, trying to keep her in touch with the family. But Stormy's replies had been few and brief. Barbara had written frequently, also, and the twins occasionally. Stormy strongly suspected they wrote only when they received a prod from their parents.

She smiled regretfully at their handsome faces. During her absence, they had changed from young boys to young men. She sighed softly. She had missed out on Barbara's first date, Amy's first kindergarten days, and oh, so many things. A closer look at her father revealed new wrinkles etched upon his forehead and a faint sprinkling of gray at his temples.

Her thoughts swung to her mother. She, of all of them, seemed unchanged by the years. Her lovely face was still untouched by age. Her brow was young and serene. Her eyes were fountains of happiness mirroring a contented soul. She basked in the light of her family's love and respect and thrived upon taking care of them. If her father was the spiritual giant of the family, carrying them through each difficult situation with an unwavering faith and trust in God, her mother was the solid foundation upon which the family rested.

They relied on the wise advice and guidance which she freely gave. The goal of her life had been to establish each of her children in the Word of God, to send them out into the world with a strong Christian faith and the knowledge of God's goodness and love. She knew that if she could teach them His ways, they would make it on their own.

"Adrian," the father's voice rang with gladness, "would you please ask God's blessings upon the food?"

"All right," Adrian smiled at the faces turned toward him. "I feel honored at being asked to share your Christmas, and I appreciate you making me feel as if I were one of you."

His voice deepened, and Stormy was astonished to see his eyes grow shy as he asked tenderly, "Could we all clasp hands and form a circle of friendship and love that will never be broken?"

Willing hands eagerly caught at one another, and the circle was made complete. A joining of their spirits took place in that split second as hearts were filled with a love that flowed from each other's fingertips. A strong feeling of loyalty sprang up so forcefully inside Stormy that she nearly sobbed with the intensity of it as Adrian bowed his head and began to pray.

His prayer was spoken with such authority, and yet such humility, that the room became filled with the presence of God. Stormy was shaken. It was as if scales fell off her eyes. She could plainly see her neglect of His desires. Had she been standing, her knees would have buckled. She realized that Jesus was in their midst seeing all her shortcomings and failures. In her mind, she could see His face grow sad. Tears flowed unbidden down her cheeks as she caught a vision of how He must see her.

She was too busy with everyday life, work, friends, and Cliff to spare any time or thought for Him, too occupied with getting the most out of life to share His love with someone else, too industrious about her own affairs and her own gain to care or be concerned with the spiritual welfare of those around her. She wanted to weep bitterly. The beauty and life of the words of praise being offered up to the King of kings tore at her hardened heart, birthing a hidden longing. She determined to again walk in the footsteps of her Lord.

As his "Amen" rang triumphantly into the quiet room, every eye was dimmed with tears. Each of them felt as if they had been personally brought to the very throne of God to receive His blessing. Stormy mopped her face surreptitiously in embarrassment. But everyone else was too busy tending to his or her own tears to notice how touched she had been by the prayer.

"Thank you, Adrian," Anna gave him a brilliant smile that shone like a rainbow through her tears. "That was beautiful. I feel as if I have been sitting in the presence of Jesus."

"Amen," Charles echoed fervently.

"Do you think Jesus would care if we ate now?" Amy piped up anxiously, her little tummy growling loudly. "I sure am hungry."

The twins burst into laughter, and Keith offered her the large platter of hot, fluffy biscuits.

"Here you go," his hand shook as he laughed, causing the plate to wobble precariously.

Several pairs of hands reached out to steady it.

"You'd better feed that hungry little belly of yours, little Sis, before it eats you alive."

"Ah, it wouldn't do that," Amy eyed her big brother in childish scorn. "I know better than that."

She was to suffer much teasing throughout the meal, but she endured it bravely. And if the truth were known, she enjoyed the attention being showered upon her.

The meal was the ideal of homestyle cooking. The table was crowned with a large stuffed bird and a huge glazed ham that had basked for hours under a sweet glaze of honey and pineapple. Homegrown and home frozen or canned vegetables were plentiful — from creamy, whipped potatoes, green beans and corn-on-the-cob to pickles, peppers, and jellies and jams. Brown gravy, salads, little bowls of tasty cheeses and sausages, and cranberry sauce were separated by saucers of spiced apple rings and rice pudding.

"By the way," Adrian looked across the table at Stormy with a mischievous gleam in his dark blue eyes, "I'd still like to hear the story of how Stormy Leigh got her pretty name."

Stormy blushed rosily in confusion. She had never thought of her name as pretty or unique, just different and odd. Warmth again surged through her as her name rolled off his lips with familiarity.

The story had been told so many times one would suppose the family had long grown tired of hearing it, yet such was not the case. They all listened attentively. Even Stormy found herself eager to hear it again and secretly watched Adrian's face to see what he thought.

Charles began to chuckle. Seeing that his daughter was not going to protest this time, he nodded to his wife, "Go ahead, Anna. I can see you're itching to tell it."

She immediately launched into the story.

"Well, Adrian, Charles and I were very excited when I became pregnant with Stormy. We were deeply in love and felt a baby would make our lives complete. We both wanted a little girl and felt so sure we would have one that we didn't even pick out a boy's name."

Her eyes sparkled, and a soft trill of laughter rippled from her lips as she continued.

"We both liked the sound of Elizabeth Ann and decided that was what we would call our little one. But as I'm sure you know, things don't always work out as planned."

Everyone's attention was focused on her, and Amy was so engrossed that she stopped eating with her fork poised halfway to her mouth. When the mound of potatoes returned to her plate with a soft plop, she never even noticed. This was the first time she remembered hearing the story.

"Charles and I woke up one morning when the baby was already a week overdue and heard pigs snuffing and snorting outside our window. Charles jumped out of bed, told me to stay where I was, and ran outside to see what was happening."

Anna began to laugh in earnest. The memory was as real as if it had been only yesterday. Her eyes met her husband's with such a look of love that everyone smiled.

"I climbed rather awkwardly out of bed and waddled over to the window. And, oh, what a sight met my eyes!"

Her laughter was so infectious that the others began to laugh with her. The old kitchen rang with the sound of their merriment.

"Charles was out there in his old red-striped pajamas and floppy bedroom slippers trying to chase twenty pigs back into the lot. His hair was standing on end, and he was jumping around waving his arms and yelling at the top of his lungs. I laughed so hard I cried — and that's when the labor pains began." Her eyes twinkled merrily at her husband's pink face.

Then she smiled at Stormy, "By the time your father had the pigs rounded up, I was waiting on the porch with my suitcase in hand. Poor darling," she looked down the table at him in sympathy, "he didn't have time to wash his hands, change his clothes, or even comb his hair. He just grabbed a coat, put me in the car, and drove like a maniac to the hospital. And it was a good thing he did! Stormy was born five minutes after we got there. But I will never forget the look on his face as we drove to the hospital.

"He looked so upset and disgusted and kept saying over and over, 'If she waited this long to come, why on earth couldn't she have waited a little longer?'"

All heads turned toward Charles, who nodded sheepishly, and admitted reluctantly, "It's true. Every bit of it."

"When the nurse brought me the baby, she said, 'This sure is a stormy little gal. She's already awakened half the babies in the nursery. She really has a mind of her own!' And I looked at you, Stormy, with your little red face all puckered up as you squalled at the top of your lungs. You waved your little fists and kicked up a storm, and I knew the name we'd picked out would never fit you. Yet, when the nurse placed you in my arms, you immediately hushed."

Her tone grew gentle and reflective, her lovely eyes softening with remembrance.

"Your father walked over, looked down at you, and said, 'Anna, we've picked the wrong name for this child. She's going to be strong-willed and independent, but she will also be loyal and loving.' I looked up at him, and the name slipped out of my mouth without thinking, 'Little Stormy. Our little Stormy.' Then you opened those great big beautiful eyes of yours and just cooed."

"And that settled it," Charles concluded. "Leigh was the name of her great-grandmother, who had red hair. So we decided then and there to name her Stormy Leigh."

"Oh, that was a good story," Amy declared, once again attacking her potatoes with a healthy appetite. "Tell us another one, Momma."

"I think we need to let your mother eat her dinner, Amy," her father smiled. "Or it will get cold. We can tell more stories later."

As the conversation became more general, Stormy found it nearly impossible to keep from watching the man seated across from her. He intrigued her beyond all reason. She would like to have asked him some personal questions, but promptly decided not to. Once she looked up to see him eyeing her thoughtfully.

She met his gaze unflinchingly, though defensively, until he said very softly, his voice a mere whisper, "It suits you well, Stormy Leigh. Your name suits you very well."

She ducked her head, squirming as his low chuckle reached her ears. He was having fun at her expense again, and she did not like it. But today she felt shy, and her quick tongue had become slow and stumbling. Was there some invisible chemistry between them that made her react personally to everything he said and did? It was strange how she could feel alarmed and excited at the same time whenever the master of Westmoor Heights paid her the slightest bit of attention!

She stole a glance at him, but he was now absorbed in a conversation with her father about the farm. He paid no attention to her for the rest of the meal. His eyes, whenever they did chance to light upon her, were once again cool and very impersonal. She was glad when it became time to clear the table. She wanted to move a safe distance from the man who had the power to turn her little world upside down. The men adjourned to the family room, and Anna and the girls began to put the kitchen in order.

"Mother, when did Adrian move into Westmoor, and where did he come from?" Stormy asked in a single breath. Her mother's dark brows rose in thought.

"Well, let me see. He moved into the house about a year ago, after spending the previous nine months restoring it. Mr. Westmoor was his great-uncle."

"What did he do before he moved here?" Her voice betrayed her consuming curiosity. Barbara looked at her wonderingly but kept quiet as their mother willingly furnished the information.

"He owns several companies that manufacture automobile parts. He seems to have done well in everything to which he has put his hand. Of course," she said matter-of-factly, "he gives all the credit to God."

Stormy looked at her, started to speak, then held her tongue. She still had doubts about Adrian's honesty, but now was not the time to voice them. Her mother went on to tell of the things Adrian had done for them and for others in the community. She was surprised to learn he had recently built a new community center for Christian young people to use.

It took longer than usual to straighten the kitchen, because Stormy's hands often were idle as she stopped to analyze what Adrian was doing for the little town. Barbara often added bits of information with as much pride as she would have for one of her brothers.

The family spent the remainder of the afternoon outside. They sped on sleds down the long hill on the north side of the house, taking turns and riding double so everyone could have fun. Then they put on razor-sharp skates and sliced about on the pond. It was an afternoon Stormy would never forget. She greedily absorbed the love and warmth of her family, finding it helped to restrain a growing sense of reluctance that came whenever she thought about going back to work.

She enjoyed her work, priding herself on her accomplishments. There really was no reason for the dread she was feeling. Finally, however, she pushed away the thought of tomorrow, refusing to look beyond the present moment.

That night, she lay in bed with a faint smile curving her generous lips, recalling the moment when Adrian had pushed her sled off the north slope. She had been holding Amy close to her, and as Adrian gave their sled a mighty thrust, she had looked up and smiled at him. With eyes glistening at her unspoken invitation, he had jumped onto the back of their sled with the agility of a male tiger. Wrapping his arms around them, he had guided their sled softly down the hill. Using his body to shield them from the spraying snow that met their every turn, his great strength had forced the sled to meet his every demand.

Stormy yawned softly, patting her mouth. It had been the best event of the afternoon as far as she was concerned. It had felt so good. A feeling of gentle strength had flowed from his arms … and yet, her body had tingled with excitement.

She was too sleepy to think about it any longer. All these disturbing feelings did not make sense! How could she be so easily attracted to a man because he was good-looking and masterful? What about Cliff? It could not be, yet her heart repeatedly whispered that it felt a lot like love.

8

The Ways of the World

The closer Stormy got to Kingston the next day, the more distant her weekend seemed. She always had been able to adapt easily to a new environment and quickly accept the new in place of the old. This asset had carried her from home to college, from college to several business-es, and finally to Eastlands, Inc. with few ties or scars. She thought she had learned it was far less painful to relin-quish things quickly than to try to hold onto things that could never be the same. But she was to find in the coming days that this principle was much harder to live by in things of the heart.

It was a glorious day for driving. The snow sparkled in the sun. The sky was a brilliant blue, and the air was fresh and crystal-clear. The world looked innocent and unspoiled. The fields were dotted with flocks of woolly sheep and herds of thick-coated cattle. Occasionally, there was a streak of red as a little fox trotted alertly down a familiar path in search of any game his keen nose could detect, or the flash of a white tail as a deer turned in flight.

All the glimpses of life and beauty were lost to Stormy. The droop had returned to her lips, and a concen-trated frown showed itself between her arched brows. Cliff ... how was he? Where was he? How had he spent Christmas?

The days at home had been nice and reviving, and she was glad for the new pictures of her family that she carried in her mind. She meant to keep her promise to return soon. She was not going to lose close contact with them again. They were precious and meant the world to her, and yet ... she was torn between wanting to be with them and wanting to get on with her fast-paced successful life in the business world.

Her car was loaded down with gifts and home-canned goodies. Beside her on the seat rocked a little figurine Adrian had given her as the family pressed last-minute surprises into her hands. It was a darling little girl, carved out of wood, a thin child with long arms and legs, flying pigtails, and an earnest expression on her pretty face. A sprig of wild flowers was clasped tightly in her hands, and she was barefoot. The little statue was so life-like, it captured each person's heart who saw it.

Anna had held it for a long time, marveling at how perfect it was in every detail. Then the familiarity of it had dawned on her. She was puzzled, but said nothing, knowing time would tell if she was right or not.

But the little gift irked Stormy. She had begun to battle strong feelings of disloyalty. Perhaps she had no right to condemn Cliff when she had, however innocently, been involved with another man. Adrian's kisses pricked her conscience. Fire raced through her veins at the memory, and she despised herself for her weakness. How could she have allowed such a thing to happen? Especially with a man she barely knew.

An emissary of the enemy of the soul whispered encouragingly that it was Adrian's fault, so she decided to blame him. He was supposed to be such a good Christian! Somehow, her mind conveniently forgot that he did not know that she was "practically" engaged. All of the special feelings of friendship she had felt toward Adrian began to evaporate beneath her guilt-ridden conscience.

She vowed never again to be disloyal to Cliff. She pictured him in her mind, dwelling lovingly on each feature and refusing to see any comparison between him and

Adrian. Yet there were some rather obvious comparisons which did not favor Clifford in the least. It was horribly frustrating to have Adrian McAllister's face intrude into her most devoted thoughts of Cliff. It must be because his face was the last one she had seen. Surely in time it would fade, and she would be rid of it!

By the time she reached the city, she was mentally and emotionally exhausted, as well as physically tired from the long drive. She longed to be back home again, throwing herself across the old faded quilt and having a good cry. Her modern, sparsely furnished apartment was empty, lonely, and cold. She stared around at her prized possessions and found no joy. How could she have gotten so used to the constant sound of noisy, happy voices in so short a time?

With lagging steps she carried her luggage and gifts inside, then curled up on the couch and kicked off her shoes. Running tense fingers through her hair, she tried to sort out her thoughts. She jumped when the sound of the phone broke the chilly silence.

"Hello?"

"Stormy?"

The sound of her mother's voice had an immediate effect on the girl. Her face brightened, and her next words carried a new lilt.

"Mother! Oh, Mother, it's so good to hear your voice again," she exclaimed, then laughed self-consciously. "I guess that sounds silly since I saw you this morning."

Little did she know the throb of love that beat in her mother's breast as she longed to gather her girl in her arms and keep her safe and sheltered. But an inner understanding told her that Stormy would have to do things on her own, learning from her own experiences and mistakes.

"Not at all. I just wished you could have stayed longer. There was no time for us to have a good, long, heart-to-heart talk as I wanted us to have."

"I know, Mother. I wanted to, also," Stormy said regretfully. "There was so much I wanted to do and not nearly enough time to do it all."

"I know, Honey. You must be worn out after that long drive. I won't keep you any longer. Daddy and I just finished our prayers, and we wanted to call and make sure you had gotten home all right."

"Thanks, Mother. I'm glad you called." Stormy was unaware of the loneliness in her voice. "Please kiss everyone good night for me, and," her voice broke with the suspicion of a sob, "remember to pray for me."

"We always do, Stormy," her mother's voice was strong and reassuring, a soft glow of warmth in the cool, darkened room. "We love you very much, and you are very precious to us. We also expect to see you again soon. Okay?"

"All right," Stormy smiled through her tears. Her mother could sense the smile, and it comforted her.

"Good night, Stormy Leigh."

"Good night, Mother."

Fighting an overwhelming sense of homesickness, Stormy hung up the phone. But as she sat staring at it, she began to feel better. No one in the world had a family as wonderful as hers. And it would not be long before she saw them again.

She sprang to her feet whistling loudly. At a flick of her wrist, light flooded the room. She put on a Christmas record, plugged in the lights that flooded her little artificial tree with silvery life, and went to the kitchenette to fix a cup of hot chocolate. Recklessly adding several marshmallows, she carried it back into the living room. Tomorrow, she would probably regret all those calories of the holiday. Cliff had a hurtful way of letting her know when she was putting on weight. But tonight she pleased no one but herself!

In the back of her mind was the whispered comment of a certain dark stranger as he held her tight on a sled that flew downhill like the wind.

Adrian had said, "I like a woman who feels like a woman, smells like a woman, and kisses like a woman."

She had blushed at his words and longed wildly for a fleeting moment to respond as if she were his woman.

Unpacking with fresh energy, at last everything was put away except for three things. She lifted down the simple, flowery print that hung on the wall behind the couch and replaced it with the plaque of Westmoor Heights. Next she placed her new Bible on the small, glass-topped coffee table. Sitting down briefly, she fingered the little figurine, also wondering about its haunting familiarity. Then she set it carefully down beside the Bible.

Standing up, she looked around the room in satisfaction. The little pieces of home that she had brought back with her added a nice, homey touch. Reluctantly, she flipped the light switch and left the room. Tomorrow was a work day. She had better get some sleep.

At the sound of the alarm the next morning, she awoke rested and ready to face another day. Slipping out of bed humming a catchy tune, she tried to order in her mind all of the things that must get done that day. A quick, hot shower, a splash of Cliff's favorite cologne, and she was ready to slip into a chic wool dress in muted shades of gold. Stepping into dark brown pumps, she threw a few necessities into a matching clutch purse and shrugged into her heavy coat. Frowning, she wondered what was missing. Ah, her gloves! They lay on the table beside her Bible, and she paused before picking them up.

Oh, dear. She had meant to get back into the habit of reading her Bible first thing in the morning. But she had failed to remember her new commitment, and it was too late to do anything about it this morning.

"Tonight," she promised softly, one finger running lightly over the soft, white surface.

Within ten minutes she was whipping into her personal parking space. Grabbing up her purse, she stepped out with a smile. Her steps were purposeful, and she looked very professional as she entered the multistoried building and strode toward her office.

Cries of "Hi, Leigh!," and "Did you have a merry Christmas?" came at her from every side. She smiled and answered lightly. It was time to get back into the old groove of her "real" life again.

When she opened her door, she felt a sharp pang of disappointment. No Cliff. Of late, he had made a habit of being in her office to greet her with a kiss, an intimate flash of sparkling blue eyes, and a husky, "Good morning, Doll." She had needed that greeting desperately this morning. Perhaps she had been *too* hard on him on the phone, although he needed to know how hurt she had been. Or perhaps she was just early. She hoped so.

She put her purse away and sat down at her desk. Pulling a thick computer printout toward her, she studied its impressive figures with a concentrated effort. But her mind stubbornly refused to grasp the information and kept drifting away to worry at her personal problem like a dog at a bone.

Maybe she *had* made too much of Cliff's date with Denise. Her heart caught painfully in her breast, skipping a beat. Fear threatened to turn into panic. What if Cliff was still angry? What if he wanted to break off their relationship? She could not bear that. Had he found someone else during the holidays? Her eyes blurred at the thought. She pushed away from the desk and walked over to stare at the ugly abstract on the wall.

It was odd how their tastes differed, she thought suddenly. He had given her the painting with pride of his own appreciation stamped on his face, and she had not the heart to tell him that she did not like it. He had taken great pains to explain its meaning to her. Finally, she had pretended she saw something in it just to escape his sharp tongue. Yes, she did see something — blobs and blotches and more blobs! The painting actually was rather awful and depressing. Oh, how she wished the plaque of Westmoor Heights was hanging in its place.

She swung around as the adjoining door opened and saw a cool, defiant Cliff. No word of greeting parted his thin lips. His icy eyes held a guarded look. No warmth softened his hard face, no welcoming arms were held out. He seemed like a total stranger, and Stormy panicked.

"Cliff!" She flew to him like a homing pigeon, throwing her arms around his slim waist and pressing her head against his chest. "I'm so glad to see you. I've missed you so much." She leaned back to look at him, and asked, "Did you miss me?"

A hint of relief appeared in his eyes as he saw her anxious face, and he thawed out immediately.

"Sure I did, Leigh," he hugged her. "Did you have a nice Christmas?"

"Oh, yes," her voice sparkled with happiness. "I did. It was so much fun. It was great to see my family again. It's been so long since I spent a few days with them, and you cannot imagine how much the kids have changed."

Almost breathless with enthusiasm and the desire to share her holiday, she did not see Cliff's eyes flash with irritation.

"With all that fun going on, I don't see how you had time to miss me," he snapped pettishly.

Stormy stopped in dismay. "I'm sorry, Cliff," she faltered. "I didn't mean to just rattle on and on about it."

"I know, I know," he muttered impatiently. "It's a long time since you had seen them, and you had a super time. Maybe we had better just get to work on that report we have to give this afternoon." He released her and stalked back into his office.

"Cliff!" the pitiful cry that ripped from her throat was lost in the slam of the door.

Tears welled up helplessly in her eyes. What was wrong? She had been more than willing to forget and forgive his date with Denise and to accept his explanation. But he acted as if she had committed an unforgivable sin by enjoying her Christmas holiday. Frantically she sought for answers. But there were none — except a rather empty explanation that he was jealous of her family. Could that be it? She grabbed at the possibility in desperation. Well, she would go out of her way to prove she loved him more than anyone else. Then things would be the same again.

So she dried her eyes, blew her nose, and settled down to a grueling day of work. She met Cliff several times during the course of the day. But each time, he greeted her curtly, as if she were no more than a casual friend. Thankfully, she had no time to worry about it until the end of the day. And by that time, things had changed for the better.

At 5 p.m., she returned to her office to collect her purse and coat, smiling over the thought of the directors' meeting she had just attended. She and Cliff made a splendid team! They had presented their ideas and recommendations in a brilliantly planned and equally shared presentation. They had received a unanimous vote to proceed with their projects.

Eastland, Inc. manufactured tiny computer components and distributed them to large companies, who in turn produced a finished product for public sale. Through several months of after-hours research, she and Cliff had discovered a cheaper, more efficient way to produce the minute parts with no loss of quality. Furthermore, they had won a huge contract from a previously uninterested conglomerate.

Success and elation shone in their faces as they left the board room, and they agreed to spend the evening celebrating. Starry-eyed, Stormy walked out into the cold December air. Everything was going to be wonderful. Maybe, just maybe, tonight would be that special night of which she had dreamed for so long.

9

A Matter of Forgiveness

At seven, Stormy was ready and waiting. She knew beyond the shadow of a doubt that Cliff would be late — he always was. But she tried to patiently overlook his chronic tardiness, sternly telling herself she must learn to accept Cliff's ways. She had tried several times gently to hint she would like for him to be on time but had met with no success. That his unwillingness to change was another example of self-centeredness did not even enter her mind.

She sat down on the couch and idly picked up the Bible. Flipping casually through the pages, she stopped to read an underlined verse that seemed to leap from the page and catch her eye — Matthew 6:14: "If ye forgive men their trespasses, your heavenly Father will also forgive you."

She had heard it all her life. But tonight somehow it sounded different. She had forgiven Cliff, but forgive Denise? She was not sure that she could. The girl knew that she and Cliff were practically engaged, yet she constantly flaunted herself in front of him. She remembered how Denise had entwined her arm in Cliff's, pressed her lovely body possessively against him and gazed admiringly into his face with seductive eyes.

Forgive her? Forgive someone whom she felt was setting out to deliberately destroy her relationship with Cliff? She felt uncomfortable and disturbed. The verse was destroying all the pleasure she had felt about her success. She laid the Bible down in irritation. She should have waited until later to read it.

Fretfully, she got to her feet and paced the small room. Where on earth was Cliff? Her temper began to flare, and she sought to smother it. The last thing she wanted was to dampen the spirit of the evening by getting upset. She made herself sit down and close her eyes, trying hard to relax. She knew the strain of the day had made her on edge, and she hoped to avoid the let-down feeling that usually follows emotional highs.

The sound of a sharp rap on her door brought her quickly to her feet. She snatched up the lovely beaded purse that matched the irridescent glimmer of beads on the embroidered yolk of her new black dress. She had hesitated a long time before buying it, feeling that its low neckline mocked her standards of modesty. Now she tugged at the draped material, trying to bring it to a more respectable height. She had bought it impulsively, knowing Cliff would rave over it. This was a dress more suited to his taste than her usual attire. He had urged her for a long time to dress differently. But now she wondered if she dared wear it after all.

Deep in her heart, she knew she had reached a point with Cliff where she must stand her ground or sacrifice some of her values for the sake of keeping his love. A spurt of common sense told her it should not be necessary to risk her self-respect or lower her standards to gain love. But the revelation dimmed as she opened the door.

"Oh, Cliff," she breathed, "you look absolutely devastating!"

Her eyes drifted dreamily over his elegant black tuxedo. He wore a white, ruffled shirt and gleaming, black leather shoes. His hair had been brushed into deep, shining gold waves, and his eyes sparkled with anticipation. There was an excitement about him that kindled an answering response in her own eyes.

"And you!" Cliff twirled her around with a slender hand, smiling with satisfaction at the splendid figure she cut in the soft, clinging black dress. "You look gorgeous, Doll. In fact," he placed a warm, moist kiss on her parted lips, "I've never seen you look more beautiful." His lips stole downwards to nuzzle her neck. "Mmmmm. You smell good, too."

Her senses were heightened by his kisses. But she became aware of a new aggressiveness in him that triggered a warning. Shying away from him nervously, she laughed uneasily, "Don't you think we should be going?"

"All right, Doll," he said reluctantly, his eyes bright and glittering. "But I had rather just spend the evening here with you."

"And let me be the only one to appreciate *you*?" her laugh trilled through the suddenly heavy, intimate silence. It was a trifle high-pitched and strained. "I want to show *you* off tonight," she smiled, tucking a persuasive hand on his arm and drawing him toward the door. "Besides, we have a lot to celebrate and talk about."

"I suppose you're right," he sighed regretfully, opening the door for her.

He had chosen a restaurant for tonight that they had not been to before. The food was rich and delicious, the lights were low and seductive, but she felt out of place. The other women's dresses were even more drastically cut than her own, showing in some cases an embarrassing amount of bare flesh.

But Cliff was in his element. Several diners recognized him and came over to talk. Stormy decided to just relax and be glad he seemed proud to have her at his side. Unfortunately, the evening seemed doomed from the moment Cliff ordered their meal. He ordered wine for both of them, and she stared at him in open-mouthed dismay.

"Cliff," she whispered, leaning forward so only he could hear. "You know I don't drink. Why did you order wine for me?"

He smiled confidently, and said, "It's time you changed some of your old-fashioned ways, Leigh." He took her hands in his. "Your choice of dress was excellent and in the right direction. Having a little drink will help set the mood for the rest of the evening. After all, it's only wine."

"But, Cliff," she protested, eyes huge and eloquent in their pleading for his understanding. "I don't want to change my ideas and standards. And this dress may be beautiful," she rushed on, seeing his face darken in anger and his brows draw into an ugly frown, "but I feel uncomfortable in it."

"Your ideas are out of date, and your standards are so high no real man could live by them," he snapped, his eyes narrowed in annoyance. "I know it takes time for someone to change their ways. But you need to keep working at it until you feel comfortable, as comfortable as I do."

He tilted his glass and drank lightly, keeping her pinned with his eye. He squeezed her hand briefly, then released it.

"If you love me, you will change," he said, his mood changing as he continued to sip his wine appreciatively.

Stormy sat in hurt silence. Disillusionment shone in the brown eyes studying the offending glass of innocent-looking liquid. Sometimes Cliff could sound so hard. He seemed to be trying to make her feel narrow-minded and prudish. And yet — she looked longingly at the handsome face turned away from her as he searched the room with his eyes — she did love him so much! Didn't she?

Her hand moved slowly toward the glass. Her fingers curled around its fragile stem. She hesitated. Pressure rose in her chest making her whole body throb with the pain of uncertainty. She felt so confused, and like a child seeking encouragement to do as instructed, she lifted her eyes to her lover's face. If he had provided encouragement at that moment, she would have lifted the glass to her quivering lips and tilted it, letting the crimson color of her sacrifice flow down her aching throat.

But even as she silently cried out to him to give her courage, she realized his thoughts were no longer on her. She turned to see the object of his fascination. Denise! Instantly her hand jerked away from the glass as if burned by the red flame it held. The glass tipped over, and she watched in horror as the wine soaked into the white lace tablecloth. She felt the chill of it as it splattered on the skirt of her dress. The glass rolled to the edge of the table and fell to the floor, splintering into a thousand slivers.

Frantically she sought to mop up the liquid, dabbing futilely at her dress as courteous attendants appeared like magic at their table. She could not lift her eyes to look at Cliff, feeling certain of the irritation she would see on his face. He hated public scenes.

With a soft, smothered cry of apology, she fled from the table. Holding her wet skirt away from herself with a shaking hand, she struggled to find her way through the maze of tables. Once she gained the haven of the empty powder room, she calmed herself by busily washing the wine from her skirt. It would probably stain, but she did not care. She would never wear it again. She dabbed furiously at a stray tear and stepped briskly over to the furnace vent in the floor, allowing the warm air to dry her dress and soothe her chilled heart.

Her dress was still slightly damp when she moved to a mirror to inspect her makeup. Thank goodness, her tears had not ruined it too badly. Then tilting her chin proudly, she marched to the door. She might as well go back and face the music. Maybe, by some stroke of luck, Cliff would not be too upset, and she would not have spoiled the evening for them.

She stood for a moment at the edge of the room, searching out their table. But what she saw made her freeze in shock. Jealousy flared like a flaming shaft through her heart as she watched an intimate little scene unfold before her eyes.

Cliff was sitting with his back to her. She could not see his expression, but Denise was in full view as she sat in the chair from which Leigh had fled. Her eyes were sad and eloquent as she leaned toward Cliff and clasped his hands in hers. She seemed to be pleading for something with every ounce of her lovely body.

As Cliff slowly shook his head, a tear trembled persuasively on the girl's long lashes. She slowly withdrew her hands and rose unsteadily to her feet. Then, as if on impulse, she held out a pleading hand to him, her lips trembling with distress. Apparently he was not moved, for the watching girl could see no movement. Denise then dropped her hand and walked away, head bent, and shoulders drooping dejectedly.

Leigh did not realize she had been holding her breath until Denise disappeared out the opposite door. Suddenly, the air left her lungs in a painful rush. She shifted her feet restlessly, not knowing how to approach Cliff. Should she pretend she had not seen anything? Should she confront him and demand an explanation? Maybe she should just be glad Denise had not persuaded him to do whatever it was she wanted. She decided the best thing was to "play it by ear" and headed across the room.

As she came into Cliff's view, he sprang to his feet and pulled out her chair.

"Are you all right?" he asked anxiously, but his eyes did not quite meet hers and a faint reddish color crept over his fair face. "You rushed out of the room so fast I thought you might have been cut by flying glass."

But you did not care enough to find out, Stormy thought bitterly.

Aloud, she said, "I'm all right. I just needed to wash out my skirt so it would not stain too badly. I am really sorry I made such a mess of things."

"Oh, it was nothing," he hastily assured her, as she stared at him in surprise. "It was just an accident and accidents happen to everybody. Try to forget about it. We are going to start this evening all over again."

His charming smile engulfed her in warmth, and she began to glow with pleasure and reassurance.

"I'm with the most beautiful girl in the world tonight, and we have a lot to celebrate. I intend to make this evening one you'll never forget, Leigh."

He reached over and took her hand, stroking each finger individually. Little shivers of delight swept through her bruised heart. This time when he ordered, he consulted her as to her preferences, treating her as if her every wish were his command, making her feel very special and very desired. This was the Cliff of her dreams, and she loved it. Like a thirsty rose, she soaked up all the attention, responding with love and delight in return.

All thoughts of Denise were pushed away. As the evening progressed, it seemed as if the incident had never happened. They laughed and talked, their feverish conversation laced with pride and success and the expectation of a soon-coming, important promotion.

"Cliff, do you really think we'll get it?" Stormy asked, her eyes big with hope.

"Yes, I think we will," Cliff was confident, his voice growing louder with determination. "Old man Adams said we were due for one, and I think he'll see to it. It'll mean a lot more money, too," he added speculatively.

"Oh, I'm glad," Stormy exclaimed impulsively. "I've been wanting to send some money home to help pay for Barbara's college tuition next fall. Mother and Dad have about all they can handle financially. I know they would appreciate any help I could give them. It was a terrible strain putting me through college although I won a scholarship and worked part time as well. I don't want them to have that kind of burden again."

The excited look faded from her face, and she faltered as she saw Cliff's disapproval.

"Can't Barbara get a job?" he barked irritably. "Most kids nowadays work their way through college."

"I know," she nervously laid her napkin on the table and reached for a drink of her tea. "And she does work summers. She has for several years. But she will still have to have financial help to go on to college."

Abruptly she changed the subject. "What do you have in mind for your raise, Cliff?"

The change in his attitude was amazing. "I have something in mind," he said mysteriously, awarding her a winning smile, "and it includes you."

Stormy's heart fluttered wildly in anticipation. Her face became radiant with joy.

Her pulse was still racing madly when Cliff opened the door of her apartment and ushered her inside. Without turning on the light, he took her in his arms and began kissing her feverishly. Then he stepped away and flipped on the light.

"Ah, Leigh," his eyes moved over her hotly. "I could kiss you all night, if you'd let me. But I don't suppose you would," his laugh was short and humorless.

Stormy stared at him wide-eyed and speechless. Was he asking her to let him stay the night?

"Cliff," she licked her dry lips, drawing his attention to them, "could I make you a cup of tea or coffee?" She turned toward the kitchen in confusion.

He caught hold of her arm and turned her toward him, "No, Doll. It's getting late, and we both have a hectic day ahead of us tomorrow. Come here."

He led her to the couch and tenderly seated her, taking his seat at her side and poising gracefully on the edge so he might see her face. "Leigh, I want to ask you a question." His voice was soft and full of yearning, yet remarkably under control. "And please take your time in answering."

Now that the moment had come, she was unprepared and frightened. Her heart beat fast in her breast.

"I think we make a great team, don't you?"

She nodded, and he went on with his well-rehearsed speech.

"I think we have a great future together. We work well together, have a lot of interests in common, and enjoy each other's company."

He stopped to catch his breath and smile at her confidently.

"To make a long speech short, I think we ought to get married. Will you marry me?"

He looked at her expectantly. Although he had told her to take her time, she knew he wanted an immediate answer. His gaze became seductive, and she threw all caution to the wind, desiring only to be in his arms again and know he belonged to her alone.

"Yes, Cliff! Oh, yes, I will," she cried ecstatically, flying into his waiting arms.

This time his kisses were more demanding, so intense they made her wince as he mashed her lips against her teeth. She hated to struggle to free herself, but he was hurting her. The pain was greater than the pleasure. Her slowing response must have communicated itself to him because he began to draw rein on his passion.

Sitting back and regarding her with narrowed eyes, he fished about in his coat pocket for a small jewelry box and opened it.

"For you, my love," he whispered in her ear, as he drew the ring from its velvet bed.

Light flashed coldly off the modest, square-cut diamond within its frame of tiny encircling diamonds, as she admired its beauty and design. Solemnly he took her hand, slid the ring on her finger, and kissed her again.

"My ring on your finger," he said softly, holding her hand up so he too might admire its beauty. The clock chimed softly twelve times, and he rose abruptly to his feet.

"I've got to go, Doll," his voice grew distant as he glanced at the clock. "See you tomorrow morning." With another hard kiss, he was gone.

Stormy slowly locked the door behind him, totally unaware of her own movements. Minutes later, she crawled wearily into bed. It had all happened too fast, she reasoned, which was why she had such a shaky feeling. The evening's events sort of ran together: Cliff's challenge to her to throw away her principles, overturning the glass of wine, seeing Cliff and Denise together, his strange proposal, and his abrupt departure.

There had been no mention of love in his proposal, and it left her with a sinking feeling of disappointment. Her head was spinning, and only the weight of the ring upon her third finger made any of it seem real.

She smiled faintly and pulled the covers up to her chin. He had been more proud of the ring than she. But then, that was being nasty and mean toward the man she had just promised to marry. Promised to marry! The strength oozed out of her limbs. She felt limp. She had promised to marry a man who had never even said he loved her!

As she fell into a restless sleep of unhappy dreams with disappointing endings, it was well that she knew nothing about the happenings taking place a few blocks away. She would have been terribly disenchanted to learn her new fiance had found a lovely, teary-eyed, young lady on the steps of his apartment. He opened his arms to her and drew her inside his door. But Stormy slept on in innocence, knowing only troubled dreams that vanished with the dawn.

10
The Valley of Decision

The new year ushered in fulfilled hopes, new dreams and plans, and a fresh gust of arctic air. Eastland, Inc. held a New Year's Eve party with a banquet and dance for its employees. Stormy was the envy of all the women present for having obtained the desirable position of the future Mrs. Clifford Callahan. But it was she who sat on the sidelines and watched as Cliff danced the night away, and it hurt unbearably.

When he took Denise in his arms for the last dance of the evening, she choked on her tears and made for the cloak room. She was having serious doubts about the meaning of the ring on her finger. She did not dance, she did not drink, she did not dress as daringly as the other girls, and Cliff seemed determined to make her see that if she stayed that way, she would never fit in anywhere. She knew he was trying to show her she was missing out on some of life's greatest pleasures. But, oh, how she wished he would just accept her as she was and respect her feelings and ideas.

The door to the little room was ajar. She stepped inside, unintentionally eavesdropping on two of her co-workers in deep discussion as they slipped into their fake furs.

"Do you think she knows?" questioned one with all the interest of a practiced gossip.

"I don't know. But it's plain to see," the other one answered. "Course they say love is blind. So I don't know. Maybe she can't see it."

"Do you think someone should tell her?"

"I'm not going to. I believe in letting things take their course. She'll find out soon enough. Besides, she ...," the woman's voice trailed off as she caught sight of the pale-faced girl. "Ah, Lois, are you ready yet? We're going to have to hurry, or we'll miss our rides."

The two women hurried out with only the briefest of nods to Stormy. They acted as if they were afraid she would stop them, she thought in bewilderment. They had never acted that way before. Surely they could not have been talking about her. Or could they? For a minute she was tempted to run after them and ask. Then she shrugged her shoulders tiredly. She was just being silly. And they certainly would not thank her if she made them miss their rides. It was late, and her imagination was getting out of hand.

She collected her coat and stepped back into the hall. As she walked down the corridor, she watched two shadows on the far wall, shadows made by two people around the bend in the hall. They melted together to form one, then separated, and one disappeared. She smiled wistfully. Lovers stealing kisses, no doubt.

But when Cliff came around the corner, her smile froze. Was it just a figment of her overactive imagination? Or did he start suddenly at the sight of her, as if she had been the last one he expected to see? She rubbed her eyes. This was ridiculous. It would make Cliff mad if he thought she suspected him of betrayal. If she really loved him, surely she could trust him.

But as she climbed into bed that night, she ached all over. Cliff had been curt and edgy on the trip home. She had tried her best to talk to him, but he had sulked and made snide remarks about being the only guy at the party who had not danced with his own girl. After a while, she had grown quiet, feeling the pressure rise again in her

112

chest. She was torn between promising him things would be different next time and holding onto her own standards.

She did not like Cliff's manners when he was in one of his moods. So she retreated into a shell of solitude and occupied her mind with thoughts of the next day. The smell of liquor on his breath and the scent of a perfume not hers made her feel ill. She was glad when he left with only the briefest of kisses and a muttered good night.

She reached out to turn off the lamp and fell sound asleep the moment her tired head met the soft pillow. No thought of the promise she had made to read her Bible ever entered her mind.

Days passed in rapid succession. Some of them found her deliriously happy, and some of them found her extremely miserable. The promotions she and Cliff received opened the door for them to be invited to a lot of parties. And constant remarks from Cliff about proper party apparel wore on her convictions, so that to appease him, she began to dress differently.

Her conscience smote her every time she spent money to buy a new party dress, money she had planned to send home. She comforted herself with the thought that her parents would have wanted her to dress well. But her conscience could not be persuaded that they would have approved of the styles she was now wearing. It was in moments like these that she felt sad and disturbed.

In time, however, she became accustomed to her changing habits and forsook thoughts of the moral upbringing that previously had caused such shameful remorse at her present lifestyle to cut into her soul.

The beautiful white Bible was packed away in a suitcase and shoved to the very back of her closet. Cliff also was responsible for this, for he made cutting remarks about it each time he saw it. Stormy honestly meant to get it back out. She only packed it away until she could make room for it in the crowded bookcase in her bedroom. But she had not spent enough time with it to really miss it. So the source of Godly guidance in everyday living was allowed to stay in darkness, where no one could see or read its precious words.

Some weeks after her promotion, Stormy found herself face to face with Denise. She was shocked to find the girl in Cliff's office. Denise looked her straight in the eye and smiled as if she was perfectly at home.

"Do you need something?" Stormy managed to ask, her voice cold and unfriendly.

"No," the answer was as smooth as cream. The girl's eyes widened innocently, "Do *you* need something?"

"What are you doing in Cliff's office?" Stormy demanded, her words spitting out angrily in spite of her attempt to remain cool and in control. "Don't you know that if you need something, you come to me first? Cliff's in a meeting."

"Yes, I know he's in a meeting." Denise's tone was mocking. The expression in her eyes matched the scornful curl of her red lips. "And, no, Miss Winters, I do not have to go through you. You don't own Cliff, and as of today, he has a new secretary — me!"

It was impossible for Stormy to hide her shock, and she could tell the other girl enjoyed upsetting her.

"Oh, yes," Denise continued heartlessly. "Connie quit today, and I'm here to take her place. Of course, I'd like to think Cliff had something to do with that."

Her smile was thin and cruel, and her baby-blue eyes glittered with hatred.

"But then I imagine you'll want to ask him about that yourself. Now, if you'll excuse me, Miss Winters, I have a lot of work to do. But if you should happen to need anything, just call."

Her voice was poisonously sweet and tinged with a gloating triumph that made Stormy furious, but she was helpless. There was nothing more she could say or do, so she turned and left the room with as much dignity as she could manage.

As soon as Cliff came out of the meeting, she called him into her office. She closed the heavy, oak door behind him and shut out the sight of the pretty, young girl filing papers in tall, metal cabinets, with her slender body posed attractively for any wandering eye to admire.

Unable to conceal the fire that flashed in her eyes, Stormy did try to keep her voice calm. But it was hard to keep a tight rein on her strained emotions.

"Cliff, did you know Denise was coming upstairs?" she asked bluntly, studying his features carefully.

"Well, yes," his eyes did not quite meet hers, and she detected a nervous twitch in his hands. "Why?"

"Did you ask for her to be promoted?"

Her heart began to thud heavily as she waited for his answer. She desperately hoped he would deny it. If he would just say he had nothing to do with it, she would believe him regardless of what Denise had insinuated.

He swallowed with difficulty, his Adam's apple bobbing in his slender neck, then immediately assumed an aggressive posture.

"Yes, I did," he stared at her coldly as if she were a complete stranger, and her hopes began to crumble.

"Why?" she cried, her voice cracking with hurt. "Why? When you know how I feel about her."

"Because she is a fantastic secretary. That's why!"

His voice grew louder, grating painfully on her nerves.

"Besides, you're supposed to be such a good Christian. Why don't you act like one and be nice to her? Don't be such a hypocrite, Leigh."

Her eyes flooded with tears, and her face twisted with pain at his words. But he ignored her distress and scowled at her.

"If you're through being childish about this, I'm going to work," he spun on his heel and stalked to the door.

Opening it wide, his next words were clear and unmistakable to both girls. "I don't know what's come over you, Leigh, but I think it's time you straightened up. You'd be a lot more fun to be around if you didn't judge everyone by your standards. You're too sensitive about everything. Why don't you stop acting as if you're better than the rest of us?"

"Cliff!"

Sobs tore from her stricken heart as he slammed the door, and the sound echoed mockingly in her ears. Somehow she found her chair and collapsed into it, quivering as pitifully as if she had been whipped. Wave after wave of anguish threatened to overwhelm her.

Was she going to have to give up all the values she had been taught in order to keep the man she loved? Was she supposed to look the other way when he flirted with other girls and just be content to wear his ring? She could not go on being torn between his ideas and her own personal convictions. She must forsake one and cling to the other. Cliff's taunting and scorn was forcing her to make a decision.

She knew he believed there was a God in some vague sense of His being an unknowable Being. But he considered the Bible too difficult to understand and useless for everyday life. Church was simply a place to go when one felt one should fulfill one's obligation. And life, he had told her on many an occasion, was meant to be lived to its fullest — and he intended to do just that. He felt he never did anything wicked and considered "sin" to be an outdated word.

Her body shuddered with great, racking sobs, and with the instinct of a hurting child, she lifted the receiver and dialed.

"Oh, Jesus, please let her answer!" she prayed over and over as she waited, "please let her answer."

"Hello?"

"Mama!" she cried brokenly.

"Stormy? Honey? Are you all right?"

The miles between them served as no barrier to the mother who instantly recognized her daughter's voice. The sound of heartrending sobs raced terrifyingly across the wires, but the mother did not panic. Instead, she reached to Heaven for instant help.

"Stormy! Take a deep breath. Do you hear me?"

She could not see the girl nod, but sensed that she had, as the crying grew more subdued.

"Now, Honey. Talk to me!"

"Oh, Mama," Stormy wailed, "I feel as if I'm falling apart. I'm going to pieces."

"Why do you feel like that?" came the soft, soothing reply.

"Cliff and I had a fight about another girl. He says I'm jealous. And he said some things that hurt badly. I feel so mixed up about some things he wants me to do and some other things he doesn't want me to do," she cried wildly. "I don't know if I'm making the right decisions. Oh, Mother, I don't think I can handle it."

The disjointed thoughts reached the mother on wings of despair, and she asked quietly, "Have you tried talking to the Lord about it?"

There was total silence on the other end of the line, and Anna knew her question was sinking in deeply.

"Stormy, you know I will counsel and guide you as best I can. But Jesus knows what's in your heart. He can help you unravel all the things you have questions about and give you the right answers better than I can."

"But, Mother," the words came dully over the line after a slight delay, "I'm no longer sure He cares or that He listens. Right now, He seems awfully far away."

"Have you been reading His Word?"

"No, not much."

"Honey, you know He has the answer to all of your problems. But you can't find them if you don't go to Him. Have you considered *His* will for your life, and are you more concerned about the way *He* thinks you should act than the way others think you should act?"

"No, Mother," Stormy answered honestly, "I haven't. I'm not sure I can pick up the pieces and start over again. What if it's not like it used to be? What if I can't ever feel like He's real again?" she cried pathetically.

"God is always the same," came the reassuring words. "He never changes. We're the ones who change. Get your eyes back on Him. Don't be afraid to take a step toward Him, He'll take two steps toward you. However," the warning came loud and clear, "you were the one to walk away. You must take the first step back."

"I really want to," the girl's voice rang with desire. "I thought when I came back to work after Christmas things would be different. I had made some new resolutions, but they all fell through somehow. I guess God thinks I'm a failure." Her voice began to drag despondently.

"Don't be fooled with that old line," her mother advised her. "No one who is trying to do what is right and please Him is a failure in God's sight. Remember! He's on *your* side. He wants you to be happy. He wants you to succeed."

"Thanks, Mother," Stormy's outlook was beginning to brighten and her head seemed clearer than it had in months, "you always did know when to pamper and when to be straight with me."

"I love you, Stormy Leigh," Pure love wrapped its arms around the girl. "We all do. We miss you, and we pray for you. Amy keeps demanding to know when you'll be home again. Can you tell me anything?"

The answer came clear and sure. "I plan on taking a long weekend off before too long. I'd like to come home for your birthday, so tell her I'll see her in about a month."

"That sounds wonderful!" her mother exclaimed, laughing joyfully. "That would be the best birthday gift you could give me. Why don't you bring Cliff with you?" she urged.

Stormy hesitated, causing her mother to wonder about the young man to whom her daughter was engaged, a young man she had learned very little about through the short, rare letters she received from her daughter.

"All right," Stormy said thoughtfully, "I'll ask him."

She heard a brief knock on her outside door and knew her afternoon work had arrived.

"Mother, I've got to get back to work. But thanks so much for helping me. I don't know what I'd have done if you hadn't been in when I called."

"I'll always be here whenever you need me, Stormy. Take care of yourself."

"I will. Love you. 'Bye."

The day went much smoother after that, and she left work in a better frame of mind. She fully intended to go home and make up for lost time with her Lord, but she was met in the parking lot by a very contrite Cliff.

"Leigh," he said uncertainly, then rushed on, "I'm sorry about this morning. I shouldn't have talked to you like that. I guess I ... I don't know, I guess I just had too much on my mind. Would you like to go out for dinner? I'd like to make it up to you."

All thoughts of her plans for the evening disappeared, as she jumped at the chance to spend the evening with him. She could always keep her appointment with the Lord when she got home. But when Cliff left that night, her mind was so full of him and the events of the evening that she forgot her promise.

She felt no desire to have a good long talk with Jesus, choosing instead to go over again and again how nice and loving Cliff had been. He had jumped to her every wish and made her feel as if she was the most important person in the world. He also had agreed to go home with her the next time she went.

Once again, life was good and exciting. Everything was going to be all right. With a satisfied smile, she fell asleep.

11
Two Worlds in Collision

The next few weeks found Stormy ecstatic with happiness when Cliff was at his best and horribly jealous whenever she saw him and Denise together. She felt like a yo-yo, up one day and down the next. A hard look had settled in her eyes from her constant battles with Denise.

The other girl took a devilish delight in hitting at her weak spots and making nasty suggestions that sounded truthful about how Cliff was so helpful and so sweet and considerate. It was, "Cliff this," and "Cliff that," until Stormy wanted to scream! Oh, how she longed to be free of Denise's constant sly digs.

So subtly did Denise plant doubt and suspicion in her heart that often she was not aware of her doubts until they came out in a conversation with Cliff. Then the war was on! Infuriated, he would jump all over her, telling her he was tired of not being trusted. Once he even stalked out of the restaurant where they were eating. She had to call a cab to get home, and always he made her feel she was to blame.

Upset and confused, she wallowed in guilt until she decided that if things were going to work out between them, she was going to have to sacrifice her desire to know the truth and operate on blind trust. The thought of losing him made her sick and drove her to try harder.

By the time she got to the long weekend planned for her next visit home, she was so tired from the extra work stemming from her new position — and from the emotional exhaustion of her relationship with Cliff — that she thought seriously about not going. Cliff had hinted strongly a number of times that he too would like to cancel their plans. But after a call from her mother showed her how excited the family was about the visit, she felt they simply had to go.

They started out early on a Thursday morning with both of them in good moods. Staying away from sticky subjects, they talked only of things that interested both of them. Stormy stopped for lunch at a restaurant she knew served good food.

As they neared her hometown, she began to point out the few points of interest that were dear and familiar, Hutchen's Feed and Grocery Store, the little white church with its tiny steeple, the school with its new addition, and the new ladies' boutique, that according to her mother, was the talk of the town. But Cliff's enthusiasm began to fade as he saw the little country town and its surrounding fields.

"It's kind of small and quaint, isn't it?" he laughed half-heartedly with disdain. Stormy stopped in mid-thought, her head spinning around to look at him.

"Well, yes, I suppose it is," she admitted, "but it's home to me, and I like it a lot better than I do the city." Surprise raced through her as she realized she had spoken a hidden truth.

"Oh, Leigh! You've got to be kidding," he scoffed, with a frown. "There is no comparison between this cow town and Kingston!"

Stormy fell silent, not wanting to shatter the peace by arguing with him. She mentioned nothing about old memories or dreams as they drove by Westmoor Heights, but she craned her neck backwards looking at it as they passed. As they turned down the lane toward her parents' home, she stole little glances at Cliff out of the corner of her eye. Her heart began to pound uncomfortably. She wondered for the first time what he would think of the old farmhouse. She turned to view it with critical eyes, trying to see it as he would.

The late afternoon sun revealed the old house in all of its weatherbeaten drabness. And to the two people in the approaching car, it was obvious that the house's kindly old features were in dire need of a face lift. The cold winter winds had peeled paint from the walls, and several of last year's dirtdobber nests ran neatly down the side of some of the windows. The house looked neat and clean but shabby. It seemed to smile at the homecoming girl, but for the first time, Stormy could imagine how it would look to Cliff.

When he brought the car to a halt, she opened the door and stepped out. She did not feel like waiting for him to come around to help her. She did not want to see the resigned look on his face or the haughty air he wore when faced with something he felt was beneath him.

"Well, this is home," she said happily.

A slight snort was his only answer. She dared not look at him to see if it was intended to express his opinion. It was strange how every fault and flaw stood out for them to see. Things she had never noticed before were now apparent. The old wooden gate was crippled and creaky. The twins had promised to fix it but had never gotten around to doing it. She touched it lightly and fond memories returned of children who could not resist swinging on it, making it sway back and forth in time to their laughter.

A scruffy cat sat on the top step scrubbing its face. It paused in its bath to purr a loud greeting and arch its back against Cliff's immaculate trousers, much to his disgust. Then the door flew open even as Stormy lifted her hand to knock, and a child flew into her arms. The cat grabbed the opportunity and disappeared like magic through the open door.

"Stormy! Oh, Stormy, you're home," the little girl cried ecstatically, hugging her fiercely.

Then as Amy drew away, she saw the slender young man who watched her sardonically. Shyness struck her dumb for a moment. Then she whirled and ran back into the house, calling to her mother at the top of her lungs.

"Mama! Mama! Stormy's home, and she's got a strange man with her! Mama! Mama!"

"All right, Amy. All right. Go catch the cat before it gets into the pork chops," Anna Winters appeared out of the kitchen with a big smile on her face.

Her trim figure was hidden behind a big apron on which she wiped her hands as she came toward them. Stormy hugged her warmly. In the background, they could hear Amy running from room to room in pursuit of the elusive cat, calling, "Kitty! Kitty!"

"Her newest addition to the family," Anna twinkled up at Cliff. "My daughter is very fond of animals, and any strays she finds are made to feel welcome."

"That could be rather dangerous, don't you think?" he asked stiffly, the thought of the ugly, scruffy cat rubbing against his clean trousers still fresh on his mind. "They carry all sorts of diseases!"

"That's true," Anna admitted, looking at him with keen eyes, "but we have a friend who is a veterinarian, and he checks them out for us and gives them shots. We wouldn't allow Amy to have pets that might be injurious to her health."

She did not snub him, but he felt corrected and shifted his feet uncomfortably.

"Mother," Stormy intervened hastily, "this is Clifford Callahan, my fiance."

"Cliff," Anna extended a slender welcoming hand, "I'm glad you came with Stormy."

The statement was simple but warm and sincere, and Cliff felt a little more at ease.

"Did you say pork chops?" Stormy sniffed the air appreciatively. "Mmmm, it smells so good my mouth is watering."

"Supper is ready as soon as you are," her mother glanced toward the stairs. "Everyone is getting cleaned up. We did the chores early, so we would have more time to spend with you. Why don't you take Cliff upstairs to freshen up. The twins are to sleep in Barbara's room, and she is to share yours. Cliff will have the twins' room."

Giving them both a motherly pat, she flashed a lovely smile at her future son-in-law, "Supper will be on the table when you come down."

Stormy headed for the stairs. Cliff, following closely behind her, remained very much on the look out for the child and the cat. But a few minutes later, they were downstairs being swooped upon by Stormy's brothers and sisters determined to shower them with affection and welcome. Stormy soaked it all up, reveling in the comfort it brought her heart, but Cliff distinctly was ill-at-ease.

"Is your family always this demonstrative?" he whispered in her ear as they found their places around the table.

She stared back at him in surprise, "Sure. Isn't yours?"

"You must be kidding," his whisper was loud and incredulous. "We show a little more reserve and taste in our displays of affection."

With her face flushing at his rebuke, she moved toward the two vacant seats. Cliff seated her politely, and she thought sadly, "You may not always be able to predict his attitudes or moods, but you can always depend on him being a gentleman around other people."

They had just started to eat when a knock on the front door sent Amy bounding down the hall. A moment later, they heard her shrill squeal of excitement. As they waited for a clue to the visitor's identity, Amy's voice carried clearly back to the kitchen.

"Stormy's home!" she announced to the guest in a high-pitched voice, "an' she brought a man with her."

Then a fraction of a second later, "But I don't like him at all." Stormy squirmed in dismay and even more horrified apprehension of what else might be forthcoming from her little sister. And she was right!

"He don't like my cat, an' he told Mama it was dangerous to have pets," Amy's voice became even more outraged. "He thinks ol' Tom's got disease — whatever that is. But I think he's just afraid of Tom. Does disease mean he's got sumpin' like fleas?" she asked as she and the visitor neared the kitchen. "'Cause I gave him a bath last night, an' that shoulda killed all that old disease!"

Upon that triumphant note, she entered the kitchen proudly leading her captive visitor, Adrian McAllister.

"Adrian!" Anna finally managed to say, not knowing whether to laugh or cry at her youngest's frank disclosures. "Please, pull up a chair, and I'll set you a plate. I'm glad you could stop by."

The kitchen began to buzz with conversation and activity as everyone sought to cover the embarrassment caused by Amy's remarks. "Maybe someday we'll all laugh about it," Stormy thought hopefully. But she could see Cliff was annoyed, and she tried to distract him.

Then she glared at Adrian. If he had not stopped by tonight, all of this awkwardness would not have happened. Apparently Cliff felt the same way. She noticed his attitude was somewhat hostile toward the man and child seated side by side across from him.

Adrian's eyes sparkled with mischief, "I'm sorry I'm late, Anna. But I did want to stop in and welcome Stormy home again."

Stormy felt Cliff stiffen. She flashed a thunderous warning to the black-haired man whose eyes had never left her, eyes that rested with cool interest on her eyes, her hair, and her lips, much to the irritation of her fiance. She knew Cliff would be quick to question her at the first possible moment, and she dreaded the thought.

"I'm sure she's glad you did," began Charles. Then at a signal from his wife, he stopped.

Not sure where to go from there, he switched the conversation to his future son-in-law. The talk at the table became general, but to Stormy, the undercurrents were uncomfortable. Any question that arose that could be debated was, and without fail, Cliff and Adrian took opposite sides. It seemed, more often than not, that Cliff got the short end of the deal, for the twins stood loyally with Adrian. After several defeats, Cliff retreated into a sulky mood that Stormy wished her parents had not been allowed to see.

She had learned to cope with his moods, but she knew that to the others, his attitude would look very much like childishness. She also knew that in his present mood, he would respond to nothing short of being given his own way.

And Amy! She was going to have a talk with that young lady later! She knew better than to stare at Cliff with those bright, intelligent eyes, showing so plainly how little regard she had for him. She was engaging in a very exasperating show of looking from him to Adrian, her expression changing to one of adoration, making it clear to all who she considered to be the best man.

There were not many subjects the family could find to discuss with Cliff. Although he did not do it intentionally, her father began to talk exclusively to Adrian about the day's work and the new ideas he had for spring planting. The family listened with great interest to Adrian's comments, but Cliff began to show unmistakable signs of boredom. Stormy sought futilely to entertain him.

Oh, how she wished Adrian had not come over tonight. He was ruining everything! He still had her father fooled by his supposed friendliness and his concerned interest. Ooooh! How she longed to expose him for what he was — a wolf in sheep's clothing. Yes, that described him perfectly. She knew all about his winning charm. He had almost fooled her too. Remembering the way she had begun to think of him at Christmas made her cheeks burn guiltily. She shot a glance at Cliff, glad he could not read her mind.

By the time supper was over, she was a jumble of aching bones and stretched nerves. There was nothing she longed to do more than crawl in bed and sleep for a week. She had eaten very little of the meal her mother had taken great pains in preparing. Her shoulders sagged with weariness. She was greatly relieved when Adrian left. Now maybe things would begin to go as she had hoped, with her family getting to know Cliff as he could be — charming and extremely likable.

Her hopes were realized, for as Cliff once again became the center of attention, he responded with the smooth manner of a man who knows and believes in his own value and self-worth. There still was the barrier of personal interests, but they listened politely, and for that she was thankful.

At Amy's bedtime, Anna switched their thoughts and conversation to a time of devotions. Barbara read from the Bible this time. The lamp light shone on her hair turning it to spun gold. She looked like an angel as she so carefully handled the precious old book. Her voice, so soft and sweet, carried a beautiful tone of reverence and love for each word she spoke. And the Holy Spirit descended upon them in a quiet, gentle way.

Stormy drifted into an old, familiar sense of well-being that suddenly was shattered when Cliff yawned loudly. His disregard for the sacredness of the moment irked her at first. One look at his face told her he was bored and restless, and as her eyes questioned him, he raised his brows in criticism. Her heart sank. Would she be able to establish family devotions in their home?

All enjoyment of the devotions fled, to be replaced with confusion, doubt, and an overwhelming desire to agree with and please the man at her side. His strong skepticism and disapproval found a receptive field in her. She found herself waiting impatiently for the last prayer to be said and rose eagerly to end the session with good night hugs and kisses.

"What do you think of my family?" she asked, with an apologetic smile, when all of them had gone to their rooms.

"They're different," he said, shaking his head. "But they'd be all right, if they just didn't try to force their religion on you children. I think it's wrong for them to insist on all of you taking part in that Bible reading and stuff."

"Oh, but they don't insist," Stormy found herself on the defensive. "It's something that we ... ah ... they enjoy," she finished lamely, not meeting his eyes. Now she did feel like the hypocrite he had accused her of being! When was she going to feel comfortable being the person Cliff wanted her to be?

"I get the idea your family is really sold on McAllister. Maybe they would prefer to welcome him into the clan instead of me," he said, watching her face closely, as her cheeks became tinted with soft rose.

"That's nonsense, Cliff!" she said vehemently.

"Oh? Well, I happen to think he's rather taken with you," his eyes darkened with jealousy. "How well do you know him?"

"I hardly know him at all!" her answer was quick, too quick, "and he doesn't care for me in the least. In fact, it's quite the opposite." Her laugh was hollow and self-mocking. Then she impulsively added something she was to regret more than once, "In fact, I have my doubts about his motives in spending so much time with my family. I wonder if he isn't trying to get our farm because it adjoins his."

Cliff was satisfied with the look on her face and took her into his arms. His kiss was possessive, but it brought no thrill to the tired girl. She failed to respond with any enthusiasm. He held her too tightly, and his kisses again hurt her lips. She exercised all of her will power not to push him away. His attentions did not soothe the aching void in her heart. Very soon, she suggested that it was time they got some sleep.

She left him at the door of his room and walked slowly down the hall. She did not see the speculative look that narrowed his eyes as he watched her, nor the discontented frown that marred his good looks as she walked into her bedroom. Barbara was there sitting cross-legged on the bed reading a book.

She looked up with a smile, "Hope you don't mind sharing your bed with me."

Stormy could not resist hugging her. She looked like a perfect little princess in a soft, flannel gown of pale blue with ruffles around the neck and hem line. Her soft, fine hair curled sweetly about her slender shoulders. Her long-lashed, big blue eyes were pure and innocent. Stormy's heart ached with love for her. If only there were some way to ensure that she would always be as sweet as she was now, unspoiled by the world.

"I love having you share my room. Reminds me of when you used to sneak in during storms when we were children."

She grinned mischievously, "Let me change clothes, and we'll spend some time catching up. Okay?"

At a nod of the bright head, she walked toward the closet, her tiredness lightening at every step. Suddenly, she realized how much she missed the closeness she and Barbara had shared as children, in spite of the difference in their ages. The years away from home had not dimmed the precious memories, and she found herself eager to regain the feeling.

Scouting around in her closet, she found an old gown and slipped it on. She was beginning to feel good. She looked toward Barbara's bent head with the light of girlishness sparkling in her brown eyes.

"What do you say we slip downstairs and make some hot chocolate to drink up here while we talk. Like we used to when we were little," she suggested, feeling young and alive again.

Barbara giggled, "It's been ages since I've done that." She slid gracefully off the bed and started toward the door.

On tiptoes, with fingers to lips to stiffle giggles, they slipped downstairs, making exaggerated signs at each creak of the stairs. They fixed large cups of chocolate and made a raid on the pantry. Neither of them saw their mother peek around the corner to investigate the noises that had awakened her, nor did they see her walk softly back to bed with a contented smile on her face. When they regained the safety of their room without being caught and without spilling anything, Stormy groaned.

"Do you know what this will do to our figures?" she asked laughingly.

"Mmmm," Barbara's muffled reply brought a grin to her sister's face.

"Try it, and you'll see."

"You're incorrigible!"

"I'm not sure what that means," Barbara laughed merrily, "but if I'm incorrigible, you must be too, being as we're sisters."

They laughed and talked, re-establishing the bond of love and friendship. Every last drop of hot chocolate eventually disappeared along with every crumb of the light, feathery cake. Still their conversation went on, stimulated by questions and answers and the sharing of hopes and dreams. But at last, sleepiness brought a lull in the talk, and they snuggled down under the old quilt.

Then something clicked in Stormy's mind, and she asked one last question, "Barbara, what did you think of Cliff?"

Her sister's answer was so long in coming that Stormy almost thought she had fallen asleep.

"He's very good looking," the words were slow and thoughtful. But Stormy was not satisfied.

"What else?"

"He can be very charming, and he has a lot of self-confidence." Barbara's answer sounded nice but was clearly evasive.

Stormy lifted herself up on one elbow and stared at the sister's face in the darkness.

"You have reservations about him, don't you?" she asked, finding herself anxiously waiting for the answer.

The seconds ticked by in heavy silence, and when the answer came, it was in the form of a question.

"Stormy, is Cliff a Christian?"

She tried to hedge, "He goes to church," then her voice became tinged with remorse. "But I'm afraid not very often. But after we're married ...."

"Stormy," Barbara interrupted, "you know as well as I do that going to church doesn't make anyone a Christian. I can remember so clearly how you always said you'd never marry a man in the hope that he would get saved someday."

"I know. I remember," the truth hit hard, and Stormy cringed under the covers. "But what can I do?" she wailed. The words trembled in the dark room like fluttering, trapped moths.

Barbara reached over and patted her lovingly, "We'll just have to pray about it. Jesus will help you know what to do. And I have all the faith in the world in your judgment."

She tactfully changed the subject, not knowing that Stormy no longer trusted her own judgment, no longer was sure what life was all about, and no longer was certain which values should be fought for and which could be discarded.

"Mother told Dad not to get her a birthday present this year," Barbara continued chattily. "And," she confided wryly, "she wouldn't like it if she knew I was telling you this. But I thought you should know and maybe help us pray about it. Things have been tighter than usual around here this winter. Dad did not have enough hay to last the winter, because bad weather set in so early. And because of that, prices were higher, so what he bought wiped out their savings account. But," her voice lightened, "he did get her something anyway. Two somethings, as a matter of fact."

"Well, for goodness sake, Barbara!" Stormy exclaimed. "Stop being mysterious and tell me what he got."

"A washer and a dryer."

Barbara puffed her pillow up more comfortably, and added, "He said since you were not home now, and I might not be too much longer, he had better get her a replacement."

"That's great! I can chip in and help him buy them. I also picked up a bottle of her favorite perfume. But why didn't she tell me they were having problems? I could have helped a little."

"She didn't want to worry you. You know how she is. I wouldn't have found out if I hadn't overheard them talking and asked about it. Dad's planning on planting an early crop to help catch up on the expense. But this is the second year in a row the weather has kept us from breaking even."

"I want you to keep me informed, Barbara. The mortgage payment is due in the fall, isn't it? I know they weren't able to make it last year. I remember Mama saying how glad they were that Mr. Berkham let them just pay the interest and renew the note. He is still president of the bank, isn't he?"

"Yes, he is."

"Well, keep me informed, and I'll try to save more to help them with the payment."

"You know, they won't want to take your money."

"I know, but when things are bad, we all need to pitch in and help."

"Sounds good to me," Barbara's voice sounded sleepy, and Stormy grinned.

"Good night, Sis."

"Good night."

The first bold streaks of daylight shot through the pale curtains much too soon for the two sisters, as did the small tornado that whirled into the room without so much as a knock and shot between them like a heat-seeking missile.

"Hi!" The missile rose to the position of a rocket and both little feet began to vibrate the bed up and down. "It's Mama's birthday! We gotta make a cake with candles, and Daddy's gonna bring home a surprise from town. He said so! Did you know it?"

"Ooooh! Grab her, Stormy!" Barbara moaned. "She's jumping up and down on my stomach."

"Ah! Got her!" Stormy pulled the little girl down on the bed. "I think she should be arrested for disturbing the peace. Don't you, Barbara?"

A tussle began between the three sisters, punctuated with shrieks of laughter from Amy as she struggled to free herself from the tickling fingers and shouts of merriment from the older girls as their eyes danced with glee.

A loud rap on the open door brought three smiling faces to greet the man standing there observing them with an amused smile on his own dark face. Amy took advantage of the interruption to make her escape from her tormentors. Barbara smiled shyly and tucked her long gown under her feet, and Stormy — well, Stormy sat with her mouth wide open, one hand darting up to her copper curls and the other pulling desperately at the blankets. She wanted to dive under them and hide.

"They were trying to tickle me to death!" Amy declared from her safe position high in Adrian's arms. She shook an accusing finger at her sisters, but Adrian only grinned and said, "If that is so, Pet, I'm sure you deserved it."

He set her on her feet, and she pouted up at him, fluttering her long lashes in disgust at his refusal to take her side.

"You'd better go and get dressed if you want to ride into town with your father and me."

Her face brightened, and with a helping smack from his broad hand, she scurried back to her room like a little rabbit.

The man turned back to the girls, finding Barbara unmoved and Stormy with the covers up to her chin. He smiled broadly, his eyes resting mischievously on Stormy.

"Good morning, ladies. Nice to see you looking so bright-eyed and pretty this morning. See you at breakfast in," he consulted his watch, "twenty minutes."

He closed the door gently behind him, and Barbara vaulted from the bed. Stormy was slower to move, her mind still seething with anger at Adrian's remark. One glance at Barbara convinced her his remark had been justified about her. She did look sweet, fresh, and pretty in her disheveled state. But she also knew the opposite was true of herself — and his eyes had been on her.

She ran over to look at herself in the mirror, while Barbara hurried out of the room to wait her turn in the bathroom. It was too true! Exactly as she had thought! Swollen, bloodshot eyes stared back at her resentfully. She had never been able to lose sleep without showing it in her face. Her red curls were tight and springy, popping out in all directions, and in the tussle, her old gown had developed a rip under one arm and a tear across the yoke.

Her face flamed as she fingered it. She never dreamed she would get caught wearing it by anyone — least of all him. She really should throw it in the rag box. But no — she was not going to! She grew defiant. It did not matter what he thought of her. If he had needed something more to laugh at, however, he certainly had it with her romping on the bed and screaming like a banshee.

She heard another door slam, and cringed again. Oh, dear. She had forgotten about Cliff! What in the world had he thought about the scrimmage going on the room next to his? She sighed and closed her eyes, shutting out the sight of her pale face. She knew she would have to answer to him — and she did.

"What in the world was all that commotion about this morning?" he crossly demanded the instant he saw her. "Five-thirty is an ungodly hour for people to get up. But to be awakened by what sounded like a massacre was a little — no, more than a little — irritating!" His fair face was warmly flushed, and anger sparkled in his hard blue eyes.

"Cliff, Honey, I'm really sorry," she laid a sympathetic hand on his arm. "I ...."

"Stormy!" Amy came running to the foot of the stairs. "Stormy! Barbara wants you to come and help her fix breakfast. We won't let Mama fix it 'cause it's her birthday," she finished importantly.

Cliff frowned at her darkly. For a moment she just stared at him with her head cocked to one side, bright eyes unreadable. Then, quick as a flash, she stuck out an impudent tongue and ran back toward the kitchen.

Stormy wanted to laugh, but one look at Cliff's glowering countenance, and the sound of his savagely muttered, "That child needs a good spanking!" kept her from laughing.

She greeted her mother with a big hug and a kiss, saying, "Happy birthday, Mother."

"Thanks, Stormy Leigh."

Smiling, she hurried to the stove to help Barbara. Her mother would have a hard time sitting still while they prepared breakfast. She preferred to serve rather than be waited on. Stormy was headed for the refrigerator to get milk and juice when she saw Cliff's brooding gaze resting heavily on Amy. The little girl sat happily on the cabinet, popping bread in the toaster and taking out the finished product.

"Mother," she said softly and hesitantly, "Amy upset Cliff this morning by sticking her tongue out at him. I don't want to be a tattletail, but ...."

Anna Winters regarded her youngest child thoughtfully. "That's not like Amy at all. She knows better. Amy?"

"Yes, Mama?" Big, sparkling brown eyes turned in their direction, and the little girl gave them a sweet, perfectly angelic smile.

Stormy felt a sharp twinge of regret at her action. She knew her mother was straightforward and would ask for an immediate apology from Amy. Yet Stormy knew that if she had not told, Cliff would not have let it rest. He expected her parents to be told of the lapse in the social graces of their youngest child.

"Did you stick out your tongue at Cliff?" Anna asked.

All talking abruptly stopped, and all heads turned to look at the child whose face flooded with rosy color — except for Adrian, whose eyes met Stormy's with a piercing look of disappointment. She could not meet his gaze.

"Yes, Mama," Amy's voice faltered.

Her eyes filled with tears as she saw the reproach in her beloved mother's eyes. The tears trembled on her lashes then fell in a twinkling as she lifted her eyes to Stormy's face in hurt bewilderment. Stormy flinched, and wanted to cry along with Amy. She had just lost the loyalty of a little sister she barely knew but dearly loved. Why did life have to be so painful at times? She looked down and a tear splashed on the diamond on her finger. She did not see Adrian's look change as he witnessed the tear, nor did she see the anger that flashed in Amy's eyes, as she glared at Cliff then turned back to her mother.

"But, Mama," she protested hotly, "he looked mean at me!"

A guilty flush stained Cliff's face, but Anna said sternly, "You know how I feel about you being impolite. You'll stay home this morning and not go into town with your father and Adrian."

"But Mama!" the child cried with horrified dismay, casting desperate looks at the father and Adrian, seeking support.

"No 'buts,' Amy," her mother's tone was adamant.

The little girl was tough enough not to burst into tears, but she was greatly subdued and sat quietly at the table occasionally salting her food with a stray tear that could not be denied.

Stormy could have kicked Cliff for his smugness. Really! Such childish behavior in a grown man was annoying in the least. But later she realized her mother had not required an apology from Amy, and that made her feel a little better.

12
A Birthday That Holds Many Surprises

Adrian and Charles left for town after morning chores, and Barbara managed to cheer Amy up by encouraging her to help make the birthday cake. But every friendly advance on Stormy's part toward Amy was met with coolness and dislike.

They finally shooed their mother to her favorite nook in the family room with a book she had never found the time to read.

After straightening her room and then scrubbing the upstairs bathroom, Stormy considered doing the huge pile of laundry. How had her mother managed for so long with the old washing machine, not to mention hanging all the clothes out to dry? Everyone had washers and dryers nowadays. A quick glance out the window made her grimace in indecision. It looked like rain, a real "toad strangler" if those black clouds were any indication.

A sudden thought hit her. If Adrian had anything to do with it, the new washer and dryer would be usable before nightfall. But she did not want to start thinking about him again. She hurried downstairs to find Cliff. He was staring moodily out the front window. He was bored to tears, and it was written defiantly in every line of his body.

"I cannot believe your parents do not have a television set," he greeted her gloomily.

"They wouldn't have much time to watch one, if they did," she replied quietly, wondering why she felt defensive when he criticized her family. "Also, most of the programs are not very informative or inspiring anymore. Mother and Dad prefer the children to spend their time reading or working on something worthwhile."

"Sounds like a living death to me," he growled doggedly.

"Cliff!" Her own temper was beginning to flare at his childishness and impoliteness.

"Well, it does," he reiterated subbornly. "And I'm glad your mother took your little sister in hand. But she should have made her apologize as well."

Something finally snapped in Stormy, something she had been trying to hold back since breakfast. If Cliff was looking for a fight, he would just get one!

"I'm not! Do you realize I could have ruined a very special, very sweet relationship with my little sister?" Hands on hips and boiling with anger, she glared at him.

He looked taken aback by her fierceness.

"I just barely know the child, and I've completely destroyed her faith in me, and all because you felt a little slighted when she stuck her tongue out at you! And no wonder! You did look at her mean!"

"She was rude!" he snarled angrily. "I can't believe you're taking up for her! She should be punished! How else will she learn to behave?"

"Maybe she thought she had good reason for what she did," she snapped, ignoring the warning sparks in his eyes.

There was silence, and he looked as if he could not believe she would dare to find fault with him. And Stormy did regret her impulsive tongue. Biting down hard on it, she closed her eyes in sick frustration. If there was anyone on her black list today, it should be herself. She had hurt two people whom she dearly loved by hasty, thoughtless remarks, and she was suffering right along with them.

"I'm sorry, Cliff," she said dully. "I shouldn't have said that."

"Sorry for what you said, or just sorry you said it out loud?" he asked huffily.

"Sorry that I ...," she started to explain when she was interrupted by an excited Keith shouting that the pigs were out.

Keith had burst through the front door with fine disregard for the mud on his boots that left two lumpy outlines of his footsteps on the floor. His face was red with exertion.

"All hands on deck! The pigs are out!"

He darted back outside, slamming the door behind him. They saw him dart in front of the window in hot pursuit of a fat, black-and-white striped pig that squealed frantically each time its hind feet struck the ground.

"What did he say?" Cliff looked startled, clearly distracted from his former thoughts.

Barbara and Amy ran from the kitchen and were joined at the door by Anna, who was quickly exchanging her house slippers for mud boots from the hall closet.

"Hurry!" Stormy urged Cliff, also heading for the closet. "If the pigs are out, it will take all of us to get them back in. And there is always the danger they'll get out in the road and cause an accident."

"Well, for goodness sakes!" he fumed, annoyed at the whole situation. "How on earth did they get out?"

"Don't know," she grunted, struggling into a pair of the twins' black, rubber boots. "Here," she poked a pair of her father's old boots toward him, "put these on."

He looked at them with an unbelieving eye. They were run down at the heels. One was badly ripped and dried mud was stuck on the toes. The flapping buckles clicked loudly as she dropped them on the floor.

"You have to be kidding!" he exclaimed incredulously.

"Suit yourself," she said, her mind racing after the pig that jumped out of the way with a loud grunt as she opened the door.

The next few minutes were a wild scene of total confusion to the young man who waited warily on the front step. Kids and pigs raced before his eyes in rapid succession, sometimes so close together that it was hard to tell who was chasing whom.

Keith pulled up in front of him with his face beet red and his blond hair flapping wildly in the breeze. "Come on, man," he cried loudly, drawing the attention of the others, "can't you at least help round them up? We need all the help we can get!"

He reached down suddenly, grabbed the hind legs of a fat, squealing pig, and began to wheelbarrow him toward the barn. The crescendo of pig squeals rose as Kyle followed close on his brother's heels with another snorting, heaving pig.

But it was Stormy's strong-handed tackle of the biggest pig yet that goaded him into action, plus the fact that he saw the old farm truck turn into the lane. Charles and Adrian immediately jumped out and ran to help, adding their voices to the noise and their hands to the dirty work.

Stormy wrestled her pig through the gate that was being operated by a very efficient Amy. She dropped its hind legs and backed out, stopping briefly to wipe her hands on the board fence. She started to praise the little girl for her help when she saw the child's interest was focused on something that brought a mischievous grin to the corners of her rosy little mouth. Stormy followed the direction of her gaze and froze.

"Oh, no!" she breathed, as she saw Cliff sneaking up on the biggest pig of the bunch.

The hefty pig had stopped to rest for a minute and view the situation from little beady eyes. But his whole body bristled with belligerence toward the humans who were trying to end a very exciting bout with freedom. He swung his head and flapped his ears in defiance.

As Stormy watched in frozen horror, she became aware that every other pair of eyes had focused on the same scene. Was Cliff trying to prove something? Surely not! He did not know the first thing about pigs. Oh, she should have insisted he stay in the house instead of encouraging him to help. Time was suspended, it seemed, waiting for some event to trigger it again. That event came in the form of Cliff. He bent down cautiously and gingerly seized two fat, muscular legs, propelling the pig onto its front feet.

There was a split second of initial surprise from the pig, which Cliff wasted by spending time casting triumphant glances at each of them. If only he would keep his mind on the business at hand, Stormy wailed silently, at least he would fare much better. Then the boar emitted a terrifying scream of rage and surged forward. Instead of letting his catch go, Cliff's expression changed to one of shock, and he hung on as the pig's lunge brought him down on his knees. A second lunge, and he was flat on the ground. As the pig regained use of his hind quarters, he proceeded to plow through the mud dragging the man behind him until Cliff's numb fingers opened. Then the pig spun away with a vicious snort, showering the prone figure with more mud.

Stormy was horrified, but Amy burst out laughing. Her merry giggles sent the twins into a fit of laughter. Even Barbara's shoulders shook helplessly. Stormy wanted to laugh, and she wanted to cry. It was funny — no doubt more to some than to others. She knew her family was laughing with Cliff, and not at him, because all of them had experienced similar situations and learned to laugh about them. They accepted with good nature the teasing that came their way. But how was she going to explain that to Cliff? It would be like trying to pacify a bull already seeing red with rage. No matter what color she painted the message, he would still be mad.

The rest of the escapees decided to join the others in the lot when Charles shook a bucket with a few pebbles in it. Hoodwinked into thinking they were about to be fed, they skipped docilely through the open gate. Amy swung it shut behind them with a heavy thud.

By the time Stormy reached Cliff, he had gotten to his knees. His pitiful, woebegone expression was quite touching as he gazed down at himself. His face was splattered with dirt and pig manure, and his hands were thick with mud, even under his fingernails. His expensive shirt and trousers were soaked in a smooth layer of colored mud that was beginning to peel off. His suede shoes, thoroughly doused, were still resting toe down in the puddle he had just emptied out of them.

"Oh, Cliff, I'm so sorry!"

Her voice was properly contrite and her hands anxious to help, but she was suddenly struck with an insane desire to giggle as she looked up at Adrian. The twinkle in his eyes caused a strange thrill of comradeship to run through her. How unexplainable! Especially in this disastrous situation.

"Here, Callahan," Adrian's big, strong hand was offered unhesitatingly to the groping one, "let me help you up."

But the moment he was on his feet, Cliff rounded on him in rage.

"I don't need your help now or ever," he snarled, with his lip curled back. "You think you're really something, don't you, being rich and stooping down so graciously to help these poor people. Don't fool yourself! They can see through you, and so can I." Raw jealousy made him ugly and vindictive. "You're nothing more than a rich parasite, trying to leech on to these people, so you'll have more for yourself later. You're out to get their farm 'cause it's next to yours, and they're so blind they can't see it."

"Cliff!" Stormy was flabbergasted. How on earth had he come up with all that? She was not sure she trusted Adrian, but to have it put so bluntly stunned her.

She looked fearfully at Adrian's darkening eyes and tightening jaw. His expression was unreadable, but a sense of forboding stole over her as his eyes met hers again. Cool, dark eyes. No warmth, no friendliness, no light — just cool and dark.

"He's just upset," she heard herself babbling, her hands fluttering toward him beseechingly. "He doesn't mean it."

"I'm just sorry you didn't do better for yourself," he said softly, a thread of steel hardening each word.

Cliff whirled on her with all the fury of a wronged lover.

"Don't apologize for me!" he thundered. "I said what I meant, and because I am not brainwashed by this namby-pamby religious stuff like the rest of you, I will say what I want!"

He swung back to Adrian, hatred glittering in his narrowed eyes, as he tilted his head back to look the other man fully in the face.

"I know what you meant by your comment. But you just keep away from Leigh. She belongs to me! I've seen the way you look at her," he seethed, his hands clenching into fists. "But she thinks you're about as low as — as," he whirled wildly about looking for a comparison, "as those pigs!"

"Cliff!" Stormy grabbed him by the arm. "You shouldn't say things like that. Come on, let's go in the house." She pulled on his arm, but he stubbornly refused to budge.

"Well, what do you say to that?" he panted in anger.

The big man smiled coolly, "I think Stormy can speak for herself. She impresses me as being able to express herself well. I don't think she needs either of us to speak for her. As for what I think of your comments about myself," he paused and eyed Cliff as a big glob of mud fell off the shorter man's belt and splashed between his feet, "I'll just consider they were spoken by someone unable to control his emotions in moments of stress and forget about them. Now, if you'll excuse me, I'll go and get ready for lunch." With a slight nod of his head, he turned and walked away.

Cliff literally was shaking with rage and humiliation as Stormy led him to the house, and all of her efforts to talk to him fell on deaf ears. He pushed her away and slammed into his room. Several minutes later when she returned to his door, he informed her shortly that he was not coming down for dinner. And, no, she could not come in, as he did not want to talk to anyone!

Finally, she became exasperated by his stubbornness and marched downstairs alone, determined to enjoy her lunch in spite of him. It was not easy, however, for he remained a forboding shadow in the back of her mind. When she tried to join in the fun wholeheartedly, it was as if his shadow would tap her sharply on the shoulder and demand to know how she could enjoy herself when he was so miserable.

After lunch, they had fun unloading the new washer and dryer and presenting them to the little mother who shed tears of joy at the sight of them. True to Stormy's prediction, Adrian had them hooked up and working before nightfall. Anna cheerfully washed a load of clothes while her daughters prepared a birthday dinner and put the finishing touches on the big German chocolate cake.

Cliff's appetite got the best of him finally. He was downstairs hanging around the kitchen when Stormy came back down after a quick shower and a thorough brushing of her damp, unruly curls. She was proud of the way her family opened their arms to him, spared him of all teasing, and pushed him cheerfully back up onto the pedestal from which he was so sure he had fallen. Adrian treated him politely, though coolly, and things went well, until Amy innocently piped up with a request.

"Would you like to hear the story about how Stormy got her name?" she asked hopefully. Her bright eyes challenged Cliff to deny her request.

"Amy," her mother admonished, "eat your supper."

"Would you?" she persisted, "it's one of my favorite stories."

"As a matter of fact," he drawled, looking the little girl in the eye, "I've always thought the name 'Stormy' was silly. I think children should be given respectable names, and I don't think 'Stormy' fits that category."

Stormy heard herself gasp. That hurt! She had never known he felt that way about her name. But come to think of it, he always *had* called her Leigh.

"I think it's a very pretty name, and the story really is very interesting," Barbara said, losing her shyness in a loving move of defense. "But why don't you tell us about yourself? We'd like to hear about your family and home."

Stormy was grateful for her sister's tactfulness and her quickness in filling a painful space of silence, and she told her so with her eyes. But Amy fixed Cliff with a glowering look of dislike. Stormy feared she might suddenly flip the mashed potatoes from her fork directly into his face. Evidently, the little girl thought better of the notion after she glanced at her mother, for she popped her fork into her mouth. Cliff never caught her interest again.

Amy could not understand what her big sister saw in that man, but then she was not sure she understood her big sister either! At first, she had liked her, but now she was not too sure. Of course, she thought as she looked hopefully from Stormy to Adrian, if her sister would just fall in love with Adrian, everything would be great. But then she could not marry him herself. Life certainly was complicated and hard to understand! How was she supposed to eat her salad when she could see Mama's birthday cake sitting on the cabinet? How old was Mama anyway? She did not seem very old, but she sure had a lot of candles on her cake. She wondered if her mother would need some help in blowing them out.

But Anna did manage to blow them all out, and when she looked up, she smiled at all of them a special smile of love and tenderness.

"I said a prayer when I blew out my candles, and I'd like to share it with you, so you can help me pray also," she said, as she looked toward her husband with love blazing from her eyes to his.

"I have a birthday surprise from me to you," she continued. "I'm so glad we could all be together for this day, especially since I have some wonderful news I was hoping to share with you when we were all together. You will have a little brother or sister sometime in November."

Shock and surprise quickly turned to happiness and excitement. The table became a hubbub of questions, and the ice cream melted in pools around the cake. Dessert was no longer the center of attention. The children were elated, ready to talk about names and ask a hundred questions each.

Charles Winters beamed proudly at his wife and showered her with beautiful, sincere compliments. Adrian, too, showed her much attention and a new tenderness and concern. Stormy had conflicting emotions of joy and concern, but Cliff was thoroughly turned off by the idea. He looked about the rejoicing family and wondered if they were all insane. It was crazy for them to have another baby! They were having a hard time supporting the ones they already had. He could not understand how a woman who had married at the age of sixteen and had five children already could be so excited about another mouth to feed. It did not make sense!

The excitement finally died down when it was discovered that Amy had eaten her dessert and Adrian's too and had a tummy ache. But after sitting on Adrian's lap a few minutes, she fell asleep. Barbara washed her hands and face with a warm cloth, then Adrian carried her to her room, laid her on the bed, and gently took off her shoes. Leaving Barbara to get her into pajamas and tuck her into bed, he returned to the kitchen.

The girls shooed their parents out of the kitchen and began cleaning up. Adrian gallantly offered to help, but Stormy quickly refused, after a glance at Cliff. She knew of his dislike for any household chores, knew also that he would insist on staying in the kitchen if Adrian did. She was not sure he would be able to stand the added humiliation of being bettered in the kitchen.

As her voice became curt with her black-haired, teasing tormentor, her mother entered the kitchen and shooed the men out like little boys.

"I've come to spend a little time with my girls. We're going to talk about babies and all the fun things that go with them. Care to stick around, boys? If so, pull up a chair," and she cocked her head to one side, a mannerism expertly imitated from time to time by her daughters.

With a muttered excuse, Cliff went to the door, and Adrian followed him with a secretive smile and a shrug of his broad shoulders.

Anna began to chuckle, "I do believe Adrian would like to have stayed. If for nothing else than to see you blush again, Stormy." As her daughter did blush, she added speculatively, "He seems to think you're really something special." She studied the girl's pink features and downcast eyes.

"Oh, I hardly think so, Mother," Stormy laughed shakily, her brown eyes lifted to search for a denial of her statement. "I think I barely make it to his tolerance list."

"Perhaps someday you will understand him better," and with that puzzling comment from her mother, the subject was closed.

"Well, girls, what shall we hope for? A boy or a girl?" Anna's youthful face crinkled mischievously. "Do we hold our lead, or do we become even?"

The sound of feminine laughter rang through the old house, causing the men to halt their conversation, shake their heads, and grin. Adrian stayed for family devotions, which the family continued to hold, tacitly ignoring Cliff's angry criticism of their "religious ways." Despite her best efforts, Stormy found her attention constantly drawn to Adrian's relaxed form as he reclined comfortably in an old over-stuffed chair.

But his attention was totally focused on the pure, lovely features of the young lady earnestly reading the Word. With a painful throb in her heart, Stormy found herself thinking about Adrian and Barbara as a couple. She was unreasonably glad that Barbara's heart had already been won by another man. By the time prayers were finished, she realized that she had received no more from devotions than had Cliff. The knowledge made her sad. She felt as if she was drifting away from her family's most treasured moments, just a solitary fragment broken off a solid unit, a lonely, frightened fragment with no way of securely reattaching itself.

Adrian rose to leave, announcing he would see them all at church the next morning. Good nights were exchanged, and they dispersed to their separate rooms. Stormy felt tired and despondent. She did not argue when Cliff insisted they leave before church instead of after as they had planned. He probably wanted to avoid any more contact with Adrian, as well as hating the idea of going to a small country church where things would be preached that would either bore him or make him uncomfortable.

He was surprised at Stormy's easy submission and kissed her ardently. The usual thrill of his touch was strangely missing to her, however. With a deep sigh, she entered her room, tears springing up at the sight of familiar things and of Barbara's bright head shining in the lamplight. She was already asleep, and Stormy wanted to cry like a baby. Oh, just to be able to reach way down and unearth all her feelings of confusion and insecurity, then drown them with tears. But she could only soak them loose with her crying, for she had no answers to all her uncertainties.

Impulsively, she softly closed her door and went back downstairs.

"Mama," the word sprang from her lips with the despairing cry of a hurt child, as she knocked softly on her parents' door. "Mama," she began to cry, "Can I please come in?"

The door opened instantly and soft, warm arms reached out to draw her close. She was held lovingly and firmly until the storm passed, and her shoulders heaved only occasionally with a sob.

"Stormy Leigh, let's sit down and talk," her mother encouraged. And talk they did. Charles heard their voices when he came back inside after checking on a sick cow. He listened quietly for a moment, then nodded his head and wisely slipped away to kneel and pray. An hour later, a silent figure slipped out of the bedroom, a smile on her face and damp curls clinging to her brow. In her heart was peace from the restlessness that tormented her, and she clung to the reassurances that had been given her, resting in their comfort.

For the mother had sown seeds of hope and spiritual understanding upon the fertile ground of her daughter's mind and was watering them with her own tears and prayers before her daughter left the room. When her husband entered, they joined in recommitting their daughter to the care of the Heavenly Father.

Early Sunday, the household began to bustle. Stormy's face was pale, but she smiled as she hugged and kissed each of her family. When she reached Amy, the child made as if to turn away, and Stormy felt her heart crack. "Amy," she said, softly and pleadingly.

The little girl turned slowly back, big tears filling her huge, solemn eyes. Fiercely she flung her arms around her sister and whispered against the soft, red curls. "I'll be better next time, I promise! Please come back soon," she pleaded, and her big sister choked out, "I will, Honey. I will."

Then Stormy was hustled into the waiting car by an impatient Cliff, who spared not a single glance for the little girl. Stormy waved until she could see them no more before settling down for the long ride back. Cliff gave an exaggerated sigh of relief, and she stiffened, prepared to defend whomever he decide to attack. After a swift glance at her set face and flashing eyes, he made no sarcastic remarks, realizing that he would not come out of the battle unscathed. However, when they were within an hour of the city, he gave vent to the feelings that had irked him all weekend.

"I still say your parents are going to have problems with Amy," he remarked suddenly.

"Why?" Stormy looked at him in amazement, "She's no different than any other child her age. She's curious, and she's inquisitive, but she is obedient."

"She's spoiled rotten, and you know it!" he snapped angrily.

Stormy declared hotly, "She's no such thing! Besides, this whole conversation is pointless! There's no reason to get upset about one little girl."

"If she were my child, I'd show her a few things! he growled savagely, his hands tightening on the steering wheel.

"Cliff," Stormy said, striving for calmness and refusing to let go of the angry words in her mind, "There is something we have not talked about yet."

"What's that?" he looked at her suspiciously, unwilling to be diverted from his train of thought, even when she reached over and stroked his arm lovingly.

"How many children are we going to have?" she questioned tenderly, her cheeks glowing at the thought.

He drew in a deep breath and said, "None!"

Stormy blanched at his cold, calculated tone and whispered, "None?" in stunned dismay. "But Cliff, I want children!" The cry of desire in her voice would have moved many a man, but not the one whose eyes remained on the road.

"There is no place in our lives for children, Leigh," he stated ruthlessly. "Children will only slow us down in reaching our goals."

"What goals are more important than having a family and sharing ourselves with children, our children?" Stormy's throat was tight, and her words rasped woodenly. She knew it would do no good to argue, but she had to try to reach him.

"The goals of getting ahead in life," he exclaimed impatiently. He shot her a look of irritation, "I thought you shared those goals. You always acted as if nothing was more important than reaching the top."

Had she really acted that way, Stormy wondered painfully? Maybe there had been a time not too long ago when she had been dangerously close to becoming totally materialistic, but she viewed her behavior now with new eyes.

"I'm sorry, Cliff," she ventured, shaking her head helplessly. "I never meant to act that way, and I certainly have no intention of becoming that type of person."

Her voice became firmer as she gained inward strength, "There are some things that mean more to me than personal gain or possessions, such as the love of the man I love, children, and a good solid family life like the one I was raised with."

Cliff snorted in disdain, "If we were to get married and start a family, we would never have all the things we want. You know that! Be realistic! Look at your folks," he pointed out grimly. "They're having no easy time feeding all the kids they have, and now they're adding another one! It's preposterous! They'll never have anything during their lifetimes. When their children are grown and gone, they'll be too old to enjoy anything!"

Stormy held her tongue as long as she could, then interrupted his tirade, "Cliff! That's enough! Stop it!"

Her sharp words, clipped and cold, managed to halt his outburst for a moment. Stormy could not hold back the torrent scalding her heart.

"When you talk like that, you make me think you don't really love me. After all, I am a part of my family! Their joys and sorrows are mine, too. When we get married, I'm not going to cut myself off from them. If you love me, you'll have to learn to love them too!"

Her ultimatum caused Cliff to retreat into a sulky silence. Stormy brooded on his words. She wanted to ask him if he considered children ever being part of their future, but she feared his reply and hated to hear the words that would separate them. They parted at her apartment door with only the briefest of kisses, and she entered the cool, dark room heavyhearted and discouraged. Surely tomorrow would be a better day. Things would get back to the welcome routine of familiar work, she thought, as she climbed wearily into bed. But her last waking thought was of Adrian. She wondered if he had noticed that they were not at church that morning.

Stormy was met mid-morning the next day by a smiling, charming, exuberant Cliff, who swept her into his arms without a mention of the weekend fiasco and kissed her breathless. She melted thankfully into his arms, more than willing to let bygones be bygones. The memory of their argument vanished like a bad dream.

"Guess what, Doll?" he asked with eyes sparkling brilliantly.

"What?" she leaned back in his arms, enjoying the feel of them around her and the sight of a wide smile on his handsome face.

"I talked to Mr. Adams about our vacations. He said personnel would work it out so we could take two weeks off together. What do you think of that?" and he spun her around dizzily.

"Oh, Cliff. That's fabulous," she said excitedly. "When can we get off?"

"That's the best part," he laughed happily. "In two weeks! Can you believe it? Just two more weeks."

After her "oohs" and "ahs" had subsided, he drew her over to the desk and lifted her onto its edge. "Leigh, I want you to come home with me and meet my parents. I think it's time they met the girl I'm going to marry."

Tears sparkled in luminous brown eyes, and a long, slim hand fluttered to her neck as Stormy swallowed with difficulty.

"Babe?" he asked softly.

Her soft, full lips trembled into a radiant smile, "Yes! Oh, yes!"

13
The Best Laid Plans

Except for a few last-minute articles to pack the next morning, Stormy was ready to go. Everything else she planned to take on her two-week vacation was packed neatly in two brand new, leather suitcases. Her apartment was spic-and-span, and she was so excited that she could barely sit still. She had skipped supper because of a nervous stomach, so now she decided to sit down with a cup of hot tea and examine the mail. When she arrived home this afternoon, she had just tossed it on the divan without a glance. But perhaps she needed to see if there were any last-minute bills.

Her eyes lit up as she recognized her sister's neat handwriting. Eagerly, she slid her letter opener through the flap of the plain white envelope. Barbara was not a consistent writer, but her letters were always fun to read and brought a smile and fond sigh from her older sister.

Stormy kicked off her fuzzy bedroom slippers and curled her feet up under her. Drawing a brightly colored comforter around her shoulders, she settled down to read and enjoy news from home. But her brows drew anxiously together as she began to read:

"Dear Stormy,

"If only I could tell you how much I hate to have to write this letter. But as far as I can tell, I have no choice.

"I don't know if you've been listening to the news lately, but a lot of people who own farms are finding themselves in a critical financial state. I'm afraid Mother and Dad are in trouble, too.

"You know how they've always tried not to worry us, but they have confided in me. And their finances are in bad shape.

"You remember we were talking about how good Mr. Berkham was to help people when they got in a bind? Well, he just sold his bank to a large city bank. It shocked all of us. But they said it was because of his health problems. Anyway, this new bank has different ideas about how a bank should be run, and they are really putting the pressure on the farm people who owe so much.

"They've already started foreclosure proceedings against the Wynsels and the Hiptons, and a lot of the farmers are getting worried they'll be next.

"Perhaps I shouldn't be telling you all of this. Mother and Dad probably wouldn't like it. But you know how things are always happening around here. Dad strained his back the other day lifting a calf feeder, and Keith and Kyle were scuffling and Keith sprained his ankle. So it has taken all of us to keep the chores done up, and Mother's been sick every day. Goodness, Stormy, I don't know what we'd have done without Adrian. He's been so good to help, and Ray, too, when he could get away from his practice.

"Plus, Mother's decided to see if she can return her washer and dryer because the pigs brought hardly anything when Dad sold them. And it's been too wet to plant an early crop of oats as he'd planned.

"The real reason I wrote all of this was to ask you if there was any way you could get off work and come home for a few days. I know it would cheer everyone up, and we really need you.

"Sorry this isn't a very cheery letter. Guess maybe I'm just too tired. I know God will see us through. He always has, and we can depend on Him. But I just needed to get it all off my chest, and I've always been able to tell you things. I guess I was secretly hoping you could take an early vacation. But I don't know how things are with you, and I don't want to cause any problems. We all miss you so much, especially Amy.

"Love,

"Barbara"

Stormy frowned in concentration. Barbara must really be upset. The letter was definitely a cry for help. She read it again. Looking up, she caught sight of her new suitcases standing by the door. Shame flooded her as she stared at them. She had a sudden vision of Barbara in homemade clothes, never once complaining, although she dearly loved finer things. And there in those two expensive suitcases were several new outfits with matching accessories that she had not really needed.

Tears filled her eyes. She wondered despairingly how she could have been so selfish? Oh, maybe she had not known all that Barbara knew, but still she was guilty of thinking first of herself. Cliff's remarks a few weeks ago about her goals being the same as his came back to prick her conscience painfully.

Well, one thing was for certain! Mother was going to keep her washer and dryer. She reached for her purse and drew out her savings book, scanning its balance with critical eyes. There was plenty in it to pay for them and still have a small balance left. Shaking her head and clucking her tongue, she regretted the times she had squandered her money instead of saving it. There could have been a much healthier figure in the little book, if there had not been so many things she had "just had to have!"

"I wonder if I'll ever grow up!" she muttered disgustedly, putting the savings book back in her purse. "But at least I can make sure Mother keeps her washer and dryer. She'll really need it with the new baby coming. My problem is how I am going to explain to Barbara about going away with Cliff for two whole weeks and not feel like a heel!"

She knew Barbara would assure her that she should go with Cliff, but that did not ease the guilty feeling in her heart. She wanted to go home and be with her family. They needed her. But she wanted to go away with Cliff, too. Yet there had been a slight feeling of reluctance whenever she had thought about going off with Cliff, a feeling that had dampened her excitement. She had felt a little edgy about this trip and wondered — but had been unable to explain it.

"Oh, I don't know what it is!" she exclaimed in exasperation, glaring at the offending suitcases.

Then she grew still — very still. Her heart began to pound with the impact of the sudden revelation that had flooded her mind. Her secret intentions had been laid bare in her soul, and she reeled as if struck a mortal blow. Yes! Now she knew.

Cliff's demanding kisses, his deepening intense passion and her constant fear of losing his love if she resisted too strongly or too often had led to a secret resolve that she had not allowed herself to even think about. Waves of color flooded to the red curls before receding and leaving her ashen and shaking. Subconsciously she had set the stage for compromise. She had known deep inside that when she came back from this trip, she would be different. She had fully intended to give herself to the man she loved. She had even gone so far as to hint at it to Cliff, pacifying for a little longer his powerful emotions that demanded a release.

She worried at her bottom lip with her teeth, a feeling of dread and insecurity beginning to envelop her.

Would her act of unconditional love bring the ultimate joy and peace she hoped? Or would it turn on her and tear her down for surrendering her cherished standards and values? Would she be able to maintain her self-respect and live with her actions? Surely one could not just give up a lifetime's teaching and training at a moment's notice and remain unscarred? Would there be permanent damage to her heart if somehow things did not work out between her and Cliff?

She had always experienced an aching desire to be needed and loved for herself. In her childhood, her family had supplied that need. Now she was reaching out with hungry hands for more. Could Cliff fully satisfy that need? Did he even understand it? She had never seen the same need in him once. She closed her eyes on that thought, then opened them with a start as the phone rang. She reached for it, cradling it against her ear.

"Hello?"

"Hello, Stormy Leigh."

"Daddy! Oh, it's good to hear your voice!"

She felt a yearning to lay her head on his broad chest and talk her troubles away, but she knew he had more problems to face than she.

"How is everyone?" she asked, purposely omitting mention of Barbara's letter.

"Well, things haven't been going all that well, but they could be much worse," he spoke cheerfully enough, but his daughter could sense a tiredness in his voice and a slight hesitancy that was puzzling.

"What's wrong?" she asked fearfully, her eyes flickering toward the letter in her lap.

"Oh, nothing too bad, nothing to worry yourself about. The main reason I called was to ask a favor of you."

"Sure, Dad. What is it? You know I'll be happy to do anything I can for you."

"I know you would, girl, I know you would." His confidence in her came like warm, approving arms across the miles, and Stormy blinked back sudden tears.

"It's just that I hesitate to ask this of you."

"What is it, Dad?" she asked quietly, her heart throbbing with love and loyalty.

"If at all possible, we really need you to come home for a few days. I know you were home only a couple of weekends ago — but ...."

"It's all right, Dad," Stormy heard herself responding to the silent plea in his voice, "I can be on my way home tomorrow."

"Tomorrow?" he asked in stunned surprise.

"Yes, I have two weeks vacation coming up that I can start tomorrow."

"Are you sure you haven't made other plans, Stormy Leigh? We wouldn't want you to give up anything you've already planned."

"Nothing that can't be done at a later date," she assured him, relentlessly shoving behind her the vision of what Cliff's reaction would be when she told him the news. "Do you need me to bring anything?"

"I don't think so, Stormy Leigh, just yourself. And thanks so much!" he said huskily. "I'd better hang up now, so the phone bill will not be too high. What time can we expect you tomorrow evening?

"I'll be home around seven, Dad," she answered brightly.

"Good night, Stormy Leigh."

"Good night, Dad."

After the line went dead, it was several minutes before she could move. Comprehension of the seriousness of her decision hit her like a ton of bricks. Cliff would never understand! How on earth was she going to explain it to him? Her heart cringed at the thought. She didn't feel up to having another heated argument with him, but what else could she have done? Her family needed her. Surely she could make him understand that. Her family would not have asked her to come, if they had known she already had made other plans. And she had not volunteered that information. Why had she not told her father about her plans?

Her basically honest nature formed only one answer. She had wanted a way out of her trip with Cliff. But that answer raised a mountain of other questions. Questions she did not want to answer! She looked at the clock and rose to her feet decisively. The department store did not close until nine. She could get there before they locked the doors.

Grabbing up the boxes her new outfits had come in, she laid them on the bed. Then she brought her suitcases into the bedroom and began to unpack them hurriedly. She folded each outfit as neatly as she could in her haste and pressed it back into its box, folding tissue paper carefully around it before closing the lid. She grabbed the receipts out of her desk drawer and stuffed them into her purse. A light jacket covered the old sweater she was wearing with her jeans, and she was ready to begin loading the car. Several trips later, she flipped off the light and locked the door.

The phone began to ring. Intuitively she knew it was Cliff. She froze. Then in desperation, she ran down the stairs as if literally pursued by the insistent rings. She must not let him stop her!

About an hour later, she was home again, her bill-fold fat with money and her mind strangely untroubled. After lengthy explanations to several people, a thorough examination of all the articles returned, and the verification of that afternoon's sales by a kindly sales clerk, she had been given back every cent of her money. A miracle! She shed her jacket carelessly onto the divan, kicked off her shoes in the middle of the floor, and headed for the kitchen. She was starving! A can of chicken noodle soup caught her eye. Soup, crackers and cheese, a big glass of whatever milk was left, and a handful of cookies. Her mouth began to water. That would finish off her food supplies. And it sounded like a feast to her hungry stomach!

She dumped the soup into a pan and set it on the burner. The phone rang, and with great irritation, she laid down the knife with which she had started to slice the cheese. She was tired and hungry and did not want to be bothered. But she adjusted the heat, wiped her hands on a hand towel, and hurried to the living room. She knew who it was, and she jerked the phone to her ear, anxious to be done with the coming ordeal.

"Leigh! Where have you been?" he demanded to know, the very annoyance in his tone causing her to bristle. I've been trying to reach you for hours."

"Hello, Cliff," she said as sweetly as she could, "I had some last-minute things to take care of and just got home." She sank heavily onto the divan, knowing she would probably need its support.

"Well, is everything okay? Are you packed and ready to go?" he asked impatiently, and she could feel the muscles in her neck begin to tighten.

"I'm not going, Cliff," she said bravely, deciding the best approach would be a direct one. But the following silence was ominous. Then he exploded!

"What do you mean, you're not going?" His voice cracked across the line like a whip, "Why not?"

Stormy felt her fighting spirit begin to rise up within her.

"Dad called me a little while ago, and they need me at home." She gave no further explanation, knowing it would not matter what she said.

"I knew it," he raged. "I knew it! Your family is always trying to come between us! They ... !"

"Cliff, they didn't even know about our trip!" she interrupted forcefully, "and I don't expect you to understand, but I *have* to go."

"No! I don't understand!" he roared, "and I never will! You went one step too far this time, Leigh." His tone turned dark and ugly, "My parents are expecting us. You'll just have to tell *your* family you can't come." Then he laughed harshly, "After all, they have enough children to help take care of them without you. Just call them and tell them you can't come! They'll have to make it without you this time."

"I can't do that, Cliff. I've already told them I would come," she protested. The faint sound of something boiling alerted her ears. "Cliff, I have soup on the stove. It's starting to boil, and I have to go check on it." She desperately wanted to end the conversation before it tore out her heart. "Please, I ...."

"Leigh! You make up your mind right here and now!" He was hard and cold. Tears slid down her pale cheeks. "Me or your family! Which is it going to be?"

"Please, Cliff!" her throat was aching and her heart hurt, "please don't do this to me! Don't put me in this position. Can't you see they need me? You'd go to your family if they needed you."

Ignoring her pleading, he pushed relentlessly for an answer, "What's your decision?"

"I guess I've already made it," she replied tiredly. "Have a good trip, and I'll see you when you get back."

"Maybe," he muttered angrily, and slammed down the phone.

"Oh, Jesus!" she cried, all restraint gone as she flung herself over on the divan and buried her face in the little pillow Amy had made her for Christmas. "You've got to help me! I don't think I can handle this. Please, Jesus. Please help me!"

The smell of scorching soup and the ringing of the doorbell reached her at the same time.

"Oh, dear," she mumbled. "Who on earth can that be? It's almost bedtime."

Well, the soup already was ruined, so she might as well answer the door first. Hastily wiping at her eyes with the back of one hand, she raked the other through her curls leaving them standing on end. It must be her landlady, probably wanting to ask how long she would be gone. Trying to compose herself, she made a feeble attempt to smile and opened the door. But her lips froze when she recognized the man leaning casually against the door frame.

"Hello," he said cheerfully. Then as she continued staring at him motionlessly, he asked, "May I come in?"

"Sh-sure," she stammered, her face flaming at her lack of manners. He stepped inside, then halted.

Swinging back to her, he asked, "Is something burning?"

"Oh, it's my soup!" she fumed. Finally gaining control of her legs, she fled toward the kitchen. "I was just going to set it off the stove when you rang."

"I see," he said amusedly, a faint smile appearing at her ungracious tone. He followed her into the neat little kitchen, looking around with interest. Then he walked up behind her to peer over her shoulder at the scorched noodles. She felt a sudden quiver of nervousness at his nearness and moved away from him, scraping briskly at the stuck food in the pan.

"Oh, great," she grouched. "Stuck tighter'n a tick! Might as well let it soak until morning."

Adrian McAllister threw back his head and laughed. The crude country expression sounded ludicrous coming from her. She probably did not realize what she had said.

Stormy glared at him. If he had not been a friend of the family, she would never have opened her door to him. And if he did not behave himself, he was going to be shown that same door, pronto!

"What's so funny?" she barked sharply.

"Oh, nothing," he said humorously. "Nothing you'd appreciate in your present mood. Is this all you have to eat?" he asked as he made himself at home opening her cabinets and refrigerator.

"Yes, it is," she snapped in annoyance, "so if you were planning on a meal, you're out of luck!"

"Stormy, Stormy," he chided softly, a warning look steeling his eyes to marble hardness. "There's no need to be rude, is there?"

Thoroughly ashamed of taking out her grouch at Cliff on him, she lowered her eyes and scuffed at the floor with a bare toe.

"No, I guess not. I'm sorry. My present mood has nothing whatsoever to do with you," she said, sounding properly repentant, but giving rein inside to the rebellious thought that he had not helped her mood any by showing up, either! What was he doing on her doorstep anyway? He was the last person in the world she wanted to see.

She looked up to catch a glimpse of what might have been concern in his eyes, but it was quickly concealed.

"If you don't mind my asking, why are you here?" the weariness that dulled her mind also dulled her voice.

"I had some business in Kingston, and when I finished, I called your father to tell him what I had learned. When I asked him if there was anything he wanted me to do for him in the city, he suggested I might look in on you. He said you were planning to come home for a few days and thought I might be of some assistance. So, here I am!" and he spread his hands expressively and shrugged.

"Well, I appreciate you taking the time and trouble, but I'm making it all right. I have everything I need."

"Except something to eat," he said pointedly, "and I am sure you'd feel much better if you had something in your stomach. Get your purse, and let's go eat."

"I'd really rather not," she hastily objected. "I'm not hungry, and I still need to pack," and her brown eyes grew distracted as she was suddenly overwhelmed by the events of the past few hours. What she wanted most was to lay her head down and cry herself to sleep.

"All right," he said gently, folding his arms and resting a long forefinger thoughtfully on his finely chiseled lips. "You start packing, and I'll be back in a few minutes," and he headed for the door as she began to protest. He turned and gave her a solemn smile and a promise, "If you're not through packing when I get back, I'll help you. Now lock the door behind me."

Her mind whirled dizzily as she obeyed. He probably would, too, and think nothing of the embarrassment it would cause her modest nature! She scurried toward the bedroom and yanked her old suitcase down from the closet. She would be through by the time he got back or die trying!

But Adrian, who had paused outside her door to listen, smiled with satisfaction as he heard her begin to move about. Action was the best possible thing for her right now. Maybe it would help dilute some of the raw pain that saddened her lovely eyes and made her sweet lips droop. He could have hanged a man named Clifford Callahan quite cheerfully, for he correctly suspected he was the cause of the girl's distress.

An hour later, he knocked on her door again. But Stormy was ready for him. She had managed to pack everything she thought she might possibly need for two weeks on the farm. She had packed with such concentrated effort there had been no time to regret the finer things she had carefully packed only hours before. All pain had vanished momentarily as her nimble fingers sorted and packed what her eyes picked out. Sooner or later, she knew the storm would hit, but for right now, she would simply do one thing at a time.

Then she had felt a very feminine urge to fix her face and hair and present a confident front to the man when he returned. He had caught her at a very vulnerable moment, and she was determined to show him that she really was the capable mistress of her own life. She had just placed the suitcase by the door as a firm knock announced his arrival. Taking a deep breath to stifle the rush of nervousness, she opened the door.

Adrian spent no time admiring the fake sparkle in her eyes or her freshly made up face, commenting only briefly as he passed her on the way to the kitchen.

"Pizza. Everything on it, plus double cheese," he said as he set his load on the table and turned around. "Satisfactory?"

"My favorite," she admitted, eyeing him curiously. "How did you know?"

Peeling off his jacket, he handed it to her and stepped over to wash his hands at the sink, saying matter-of-factly, "Your mother told me."

"Oh?"

She could think of nothing further to say, but she did wonder what else her mother might have told him. However, she refrained from asking! She started to take plates from the cabinet, but he stopped her.

"No dirty dishes tonight. We'll just use napkins and fingers. I've brought soft drinks with me, and when I leave there won't be anything for you to do except tumble into bed. Now, shall we eat?"

He held out her chair to be seated, and as much as she hated being obligated to him in any way, it still brought a warm glow to her chilled heart to be treated like a lady. The meal was very enjoyable, and she found herself being drawn out to talk about herself and her favorite things. A new experience indeed! However, she also found him a ready listener to her anxious questions about all the difficulties facing farmers. And he did much to lighten her fears while still being truthful and realistic. It was nearly 11 p.m. when he rose and began to clear the table, stuffing the cartons back into the brown sack.

"It's past time for all little girls to be in bed," he announced authoritatively, and she automatically rebelled, stiffening until she happened to see the twinkle in his eye.

"Aye, aye, Sir," she saluted him meekly and laughed at the surprise filling his eyes at her easy submission. She followed him to the door.

"You're really something, Stormy Leigh. Do you know it?" He tilted her chin and looked deeply into her eyes, "Drive carefully tomorrow."

A moment later, Stormy was still standing in the doorway, lips parted and eyes bemused. Coming to herself, she quickly closed and locked the door. What was the matter with her? Honesty told her she had expected him to kiss her. But what was worse, she had actually wanted him to, and was even now suffering the undeniable pangs of disappointment because he had not! Was she so fickle she could profess to be in love with one man, and yet fall willingly into the arms of another? She fussed and fumed over the matter, and the episode was still on her mind when she crawled into bed. But it did serve to keep her distracted from more painful problems until she fell asleep.

Perhaps she would have been greatly comforted had she known that Adrian had been sorely tempted to comply with the unspoken desire he saw in her eyes. Only by sending a swift prayer heavenward was he able to control the fierce urge to take her in his arms and kiss away the pain. Yet his knowledge of the principles of his God kept him from touching a woman promised to another man.

No matter how selfish or shallow or utterly worthless he considered that man to be, he must remove from his mind the temptation to surrender to his own emotions and needs. He must turn his thoughts to the Lord. He accepted the peace offered him by the One who knew him best and fell soundly asleep to dream of winning a girl for himself. One that was truly beautiful and loved him in return. Oddly enough, however, the girl in his dreams resembled Stormy Leigh Winters.

14

A Truce Is Declared

The alarm clock crowed like a rooster at the first burst of dawn, and the girl whose coppery curls tumbled in wild disarray on her pillows stirred restlessly. Her sleepy eyes focused grumpily on the clock. Indeed, if it had not been for the absolute necessity of an early start, she would have aimed a pillow at its glass face. An alarm clock might be one of the necessary evils of life, but she hated it with a passion. And she had muffled it with a pillow more than once.

Reluctantly, she left the warmth of the bed and stumbled to the bathroom. But an hour later, in a much better mood, she put her suitcase in the car, strapped herself into her seat and drove off into the crisp morning. She would not let herself dwell on Cliff, preferring to believe that all would be right when they saw each other again. Cliff got angry easily, but was not one to hold grudges. She might as well become accustomed to his moods. At this point, she certainly had no fairy tale dream of things being different after marriage.

But after long hours of driving, her mind began to drift. She wondered if she would see Adrian again soon. Her face grew rosy at her thoughts. She must get a grip on herself and stop thinking such preposterous things. Cliff was her fiance. Not Adrian, who was neither lover nor friend. She must be true and loyal to Cliff, not like the girls in the office who tried to secure a firm grip on one man while playing the field with others.

She did all right until she slowed to gaze at Westmoor Heights. Then her mind slipped off into old familiar dreams. There was no way she could control the feelings. It was as if her first awakening moments of romance were linked to the big stone house.

When she first caught sight of home, she saw a small figure in red jump up and down and go streaking toward the house, a long mane of dark hair streaming behind her. She pulled in the drive, and the front door burst open. The twins raced through it as if released from school. They greeted her as if they had not seen her in months, instead of only a couple of weeks.

"Stormy! Stormy!" echoed gladly in her ears as she stepped from the car and was instantly smothered in hugs from her neck to her waist. Escorted to the door like some returning hero, she laughed and cried and felt her heart begin to thaw. Tears coursed down her cheeks. It was some time later before she was allowed to go upstairs and change clothes. Then, with a gay heart and a genuine smile, she rejoined them in the kitchen. The table was set and the food was being dished up. Much ado was made over her, and much teasing went on as she was led to a seat decorated with red-and-white streamers and a place card that said, "Home Coming Queen."

"Home Coming Queen?" she questioned with a quirk of auburn brows.

"Yeah, don't you think it fits?" Keith teased gently as he seated her, "I thought all women considered themselves to be queens!"

She punched him in the side, and he yelped in mock pain.

"We just wanted to do something a little special, what with you coming home on your vacation and all," Kyle drawled shyly. "You coulda spent it with that Cliff guy and probably had more fun."

"Nonsense!" she laughed bravely, enduring the knife-like stab of remorse like a true soldier. "What could be more fun than spending my vacation with all of you? Cliff and I will have many vacations together later on." She looked about at their intent faces and grinned. "Now, come on! No more long faces! We've got two long weeks to enjoy being together. And I'll probably be home again before I change my name and become an old married lady. Besides, I think we'd better start eating if we hope to get any potatoes. I have a sneaky suspicion Amy's been devouring them a spoonful at a time!"

As all eyes turned on her, the little girl smiled angelically and moved away from the bowl of creamy potatoes that bore signs of her hunger in its dimpled surface. She made it safely to the table and pulled out her chair before the spoon she had tucked into the back waistband of her skirt fell to the floor with a tell-tale ring. Laughter rippled around the table, and after carefully maintaining her air of innocence until it seemed likely she would not be scolded, Amy began to giggle.

Stormy had meant to stay awake for a while that night to do some serious thinking, but she fell asleep as soon as her curls kissed the pillow.

Sunday morning rolled in nippy and cool with low-hanging, heavy clouds of predictable rain moving sluggishly across the heavens. But it was warm and cozy in the Winters' big kitchen with morning chores done and freshly scrubbed faces greeting the huge platters of sausage, ham, eggs, biscuits, and gravy with shouts of hunger and appreciative sniffs. A leisurely breakfast was soon replaced by the bustle of clearing away the dishes and dressing for church.

Then there was the rush through the sprinkling rain, an excited chorus of continuous chatter all the way to church, a more drastic scramble through the more pro-

nounced pelting rain, and a quiet, reverent hush as they
lined up and marched down the aisle to fill a whole pew.
Their voices blended sweetly together as the sacred old
hymns were lifted to God with joyful hearts, and they
shared the intimate glances that told of a closeness of spirits.

They listened attentively to the message of hope that
was expressed so simply and yet so beautifully by the old
saint of God who had faithfully led them through the
years. They trusted him to tell them of the ways of God
and to encourage them to stand firm upon His Word. Even
little Amy, in her Sunday-best dress sitting primly
between her sisters, listened gravely. Then having spent
time in the precious presence of the Lord and being spiri-
tually refreshed, they adjourned outside to exchange
Sunday lunch invitations.

Stormy's eyes roamed the milling people, searching
for a dark head and shoulders that would tower above
most. Her family had sat close to the front of the church,
and she had been unable to satisfy her curiosity as to
whether he was there. People warmly welcomed her
home, pumped her hand enthusiastically, and asked in a
friendly manner how long she would be home. She smiled
until her cheeks ached, but she thoroughly enjoyed visiting with friends and kinfolk. She asked as many questions
as she answered. It was not until a soft, velvety hand was
placed limply in hers that her social equilibrium failed.

"Why, Stormy Winters!" a rich, husky voice purred.
"How long has it been since I last saw you? Why, the last
time I saw you, you were a tall skinny girl, all arms and
legs and lots of red curls tied up with rubber bands!"

Stormy flinched involuntarily, but her expression
revealed nothing more than the utmost grace and charm
as she retaliated.

"And you were a short, chunky girl with lots of
freckles and buck teeth! Yes, it has been a long time!"

Immediately, she regretted her hateful dig, but she could not retract it, so she smiled in an effort to reduce the sting. However, the other girl simply laughed and shrugged her shapely shoulders, her black eyes flashing with amusement.

"You're still quick with the tongue, aren't you, Honey?"

Stormy flushed hotly, realizing she had been put in her place.

"I guess so," she muttered miserably.

Vivian Langley — beautiful, willful Vivian, who always got her own way and always managed to win. She had been the teacher's pet, the school's pride, and the prettiest girl in town. Stormy knew the statement she had just made had been what she had wished on the girl rather than an accurate description. In truth, the girl was olive-skinned with very little tendency to freckle when she was small and even less tendency now. It had been Stormy Winters who had borne the brunt of a nose that still freckled easily whenever the sun reached her with its warm rays.

Vivian had been blessed with hair the color of a raven's wing — soft, silky hair that flowed away from her face and down her back like a black veil. Large, lively, black eyes, lashes of an enviable length, a slender, delicately flared nose poised perfectly over full red lips that were further complemented by a matching pair of bewitching dimples that winked when she smiled. Her small head was held regally above a petite, feminine form whose earlier plumpness had rounded into very enticing curves. She was beautiful, intelligent, and excitingly feminine. Beside her, Stormy felt like an overgrown red ox!

"Ah," Vivian looked pointedly at the dainty, perfectly manicured little hand that Stormy still grasped.

"Oh! Sorry!" Stormy dropped her hand as if it had burned her, then watched in fascination as it moved elegantly upward to rest lightly and ever so possessively on a masculine arm.

"Adrian, darling," her voice crooningly beckoned the attention of the handsome man at her side, "this is Stormy Winters, a girl I used to go to school with years ago."

And from the tone of her voice, Stormy thought bitterly, I never did graduate! Her smoky brown eyes turned hostile as she raised them to encounter amused blue ones.

"We've already met, Vivian," he smiled, directing his gaze to the lovely little vision before him.

"Oh?" Black eyes darted back to the stony face of her school mate, "In that case I guess introductions are quite unnecessary, aren't they?" Assuming a charming, suddenly disinterested attitude, she swept by Stormy with a casual, "We'll have to get together some time and talk about old times."

"Huh! That's what you think!" Stormy muttered under her breath, her flustered brown eyes watching the handsome giant following docilely in the wake of the school princess. In that instant, she knew that her day was ruined totally and irrevocably. Reason argued that such dramatic assumptions were silly, but it was still true. She moved along with the crowd through the narrow, double doors and down the whitewashed steps to be greeted by a panting little girl.

"C'mon, Stormy!" she implored. "We're all waiting on you, an' the preacher's coming home with us. We're going to have him for dinner!"

In spite of her resentful feelings, Stormy had to chuckle.

"He's going to have dinner with us," she corrected as the child grabbed her hand and tugged.

"That's what I said!" Amy looked at her as if she were deaf, her soft forehead wrinkled in displeasure. But no one seemed put out that the older sister had prevented them from leaving earlier. Rather, there was a proud look in their eyes as they watched her approach the car, a look that made her sore heart feel much better.

"Here!" Amy directed, "You sit back here with me, so we can visit." And quite meekly her sister clambered in behind the small figure and dutifully gave her a great deal of attention during the trip home.

All in all, it was a very quiet day spent in the company of the pastor and his round little wife whose snowy hair could not age her youthful, saucy green eyes. And it was not until after church that evening that Stormy found the chance to ask some questions that had been nagging at her all day. She and her mother were busily popping great bowls of corn for the rest of the family, and she popped a kernel in her mouth before speaking.

"Mother, when did Vivian come home?"

"Mmmm, must have been some time last month," the answer was muffled as Anna bent to retrieve a dropped potholder, "she's grown into a very stunning young woman."

"Yeah, I guess so," Stormy said hastily, not wanting to dwell on the perfect features of someone she envied, "but I thought she was married. Where's her husband?"

"Her mother told me he died about six months ago of some kind of cancer. They didn't have any children, and she's come back home to live with her parents. Her mother's worried about her, says she has really had a rough time and needs a lot of attention to restore her confidence."

"Huh!" a dark grunt sounded, barely audible.

"However," Anna Winters continued, "I always felt her problem was that she had received too much attention since she was a child."

"Me, too," the words were louder and staccato.

"It's quite obvious at times that she is spoiled."

"She has surely latched onto Adrian, hasn't she?" The words rushed out unchecked, and Stormy held her breath awaiting her mother's reaction.

The slender back turned to the girl gave no indication that her mother had noticed the barbed resentment in each word, but the brown eyes so like her own twinkled merrily as Anna watched the kernels she had dropped into the hot oil. She made her voice casual as she answered her daughter.

"Yes, they seem to have hit it off like two peas in a pod. Of course, Adrian is the sort of man Vivian's always liked — good-looking and rich. But then again, it's about time he settled down. He's always said he'd like to get married and have children."

She backed away from the stove carefully holding the hot skillet of popped corn and looking for the bowl that Stormy should be holding out for her. She quickly hid a grin as she saw a laser-like look of glittering distaste that could have burned a hole through the bowl, and she ignored the flushed face that glanced her way when the bowl was tardily set before her.

"Where was Adrian tonight?" The question was the first one Stormy could think of to successfully dispel the image of perfectly angelic children with glossy black curls, blue eyes, and dimples.

"He was teaching a boys' class — the one the twins are in."

"Does Vivian teach a class also?"

"Not hardly," Anna stated dryly, "Nor is she likely to."

"Oh? How come?" curiosity boiled up again.

"Vivian makes no bones about the fact she only goes to church because Adrian does."

"Well, he ought to be able to see through her!" The criticism snapped in the air raised her mother's eyebrows.

"He probably does," she answered easily.

And Stormy had to be content with that, as her mother disappeared through the doorway with a tray of glasses filled with soft drinks or iced tea.

She was awakened early Monday by the sound of little feet slapping barefoot across the floor, but had no time to prepare herself before a small bundle of boundless energy landed on her middle and began to pull back her warm quilt.

"Morning, it's morning," she was told enthusiastically in a sing-song voice to which she answered with a groan and a useless tug at her covers. But the little girl was undaunted. "Wake up, Stormy! Wake up!" She bent down to look into her sister's sleepy face, "You've got to come and see Ol' Tom's kittens! Ol' Tom had kittens!"

"He what?" Stormy ceased her struggles and blinked up at the bright, brown eyes. The tangled brown head tilted cockily. "Well, they're not really his. They're Mousey's. But he's real proud of them!" She bounced up and down experimentally to see if it would spur her limp sister into moving a little faster. It did!

"And who, pray tell, is Mousey?" was the sleepy question accented with a huge yawn as bare feet timidly tested the cool floor.

"She's Tom's wife," was the natural answer spoken very matter of factly, "and she's real good about catching mouses in Daddy's barn."

"Mice," Stormy said, muffling another yawn and looking longingly at the warm nest she had just left. "Suppose you give me a few minutes to get dressed, and we'll go see these kittens of Tom and Mousey's. Meanwhile, I think you forgot to comb your hair, didn't you?"

A startled hand streaked to the thick, tangled mane, and a quick nod affirmed it to be true as Amy jumped off the bed. "See ya later!" she said and scampered out of the room.

Somehow getting up early to go to work at Eastland, Inc. and getting up even earlier to start a day's work on the farm were two entirely different matters, and of the two, Stormy found she preferred the latter. With everyone calling "good morning" to each other and a lot of good-natured teasing going on, it was fun.

She ran downstairs dressed in jeans and a blue-checked shirt, feeling like a little girl again. Her clear sparkling eyes gave no evidence of the tears that had soaked her pillow during the night, as memories of the bitter words between her and Cliff kept her awake. In the quiet darkness, it had been easy to imagine she had lost him forever. But the morning's activities soon dispersed the torment of the night, and she counted the days until she could see him again.

With breakfast over, she was climbing into the hayloft as the sun peeked shyly over the tops of the giant trees in the east meadows. The air was chilly, and she shivered, more from nervous excitement than from actual cold. Cool mornings and evenings had always given her a sense of anticipation. She had never quite understood the feeling, but it always happened.

Amy carefully, ever so carefully, picked up the tiny, mewing kittens and offered them to her until she had emptied the soft, warm hollow where they had huddled. Stormy's lap was filled with yawning, stretching little creatures whose unopened eyes were disguised by tiny pink mouths hissing exaggerated warnings of mighty strength.

"Once they get used to you, they won't spit so much," Amy consoled her, her brown braids bobbing confidently. She reached for a black kitten and stroked it tenderly, crooning softly as she placed it back in the nest.

"Daddy says not to handle them too much when they're just babies," she explained, reaching for a second kitten, a tiny calico ball of life.

"What are you going to do with five baby kitties?" Stormy asked, just to hear the little girl's explanations.

A long, drawn out sigh met her question head on. "Well, I just don't know. I'll have to figure out something. Daddy says I can't keep all of them, but maybe he'll change his mind when they are big and beautiful and can help their mama and daddy catch mouses. 'Course I think they're awful pretty right now, don't you?" she asked earnestly.

"I sure do!" Stormy hugged her impulsively, "but we'd better go and see if we can be of help to someone. The babies probably need to go back to sleep."

"Oh, yes!" Amy nodded emphatically. "They need to sleep a lot and eat a lot. But I was wonderin'," she laid a persuasive hand on Stormy's arm and gazed earnestly in her eyes, "if you could tell Daddy how nice they are. I just gotta keep them all together! They're a family, you know."

"I know, Honey," Stormy patted her hand. "We'll see what we can do." Her eyes misted as she followed the tip-toeing child from the loft. Oh, how she wished the only pain Amy would ever encounter in life would be the pain of having to separate her kittens. If life could only be so simple.

She felt she had missed out on so many precious memories by not coming home more often. Some way, somehow, she had to make Cliff understand how very important she had discovered her family was to her. If he would only give them half a chance, he could not help but love them too.

They returned to the house to find their mother had been forced back to bed with a splitting headache and morning sickness. Protesting soundly that she could work, she nevertheless confessed her relief that Stormy was there to take her place. The children had two more weeks of school, and she hated to keep any one of them home with her, knowing those last weeks were important.

Stormy helped Barbara pack lunches and search for school books until the school bus wheezed to a stop in front of the house and tooted a weak-sounding horn. Then she stood on the front steps and waved goodbye as they ran to climb aboard, feeling very much like a mother.

Barbara had never asked for a car, although she wanted to have one. And she would have to have one when she started college, but she would never ask her parents to give her one. She knew they could not afford it, so she had been carefully saving her summer job money for the last three years. Stormy pondered the situation, squinting her eyes to watch the bus disappear around the corner in a puff of dust.

The twins would turn sixteen the first of June, and they too would want a car. Perhaps if they pooled their meager savings with Barbara's, they could buy one together. She would have to mention it to them. She might even be able to help them a little. She turned back toward the house.

By the end of the day, her steps were lagging, but it was a good sort of tired feeling, a feeling of having done something worthwhile and of having helped people she dearly loved. She had dashed back and forth between her parents all morning, checking to see that her mother was resting comfortably and that her father was not over-taxing himself by lifting something too heavy and further straining his back. There were so many things to be done this time of the year on a farm, things needing attention in the fields, around the barns, and in the house and garden. Those things crying out for attention made her very conscious that her parents easily could do too much from sheer necessity.

She had finished shoveling hay and manure off the concrete floor of the pig pens and was hosing it down when she heard an approaching vehicle. She gave the floor another sweep with the water hose, climbed over the board fence, and padded over to the faucet in her over-sized, rubber boots. She began to coil the hose up, but as the sound grew nearer, she glanced curiously around, expecting to see Ray Carlson, her old beau and Barbara's boyfriend.

But the sight of the broad-shouldered man jumping lightly from the husky, red truck made her heart skip a beat and sent a small tremor of shock down her spine. Dismay caused her lips to droop, and her lashes fluttered uncertainly. How she wished she could hide from the laughter she saw dancing in his penetrating blue eyes! Why did it matter whether it was Adrian or Ray? Ray had seen her many times in such garb, and she had never thought a thing about it. But she cringed from appearing less than her best in this man's sight. It didn't make an ounce of sense. Irritation boiled up in great waves, so that she only nodded curtly at his friendly greeting.

"Dad's in the barn," she jerked her tangled red curls toward the building and brushed by him, "Got to go in the house and check on Mother."

"Stormy," his voice, soft yet taut, slowed her steps, and she faltered, looking back at him reluctantly. "Set the table for four, your mother invited me to stay for lunch."

Angrily, she spun back around and stomped her way to the house, her boots squishing loudly with each step, and her ears burning fiercely from the low chuckle that sped her on her way. Sure enough, her mother was on her feet and moving around, her eyes bright, and her movements free from pain.

"Hi, Hon. You clean up while I start lunch."

"But, Mother," she protested, "are you sure you feel like it?"

"Yes, Dear. I feel fine now, and I'd like to get some things done. Now hurry. Daddy's going to want a quick lunch, and I need your help."

"All right." She dashed upstairs, her mind racing ahead, and in a scant ten minutes, she was back in a soft, pastel blue dress that was very pretty and very feminine. For some vague reason, she had also yielded to temptation and caught her damp curls back with a matching, slender ribbon, applied a light coat of makeup, and a splash of her favorite cologne. She was breathless.

"My, but you look pretty!" her mother complimented her with knowing eyes.

"Oh, I just wanted to look and smell better than I did when I came in," she excused herself with lowered lashes and an offhand manner, hoping her mother would not tease her. And she didn't. After a brief study of the sweetly pink cheeks and restless hands that jerkily placed the napkins and silverware around each of the four places, Anna went back to the pleasant task of preparing the meal.

Fried ham and potatoes, brown beans expertly seasoned, a green salad, and corn bread were waiting on the table when the two men entered the back door. Claiming kinship to starvation, they washed hurriedly and came into the kitchen, their male voices raised in hearty laughter over some amusing incident. They ate hungrily and talked avidly about the farm with polite attention directed toward any comments made by the women.

Anna was eagerly included in their talk and urged to take part in the suggestions and decisions, her keen mind and common sense commanding a respect from the men. But Stormy felt a wee bit left out and more than a little put out at the visitor's actions toward herself. In no way, did his eyes reflect his delight in her presence or his awareness of her eye-appealing attire. His manner was cool, although courteous, and she found herself greatly regretting her rudeness at his arrival.

It seemed ridiculous yet extremely important that he notice her. But in no way could she make him notice her without seeming forward or obvious. So she remained a little offended throughout dessert and wondered frequently and peevishly if he would have acted differently if Vivian had been there.

She contented her aggravated feelings by making preposterous comparisons between him and Cliff, in which Cliff always came out the winner. Indeed, she was glad to begin clearing the table. Adrian offered his services to her father for the next few afternoons, and her father accepted his offer enthusiastically. Old suspicions reared ugly heads, and Stormy glared down at his black curls as she passed his chair. The men went back outside, and resentment clouded her thoughts as she slammed the dishes down loudly in the sink. Why would a man rich enough to hire people to do his own work volunteer to work for a man who was not even related to him? Why?

She cleaned house all afternoon, working as hard and fast as she could to help banish an inconsolable self-pity that told her she was a loser all the way around. Cliff had not called and probably would not. Adrian thought of her as a child and treated her that way. She was feeling downright miserable. She had examined her looks with a very critical eye after seeing Vivian at church and despairingly decided that a curly shock of hair, a snub nose, and too generous lips did nothing to attract or interest the opposite sex. Large, brown eyes made the swift calculation that she had achieved nothing short of a miracle when she won Cliff's love. That recurring thought made her more anxious about the absence of communication between them.

By the time she finished cleaning upstairs, it was time for the children to come home from school. A delicious aroma met her as she ran downstairs and began to relax, welcoming the children's chatter as they burst through the door. Chores were done quickly and smoothly with everyone working together. As they took their places around the table, Stormy was able to appreciate the vigorous appetites that attacked the tender beef roast her mother had spent the afternoon preparing.

Barbara was aglow with the promise of being considered for a very essential and highly coveted scholarship. She also had inquired at the Hutchens' Feed and Grocery Store for a temporary position as a summer sales clerk and been offered the job of bookkeeper instead. The better position meant better pay, and she was radiant as she shared her hopes with her proud family. She and Ray planned to attend a church rally that evening, and she hurried away after supper to dress.

She had urged Stormy to go with them, but her sister had declined, not wanting to make the traditional "three's a crowd." She also had an inkling that Adrian and Vivian would be there together. Despite repeated silent remarks that she did not care and that they deserved each other, she was still left with a very unsatisfactory, hollow feeling in the pit of her stomach, a feeling she eventually blamed on missing Cliff.

Family devotions found her unusually responsive. She knew she badly needed the inner peace and joy that shone on her parents' faces, in spite of the major problems they faced. Through the years, they had tried and proved God, finding Him totally dependable. She longed to be able to completely trust Him also. She needed a Friend Who would understand her and yet love her unconditionally. She was not sure if she could find Him through the tangled web of independence her years away from home had woven in her.

Yet the words from 1 Peter 5:7, "Cast all your cares upon Him for He careth for you," quoted by her mother with such fervor, the blessed light of assurance shining in her lovely eyes and ringing fervently in her clear voice, caught at Stormy's yearning spirit and offered hope. The family time of prayer began with thanksgiving to the One Who daily supplied all their needs and whose promises never failed. Then petitions were offered up by each person, explaining to the Lord in their own words, their needs and desires. Finally, a joyful praise of thanksgiving was lifted to Him Who is worthy of all praise.

Stormy went to her room and dug her Bible out of her suitcase, hungrily finding the verse that touched her bruised and weary heart. She knelt humbly beside her bed, buried her face in the covers, and poured out her heart in a repentant prayer to her Heavenly Father, asking to be forgiven for her lack of concern for His will and to be led to a new and better understanding of His Word. She felt as if she were illuminated on the inside when she slipped between the covers. All was well. She would rest in His care.

The rest of the week fell into an ever-changing pattern of working, caring, and sharing. A strong bond of love was renewed between Stormy and her family, and it did her good to know they listened to what she had to say and cared about how she felt. She was able to go through the days with a smile on her lips, hiding the hurt of her continued estrangement with Cliff from anxious eyes.

More than once, she seriously considered calling Cliff's parents to see if she could talk to him, but she was too proud. Adrian treated her the same each day during the noon meal that he shared with them, and she soon lost a good portion of her nervousness. She resolved to think of him only as someone whose actions still needed to be closely observed, but otherwise he could come and go as he pleased.

Thus, a silent truce was declared between the fiery, spirited girl and the big immovable man, as each worked in separate ways for the people they loved.

15

A Working Vacation

The first week of Stormy's vacation was soon gone. Charles was greatly appreciative of the help Adrian had given him. His back was becoming stronger every day, and he and the twins would be able to handle the farm without any problem that summer. But Stormy knew her father still had to be very concerned about their financial status, so she approached him one evening after supper when the kids had all disappeared to the barn to see Lucy's new litter of spotted puppies. Her mother was drying the last of the dishes, and Charles was quietly reading the little town's daily newspaper.

"Daddy," she said, pulling out a chair and sitting down beside him, "can I talk to you?"

"Why sure, Stormy Leigh. What's on your mind?" He folded the paper and laid it aside, giving her his full attention.

"Daddy, is the farm in trouble? I mean financially?" she asked, searching his tired face with troubled eyes.

"Yes, Stormy, it is," he answered her frankly, his voice quiet but undefeated.

"Serious trouble?" she persisted, feeling she had to know the worst however bad it might be.

He sighed deeply, his eyes lingering on the smooth lines of his wife's face as she seated herself across from them. Then he looked squarely at Stormy, "Yes, we're on the verge of losing the farm."

Stormy swallowed hard. The bald truth had been what she expected. Yet it took her breath away.

"I want to help," impulsively she laid a strong, young hand on his rough one. "I don't have much, but I want to help."

"We can't accept your money, Stormy," her mother spoke firmly. "What our children earn is theirs."

"Mama, I will not let you take your washer and dryer back!" Stormy burst out, "I know how long you waited and saved for them, and I just will not let you take them back!" She was on the verge of tears.

"It's all right, really," her mother soothed gently, "and we really do appreciate you wanting to help. But I made it fine without them, and I'll make it fine again."

"No, Mother! I don't mean to sound dictatorial or bossy, but I made up my mind before I came that I wouldn't let you take them back!"

"How did you know I was thinking about returning them?" her mother questioned.

"Barbara wrote and told me, and I'm glad she did!" Stormy defended her sister. "Please, please let me help you. You've both done so much for me, and I can do so little anyway."

Stormy could see indecision in her parents' eyes as they looked at each other, and she knew how bad the problems must be for them even to consider it.

"Just consider it a small loan," she pleaded, "when things are good again, you can pay me back."

Her father's eyes misted, and his voice grew husky with emotion, "Anything you want to contribute will be greatly appreciated, daughter, and we sincerely thank you."

"Thank *you*, Daddy ... Mother," she hugged each of them, then turned and ran upstairs to get her money. But she determined never to let them pay it back. She was giving it because she loved them and wanted to share in their hardships as well as their good times.

When Sunday morning rolled around again, she found herself eagerly anticipating going to church. Her soul searching for the truths she had abandoned had stirred an inner hunger that would not be stilled. The old minister's message to his flock contained the cry of the Father to His children to rest in Him in the midst of their troubles. Again Stormy heard the principle of "cast all your cares upon Him." Her heart leaped afresh at the familiar verse, and she received its comfort gladly.

A look of wonder softened her eyes as she glanced at her parents, noting the smile of contentment and the look of love they shared. She knew instantly why they had risen above the many trials and hardships she remembered from her own childhood. They had learned to completely cast all their cares upon their Father, Who had never failed them. They rested in the quiet assurance that He never would and that their future was secure in Him.

"I've always known that," Stormy mused silently, her eyes flickering back to the minister. "They have told me that all my life. But I never had a revelation of full understanding until this moment, and I did not know they had that kind of faith. Oh! I want it too. I know I don't have it now, and maybe it comes through years of trusting and proving Him. I don't know. I just know I want it. I want the kind of peace in my heart that will keep me steady and strong when everything around me is going wrong."

So it was that she listened with all her heart and received much strength that day.

Vivian appeared at her side after church and drew her aside for a moment. She was dressed very becomingly in a delicate pink dress with white eyelet embroidery caressing the edges of the wide collar that fell softly over her bare, brown arms. She looked dazzling.

Pink! A color Stormy had always loved but did not feel went well with her coloring. Nowadays, women did not pay much attention to the old adage that "redheads can't wear red," but she had never felt comfortable in any shade of red. She smiled into the beguiling black eyes and watched the fluttering, long lashes lift often toward Adrian as he stood conversing with a group of farmers. She steeled herself for whatever the lovely, elegant Vivian might decide to say.

"How have you been, Stormy?" she drawled huskily, smoothing her lace collar with the tips of perfectly manicured pink nails.

"Just fine. And you?" she answered cautiously, hiding her own hands behind her back. A week's work on the farm had dulled the buffed finish of her nails, because she could never remember to wear work gloves. Also, a torn nail had bothered her horribly since the service was dismissed for fear it might accidentally scratch someone when shaking hands.

"Oh, just wonderful," Vivian responded, her black eyes fixed dreamily on Adrian, "just wonderful!"

"That's good," Stormy wondered where the seemingly aimless conversation was headed and was about to excuse herself when the little velvet hand left the lacy collar and gripped her arm with surprising strength.

"How long are you going to be home?" the question was blunt, the onyx eyes suddenly hard and cold, and Stormy blinked owlishly in surprise.

"An-another week," she stammered, and despised her inability to act mature around the other woman.

"You're just here on vacation?" the grip relaxed slightly, then the petal pink nails dropped to twist a sparkling diamond dinner ring back and forth on her finger.

"Yes," Stormy followed the woman's gaze back to Adrian and flushed hotly as she saw the amusement in his eyes. She could just imagine what he was thinking! She knew she looked like an overgrown farm girl beside this stunning creature. But she was not about to preen herself in his sight as the darling little Mrs. Langley was doing. She jerked her eyes away from his dark face and fiercely studied her big feet in sensible brown shoes poised awkwardly next to the tiny ones in fragile pink slippers. Fairy princess feet versus clodhoppers! Huh! It was injustice at its worst. It just was not fair!

She bit down hard on her sharp tongue to keep from blurting out to the petite, pink lady that she did not want to talk to her any longer and would prefer not to ever see her again. Instead, she raised a polite, bland face to the next question.

"Adrian tells me he's been helping your father this week. Is your father having problems?"

That question *did* earn Vivian a cold stare, and she hastened on defensively, "I didn't mean to pry, of course. It's just that a lot of farmers are about to lose everything they own. I was simply concerned." Her eyes narrowed slightly as she prepared to try to dig the truth from Stormy.

"Why don't you ask Adrian? He knows more about it than I do," and brown eyes for once out-stared black ones, which shifted restlessly back to the man in question.

"Of course, dear."

At her patronizing tone, Stormy's emotions reached the boiling point. But she managed to bite her tongue.

"If you don't want to answer, that's fine. I'm sorry. I didn't realize you were still such a sensitive child," the last words being spoken intentionally louder so that they almost certainly reached the ears of the big man briskly moving their way.

Stormy mumbled an excuse and fled. It was she who waited in the car that day, miserable and angry. All the newfound joy she had experienced during the service disappeared like a puff of smoke, and she unconsciously took back to her heart all the cares she had lain at the Master's feet. Once again she was weighed down with pain and frustration.

"One woman," she thought bitterly, "one woman with the beauty of the night in her eyes and the lash of an adder in her tongue. How can she make me feel so useless and ugly, not to mention childish, by a simple gesture of a graceful hand or a careless word from made-up lips?"

Anna Winters was surprised to see her eldest sitting alone in the car. She turned to her anxiously as she took her place in the front seat.

"Stormy Leigh, are you all right? Several of the ladies were disappointed not to talk with you."

"I'm sorry, Mother," Stormy smiled wanly, "I have a headache and don't feel very well," and a bad headache it proved too! She spent most of the afternoon lying on her bed with a cool cloth on her forehead listening to the sounds of talk and laughter that drifted upstairs.

Ray Carlton had been invited to Sunday lunch, and he and Barbara suffered the brunt of the twins' teasing that day.

Although Stormy felt better by church time that evening, she decided to stay home and spend a long, lonely evening by herself. Her mother wanted to stay with her, but she insisted they all go on to the service. After they had driven away, she moodily wandered outside and sat on the porch swing, stroking Ol' Tom's still-scruffy fur. But he reminded her of Cliff and that made her want to cry, so she put him down and went to the barn to climb up in the loft and play with the kittens.

They were just learning to play with each other, and their antics reminded her of Amy, whose love for animals was unmatched by any other person she knew — except perhaps for Ray's. Thinking of him and Barbara and their beautiful, growing love made her own heart swell with loneliness. Restlessly, she left the kittens and went to look at the new puppies piled on top of one another asleep. Their occasional grunts and wiggles made her smile, but soon she turned back to the house with a sigh.

She wished she had gone on to church. As much as she loved the farm, it was too quiet tonight. She bit her lip in discontent, then impulsively headed for the telephone. She would call Cliff! All pride was gone, replaced by a fierce desire to hear his voice again, even if she had to beg for forgiveness. She did not have the telephone number, but after several attempts, she managed to get it through the operator. Excitement coursed through her as she imagined his pleased surprise at her call. She hoped he would confess how much he had missed her.

"Hello?" she cheerfully answered the curt voice on the other end. "May I please speak with Cliff?"

"I'm sorry. He's gone out for the evening."

"Gone out?" she echoed weakly, her excitement draining away. She felt frustrated and a little sick.

"Yes. That's what I said," the voice grew impatient, and after a moment, asked, "May I ask who is calling? And would you like for me to give him a message?"

"Uh ... uh, no thank you. It isn't important. Goodbye." Stormy buried her face in her hands, giving way to a storm of tears. After a good cry, she marched upstairs and bathed her face in cold water. It had done absolutely no good whatsoever to carry on like a baby! Why on earth had she gone to pieces when told he was out for the evening? What did she expect? That he would be home mooning around like she was? Ridiculous!

She snorted, drew water up her nose, and began to cough and sputter. When she could once again breathe, she glared at the red-faced reflection in the mirror. She was going to have to stop suspecting him of cheating on her all the time, or she would soon be a mental case. Where was all the trust that was supposed to come automatically when you loved someone?

"Shame on you," she scolded the girl in the mirror, "it's high time you shape up, or no one is going to like being around you."

Thoroughly rebuked and disciplined, she dried her eyes, powdered her red nose, and marched back downstairs. Her family would be home in about thirty minutes, and she was going to have a delicious snack ready for them. Cookies with chocolate chips and walnuts were hot and ready to eat when the lights of the old station wagon bounced off the barn wall. Humming happily, she ran through the hall to meet them at the door.

They trooped in noisily, asking in unison how she felt and telling her how much they had missed her at church. She wished again that she had gone. Certainly it would have done her more good than moping around the house. She turned to close the door and was startled to see a long, sleek vehicle turn in the drive with two heads silhouetted close together.

"Mother, are you expecting someone?"

"Yes, dear." Her mother's head appeared around the bedroom door as she added, "I asked Adrian to stop by. I want to treat him for helping your father last week. I'm going to change clothes. Keep them entertained for a few minutes, will you, dear?" Her head disappeared back into the bedroom, and an unreasonable panic seized the girl at the front door.

Entertain him? How? She could not even seem to speak civilly to him when they were alone. Alone? Hardly! She had forgotten the second head in the car, and now it moved up the walk at Adrian's side, with its soft black hair flowing like a cloud around plump, shapely shoulders.

"Hello," she gasped, "Won't you come in?" She wanted to laugh and cry at the sound of her voice. Talk about the voice of a crow! She felt them glance at her strangely as she ushered them toward the kitchen.

"Please, go on back. Mother and Dad will be here in a moment." Ah, that was better, more normal sounding. They stood silently by the table as she moved toward the cabinet without remembering to ask them to be seated.

"Where did you run off to so quickly this morning?" Adrian asked curiously, "I wanted to ask you something."

Whirling around fiercely, her temper suddenly flared at the painful memory his words evoked, she spouted off without thinking, "I wasn't running away!"

"Okay! Okay!" he held up his hands in surrender, "you weren't running away."

Stormy swallowed hard and prayed for help in the form of one of her family, anything to avoid the mockery in Vivian's eyes. She fumbled at one of the glasses she was placing on the table and knocked it over. It rolled to the other end of the table, and Adrian caught it with a deft twist of his wrist. He walked around to her and placed it back on the table.

"Well, may I ask you now?" The request was made very matter of factly, and Stormy's heart thundered treacherously. She dared not lift her eyes from the table to meet the black ones whose intense interest in the conversation could be felt in a piercing manner.

"Surely," she said shakily.

"I'd like to talk to you sometime about the computer I use to store my farm records. I feel we may be outgrowing it, and I could use any advice you could give me."

Her eyes lifted in complete amazement just in time to catch the intense look of violent jealousy that transformed Vivian's beautiful face into one of undeniable ugliness before self-restraint was firmly applied, forcing it to relax into a watchful, catty smile. Thrown off-guard by the unexpected request and the look of black antagonism in the other woman's eyes, Stormy was momentarily speechless.

"Well?" Adrian prompted, his hand reaching out to turn her attention to him, "do you think you could spare me some time in the near future?"

"Oh, yes. I think I probably could if …," unexplainably she melted under his eyes and heard herself begin to prattle like a school girl, "I mean I probably could find the time and help you decide if you need a computer with a larger memory." She finished weakly, feeling like a fool.

"Adrian!" A high-pitched shriek interrupted them, and Adrian swung around to catch Amy in his arms. He gave her a bear hug and then swung her upward to touch the ceiling.

"Hi, Kitten. How are you?"

"Fine," she answered in a delightfully grown up voice, which she promptly lost as she caught sight of the big platter of cookies, and yelled, "Cookies! Cookies! Mmmmmmm! Chocolate chip cookies!"

When Stormy finally emerged from her daze, she was happy, also free from her earlier depression. Nothing bothered her the rest of the evening, not even the dark frowns she encountered from Vivian nor her barbed remarks. Her cookies were a great success, and for once, she accepted herself as she was. Blue jeans, a soft blue sweater, and tennis shoes might not make much of a showing next to an ivory pleated silk dress with a black patent leather belt and matching heels, but she did not care.

Adrian had asked for *her* help in the presence of Vivian, and that had set her heart to singing. But the couple did not stay long, for Vivian soon tired of the domestic scene and cooingly suggested they leave as "these good people have to get up early, darling." Adrian, of course, rose immediately and courteously thanked his host and hostess for their hospitality.

Stormy sat very still, hoping he would speak to her before they left — and she was not disappointed, for he turned back at the kitchen door.

"I'll talk to you about it more tomorrow," he promised with a smile.

A shy smile accompanied her slight nod to him. She suffered the sharp sting of a cold look from Vivian, but it left her unaffected. To top it off, Amy came and slipped a warm little hand into hers and gave her a sweet little hug.

"You make the best cookies ever, Sister," she declared, her eyes proud and glowing. "And you're much prettier and nicer than Vivian. She's an old grouch!"

"Amy!" Punishment threatened in the form of her mother, and the little girl skipped quickly away calling back over her shoulder as she went, "Well, it's true!"

The next week was packed full of memories for Stormy. Her mother was feeling much better and able to be up and around more each day. Her father professed himself to be well, and the hay crop coming on promised to be such a success that he was in high spirits, repeating now and again, "Might even have enough to sell some."

She helped clean house and fix meals, attended to the never-ending outside chores, and became involved in every project going on around her. The twins had decided to build their mother a wall-length bookcase for her Christmas present, and Stormy eagerly offered to help sand and stain the wood that was being cut and shaped by two pairs of very talented hands.

Her love and fondness for the boys grew. They never quarreled, and they respected each other's opinions. Given to fun and with optimistic personalities, their company began to cause Stormy's own natural humor to reassert itself. Often her wittiness matched their own, and all three would fall into such gales of laughter that work would stop while they wiped the tears from their eyes. They counted her "one of the guys," and accepted her in everything from discussion of the latest cars to playing basketball.

Barbara's heart was satisfied by the latest fashion magazines that Stormy had remembered to bring home. The two sisters spent many hours poring over them and exchanging ideas about dress designs. Barbara's flair for designing and her avid interest in clothes made Stormy wish there was some way her talent in that area would be put to use. But Barbara felt her life's calling was as a teacher at Shelton High School, so Stormy said nothing to confuse her resolve or to divert her thoughts in another direction.

She baked all sorts of goodies, sharing old and new recipes with her mother, whom she considered the best cook in the world. She spent long hours talking with her father, listening to his stories of God's provision over the years and grasping for the spiritual wisdom he had gained.

True to his word, Adrian McAllister had spent his lunch hour the day after his visit to the farmhouse with Vivian talking to Stormy about a possible new computer. She grew to respect and admire his keen mind and the foresight that placed him ahead of many of the older farmers, who would never accept the fact that computers had become a way of life. He had seen immediately how they could be harnessed and made to pull the plow of tedious bookkeeping. He used his computer to keep tabs on all the farm proceedings.

Adrian listened closely to all that she said, easily grasping the technical information she gave him, and the next day reported success in obtaining the equipment that she had suggested. His interest in her field provided common ground for them to advance across. A number of stimulating conversations on the subject established a fragile boundary of peaceful harmony between them. And his masculine attention did much to restore her confidence in herself, not only in her profession but as a woman.

The days passed too swiftly, and Friday night the family assembled in the auditorium of Shelton High for Barbara's graduation. The event brought back old, almost forgotten memories to Stormy. She felt as if a lifetime had passed since her own high school graduation. Sentimental tears stung her eyes and her smile wobbled, but no one noticed. She was so proud of her beautiful younger sister and so excited about the future she faced with confidence and natural grace.

Barbara appeared very mature as she rose to give the valedictory address for her class. Her clear, lilting voice proclaimed to the world that she and those graduating with her believed that with God's help they could do anything they set out to do and be an example of progress to those who followed them. In this small town, no worldly board of directors stopped her from using the name of the Lord in her speech as had happened in many places in recent years.

Oh, yes! The family was very proud of Barbara. Their love shone in their eyes and faces as they flocked around her after the formalities. Stormy deeply admired Ray for his love for all of her family. He did not whisk Barbara away for himself, but became one of the family, allowing them all to share in the happy event. He and Stormy spent some time reminiscing about their own school days and the friendship they once had as teenagers. The whole family spent a merry evening together, rejoicing in the victory of accomplishment of one they loved. And Barbara basked in their love and attention.

Early Sunday, Stormy woke with a start. Today was the last day of her vacation, and she had a full day of travel ahead. She slipped out of bed and padded barefoot across to draw aside the curtain. Curling up by the window sill with a soft, comforter tucked around her feet, she gazed across at the big house on the hill just as she had done every morning for two weeks. But no longer did she become lost in romantic dreams. Her thoughts were too involved with other matters. The house still was comforting in a solid, familiar way, and she loved it dearly. She wondered if Vivian would someday be its mistress. It certainly seemed possible. She disliked the idea, but really it was none of her business.

Sighing, she knew it was time to lay aside childish notions and face the future more realistically. She could now look back on her temptation to give herself to Cliff before marriage without shame — because temptation was all it had been. Thanks to the hand of the Lord moving on her because of her parents' prayers, she had escaped that snare of the tempter and knew she would never be in danger of it again. It was too important to wait for that special and right time in marriage, and too easy nowadays to spoil that wonderful moment of sacred, giving love. By doing what she believed in her heart was wrong, she would have had to live in the shadow of that spoiled time for the rest of her life.

Yes, she knew God would have forgiven her, but what damage would she have done to her soul, and what scars would she have on her heart? She was so thankful the Lord had intervened in the form of calling her home to help her parents. Now she could enter marriage with Cliff with a pure, undefiled body and have the respect for him that she should have. Marriage was an act of commitment and should be consummated by an act of true, unadulterated love. She smiled. It was time to head back to Kingston.

She left the farm after lingering goodbyes, numerous promises, and some tears. Her little car was piled high with goodies of all sorts. Money might be scarce, but life on a farm meant having plenty to eat.

Amy looked at her solemnly, big brown eyes glistening with tears, and glossy braids swinging slowly back and forth as she sorrowfully shook her head.

"Don't know what we're gonna do, Stormy," her little voice trembled as she jutted her jaw out manfully, "won't be nobody to help me watch the baby kitties and puppies." She gulped loudly, tears beginning to flow over their fluttering restraints, "An' ... an' who'll milk some extra milk so's Tom and Mousey and Lucy can have drinks, an'...."

Stormy swooped down, gathered her close, unable to bear the sight of her tears, and cried softly, "Oh, Baby, it isn't like I won't be coming back."

She rocked Amy in her arms and patted her comfortingly. The little girl clung to her before pushing away to look at her seriously, her tear-stained face intense and pleading.

"Couldn't you just marry Adrian, an' stay home an' not go away any more?"

"But what about Cliff, Honey?" Stormy asked, hoping to distract the child and quiet her distress, but that was definitely the wrong thing to say.

"But I don't like Cliff!" Amy wailed loudly, and the twins shifted their feet uncomfortably. They were in complete agreement with their little sister, but they could say nothing.

"Amy," Keith stooped down and disengaged her arms from their stranglehold around Stormy's neck. "You mustn't make Stormy feel badly. She loves Cliff, and we want her to be happy. Come here."

Unhappily, the little girl fled into her brother's arms but continued to hiccup miserably.

"Oh, Amy, I love you!" Stormy took the wet little face in her hands and kissed it. Then giving Keith a quick, hard squeeze, she hurriedly got into her car. There were cheers and shouts as she drove away, but Amy's sad face stayed with her for many a mile.

16
A Need for Perfect Peace

The closer she got to Kingston, the more excited she grew. What had sounded like an ultimatum in her last conversation with Cliff had dimmed to a shadow of its original threat. Surely he would not still be angry. Her family's need for her was too important for him not to understand. They would kiss and make up, and everything would be wonderful again. Mindlessly, she hummed a little tune, planning what she would say and wear when she saw him again. Music sang in her veins, and her heart soared like a kite on strings of love.

She considered driving to his apartment, then decided against it. He might not have gotten back yet. She would wait and call later in the evening, and if he was too tired to come see her, she would at least have the pleasure of talking to him over the phone.

Stopping at a small grocery store to pick up a few supplies, she went directly home. After visiting a few minutes with her landlady and picking up her mail, she staggered up to her apartment with her arms loaded down. The rooms were stuffy from being closed up, and she threw open the window, welcoming the brisk gust of air with a deep breath. After several trips to the car, she was glad to be able to put away the groceries and then take a long, relaxing bath. Dressed in a long, soft, fleecy gown, she made herself a sandwich, poured a glass of milk, and settled down to go through the mail.

An hour later, she laid the last newspaper aside, stretched, and rose to her feet. Ignoring the suitcase by the door, she headed for the phone. She would unpack later. She had waited as long as she could to call Cliff. Breathlessly, she dialed his number and listened to it ring ... and ring ... and ring. That was odd! She thought he would surely be home by now. It was 10 p.m. Could something have happened? Maybe he had tried to call her during the day, and she had been on the road. Something bad could have happened, and she would have had no way of knowing.

Then she laughed nervously at herself, fighting to chase away disturbing thoughts and fears. She would just call him later, but he did not answer his phone at eleven or even at midnight. She finally went to bed. If she was going to work tomorrow, she needed some sleep. Isaiah 26:3 caught her eye as she opened the Bible at random: "Thou wilt keep him in perfect peace, whose mind is stayed on thee: because he trusteth in thee."

"Lord," she thought, "that's exactly what I need — perfect peace. I do trust You to take care of things for me, and I will do my best to keep my mind stayed upon You, because I realize Your promise will come true only if I meet the condition. Your promises do not fail, people do."

She decided to stand firm upon the promise and wrote it down on a piece of paper, then tucked it away in her purse. The Word of God was beginning to come alive to her again, and she had found herself seeking it out often during the past two weeks. This night, she read until she fell asleep and woke up early the next morning with it clutched to her breast. She laid it gently on her night stand, thankful that she had not crumpled or torn any of its pages during the night.

It seemed strange to realize there was really no need to get up so early, and she really had not had enough sleep. But she crawled out of bed and went over to the window. When she drew back the curtain, she was greeted by a damp, foggy morning that obscured everything from her vision except the wall of the apartment building next door. One look at its bleak, gray walls made her turn and crawl back into bed. She wanted to call Cliff, but did not, knowing he liked to sleep as late as he could.

She arrived at her job early and enthusiastically started in on the work stacked on her desk. Dressed in a brown business suit, plain white blouse, and brown heels, she presented the perfect picture of what Cliff liked to see in the office. She set the scene strategically: her neat, professional outfit; the sweet, elusive perfume that floated around her as she walked; and a prettily wrapped package of his favorite chocolate mints waiting on his desk. She did not expect to see him before 9 a.m., and by that time she hoped to be able to help him with *his* work.

She was totally unprepared for the sound of laughing, intimate voices outside the adjoining door at 8:30. She listened curiously, trying to distinguish the voice. Cliff! Her heart began to race, and she sprang lightly from her chair. Swinging open the door of his office, she froze in mid-step. A curious numbness gripped her, and she felt light-headed. The couple sprang apart at the sound of the opening door, their faces red with guilt. But in the split second before they parted, the stricken eyes of the tall, slender girl had beheld a scene that caused her such tremendous pain that she thought her heart would burst. Her senses reeled, making the room whirl dizzily, and she held the door with all the strength she could muster.

"No!" she whispered, her voice rasping, her throat dry and throbbing, "No, it can't be true."

The two people facing her saw her brush a shaking hand across her eyes as she sagged weakly against the wall. But they did not, could not, reach out to help her, their own shock at her unexpected appearance freezing them motionless. Stormy straightened up slowly, her eyes

211

great pools of horror and bewilderment that shamed Cliff and Denise so that they avoided looking directly at her. No one said a word, and she turned her back on them. With all the dignity her wounded spirit could muster, she stepped back into her own office.

Closing her door, she leaned against it for a moment before dragging herself over to her desk. She did not collapse, nor cry, nor react further in any way. It was as if the passionate kiss and embrace she had just witnessed had drained her of all feeling. And yet a terrible void had stolen the place of her heart, and her spirit was bruised beyond pain.

Gradually her body began to function, following its normal routine. Had she realized it, she would have been grateful. But for the moment, she did not know what she was doing. She felt nothing. She was numb. She supposed the shock would wear off soon. Then she would be angry or wake to an all-consuming pain. Then she would have to reckon with the devastating emotion of betrayed love. Her fingers moved feverishly, spurred by a inward churning, as work provided an escape from tortuous thoughts. At noon, she stiffened her morale and decided to go down to the lunchroom as usual, but when almost there, realized she had forgotten her lunch and had to go back and get it.

A terrific headache began to cloud her mind. She knew she must eat something although the very thought of food was nauseating. As she moved sluggishly back down the stairs, her mind came alive, and she began to feel all the excruciating emotions she had known would soon surface. Suddenly, she felt excessively sensitive and paused outside the door wondering how many of her coworkers had known all along what was happening.

"But if they knew, why didn't they tell me?" she screamed inside. "Why did I have to find out this way?"

"Excuse me," she said, and the other woman coming out of the lunchroom looked at her white face curiously, but made no comment. Pushing the door farther open, she walked in closely followed by an older woman, who stopped hesitantly.

"Miss Winters, are you all right?" she asked worriedly, catching the attention of another woman who had just entered and who looked at her with interest. Stormy plastered a bright smile on her face, determined not to let her pain and humiliation show.

"Yes, Edna," she said tightly, "I'm fine. Thank you."

The older woman shrugged and started to turn away. Then Stormy felt she just had to know the truth, and she placed a restraining hand on Edna's arm and asked if she could talk to her for a few minutes. Edna reluctantly followed her into a large supply room across the hall.

"Edna, I want you to be honest with me. Okay?" The firmness in her voice made things clear, as she began to search for the truth. At the woman's slight nod, she continued, "How long have you known about Cliff and Denise?"

Edna's mouth opened, closed, then opened again, and she did not hedge. She knew exactly what Stormy was talking about.

"I'm really sorry, Miss Winters," she faltered, actually wringing her hands in her agitation. "I told the girls someone should tell you, but they thought we ought to mind our own business and not cause trouble between you and Mr. Callahan. I always thought you were too good for him. But I didn't say anything, because I could really only speculate about what was going on."

"Edna, it's all right," Stormy tried to stem the flood of words that gushed out like a suddenly undammed spring. "Just please tell me what you do know. I don't want any speculation or wild guessing. I just want what you personally have heard or seen," her voice trailed off into a sob that was immediately stiffled.

Edna fidgeted, "Well, I uh ... I saw him flirting several times with her. Some people might not call it flirting, but I do," she continued defensively.

"If you would, Edna, then I'm sure I would too," Stormy said quietly. "Go on."

"He made eyes at her, letting her know he liked the way she moved and all. You know what I mean," Edna's spinsterly face colored vividly, but she continued faithfully with her indictment. "And I've seen him put his arm around her waist and hug her in a very familiar way. Then I did catch them in here once," she waved an arm back toward the shelves of supplies, "but I did not see what they were doing. They were standing real close when I opened the door and moved apart real fast. I guess that's about all."

She looked expectantly at Stormy, saw the bowed shoulders, and clucked angrily with her tongue, "Miss Winters, there are others that have seen and heard a lot more than me. I'm sure they would tell you if you asked them."

With a heart aching from a burden that had grown steadily heavier and her eyes bruised with the knowledge she had expected to hear, Stormy raised her head and looked at the older woman.

"No, Edna. I think I've heard enough. I would just like to know how long it's been going on."

Edna's eyes shifted to the floor. She was not able to look at the naked pain in her co-worker's lovely eyes any longer.

"I'm not too sure," she confessed thoughtfully, "I suppose I started noticing it back around Christmas. But

Leigh, he's not worth your love or your hurting over him!" she sputtered, a new fire in her eyes.

"Everyone says he is just swinging his way to the top on your 'smarts,' pardon the expression," she said hastily, fearing she had said too much but strangely exhilarated by the chance to express her opinion about a wrong too long left unexposed. She raised expectant eyes to her championed heroine.

Stormy smiled, but it was a poor, quivering ghost of a smile that flickered and fled. "Thank you, Edna. That's all I wanted to ask you. Except, would you please not mention our conversation to anyone?"

The request was simple and stated with a lady-like grace that the other woman greatly admired.

"I won't say a word!" she promised, satisfaction gleaming in her smug smile. She now had a tidbit to hug to herself that would make her seem more important to others who often ignored her. But she fully intended to be loyal to Miss Winters, and indeed no one could induce her to say more than that she and Miss Winters had talked, and that Miss Winters was a really nice person, very undeserving of a cad like Clifford Callahan.

As the door closed behind Edna, Stormy sank down into a pitiful huddle on a box of business forms. She felt sick to her stomach, and there was no relief in sight for the tears that kept bubbling up. She buried her face in her hands and cried great sobs that shook her from head to toe, their force emphasizing the agony of her heart.

A few minutes later, she lifted her bright head. Into her eyes had settled a dull, lifeless look, and her lips were white and set. She stared at her lunch bag, wondering if she would ever want to eat again. Her soul now shrank from entering the lunchroom full of laughing, talking people whose prying eyes and sharp tongues could attack her and tear her apart the instant she set foot among them. She harbored no ill feelings toward any of them, but she also realized many of them envied her the position she had attained. They would feel no remorse about tearing her to pieces with cruel remarks.

She reached for her purse, intent on finding her car keys. She would leave. Go somewhere — go anywhere — and call back to say she would not be coming back ever! Her groping hand touched a piece of paper, and she drew it out impatiently, but her eyes fell on it as her hand began again to hunt for the car keys. Slowly her hand stilled as her brain began to absorb Isaiah 26:3, which she had written out so trustfully the night before.

"Oh, Jesus," she began to beseech Heaven, her eyes lifting in despair. "I know You can see me right now! I know You are with me right now! You know my world has just fallen apart. I'm falling apart too," fresh sobs shortened her breath. "Lord, I can't make it on my own. I just can't. All I want to do is run away. I've got to have Your help, and according to Your Word, if I trust You with all my heart, soul, and might, I can come out of this situation with peace.

"I know I've been so far away from You that we have not been on speaking terms, and I know it was I who walked away. But Jesus," she prayed earnestly with child-like faith, desiring His promised nearness, "I do love You. I can remember how close I felt to You as a child, and I long to feel that closeness now."

She knew He understood and had answered when the dark cloud of anger and pain began to dissolve, leaving her with a sweet peace and real joy. She had started on the journey home and would learn daily how to walk with Him, as she suddenly understood that what He cherished most was an honest heart and a repentant spirit.

She did not for a moment suppose all would be perfect from now on, but she had a Friend to go to when things went wrong. He had promised that He would work everything out for her good. All she had to do was trust Him. She could find nothing good in her heartache. But she clung to Him with the blind reasoning of a child who recognizes its father can protect it from dark and frightening fears. She smiled at the little piece of paper in her hand.

"Thank You," she whispered, placing the paper back in her purse. She picked up her lunch and rose to her feet. She still had thirty minutes left of her lunch hour. Uncertainty flickered in her eyes, but purpose rose in her heart and chased it away. She opened the door of the supply room, crossed the hall, and stepped confidently into the lunch room.

She was met with a few knowing looks and whispers, but there also were some who welcomed her to their table. The rest of the hour was spent conversing about clothes, food, and children. Stormy tried to respond to the lightheartedness, but it was a trial that sorely taxed her strength. She was glad to disappear once again into the quietness of her office. She was glad she had not run away, but she wondered how much longer she could survive with Cliff just next door. She was working feverishly when the door opened. She looked up to see Denise watching her.

"I want to talk to you," the other girl said brazenly.

"I don't see that we have anything to talk about," Stormy's voice was stiff and cool, yet dignified. It must have touched a raw nerve because the other girl's lovely face flushed. She jerked her head angrily, her voice full of defiance.

"Well, I say we do. And I'm going to say it before I leave!" She was beautiful even in her rage, and all too easily, Stormy could see her attraction to the opposite sex. Dressed every day in figure-hugging dresses and sweaters, her face made up to enhance a contradictory image of innocence, she could undoubtedly win the interest of almost any man. She was shallow, but undeniably desirable. Stormy's heart writhed in anguish. She did not want to hear sordid details from this girl. She wanted to be left alone to nurse her broken heart in solitude.

"Do you hear me?" the girl advanced to her desk and perched on the edge, hiking up her skirt to an indecent height. "I just want to explain why you lost Cliff."

"I would rather not hear your explanation. I don't feel I could credit any advice from you," Stormy's tongue came unleashed. The sting of it widened the baby blue eyes watching her.

"My! My! Aren't you even curious about how I stole Cliff away?" she asked maliciously and was rewarded by seeing Stormy flinch and grow pale. She continued vindictively, "You just don't know how to play the game right." She examined her long red nails with interest before directing her bold gaze to the quiet girl whose steady eyes never left her face.

"And just how *far* did *you* play the game, Denise?" The words rang out more as an accusation than a question. The blond girl squirmed off the desk and began to pace the floor.

"Far enough to get what I wanted," she spat out. "I didn't hide behind some silly, lily-white religious idea. If you don't give a man what he wants, he'll just find it somewhere else."

"Then he isn't worth having!" Stormy cried in agitation. "Why should a woman have to lower her standards and lay down her self-respect at the feet of a man for him to trample on. That kind of man will sleep with any woman who makes herself available!"

Vivid red flared up the girl's slender throat into the roots of her blond hair. "I love Cliff!" she declared self-righteously. "And I've loved him a lot longer than you. Maybe that doesn't make what I've done right, but it was worth it to me!"

"Just how long have you known Cliff?" Stormy's interest was caught in spite of her abhorrence of the conversation.

Denise stopped pacing to muse dreamily. "We went to school together. He was always the best in everything, I thought. He used to be nice to me and sometimes carried my books home for me. We lived next door to each other. Then he went away to college and," her eyes darkened with remembered loneliness, "I missed him so much. Why I almost camped on his doorstep when he came home." She laughed self-consciously, darting a strangely childish look toward Stormy.

"Then he moved here and went to work for Eastland, so I followed and got hired as a secretary. I didn't go to college. My folks didn't have the money, and I could not find a job that would pay enough. I was not smart enough to get a scholarship," she shrugged her shapely shoulders regretfully.

"Anyway, Cliff helped me get on here, and I could see him every day. Sometimes, he would drive me home or take me out."

Then her face hardened again, and she turned sneeringly to Stormy, "But then you came along and thought you could take him away from me. He's mine, I tell you!" Her voice was loud and belligerent. Gone was the docile sweetness of the previous moment. She marched back to the desk to glower, "You can have me fired if you want to, but that will not change the fact that Cliff and I spent the last two weeks together at his folks!"

Stormy's slender hope collapsed. She was shaken to the core of her being. Her head felt light again, and she moistened her lips. But she could make no reply to the remark that had destroyed any illusion that the affair had not been serious.

"Oh, yes," the other girl continued heartlessly. "He even told his folks that after all these years, he was going to marry the girl next door. Now, what do you think of that?" she began to laugh, her face aglow with triumphant happiness. Suddenly she stopped and snapped her fingers.

"Why I bet you tried to call him last night, didn't you? Probably wondered where on earth he could be." Without waiting for a confirmation, she continued smugly, "Well, he was at my place."

Stormy thought she would scream if the girl said another word. Her wounded heart was beating frantically under the attack of Denise's jabbing statements. She rose to her feet, the muscles in her throat working convulsively.

Denise watched her cattily, knowing she was defeated and curious as to her next move. She had won, and the morality of her technique for doing so was unimportant to her. She had succeeded in getting what she desired most in life and could feel a sort of pity for the girl whose place she had usurped. Denise studied Stormy's ashen face as she moved gracefully around the desk and had to marvel at her composure and self-discipline. She really had expected a dramatic scene of weeping and begging. But Stormy had in no way indicated that she still felt anything for Cliff.

Mystified, Denise continued to watch, her eyes narrowed. Then they widened in astonishment as she looked into the calm, brown eyes now facing her and realized that only pity for her was mirrored there. She suddenly saw herself as Stormy saw her — a poor, little girl who had sold herself for empty promises and a loveless future.

"You are more than welcome to him, Denise," Stormy's voice was serene, almost casual, and free from the condemnation Denise had tried to put on her. "He is all yours. And good luck."

She opened the door for Denise to leave, and closed it gently behind her as she flounced through. But then she staggered back across the room on legs too weak to support her and dropped into her desk chair. Laying her hot cheek against the cool glass surface of the desk, she closed her burning eyes. In spite of her cool-appearing exterior, she was a quivering mass of jelly inside. If the ordeal with Denise had lasted much longer, she would undoubtedly have lost control of the situation.

She still had an hour before going home, and her body rebelled against the limits to which it had been pushed. Exhausted to the point of fainting, she pressed on, even staying late to complete her work. She could only hope her figures were accurate and stayed longer to recheck them. She had not seen Cliff since that morning and did not care if she ever saw him again. She had tried to be fair and not take all the evidence she had been given as absolute proof of guilt until he admitted it himself. And, oh, how she hated the thought of that happening.

Finally, she opened the door between their offices, her soul cringing at the memory of the morning. The package she had laid on his desk was still there, and his jacket was thrown over his chair. She had picked up after him, and now bitterly knew that Denise would be doing what she had considered a delightful chore. She could recall other little "acts of love" she had done for him, trying to please him and make things go right for him. She shook her head, unwilling to think about it any longer. She picked up the package of candy and left the room.

17
The Truth Is Exposed

When Saturday morning came, she lay quietly in bed thinking over the past few days. Late Monday, she had given way to a storm of tears. In despair, she had called home. She smiled faintly, remembering the call. Dear Daddy! He had known exactly what to say to help stop the flood of self-pity in which she had been drowning. His dear, grave voice had been like a soothing hand on her troubled mind. She had poured her story into his sympathetic ear, and he had listened with all the patience of a saint.

But when she had sobbed out her intentions of quitting the very next day and coming home, he had talked to her gently, encouraging her to wait a few days before taking such dramatic action. So she had waited and tried to be strong, wearing a brave face to work the next day to meet her unfaithful fiance.

In a very composed manner, she had approached him, her face a lovely study of sadness that drew dark shadows beneath her moist brown eyes and made the curve of her lips droop.

He had looked up at her, and she had seen the cowardice in his eyes for the first time. He was not the man she had thought him to be. Why! He really was weak in character and had been manipulating her selfishly through her emotions and her love for him. He had not an ounce of godliness in him! And she had wanted to marry him? Her emotions might not yet be totally convinced of his instability, but her heart had been recaptured from under his feet.

And she would determinedly nurse it back to health again.

"Hello, Cliff," she had said in a voice carefully devoid of judgment, but it made him squirm and reddened his face.

"Hi, Leigh," he had recouped quickly, with a bold look of defiance.

She had pulled off her ring and without a second's pause dropped it in front of him. It made a tinny sound as it rolled toward him. He had said nothing, just stared at the ring. She had wondered if he would make any kind of explanation, even hoping he would have the manhood and courage to at least apologize. But he had not. Instead, as usual, his feelings had been all for himself.

"I guess I blew it, didn't I?" His tone had been that of a martyr. "I didn't intend for things to go this way. It just happened. I guess you don't love me anymore." She had eyed him in perplexity.

"I don't really know whether I do or not," she had admitted honestly, "I just know I don't want to marry you."

He had kept quiet, and she had walked away leaving him sitting there. The remaining days of the week had been long and wearisome. The joy she had found in her job was gone. She dreaded to go to work each morning. She and Cliff were barely speaking to one another. But there were no angry scenes, and Denise flitted around him like a little humming bird. He did not send her away, and Stormy sadly concluded that she had been blind to his infatuation with the girl. He seemed to be tied to her in some sort of way, and Stormy realized all over again that she had never really known him.

Thursday afternoon, her curiosity had finally gotten the better of her, and she had approached him to ask why his affections shifted from her to Denise.

"Because she was there, and you weren't!" he had angrily blurted out. She drew in a sharp breath as his words pierced her heart. "You were always too old-fashioned to show a man a good time," he had added cruelly, his lips thinning into a sneer, as he arrogantly placed the blame for his actions on her.

"And just what do you call a good time, Cliff?" she had asked evenly, her face white and drawn. "Sleeping around?"

"I don't want to talk about it!" he had cut her off abruptly and shoved back his chair.

"I don't especially want to talk about it, either," she had said in a quivering voice. "Denise told me enough to sicken me. I just want to know why it happened."

"Because Denise loved me enough since we were kids to give me anything that would make me happy, and you didn't! Well, now you know!" he had thrown out the words sarcastically, his eyes cold and hard. "Are you happy? You should be! You're still as pure as the driven snow!"

If he had hoped to shame or anger her, he was doomed to disappointment, for a sweet glow had shone in her eyes as she drew herself up with dignity and grace.

"Yes, I am," she had said softly and happily. "And I'm so glad."

He was fascinated by her loveliness as the afternoon sun caught her in its last blaze, kissing her curls into a fiery halo and casting a light upon her fair face. She was beautiful in that instant — incredibly beautiful to the man who knew finally that he had lost her. Fool that he was, he had lost her. It was the last time he had a chance to win her back, and he had hesitated too long. Winning her would mean too many changes in himself and his lifestyle.

But the memory of her beauty at that moment was to forever haunt him with regret.

Stormy had gone back to her office and asked for an appointment with Donald Adams, the president of the company. He had seemed pleased to see her, welcomed her cordially into his office, and seated her courteously. He had listened gravely to her resignation. When she had finished, he had sat for a moment scrutinizing her face in a friendly manner. Then he had crossed one leg, fixed the pleat in his trouser leg, and flicked away a piece of imaginary lint.

"It's really because of young Callahan, isn't it?" he had observed, and she had eyed him in astonishment before nodding agreement.

He had moved a hand expressively over his silver hair and said, "I see and hear much more than people give me credit for. But, Leigh, he is not worth your breaking your heart over. Is there any hope of your getting back together?" he had asked gently, not wanting to pry, and she had accepted his question in that light.

After her firm, "No," he had nodded in satisfaction and said, "Leigh, I want to tell you something. I have never been one to brag on my employees, but I think very highly of you." Waving away her thanks, he had continued, "But Clifford has made it to the top on your skirt tail, my dear. He has made gains for himself out of your intelligence and ability, and I feared that he might be using you for that very purpose. That is one reason I hate to let you go. He knows that if you go, it is possible he will automatically fall into your position. So don't expect him to beg you to stay."

"But I don't understand," she had cried, "I don't hold any more authority than he does!"

"Not presently," Mr. Adams had admitted, "but I know and Callahan knows, that the directors have consid-

226

ered voting in a new title and position, one that would head up your floor and consist of four departments. You were the unanimous choice. However, if you leave, Cliff is the only other person we have with the capability to do the job. I would imagine he feels he will get it if you leave."

"Oh, my," she had felt sick and swayed back dizzily into her chair. Immediately, Mr. Adams had been at her side.

"Are you all right?" he had asked anxiously. "I didn't meant to upset you more. I only wanted you to know the score."

"I'm all right," she had smiled wanly. "But I still feel I must leave."

As she moistened her lips and sat up straighter, he had resumed his seat and said suddenly, "Would you consider just taking a few months leave?"

Rewarded by her hesitation, he had said, "All I ask, Leigh, is that for right now you just take a leave. If, say, in three months you still want to quit, I will not say another word. Just please take some time to consider."

She had agreed and promised to let him know something by the first of September.

"Goodbye, Leigh, and the best of luck," he had said while showing her to the door. She had returned to her office and started packing away all the little things that had made it "her place" for so long.

She yawned and stretched. That had been Thursday. Friday she had packed all day, driving herself to the point of exhaustion. Now, her apartment looked naked in the early morning light. Striped of all personal keepsakes and belongings, it no longer seemed like home to her. In a few days, the rent would be up, and she had told the landlady to let someone else have it, giving up her deposit in lieu of a proper notice. She looked at the bare walls. Surely she should have a feeling of nostalgia or something about leaving — but she did not. She was glad to be going home.

She began to feel excited. After the stress of the last few days, she desperately needed a lift in her spirits. Quite unaccountably, she felt happy. She was munching on a sweet roll when the doorbell rang, and she padded over to open it in her big, fuzzy pink slippers. Her love for pink manifested itself in her nightwear, even if she did not dare wear it out in public.

She belted the soft, pink, quilted robe a little snugger and smoothed her unbrushed curls with a heavy hand. She really should have dressed first, but hunger had driven her straight from the shower to the kitchen. She had not felt like eating all week and had practically fasted. This morning, it seemed her body wanted to make up for all the lost time! Oh, well, it could only be the landlady this early.

When she opened the door to find two men, she panicked and involuntarily began to close the door in their faces.

"Leigh," Cliff called, "I've got to talk to you!"

The door swung open under his hand, and he stepped toward her pleadingly.

"You're too late, Callahan," the other man said in a deep, hard voice that stopped Cliff in his tracks. "She's going home."

Stormy's laugh rang out prettily, "He's right, Cliff. I'm going home. By the way, my condolences on the postponement by the directors of a head supervisor's position. Mr. Adams told me yesterday."

The expression of entreaty in the blue eyes facing her turned to bitterness, and the charm that once had fascinated her turned sour. She had learned the truth about him, and it had set her free from a lifetime of misery and scorned love.

He glared at her and then at Adrian, and spoke nastily, "I always did think there was something between the two of you, and *you* were always accusing *me!*"

Jealousy made his voice ring, but then the man behind him clamped a heavy hand on his shoulder and propelled him out of the room. Closing the door behind himself, Adrian looked down at Cliff and shook his head.

"You had your chance, Callahan. It's time to move on."

"You'll never get her!" Cliff gritted his teeth angrily. "She thinks you're out to steal her father's precious little farm. She'd never marry you in a thousand years."

"Whether she will or not is her decision," came the even reply, "but you're out of the running, so you might as well be on your way."

He turned his back on the other man, opened the door and stepped inside, closing it forever to the man whose selfishness had put an end to his own schemes. Adrian faced an empty room and smiled. He sat down on the divan, leaned back, closed his eyes, and waited.

Stormy had stood still for a moment after the door closed behind the two men, her mind racing. Then she whirled around and ran to the bedroom where she quickly slipped on the clothes she had left unpacked for the trip. Holding her breath to steady her hand, she applied eye makeup, brushed her hair hard and fast, splashed cologne on her wrists and throat, and opened the door tentatively to peek out. Yes, he was still there. She had known he would be. She assumed a nonchalant air and opened the door farther.

"'Bout ready to go?" the voice spoke even before the dark eyes opened and the man sprang to his feet.

"Uh … uh, yes," she stuttered, suddenly very ill at ease with this man who always seemed so in control of everything. "But what are you doing here? And how did you know I — I," she spread her hands helplessly.

"Your father," was his only comment and nowhere in the steady blue gaze was there indication that he would always be there if he should believe she needed him.

"Have you finished eating?" he asked, looking at the half-finished roll she had hurriedly placed on the coffee table.

"Yes," she said, her appetite once more swallowed up by the fast pace of events.

"You don't eat very much to be such a big girl," he stated dryly, and her temper began to spark.

The remark was strangely reminiscent of the one he had made at their first meeting, and her tongue was tipped with sharp words. Only a glimpse of the teasing light in his eyes, before he dropped them again to the roll, prevented her from lashing out at him. In fact, his heavy brows rose in mock amazement at her silence as he popped the rest of the roll into his mouth.

The action somehow embarrassed her with its intimacy, until a picture of Amy registered on her mind: Amy with a doughnut in her hand insisting that Adrian take a bite, and then she would take a bite, until the goodie was gone. A curious reluctance surrounded the admission that Adrian probably saw her as a larger edition of her little sister — just someone to be looked after, teased, and whose whims must be catered to on occasion. She moved restlessly.

"My truck's outside," he said, intently watching the changing expressions on her face. "I figured you'd need some help moving home."

Dumbfounded, she gawked at him, her mouth falling open.

"That's right, little girl," he grinned mischievously. "I'm going to help you move back home. So let's get started, shall we? Which box goes first?"

Stormy had spent most of Friday trying to decided what she could carry in her little car, and what she would have to ship or leave behind. Now this man appeared out of nowhere and announced he was moving her home! Grateful she *should* be, but right at this moment, she wanted to box his impudent jaw!

As he picked up the box she pointed to, her eyes fell on her Bible. "Thanks, Lord, for sending me some help," she said silently, then paused and looked up quizzically, "but did You have to send *him?*"

A whistle alerted her that Adrian was fast on the move, and she scooted another box toward the door. He laughed at her red face as she straightened up.

"Little girl, you finish packing. I'll handle these," and so saying, he lifted the heavy box easily and left the room.

"Little girl? Huh!" She snorted at the broad back that disappeared from sight. "Little girl — indeed!" Untruthful though they were, nevertheless the words left her with a pleased feeling. It had been a long time since a man had made her feel small and dainty, much less called her little. Just as long as he was not referring to childishness — her eyes narrowed suspiciously. But this time his whistle brought a smile to her lips, and she began to happily pack the few remaining things. She turned her key over to the landlady and joined Adrian who was standing beside her car.

"That's quite a haul for a hope chest," he laughed. "Maybe it'll make some guy feel lucky someday." He watched her covertly to see if she was really over Callahan or if she would take his remarks as a dig. He wanted to make her mad, so that she would rise up over the sorrow he suspected she was feeling. His words had the desired effect, because she rose to the bait.

"Just having me will make some guy feel lucky, Adrian McAllister!" she retorted, stung on a raw nerve.

"Yes, my lady," he bowed low before her as she crossly jerked the car door open. "'Tis certainly true! 'Tis certainly true!"

She slammed her door, glared up into guileless eyes showing only the deepest admiration, and glowered threateningly, "I hope — oh, I hope that you marry a woman that — that!"

"Yes?" his darkly handsome face loomed in her open window.

"That's bigger than you are," she finished weakly.

He threw back his head and laughed. The rich sound of it tickled Stormy's spine, and she shivered. When he finished laughing, he leaned in the window again.

"Do you know where Rose's Restaurant is? Halfway between here and Shelton?"

"Yes, I know where it is," she snapped, still nettled.

"Good," he chucked her under the chin, "meet me there for lunch."

Without waiting for an answer, he walked away. She sat fuming until he moved his truck out of the way and motioned for her to take the lead.

"Oh! Ornery creature! Serve him right if I didn't stop at Rose's!" Maybe she would do just that. Drive by and honk as she went! But common sense told her it wouldn't matter to him in the least. He would stop and eat anyway. Rose did serve the best food between Kingston and Shelton, and Stormy knew she would be the one to suffer. So she gave an exasperated sigh and stepped down on the accelerator as an impatient honk sounded behind her.

When lunch was past and the trip half over, Stormy was feeling fine. The meal had been delicious, and yes, she would grudgingly admit, she had enjoyed Adrian's company. At least, it had been better than eating alone with only miserable thoughts for company, she defended herself. They had talked about computers, farms, food, and so on, and she had managed to gain a smidgen of insight into her companion's opinions and lifestyle. Their conversation gave her food for thought, and she arrived safely at home without having been swamped by memories of Cliff that constantly hovered only a curtain of thought away.

Supper was ready and waiting, and eager, willing hands made short work of unloading the car and truck. The twins complained good-naturedly that they would probably have to move out into the barn and give her room for all her stuff. They might even have to knock down a wall — and build on a room, too. They did so enjoy teasing her. And she marveled that she could respond so easily to them, when Adrian's teasing always set her teeth on edge and made her fly into a rage.

"Oh, Mother," she squealed, as they all trooped to the kitchen, "My favorite! Smothered Swiss steak! Mmmmm!" She hugged her mother ecstatically, "You can't possibly imagine how good that smells. I'll just run upstairs to freshen up and be right back."

Adrian caught her by the arm as she rushed by him. "Remember," he laughed, "big girls like you don't eat very much."

She drew her lips into a thin line and fastened glittering brown eyes on him. With hands firmly planted on hips, she said clearly, "I'd have you know, Adrian McAllister, I'm just about fed up with your smart remarks!"

The family froze, their eyes riveted on the girl whose red curls fairly danced with fury, but the big man only smiled into her scowling, puckered face. "In that case," he said, "you're certainly too full to eat very much, so we won't have to bother saving you any!"

"Oh, you ... !"

She ground her teeth, pushed past him, and flounced upstairs to bury her face in a cool, wet cloth. She could hear laughter and knew that Adrian was accepted as one of them. His teasing would not bother them, but her angry, cutting remarks would. She shoved back the damp curls around her face. Somehow, she would just have to learn how to keep a tighter lid on her temper!

"Father," she prayed impulsively, "You know I want to be good and sweet. Please help me. My angry words and ways don't seem to bother *that man*, but they do hurt others I love. Please teach me to control my temper and be temperate in *all* things so I may please You."

Feeling much better, she robed herself in her prettiest smile, changed the flash in her eyes to sparkles, and chose not to be provoked for the rest of the evening. For her exceptional behavior, she was rewarded with a friendly, "Goodnight, Stormy Leigh" and a pat on the head from her co-traveler as he left the house. Treated like a child again! But from behind gritted teeth "the child" smiled angelically, and only a faint, sweet growl was heard coming from beneath her breath as the door closed behind him.

18
Some Hopes Go Up in Smoke

It was half past eight Sunday morning when Stormy woke up, but she thought it was much earlier because of the darkness of the room. When her eyes focused better, she sat up and looked at the window. She smiled. Her family must have formed a conspiracy to let her sleep late, for she had not heard the usual early-morning ruckus of voices and feet. And someone — probably her mother — had slipped in and draped a blanket over the window to keep out the sun.

A rush of love for them enveloped her and misted her eyes. They were a beautiful family who showed love through words and actions. She eased out of bed and padded over to her window. Gently pulling the blanket down, she was rewarded with the beauty of a glorious day. The sun was brilliant, lighting the windows of Westmoor Heights with crimson fire. At a knock on her door, she turned.

"Yes?"

"It's Mother, Stormy Leigh. May I come in?"

"Surely, Mother. Come on in."

Anna Winters stepped into the room anxiously eyeing her tall daughter and asked, "How are you feeling?"

"I'm all right, Mother." A dreamless night's sleep had done wonders for her after the sleeplessness of the past week. "I feel good. Thanks for letting me sleep so long." She laughed gaily, "It was probably hard to keep things quiet this late!"

Her mother laughed too, "It *was* rather difficult! Everyone wanted to cooperate except Amy, and we almost had to 'hogtie and gag' her. She's downstairs right now insisting that you have been *expecting* her to wake you up. That child!" Anna shook her head ruefully and smiled.

"Poor, precious lamb!" Stormy laughed again. "She does make a good alarm clock."

"Indeed she does! And it will be an asset for her if she manages to keep the ability and want-to when she grows up."

She crossed the room and looked into the sleepy brown eyes. "I just want you to know that I'm so glad you're home, Honey," she hugged the girl to her and patted her back, holding her tighter at the sound of a ragged sob.

"Mama," the girl reverted to the childish version of mother that she always used in times of stress, "can I talk to you sometime ... sometime when I can talk without crying?"

"You know you can," her mother answered her reassuringly, a glad light of welcome in her lovely eyes. "Whenever you're ready, I'll be more than happy to listen. I know you've been through something extremely hard. We want you to know that we just love you, and we're on your side."

"Thanks, Mother," Stormy drew in a deep breath. "I'll be downstairs in just a few minutes."

"Do you need me to press something for you to wear to church?" Anna asked, looking toward the packed suitcases.

"No," Stormy moved toward the closet. "I thought I would wear that little blue-print dress I haven't worn in years." She smiled a sad little smile that twisted the heart of her mother, "I think I'm in the mood for something old and something blue."

"All right," Anna forced herself to sound cheery, "we'll see you in a few minutes."

Stormy had several new dresses in her suitcases, but she could not bring herself to wear one of them, her weeping heart reaching out for the old and familiar. The blue dress had been a favorite of hers, and she hoped it would still fit. It did, although the weight loss she had suffered over the past week helped. It had a contrasting collar and a double roll of ruffles around the full skirt.

She buckled on simple, low-heeled white sandals and viewed herself in the mirror. The outfit made her look younger, as if the things she had experienced had not aged her. For a moment, she longed to go back in time and relive a part of her life. But no, it was not wise or right to look back and wallow in regrets and self-pity, so she lifted her chin and brushed more color into her pale cheeks.

Amy was apologetic when she got downstairs, immediately saying, "Mama wouldn't let me wake you up this morning. I told her you'd probably oversleep and miss church. But I did like she said." She looked up at her sister for approval and was rewarded with a hug.

"I missed you, Sugar. You can come wake me up tomorrow morning. All right?"

A wreath of smiles swathed the round little face. "Okay," she said and took Stormy by the hand as they started for the car. "I want you to sit by me."

It was amazing the way such a little girl could make her feel so loved and wanted, and a lump stuck in her throat. Impulsively, she bent down and hugged Amy only to be met with puzzled honesty.

"Why'd you do that?" she asked, as she readjusted her little white straw hat.

"Just because I love you." A long, slender finger touched Amy's pert little nose, and it wiggled.

"Oh!" Little round arms wrapped themselves around her and squeezed hard. "I love you, too."

Stormy was surprised to learn how hungry she was to hear the Word preached. She found the message to be healing for her soul and comfort to her bruised heart. When she stood up to leave the church, there was a smile on her face that no question about the loss of the ring from her finger could cause her to lose — if the question was from someone who cared.

However, the first person who spotted the bare ring finger was a dark-headed vivacious woman whose prying eyes darted over the old blue dress first.

"Why Stormy Winters," she shrilled, "I thought the last time you were here, you were wearing an engagement ring."

"That's right," Stormy turned from her to smile into the sympathetic eyes of Mrs. Hutchens, whose husband owned the local feed and grocery store.

"Mrs. Hutchens," she said with genuine warmth, "I have been wanting to tell you how much Barbara is enjoying her job."

The kindly woman looked deep into her eyes and longed to swish her away from the presence of Vivian Langley, whom she knew was bent on snooping into something that was none of her business.

"We think the world of Barbara. Always have. Feel like she could be one of ours. We tried to get her to take a vacation between finishing school and starting to work, but she wouldn't hear of it."

"She's always been a hard worker," pride laced the words, "and she's as good as gold!"

"She sure is, Stormy Leigh." The woman moved back into the mass of people, "Come in and see us sometime."

Vivian, who had been impatiently tapping one tiny foot, bluntly resumed her questioning.

"Aren't you engaged anymore?" The sharp words penetrated Stormy's mind, and she reluctantly turned to face the relentless, aggressive woman.

"No, I'm not." She offered no explanation. "Now, if you'll excuse me, I must go. My family is probably waiting for me," she turned and walked away from the dissatisfied woman whose eyes narrowed thoughtfully.

Vivian knew the girl presented no threat as far as looks were concerned, especially in her simple, outdated dress, but she could present trouble simply from her nearness and close association with Adrian. It would behoove her to change her tactics and pressure him a bit more aggressively. Elapsed time could provide a problem in the person of Stormy Leigh Winters.

There were no guests for lunch at the Winters' house that day, and the family sat around the table catching up on each other's news after the meal. They talked about Barbara's job and of how the Lord had blessed her with a much better position and pay than she had anticipated. She was highly hopeful of winning that scholarship to pay for her tuition, and the better pay would provide for all the little extras.

Charles Winters talked of the rains that had prevented him from planting an early crop but had blessed him with an abundance of orchard grass that he planned to cut next week. He foresaw there would be enough to feed his cattle through winter and still have some to sell. His sons loved to work on the farm, and their strong backs and willing hands would provide him with all the help he needed.

He talked of giving up his hope of buying a new, round hay baler such as many other farmers were using. When the boys left home, he would need one. But this year, things had been much too tight financially for him even to consider buying one that he knew would sell cheap. Also, he had refused an offer from Adrian to borrow his, choosing to bale his hay with the square baler he had used for years.

The twins had to tell her of their car shopping adventures. They were still searching for their dream car but were ready to settle for a little Volkswagen they had found. Barbara was going to pool her money with theirs, and they were ready to settle the deal.

Amy was like a little bird let out of a cage. Her plans for the summer ranged from fishing in the creek to persuading the twins to build her a bigger doll house.

Stormy ventured little about her plans. In fact, she really had none. The idea of having no plans made her feel glad but also restless. So she offered her services to anyone needing them and was immediately accepted by everyone. Barbara wanted some training on running the small computer the Hutchens' were installing. The twins wanted to borrow her car on occasion. Her mother and father welcomed her help in the house and on the farm, and Amy declared she would take her fishing as everyone else *pretended* to be too busy. It was a fun afternoon for them all, and before they knew it, it was time to go to church again.

But Tuesday morning, disaster struck. There had been a stiff breeze blowing all morning that felt good after the heat that had come early. Stormy opened the windows wide before starting to clean the house. Her mother put a chicken on to bake and was kneading dough to make rolls after she finished cleaning upstairs.

"How are you feeling?" she asked as she entered the kitchen. Her mother had been forced to lie down for a little while after breakfast.

"Much better, Dear." A pale face turned toward her. "Once I get completely over being sick in the mornings, I'll be fine. I just hope and pray it does not last the entire nine months." She grinned and winked at her daughter, "Must be another boy." She patted her stomach lovingly.

"Um … or another girl like me!" Stormy laughed and went to look out the window. "I love the smell of bread dough," she mused. A frown creased her forehead. "Mother, come look!" and as her mother appeared at her side, "Doesn't that look like smoke?"

"Yes, it does," her mother answered uneasily. "And it looks as if it could be coming from one of the hay fields. Maybe you had better go and check on it. Even if it's not one of our fields, they may need you to help put it out."

"All right," she called, running down the hall to get her old shoes as she heard the sound of a truck racing up the drive.

"Anna!" She recognized Adrian's voice and an icy hand of fear clutched her heart as he threw open the front door. "Anna! I need buckets and some rags, blankets, burlap sacks, and anything you have to fight a fire."

"Coming, Adrian," Anna called as she ran outside in her bedroom slippers. She lost no time in gathering the things he requested. "Is it our field?"

"I'm afraid so, Anna," he said as he began to toss the buckets and other objects into the back of the truck.

"I'm coming with you," she said determinedly.

"No! All the smoke and exertion would not be good for you or the baby. And I don't have time to argue," he added firmly as rebellion rose in her desperate eyes. "Just stay here … and pray!"

"Are you ready?" he asked the silent girl whose heart had sunk with dread and apprehension at his words.

She nodded, jumped in the truck, and barely had closed the door before they were speeding back toward the boiling clouds of smoke.

"How did it start?" she cried, looking at his drawn, worried face.

"Don't know," he answered shortly, and feeling rebuffed, she retreated into silence until they reached the field. There her worst fears were realized. "Oh, God, no," she whispered, stunned at the sight of the crimson line of fire racing madly out of control and mowing down the ripened hay and her father's hopes at the same time.

By the time she could move, Adrian was tossing the things he had brought to the twins whose despairing young eyes showed their understanding of the tragedy.

"Where's Dad?" Stormy shouted above the wind that whipped the fire into a blazing inferno.

"He's gone to get my tractor and plow to make a fire break and to call the volunteer fire department," Adrian shouted in her ear. "Here! Take these!" he thrust into her hands a bucket and a pair of ragged blue jeans, and she took off in a run after the twins who headed as fast as they could go to the pond at the edge of the field.

Tears of frustration and anger mingled with tears from the heat and smoke, as she ran back and began to beat at the fire with all her might.

"Why, God? Why did this have to happen! You know how badly we needed the extra money from this crop! Now it looks as if we will not even have enough for our own cows!"

She drew in a deep breath and choked on the thick air suffocating her. She heaved helplessly for a moment, then began to beat the fire again, continuing with her bitter accusations. "God, You know Dad can't afford to buy

244

any hay! You know we're in danger of losing the farm right now! How could You let this happen when we were depending on You to help us?"

She cried and beat, and cried and beat, trying to master the flames that mocked her efforts. Her hands and face were soon black with soot and her lungs ached unbearably from breathing the searing, stiffling air. The soles of her shoes burned her feet as she moved across the heated, smoking ground, and her tears made little sizzling sounds as they continued to rain down her face and fall on the ground.

Rushing back to the pond on rubbery legs to refill her bucket, she squinted blurry eyes and saw several more trucks parked at the edge of the field. More help! They were all around her now, shouting encouragement as they ran past. People whose faces she could not distinguish but whose voices gave her hope. The fire became uncontrollable as it swept gleefully out of the field containing the pond, leaving it a smoking ruin. But the firefighters were hardy and determined, and by late afternoon, they had forcefully subdued it.

Stormy listened numbly to their condolences and their offers of help which her father accepted with heartfelt thanks and appreciation. But she knew many of the neighbors walked away wondering in their hearts if this would be yet another of their friends who would collapse while fighting to keep his farm. The thought broke her heart.

"I'll take your plow back, Adrian ... and ... thanks." The words so simply spoken touched the heart of the big man, and he laid a hand on his friend's shoulder.

"Think nothing of it, Charles. You'd have done the same for me."

Charles turned away to hide his tears and walked slowly over to the tractor. The twins took the other tractor on home, knowing their father would be cutting no more hay that day. Blindly, Stormy started walking back toward the house, but she had taken no more than three steps when she was swept up in strong arms.

"No, little girl," the big man said gently, "I'm taking you home."

Her head sagged wearily against his shoulder without protest. A part of her mind wondered at the ease with which he carried her across the rough field, and her heart sought and found comfort in the arms that held her close. The strength of the hard body she leaned weakly against was a refuge to her unutterably weary body.

He lifted her easily into the truck, checked to make sure he had collected everything he had brought with him and then climbed in beside her. With one hand on the wheel to guide the truck over the uneven ground, he reached over with the other one and took her grimy one.

"It'll be all right, little girl," his voice was hoarse. "God has not forsaken your father, and He never will. You must believe that! Don't blame Him. He didn't do this. Just look to Him for strength and comfort. He loves you very much."

She did not answer, and he said nothing more. When he stopped the truck, she opened the door and climbed out. She started toward the door of the house, but he stopped her.

"Stormy Leigh."

She looked up at him dully. The whites of his eyes were red, and he looked heartbreakingly weary.

"Remember what I said."

Mutely, she nodded, afraid to speak for fear the tears would start and never stop, and walked away.

The family was unusually quiet that evening. But the father's voice rang out strong and true as he gave thanks to God that all had not been lost in the fire, and thanks for the good neighbors who had volunteered their time and help, and thanks that no one had been hurt by a force that could have destroyed more than just a crop.

But Stormy's newly regained faith was splintered. Her heart sought to believe in the goodness and the stability of God, but her mind thrashed and re-thrashed the problems that seemed insurmountable. She could see the peace on her parents' faces as they arose from their knees where they had poured out their hearts to God, but she could not as easily lay down her own load.

The next morning, she ached beyond measure. Her eyes were gritty and painfully swollen, and she felt miserable. She dragged herself out of bed, with Amy's annoyingly cheerful help, and dressed.

"Amy, how in the world can you be so happy when Daddy's lost almost all of his hay!" she finally snapped, and the child looked at her with hurt, surprised eyes.

"But Daddy said Jesus would take care of everything, and we shouldn't have to worry about it."

She looked at Stormy anxiously. "Are you worrying, Stormy? Do you want me to help you worry?"

Shame rushed over Stormy, and she shook her head, dropping to her knees in front of the child. "No, Amy. Daddy's right, and I'm just being an ugly old grouch this morning. Please forgive me."

"Okay," a wet, little kiss landed on her cheek. "Mama's making blueberry pancakes this morning. Boy, am I glad you're home!" A mischievous smile rounded her saucy little cheeks, and she swung her long pony tails, "Now we get to have all kinds of goodies."

A special breakfast perked up Stormy's spirits, and she went outside with her father and the twins to assess the damage. The day was cloudless and lovely, a sharp contrast to the charred fields that lay at their feet. But Charles Winters smiled and turned to his children.

"Looks like a good day to cut hay. Adrian called me this morning and offered to help and bring two of his tractors with mowers. If we use his two and our two, we'll have the hay drying in the sun by noon ...."

When noon came, and they returned to the house, Stormy was famished. The fresh air and scent of freshly mown hay had ripened her appetite and greatly improved her frame of mind. She was still worried about the farm, but she had spent the better part of the morning apologizing to God while operating one of the tractors and mowers for having accused Him of not caring about them.

The fact that the fire had started in the field next to Adrian's caused an old, ugly suspicion to rise in her mind, but she tried her best to hold it at bay. Surely Adrian would not have intentionally started a fire, then helped to fight it? It must have been someone carelessly throwing a cigarette out of a passing car. Yet she knew without a doubt that he would snap up the farm in a jiffy, if her father ever lost it.

Oh, how she wished she were not so subject to imaginings and bad moods! If only she could have the sweet, trusting nature of her sister. Barbara had no trouble trusting God or Adrian. She took them at face value and believed in them. She would only shake her head at her sister's fears.

19
Love Your Neighbor

The days were crammed full of work. After the hay dried, they raked and baled it, and hauled it to the barn. It would not be enough to see them through the winter, but they were grateful for what they had and refused to complain about what might have been. They celebrated the end of the hay season with a homemade ice cream party and invited all the neighbors who had helped them on the day of the fire.

The women brought their favorite recipes, and the children took turns cranking the older ice cream freezers while the newer ones spun merrily on the ends of their electric cords. The men brought musical instruments and played for hours to everyone's delight. There were guitars and banjos, harmonicas and fiddles, and each musician knew how to make his instrument talk!

Stormy was astonished to see Adrian pick up a long, silver Shepherd's flute. He fingered it delicately and placed it softly against his lips to draw from it such sweet, haunting music that everyone stopped to watch and listen. The way his body swayed slightly in time to the music fascinated her. Black curls clinging to his forehead, his strong, tanned neck shone softly in the moonlight, while the artificial light caught the silvery brightness of his flute. He looked strong and masterful in faded blue jeans and a blue chambray shirt open at the neck. His sleeves were rolled up, and the thick, black hair on his forearms suggested a mature masculinity, as did the thatch of dark, curly hair appearing above the last snap on his shirt.

Her eyes widened in alarm, as he lifted his eyes to her face. She blushed and turned away hurriedly. Why on earth was she allowing herself to notice this man! Had she not known enough hurt at the hands of a man to last her a lifetime? Why should she think this one would prove any different from Cliff? Notwithstanding her reasoning, her eyes drifted time and again to the trustworthy clearness of his eyes and the gentleness of his smile. She recalled how safe his arms had felt on the day of the fire, how she had buried her tired, dirty face against the damp, smoky fabric of his shirt, and how she had realized he cared about her hurt and grief.

When everyone had settled down around the long, back porch with heaping bowls of fast-melting ice cream, many deep sighs of enjoyment were heard as the end of a long, hot working day was celebrated.

John Riley, their nearest neighbor to the south, suddenly spoke up, "Say! Did you hear about Harvey Jackson?"

At their mystified looks, he continued, "He had just finished cutting his hay when the finance company showed up and repossessed his tractor."

There were exclamations of dismay and concern.

"Yep. He told them if they would just let him keep it until he got his hay done up, he'd get enough money from selling it to make his payment. But they wouldn't listen. Said he's too far behind now. And he had a really good stand of grass, thick and heavy. He could have showed a real profit this year." He shook his head sadly and clucked his tongue, "It's a real shame."

Stormy's heart swelled in pity for the poor man, and she spoke up impulsively, "Couldn't we do something to help him?"

Her words rang out desperately, and all eyes focused on her. Helplessly, she turned to her father, "Daddy! Can't we do something?"

"Good idea, Stormy Leigh," he said quietly and rose to his feet. "Men, Harvey Jackson isn't a Christian nor a churchgoer — but we are. And I think it's time we began to unite together as they did in the old days. We have always helped one another from time to time, but things are changing fast now, and if we don't all stand together, we may all fall together!"

His bold statements were met with vigorous nods, as the spirit of oneness began to fire them with enthusiasm. "He's right!" began to echo over the porch until he motioned them to silence.

"It's forecast to rain Thursday," he looked up at the sky, "and I know some of you still have your own hay to put up. But if the rest of us could each contribute some machinery and manpower, Harvey Jackson just might survive and still be around when one of us needs help."

The idea caught like wildfire, and before the evening ended, plans had been made to meet at the Winter's farm early the next morning with all available men and equipment. The women offered to prepare food and take it to the Jackson farm at noon. And there was a live current of excitement that coursed through the group as if they had just unleashed a tremendous power that could possibly sustain them all.

Stormy, dressed in old blue jeans and a brown plaid shirt, was ready when Amy stormed her room the next morning. Last night had been the first since she came home that she had not cried over her lost dreams with Cliff. Her last thought of the night and her first thought of the morning instead had been the love in her father's eyes as he hugged her good night and whispered in her ear, "I'm so proud of you, little girl, so proud!"

A small convoy left the Winters' home that lovely morning, a convoy of various sized tractors, hay rakes, and balers. Stormy drove their old farm truck at the end of the convoy. She and Keith would be hauling the bales of hay that tumbled from the baler. Their father was somewhere up ahead in his big tractor, and Kyle was bumping along behind him on the little gray tractor.

Apparently the word had spread, for they picked up at least four more tractors and two more trucks during the ten-mile trip to the Jackson farm. Stormy was not surprised to see Adrian astraddle a big, green, late-model tractor, his big smile gleaming as he greeted his neighbors. He stopped to speak to Keith and laid a friendly hand on his shoulder. But his only notice of Stormy was a brief nod that left her childishly aggravated. Though still early, the day was sultry, and heavy, dark clouds rumbled ominously in the distance, threatening to lose patience at any moment and sweep the valley with a deluge of fierce rain.

As long as she lived, Stormy would never forget the look on Harvey Jackson's face as they rumbled up his drive. He and his big, raw-boned wife came running out of the house, shock and disbelief draining their tired, strained faces of any color. Mrs. Jackson began to weep unrestrainedly, and her husband had the look of a pardoned man. Hope lit the fire in his dulled eyes, but he could barely talk, so choked up was he by overwhelming emotions. His stooped shoulders straightened, his steps grew lighter, as he ran before them to throw open the gates.

There was not a worker whose heart did not rejoice in a chance to bring hope and help, and a strong feeling of kinship was born that day between them and the Jacksons. Everyone worked hard all morning. At noon, they jumped aboard the trucks and rode back to the house for a quick lunch.

The women had the food ready and waiting. There were hams, cold chicken, potato salads, cheeses, home-made breads, and all sorts of desserts. Cold lemonade and punch were drunk by the gallons. Within an hour, however, they were in the fields again.

Tired, dirty faces smiled happily as the convoy drove away into the dusk. One man's sincere thanks and inability to praise them enough made a sweet glow in their hearts. It was a day that would not soon be forgotten.

News of what they had done spread quickly. By Sunday morning, the entire community was talking about it. It was enough for those who had helped Harvey Jackson to see him in church with his family, once again in possession of his tractor.

At the end of the service, he stood in faded blue overalls and, in slow halting words, tried to express his gratitude. He felt that if these people who professed to be Christians were so governed by their love for God as to take time away from their busy lives to help a man they scarcely knew, then what they had was real. He had been so greatly impressed he had wanted to see what made people do what they had done without hope of pay. In their faces, he had seen Christ, and in their lives, the goodness of God. He and his family wanted to be a part of them. He humbly offered his services to anyone needing help and awkwardly resumed his seat.

The congregation exploded with applause. It was decided that anyone needing help should contact Charles Winters, and he would see to it that the need was met. People opened their eyes to the joy of giving and helping and each wanted to contribute.

After another week went by, Stormy began to grow restless. Barbara was working every day, and the twins had hired out to other farmers for the remainder of the hay season. Their satisfaction of being able to add something to the nest egg shone in their faces. Anna was feeling much better, and Charles seemed able to cope with the chores. Stormy began to feel useless. She was constantly assured that she was needed, but she missed her job and her paycheck.

"Mother," she said one morning, as they washed the breakfast dishes, "I think I'll see if I can find a part-time job."

"Oh?" her mother's thickening figure turned, "do you have some place in mind?"

"No," the girl confessed, absent-mindedly washing a glass a second time. "I guess I need to go see what's available." She rinsed the glass and laid it in the dish drainer. "I thought I'd run into town this morning and look around. I could pick up some things for you if you want to make a list."

"All right," her mother agreed, drying the glass and placing it in the cabinet. She watched her daughter leave the room, a small pucker forming between her finely shaped brows. She longed for Stormy to confide in her. She went to a drawer, took out a pad and pencil, and began to make a list. Then, as if inspired, she snapped her fingers. Her eyes twinkled with mischief, and she chuckled. But she said nothing to the girl who returned with her purse in hand. Handing her the list, she complimented her on her pretty, yellow dress and wished her well. After watching Stormy drive out the lane, she placed a quick call, then returned to her work with a lighter heart and a secret smile.

Stormy felt a little nervous and unsure of herself. She had not had to go job hunting in two years. It felt strange. On impulse, she stopped in at the new dress shop. A tall, elegantly dressed woman greeted her as she pushed open the door and stepped in.

"Hello. May I help you?" She spoke in a pleasant, cultured voice.

"I just wanted to look around." Stormy slipped the strap of her purse up onto her shoulder. The woman smiled in a friendly fashion and turned back to the counter.

"I'd also like to know if you might have a position open for a sales clerk, bookkeeper, or anything else," Stormy added hastily.

"No, I'm sorry, I don't. Are you looking for a job?"

"Yes, but I'd still like to look around," Stormy looked with interest at the racks of clothing.

The woman came over and introduced herself as Susan Miller, then proceeded to talk about fashions and business in a small town. Stormy enjoyed talking to her and mentioned that her sister had a natural flair for designing clothes.

"Oh, really?" Susan eyed her thoughtfully. "You surely can make good money being a designer."

"So I've heard," Stormy held a wintergreen blouse next to herself and viewed it in the long mirror, "but she wants to go to college and then come back and teach school."

Susan Miller tapped a pen against her lips and said, "If for some reason her plans change, have her come and see me. I think I know someone who might be interested in her talents."

"All right," Stormy peeked at the price tag. It was just barely in her price range.

"I'll take it," she said happily. Accepting the other woman's invitation to have coffee some time, she went back to her car and put her package inside. Where next?

Stormy Leigh

She tried the post office, bank, and hardware stores, but with no success. She checked with insurance companies, real estate offices, and even the two nicer restaurants, but without results. Tired and footsore, she decided to call it a day.

Just as they finished supper, Adrian drove up. He spent a few minutes with Charles, then wandered into the kitchen. Stormy and Barbara were clearing away the supper dishes.

"Hi, Adrian!" Barbara flashed him a lovely smile and scooped a stack of dishes off the table in one deft movement. "What are you up to?"

He drew out a chair and sat down, "I need some help from your sister."

"Me?" Stormy fluttered nervously, then felt stupid. Who else could he have meant?

"Yes, you, Miss Computer Lady," white teeth sparkled in his face.

Stormy stumbled on her way to the cabinet and wished frantically that her heart would quit acting so crazy.

"Here," he patted the seat of the chair next to him, "come sit down for a minute."

"Oh, I'd better finish cleaning up," she said hastily.

"Oh, that's okay, Stormy," Barbara interfered innocently, "I'll finish up. You all go on out where it's cooler." Stormy sent her a furious look, but she was too busy wiping the table to notice.

"Thanks, Barbara." Adrian rose lithely to his feet and looked expectantly at Stormy, his black brows raised in question and gave her an amused smile that set her on edge.

256

Flushing, she hurried past him and marched out the front door. She sat down on the porch swing and dug her feet into the rug beneath her like a nervous child. She expected him to sit in one of the other chairs scattered about the long porch, but he sat down beside her. The old porch swing creaked under his weight.

Facing her, he shifted his long frame until he could lay his arm comfortably along the back of it. Stormy angrily scolded herself for the thrill that tickled her spine and made her feel like a schoolgirl on her first date. She swallowed hard and felt the fire in her cheeks.

"Stormy Leigh, I'm at the place where I need that bigger computer you advised me to buy," he stated bluntly. She watched him warily out of the corner of her eye wondering what he was leading up to. "I also need someone to program it and reload all the data stored in the other one. I'm getting behind in my records, because the computer I have can't handle the load — as you know from our other talk."

She faced him then, looking suspiciously for telltale signs that her mother might have had a hand in this, but his eyes remained steady and unflinching as he continued, "I'm looking for someone to take on this job, and you were the best one I could think of. Are you interested?" He asked the question casually, as if it mattered not at all to him whether she was or not.

"Well, I suppose I could," she answered as nonchalantly as she could, trying to ignore the wild fluttering of her heart. "But I'd only be able to work part time. I ought to be home some of the time in case Mother and Dad need me." She fully expected, and half hoped, he would turn down her unenthusiastic response, "I would imagine you'd need someone full time."

"No," he drawled slowly, studying her red face intently. "I think part time would work out just fine. How much per hour would you work for?"

"I — I don't know," one hand uneasily shoved back a stray curl.

"Well, I'm sure there'll not be a problem about that aspect. We'll work something out after you've had time to think about it." He stood up as though suddenly bored, "See you about six in the morning?"

"Six in the morning?" she echoed feebly.

He frowned, "I thought maybe you could work from six until ten or twelve each day. Is that all right?"

"Oh, sure," she waved a hand weakly. "That'll be fine." She wanted to say that it sounded great, but the words stuck in her throat. With a short nod, he strode down the steps to his truck.

The next morning, she tried on three different outfits before finally settling on a skirt and striped blouse. The indecision made her late for breakfast. She gulped down her milk and toast so fast she almost choked. Dashing around to gather up things she thought might be needed only increased her nervousness. Finally, she raced to her car and drove away in a cloud of dust.

Anna Winters had patiently helped as much as she could and sighed with relief when Stormy disappeared out the end of the lane. Her little hint to Adrian had been seized upon with enthusiasm. He had responded with as much speed as she could have wished. Now only time would tell whether she had done the right thing or not.

Stormy parked on the paved drive in front of the house and ran lightly up the wide steps. The brisk breeze tossed her heavy hair, lifting the mass of curls that had lengthened considerably during the time she had been home. She had no idea of her appeal to the man opening the door, no idea of the beauty of her eyes, the lovely color highlighting her fair skin, or the fascinating curve of her lips. The wind whipped her clothes around her feminine figure and blew red-gold curls away from her high forehead.

"Hello, Stormy Leigh," he said huskily, wanting to draw her into his arms, "how are you this morning?" Shuttering his passionate gaze, he stepped back politely for her to enter.

"Fine," she wet her lips with the tip of her tongue, unintentionally drawing his attention to them. "It's really windy out there!" She took another step, anxious to move away from his piercing eyes and looked about with pleasure at the familiar setting she loved so much. The heavy, expensive furniture looked as if it had always been there, and she longed to just go around and touch everything as she had when she was a child.

Adrian watched her curiously, noting her fresh look and changing expressions with interest.

Suddenly, she whirled around, "Well, when do we start?" she said nervously, clasping her hands together.

"Right now, if you're ready."

She nodded her bright head, reminding him much of Amy.

"Have you had breakfast?" he asked over his shoulder as he led the way to the office.

"Yes."

"Good."

He drew out a chair and motioned for her to sit down. "Welcome to Tabby," he said.

"Tabby?"

"The first serious work she ever did for me was make a list of tabulations. Hence — Tabby."

"Oh, I see."

"And this one," he uncovered a larger setup beside Tabby, "Has no name as yet. Perhaps you would like to do the honors."

"Well," she laughed uncertainly, "how about Einstein, since he's going to be the brains of this operation."

"Einstein it is," he patted it gently. "Hope he lives up to his name."

He pulled up a chair and sat down beside her, his face serious as he began to speak. "As you know, computer technology has become indispensible in business in this country, even in farming. Many older farmers, however, are reluctant to accept the changes necessary to survive. Some of them really cannot learn the new technology or adapt. Now I'm not talking about your father," he held up a hand of caution at her expression.

"He happens to be one of many who would love to be able to use the newest advances in technology, but he has neither the cash flow or available credit to do so. For those who can stay in step with each new dimension of progress, technology can bring increasing prosperity. But time and our economic system do not allow anyone to rest or sit back and be content with past accomplishments. It seems as if each morning brings something new nowadays, and it is a constant battle to stay in the forefront."

He smiled at her intent face, "I said all of that to say this. Your father has longed for a computer set-up ever since I got Tabby. He realizes the amount of work it can save him, and also how a computer can help him produce more from what he has. So, as soon as everything is switched to Einstein and running smoothly, Tabby will become his."

"You don't mean you would just give it to him!" Stormy gasped incredulously.

"Yes."

"But why? These things cost a lot of money."

"Because he is my friend, Stormy Leigh. And I love him like a father. I know he can't afford to buy a system like this, and I feel I owe him for helping me get acquainted and accepted in the community when I first came here."

She said nothing, and he scooted his chair back. "You know your job better than I do," he said calmly, looking down on the bent red head, "So I'll show you Tabby's software, answer whatever questions you have, and then let you get to work. After you have exchanged the data, we'll discuss the new enhancements I would like to have. All right?"

"All right," she became very businesslike, enjoying the challenge.

"I'm going out to do some chores, so I'll check back with you in a couple of hours."

"Okay," the answer sounded absent-minded, and Adrian grinned. She never knew when he left the room. But when he came back, she hit him with a dozen questions.

"Whoa! Wait a minute!" he laughed, throwing a hand up in protest. "It's time for a break, and I could use a snack. Nora is bringing in some rolls and juice, so let's just relax for a few minutes. I can spend the next hour with you, so we'll have plenty of time to answer all of these questions you're bursting with."

Suddenly ill at ease, Stormy fell silent. As long as they were involved with something in which she was competent, she felt confident. But the moment they moved to a more personal footing, she floundered about like a fish out of water. She had never experienced that feeling with Cliff or any other man but Adrian for that matter, and she wondered wretchedly what made her tighten up like a coiled spring.

As if sensing her new reserve, he opened the side door and invited her outside onto a small, shaded patio. The wind had died down considerably, but dark clouds still danced like little, black lambs across the skies.

"Sure wish it would rain," he said, staring off into the distance, as she perched uneasily on the edge of a stuffed lounge chair. He turned before she ever heard a sound and greeted the woman who stepped through the door with a loaded tray in her hands.

"Thank you, Nora. That looks great!" he smiled warmly at the tall, thin woman who placed the tray carefully on the table and disappeared again with only the briefest of shy smiles.

"She's rather timid," he explained, pouring icy orange juice into two tall glasses. "But she's the best housekeeper and cook I've ever had." His eyes drifted back to the clouds, and he switched the subject before Stormy had a chance to ask him about his past. Had he always been rich? And where had he gotten all of his wealth? She wanted to credit him with getting it some crooked way, but his reputation said otherwise. So what if he had come by it honestly! That didn't mean he would not stoop to grab more ... like her father's little farm!

As if in answer to her angry indictment, he spoke, "If it doesn't rain soon, a lot of the farmers won't make it. A drought will break their backs — and their pocketbooks."

Stormy knew who he was talking about and knew he was right. She gritted her teeth and glared up at the brassy heavens.

But Adrian searched the same heavens with pleading in his eyes.

"We must pray harder," he said in a low, fervent voice. "God help us. We must pray harder!"

20
Days of Trouble

Stormy tremendously enjoyed her job. It satisfied her delight in challenges and yet gave her time to do other things. After the first week, she was left on her own. Adrian was seldom around. The pay was excellent, more equivalent to a full-time job than part-time in her estimation. Things also had been steadily improving for her family — until one week in July when two blows were suffered without warning.

Stormy came home from work about 10 a.m. one day and helped her mother pick her fourth bushel of green beans. After a quick lunch, they made themselves comfortable around the table where they could feel the stirring of air from the old-fashioned ceiling fan and began to work. Stormy's strong, nimble fingers snapped beans quickly while her mind wandered.

"What's on your mind, dear?" her mother asked, her own fingers making short work of the long beans in her pan. A soft sigh escaped the lips of the girl.

"Oh, I was just thinking about Cliff."

"Would you like to talk about it?" she offered without undue pressure.

"I wonder if I'll always be a failure with men," her voice held sadness and a touch of self-pity.

"Why would you feel that way?"

"I don't know. I guess because Cliff chose Denise instead of me ... and he's probably the only man who'll ever fall in love with me!"

She began to feel ashamed as she heard the self-pity become more pronounced. "I'm no beauty!" she blurted out self-defensively, breaking a bean with a vicious snap.

"You're wrong, you know," her mother paused and looked at her steadily. "You are a very lovely girl, and you have a special smile that people watch for — after they first see it," she added dryly.

"I guess I haven't been too cheerful lately, have I? I've never been good at hiding my feelings."

"Are you still unhappy?"

"Ummm, sort of. I'm happy to be home and wouldn't mind living here the rest of my life if I could, although for years I've thought a career was the only way I could be happy. But I still feel mixed up and confused," she looked helplessly at her mother for understanding.

Sympathetic eyes met hers, "Why don't you start at the beginning and tell me everything," she invited. "Maybe bringing your thoughts and feelings into the open will help."

Needing no further urging, Stormy started her tale. Beginning with meeting Cliff and ending with his accusation that she had not met his needs. She stumbled, red-faced, over nearly giving in to his seduction, but gained confidence as she related how her very soul reacted in anguish at the thought of giving up her virginity without the commitment of marriage.

Her mother listened carefully and said little.

"Mother, I think God had a part in helping me not to fall," Stormy's voice was sure, but her manner was shy as she glanced at her mother.

"I know He did!" her mother's voice rang with lilting conviction. "We had been praying for you every night, asking that God would protect you and give you wisdom. And He did."

Stormy went to the refrigerator and poured a glass of milk for her mother and one for herself. Taking her seat again at the table, she picked up her train of thought.

"Mother, how did you and Daddy learn to trust the Lord. I mean all the time. No matter what happened. How do you keep from worrying and being afraid?" The hunger in her eyes and the yearning earnestness in her voice was so touching her mother laid the beans aside.

"I know you are facing one of the greatest crises of your lives," Stormy continued, "with several couples in the community already filing for divorce because of the economic stress. I heard the other day that Mr. Balks' death was ruled suicide. But you and Daddy are closer now than I can ever remember you being.

"And although you are pregnant and of an age when having a baby is not easy, you are basically in perfect health, while some people are losing their health as well as their families and farms. I don't understand how you do it! You do most of the bookkeeping as well, so I know that you — more so than the rest of us — know the financial shape we're in. Yet you remain so calm and seemingly at peace!"

She shook her head in wonder, her eyes shining in admiration, "You keep yourself looking lovely. You're always building us up. You always have a smile and an encouraging word for Daddy. At times, I really don't know how you stand up so well under all of it. Especially when, most of the time, there is no extra money and not much hope of getting any."

Anna smiled and quoted, "'God is our refuge and strength, and a very present help in trouble' (Ps. 46:1), and 'Perfect love casteth out fear' (1 John 4:8). I think those verses should answer all your questions, my dear. I have depended on those promises all of my life to see me through things that looked impossible."

She looked at Stormy thoughtfully, "Remember when you were a child? Did you ever worry or fret that your father and I could not — or would not — take care of you? Did you ever feel you had to make it on your own because you weren't sure you could depend on us?"

"No! Of course not!" Stormy exclaimed. "I always knew I'd be taken care of. I didn't feel the least bit anxious about that. It didn't even enter my mind to worry."

"Why not?" her mother probed softly. "Why did you feel that way?"

"Well," Stormy wrinkled her forehead in concentration, "I loved you and knew you loved me even more, and I ...," The light of understanding began to dawn in her eyes. "I trusted you," she ended triumphantly.

"Do you recall what Jesus said about your Heavenly Father?" She began to quote Matthew 6:25-33:

"'Take no thought for your life, what ye shall eat, or what ye shall drink; nor yet for your body, what ye shall put on. Is not the life more than meat, and the body than raiment? Behold the fowls of the air; for they sow not, neither do they reap, nor gather into barns; yet your heavenly Father feedeth them. Are ye not much better than they? Which of you by taking thought can add one cubit unto his stature?

"'And why take ye thought for raiment? Consider the lilies of the field, how they grow; they toil not, neither do they spin: And yet I say unto you, That even Solomon in all his glory was not arrayed like one of these. Wherefore, if God so clothe the grass of the field, which to day is, and to morrow is cast into the oven, shall he not much more clothe you, Oh ye of little faith? Therefore take no thought, saying, What shall we eat? or, What shall we drink? or, Wherewithal shall we be clothed? ... For your heavenly Father knoweth that ye have need of all these things.

"'But seek ye first the kingdom of God, and his righteousness; and *all* these things shall be added unto you.'

"Oh, Stormy Leigh," her mother sighed fondly, "if people would only turn their eyes to God. He wants to supply their every need. Instead, they run around trying to work things out on their own. Then when they fail in their expectations, they blame it on God! People can be very odd in their ideas. They run from the Source of help and turn to the deceiver for hope. He leads them down a merry path, and then while the world comes crashing down around them, he stands back and laughs!"

She paused for breath, then smiled and continued, "God is the originator of love and trust, and we, His children, should love and trust Him above all others. We have Him with us always — in *and* around us. We have no need to fear. It seems natural to turn to Him for help. After all, He *is* our Father.

"However," she cautioned wisely, "He also knows what is best for us. We try to be good parents, and in so doing, we constantly make choices about what's best for our children. We don't always give them everything they want, even though it may almost break our hearts to withhold from them their heart's desire. But we do what is for their best good. We know some things they want will bring them harm or cause them to grow up into adults who are not responsible and God-fearing."

She smiled again, not wanting to sound as if she was preaching at her daughter, then said, "Certainly our Father, in whom is all wisdom, knowledge, and understanding, knows what is best for us. And we can rest assured that He will withhold no good thing from those who walk uprightly before Him, according to Psalm 84:11. Our job is to trust Him."

"But, Mother, how can I get that trust?" was the next question.

"Can you imagine the pain and hurt your father and I would feel if we thought our children felt they could not depend on us? Your Heavenly Father has feelings, too, dear. And our unbelief and fearful ways bring Him sorrow and sadness."

"Oh, I wouldn't want to hurt God!" Stormy's eyes grew round and concerned. "I love Him!"

"One more thing," her mother picked up the beans and again began to break them, "lasting love and trust are not obtained overnight in a few, brief sessions. They are made to grow and develop into their fullness over a period of time. The longer you're around someone, and the more you associate and communicate with them, the easier it is to trust and believe in them.

"So many people ignore God until they really need Him. It's no wonder they feel He is so far away, when they've been out of touch for so long. God desires continuous contact with His children. He loves for them to talk to Him, and He longs to bless them. Would you not feel sad and lonely if your children refused to talk to you? Wouldn't you feel something was wrong when they were too wrapped up in themselves and what they're doing to give you the time of day, much less sit down and talk with you?"

"Mother," Stormy looked at her mother in awe, "you should be a teacher! You make it all sound so simple."

"It is, dear." The sound of a truck outside and laughter announced the twins' arrival. "You'll find that everything about your relationship with God can be simple and child-like — not 'childish', but child-like. Childish faith is a narrow, selfish belief that disappears with time and trouble and is really not faith. But a child-like faith will grow and carry you through anything you have to face."

They rose to greet the twins, and Stormy placed a quick kiss on her mother's cheek. "Thanks, Mother," she said huskily. "I've really been needing this, and I promise I won't forget what you said."

After supper that night, Amy insisted the twins keep their promise to take her fishing. They willingly agreed. Grabbing their rods and fishing tackle, they headed for the creek with her hot on their heels. Stormy and Barbara sat on the porch swing and talked about their jobs and about Barbara's college plans. She hoped to hear from her scholarship application any day.

Their parents were in the small room adjoining their bedroom. In a previous more affluent generation it had been a dressing room, but it had been used for a nursery and/or sewing room during their time. Now they were discussing what needed to be done to turn it back into a pretty, fresh nursery again.

As the evening shadows lengthened, and the girls were laughing at Ol' Tom's playful antics, they suddenly began to hear a shrill sound.

"What was that?" Stormy asked, frowning into the darkness.

Barbara shrugged her shoulders and scanned the darkening fields. "I don't know," she said, "but Amy and the boys should be back anytime. It will soon be too dark to see."

The high-pitched sound came again faintly, and Barbara opened the back door to call, "Daddy! Would you come out here for a minute?"

"Sure, Honey," He stepped outside asking, "What is it?"

"I don't know. But listen!"

They all listened, and the sound came again, clearer and at last horrifyingly familiar.

"That's Amy!" the father exclaimed as his wife appeared at his side.

"Stay here, Anna!" he warned sternly. "It's getting too dark for you to go running out there. You might trip and fall."

Then he took off running toward the line of trees at the edge of the meadow with the girls pounding along at his side.

"Daaaddy! Daaaddy!" the child continued to scream. "Daaaddy! Oh, Daaaddy!" As she burst through the tangle of trees, they saw her stumble and fall. Stormy's heart gave a painful wrench, and she clutched her aching side. Amy staggered drunkenly to her feet before they could reach her. They could hear her crying loudly, as she ran as fast as her little legs would carry her. "Daaaddy! Daaaddy!"

Sobbing brokenly, exhausted and trembling, she fell into her father's arms. He clutched her tightly, holding her head firmly against himself for a few seconds before easing her back to the ground.

"Amy, what is it?" he questioned urgently. "What's wrong?"

"Oh, Daddy! Kyle!" she sobbed hysterically, her voice rising to a scream, as she pointed a chubby, shaking finger back toward the creek. "Kyle! Kyle!" she cried frantically even as she clung to him and heaved with racking sobs. It was plain that she was in shock, and knowing she was not able right then to tell him anything more, Charles turned to his daughters, his face white and tense.

"Take her back to the house, Barbara," he ordered, gently releasing himself from the rigid fingers that clutched at his shirt. "Hurry!" He left his tiny daughter and began to run toward the creek. There was no way Stormy could keep up with him, for he was running with the speed of a deer. The unknown danger to his son triggered a great flood of adrenal in his veins. She did not dare look back for fear of losing her footing, but kept her eyes balanced between her father and the rough, uneven footing barely visible in the twilight.

He pulled up short on the bank of the dark swirling waters of the creek, cupped his hands to his mouth, and called, "Keith! Kyle! Where are you?" He called again and again in growing frustration.

"Stormy Leigh," he swung around to her, "where have the boys been fishing this summer? Upstream or down?"

"Down below the swimming hole?" she guessed, praying that she was right.

He was off again, moving sure-footedly among the rocks and trees. A few minutes later, he paused to call again and was rewarded by a faint call from across the small rapids they were approaching. Very shortly, they stumbled across the boys near a small, quiet pool of water. It was almost too dark by then to see the scared faces of the two boys watching anxiously for them, and Stormy wished desperately for a flashlight!

"Dad!" Keith ran to meet them. "Kyle stepped on a copperhead, and it bit him! And we were just fixing to come home, too!" His young voice broke in a sob, as his father hurried past him to Kyle huddled up on the ground.

Stormy winced sharply as she twisted her ankle on an unseen rock, but she manfully bit her lip and hobbled after him. Her father had knelt beside Kyle and was examining the cut and the tourniquet Keith had made.

"You'll be all right, Son," he said, picking up the heavy youngster in his arms. "We're going home."

They were met just out of the woods by Adrian, who took the boy from his exhausted father. With only a second's glance at the torn jean leg and the tourniquet, he headed for his truck.

"Charles, we'll go in my truck," he lifted the boy up into the cab. "You hold him, and I'll drive!" And they were gone in a flash with only winking tail lights to soothe the hearts of the rest of the family.

Amy had calmed down, but when she saw Keith, she ran to him and buried her face in his shoulder. He held her close, one hand stroking her hair. He looked as if he had aged, and his face was white and strained. Dried blood from his efforts at sucking the venom from his brother's leg encircled his mouth and spotted his shirt.

"Mother," his voice trembled with fear. "Will he be all right? I did all I knew to do."

"I know you did, Son," she wiped his face with a cool, wet cloth, "you did well, and I'm proud of you."

"But ... I'm scared. He ...," he stopped, his face crumpling and his young shoulders shaking as he fought to hold back the tears and the fear that had just caught up with him.

"Let's just ask Jesus to take care of him," his mother said, and they did. Even little Amy added her petition in a quivering little voice that the Lord knew well, and her simple, trusting words warmed their hurting hearts.

Charles called in about an hour and said the doctors were sure his foot would not have to be amputated as sometimes happens when too much time intervenes before anti-venom shots can be given a snakebite victim.

It was late when Charles and Adrian returned. They reported Kyle was resting as comfortably as possible, but that he was very sick and would be in the hospital for several days.

"I've got to go and stay with him tonight," Anna said determinedly, taking off her apron.

"I knew you'd feel that way," the worn face of her husband creased into a loving smile, his eyes resting tenderly on her tired face. "That's why I had Adrian bring me home."

Anna turned to the children, "Stormy, Barbara, I'm going back with your father. Can you handle things here?"

"Yes, Mother," they said in unison. Anna's eyes rested with misgivings on her youngest, who still hiccuped occasionally and watched her beloved family with scared eyes.

"Amy," her voice was soft and soothing, "I want you to mind your sisters while I'm gone. Be a good girl, and go to bed when they tell you. You're not to worry about Kyle. Jesus is watching over him, and he's going to be fine. All right?"

The pale, solemn little face nodded gravely, and Amy ran to throw her arms tightly around her mother, hiding her face against her soft, warm body. Then the parents left for the hospital, and shortly thereafter, Adrian left also.

"Do you girls need anything?" he asked, his hand on the door knob.

"No. We'll be all right," Barbara assured him. "Thanks so much for coming as soon as we called. It really helped Dad to have you with him."

"No thanks necessary," he said kindly. "Anytime you need me," his eyes shifted to Stormy's face, "just call."

Stormy acknowledged his volunteered services with a mere downward flutter of her lashes. She was grateful for his help, very much so. Yet something within her rebelled at the idea of her family growing to depend on him so much. She feared some day they would be painfully disillusioned. She swept Amy up in her arms and headed for the stairs, leaving Barbara to show Adrian out.

Kyle returned home pale and sickly within a few days. His leg was healing nicely with very little apparent scarring, for which the family wholeheartedly thanked God, and began to believe Him for the money with which to pay the hospital bills.

Anna tired easily, both from the heat and from her condition, so the majority of the work load fell to Stormy's lot, and she did it gladly. Adrian accepted Stormy's request for a few days' leave from her job and even offered to pay her for those days anyway. She refused his generosity, but thanked him for his kindness. She looked after her mother and Kyle with ease and dexterity, but Amy presented a very perplexing problem.

From the night Kyle was bitten by the snake, Amy scarcely ventured outside by herself. Before, she had been practically fearless. The very night of the accident, Stormy had been awakened in the middle of the night by the sound of a pleading little voice and the feel of a cold little body wriggling under her covers and snuggling up against her.

"Stormy, can I sleep with you?" had become a nightly sound, and Stormy always agreed. Often Amy suffered from nightmares and woke up her big sister with her screams.

Under no pretext could they talk her into going outside and playing by herself. She insisted that "something bad" was out there to get her. Trying to talk things out only made matters worse, for she usually ended up in tears or a tantrum. So she was underfoot all the time and very demanding in time and attention. Stormy worried about her constantly until her attention was diverted, and she had to add Barbara to her evergrowing list of concerns.

The long-awaited scholarship letter arrived one day, addressed to Barbara Sue Winters. The family waited impatiently for her to come home from work to share the good news. They were seated around the supper table when she finally arrived. They asked the blessing, passed the food, and began to eat as she opened the letter. The suspense was almost unbearable as they waited with bated breaths. Totally unexpected was the sight of her lovely, sweet face crumpling, hot tears scalding the letter as she shoved back her chair and fled upstairs.

The offending document that had destroyed her hopes lay stiffly beside her plate. Her father slowly reached for it. He scanned its contents and looked up sadly at the silent, distressed faces surrounding him. Folding the letter back up and placing it carefully in its envelope, he spoke heavily.

"It expresses the sincere regret of the foundation that she did not win the scholarship and gives the name of the person who did. I'm afraid it's been quite a blow to our little girl." He looked at his wife with troubled eyes, "She's been expecting to win ever since she applied."

"I know, dear," her eyes sought to reassure him, "But God knows what is best for her, and in the long run, everything will work out all right."

"Yes, Mother," he smiled, his tired countenance lighting with confidence, "You're right. And we know, according to Romans 8:31 that if God be for us, who can be against us? And He *is* for us and our children."

But Stormy was not so sure. Her fledgling faith began to waver, although she fought to hold it steady and believe as her parents believed. Why, if God loved them, did He allow bad things to happy? Surely there was nothing but good in Barbara wanting to go to college, especially when it would profit the whole community when she gained a teaching degree!

She tried to reason it all out in her mind and only succeeded in becoming exceedingly miserable — as always happens when people try to figure out spiritual things with the mind and emotions. Once again, she became guilty of complaining to God about their problems. She knew He *could* do something about it all! Why didn't He?"

The peaceful household began to disintegrate under the pressure. Kyle grew fretful and anxious to be up on his feet. Amy plagued everyone with whining demands. Barbara excommunicated herself from her family, moping and crying a lot, apparently unable to come to terms with her disappointment. Stormy worked herself into a frenzy, trying to meet all their needs while working out her own feelings of inadequacy and frustration.

Then into this thick mixture of problems walked Clifford Callahan, stirring up a thick fog of dust with his arrival, dust that swirled through windows left open to hopefully catch any breeze that might alleviate the intense heat.

Grumbling loudly at the visible appearance of a film of dust on her freshly polished furniture, Stormy strode angrily through the house. Her curls were covered with a red bandana, and she jerked at wet rubber gloves as she opened the door. She received such a shock from seeing his face at the door that she was momentarily disoriented and speechless.

"Hello, Leigh!" he greeted her warmly, carefully avoiding staring at what to him was her outlandish garb.

"I ... uh ... well, uh, hello yourself," she automatically lifted a hand to free her hair and stepped back awkwardly. "Would you like to come in?"

"Sure!" he laughed, a bit too heartily, and Stormy began to wake up and wonder what on earth he was doing on her doorstep.

Amy wandered listlessly into the room, took one look at the neatly dressed young man and ran to the kitchen, screaming at the top of her lungs, "Mama! Mama! *That* man is here again. That man who took our Stormy away. Oh, Mama, *don't* let him take her again! Please, Mama ...." Her voice grew muffled, firmly shushed by her mother, and silence hung heavily in the air between Stormy and Cliff.

"Please, sit down," Stormy motioned him to a chair, took off her apron, wadded up her gloves and bandana in it, and laid it aside. "So," she smiled brightly, "what brought you way out here?" Only her tightly clenched hands betrayed her nervousness.

"You," he said intimately, patting the cushion beside him. "Why don't you come and sit beside me, there's room." He smiled one of his most captivating smiles, but she shook her head, her thick hair swinging loosely about her shoulders.

"I'm not too sure we have anything to talk about," she said, determined not to fall under his spell. Keeping her distance seemed important.

"Sure we do," he wooed her. "I've missed you more than you will ever know. I was hoping you would say you'd missed me too. Have you, Leigh?"

His eyes beckoned like warm fire, and she was tempted to succumb to his charm simply to be held in his arms and whisked away from the turmoil that seemed to dog her every step lately. Maybe she had been too harsh on him. After all, good men did fall into temptation and rise to be true again. If God could forgive him, surely she could! She lost touch with reality in search of an easier way and fell under the spell of his controlling personality again. He was quick to sense it and press his advantage.

"Oh, Darling," he fell to his knees in front of her, impressing her with a humility she had never expected to see. "I need you! Can't we just let bygones be bygones?" He raised her hand to his lips and fervently kissed it. Her pulse began to race unsteadily. "Please come away with me. Come back to Kingston. We'll get married, and I'll prove to you how happy I can make you!"

But her spirit was quick to sense a false note, a lack of real repentance and remorse.

"No, Cliff, I can't." She firmly recaptured her runaway imagination and sternly bridled her emotions. "My family needs me, and there is no way I could leave them right now."

Immediately she had evidence that intuition was right. Petulance thinned his lips, turning them cruel, and she realized he was trying hard not to get upset but to play a role he thought she would accept.

"But, Leigh ...," he began.

"Stormy," she corrected.

"What?" he lost his train of thought and stared at her.

"I go by Stormy and always will from now on." The very words brought reassurance that she was right to stand by her family. The sound of her first name, given her in such love by her parents, made her feel good and warm inside.

"Okay, Stormy!" he echoed irritably. "Do you have to play the part of a martyr?" He once again projected his own attitudes onto her. "Honey, your family can take care of themselves," he said, taking on a sweetly beseeching tone in response to her fiery look. He spoke as if talking to a headstrong child, "Why I bet if you asked them, they would tell you so themselves. You need to look after your own interests. Besides, don't I count? I need you too." He tried to bargain skillfully, watching like a hawk each expression that flitted across her face.

"What about Denise?" she asked coolly. "Where does she come into all of this? Have you tired of her already?"

"Leigh! Uh, Stormy. That was all in the past!" His face flushed in irritation but his eyes avoided hers. "She means nothing to me."

As she looked at him, she knew he was lying, that he wanted to have success and love too in the form of two different women. Need her? Yes, he probably did — to further his career. But love her? No. His love, small and selfish though it was, was reserved for Denise, the girl who had trailed him for years, winning his heart if not his name.

"No, Cliff. I can tell by your manner that the matter is very much in the present, and the stakes are too high for me." She rose to her feet and stepped away from him, although the emotional habits of the past still caused her to yearn after him on one level of feeling. "If we were to marry, we would lose in every way that is important. I can't afford that, and whether you realize it or not, you can't either. Oh, yes," she motioned him to be silent as he began to protest, "I know you think you have all the answers, but you don't. You'd willingly marry to further your career and cheapen yours and Denise's love even more."

His face grew sullen, and his lips curled in anger as he realized he was not going to get his way. Suddenly, he was very unattractive to her. Confident now in every sense, she threw back her glorious mane of hair and faced him.

"My Christian standards, not to speak of my love for my family, come far before a loveless, one-sided marriage in which I would bind myself in love and loyalty to a man who could never conceivably return that devotion. That's not for me!"

"You'll be a spinster and grow old in this one-horse town!" he gritted his teeth in vexation, "and one day you'll wake up and see your stupidity. You'll wish you could undo the decision you made today! Or maybe you're hoping to win that McAllister guy." His face twisted in an ugly scowl. "If so, you've lost out. I just saw him leave a jewelry store with a ravishing, black-haired dame on his arm. She was drooling all over him, and he was eating it up," he added, as her face whitened.

"You know, Cliff," she said evenly, "you could seldom ever find anything good to say about anyone except yourself. You're despicable." Walking to the door and opening it, she said, "Give my regards to Denise and my sympathy. I wish her luck. She is certainly going to need it!"

Furiously, he stepped outside. "I won't be back, Leigh. You've had your last chance!"

"And that was one more chance than I needed," she laughed merrily. "Goodbye, Cliff." She closed the door and went back to work with a smile on her face, ignoring the sound of the car roaring madly down the dusty road.

Amy crept into the room and softly touched her arm, her eyes dark and fearful. "Are you going away again, Stormy? Are you?"

"No, Angel," she stooped and looked into the puckered, anxious little face, "I'm not. I won't ever leave with him again."

"Oh, I'm so glad," Amy whispered, hugging her fiercely. "I'm so glad!"

"Me, too!" her sister whispered back, returning her hug. "Me, too!"

21
The Course of True Love

The heavens gave no sign of relief to needy farmers, and the earth became scorched and cracked. The thick grass that had flourished at the start of the season lost its lushness and faded to dry, brittle stems that crumbled at a touch. Charles Winters began to dig deep into the replenished savings account to buy grain to help sustain the cows, any unborn young, and the new calves born in the Spring.

Then the mail carrier delivered two troublesome pieces of mail. The wolves of worry and hardship constantly gnawing at the family's survival and peace of mind loomed nearer.

Amy, innocent little Amy, delivered the first piece, chortling loudly that *that man* was no good! He didn't love Stormy, or he wouldn't have his picture in the paper with another woman ... a woman in a wedding dress! See?

She thrust the *Kingston Chronicle* into Stormy's hands, as she and her mother were standing around the table cutting up tomatoes for canning. Then Amy stepped back to see her sister's reaction, her little hands planted firmly on her hips in perfect imitation of the one who stood looking at the paper.

Anna took one look at Stormy's shocked, white face and quickly stepped over to view the wedding picture of Cliff and Denise. Stormy began to shake, and Anna turned sharply to Amy.

"Go outside and play, Amy!" she ordered. Immediately the child began to cry fearfully, "But Mama, something bad might get me!" she wailed, heading for the accustomed security of her older sister's arms.

But Anna caught her by the arm, and landed a swat on the little girl's backside, "I said, 'Go outside and play!'" Amy took off like a whipped puppy, her feelings hurt more than her behind.

"Here," Anna said as Stormy lifted distressed eyes that were swimming with tears, "Sit down." She drew up a chair, and Stormy dropped weakly onto it, one hand clutching the paper to her breast.

Gradually the color came back to her cheeks and lips, and she lifted her gaze to her mother. "It's just such a shock," she began, tears bubbling up and out. She laid her head down on the table and cried her heart out. Calmly her mother stroked her head until only the sound of sniffles were heard. Then she poked a couple of tissues under the folded arms and said, "Blow."

Stormy obeyed and pushed the damp hair away from her face. "I'm sorry. I didn't mean to act like a baby," she hiccuped miserably.

"Sorry for what?" The cheerful answer caused her to look up into her mother's twinkling eyes. "I'm just glad it wasn't you in that picture! He'd have only broken your heart. I have a feeling it's only your pride that's hurting right now. It will mend much easier than a broken heart. Am I right?"

Mutely the girl nodded. Then she began to laugh. "Oh, Mother! I have wasted so many tears on him it's ridiculous! Really, I pity Denise. She'll have her hands full trying to live with him. Whew! What a relief!"

She went to the sink to run cold water over her hot face. "I guess I've been expecting something like this," she admitted, "but I couldn't seem to take it when it came. And it really *is* just a matter of pride. All the time I was crying, I was picturing what people at work were saying about poor little Leigh Winters and thinking that I would never be able to face going back to work there. But Mother, I can go back if I decide to, for 'I can do all things through Christ which strengtheneth me,'" Philippians 4:13 says.

"Amen!" her mother agreed.

But another piece of mail bearing the return address of the Shelton Bank afforded a more serious qualm. A white slip of paper was the notice of the Winters' mortgage. The payment must be made on time this year because the note had been renewed last fall, and the bank would not renew it again. There was not nearly enough money in the bank to pay the interest, much less the note. A grim picture indeed was painted for the little family. They had until the middle of the fall to come up with a solution. They discussed the problem at great length, but could not find an answer.

The calves were too young to bring a good price, and beef prices were down anyway. The corn, once green and stout, had become stunted, tassling out too early as the drought continued. Their burdens mounted higher, but their faith gave them strength. They encouraged themselves in the Lord, holding fast to His promises.

Adrian came over after supper one night and lifted the spirits of at least one of the Winters' family. He brought a surprise for Amy — a pony, a woolly, brown, sweet-natured little Shetland mare that won her heart on sight.

"For me?" she squealed, jumping up and down excitedly, "a real pony for me?"

It was the beginning of the end of her nightmares. Her first glimpse of the mortality and fragility of human life had disoriented her, and a look at the reality of the truth that life goes on in spite of its frailty righted her universe. To her family, it was as if a miracle happened right before their eyes, a miracle in the shape of a friendly little beast.

Adrian assured them he would supply all the feed and the necessary riding equipment for the mare. However, she was now pregnant and would foal around the end of January. He instructed Amy in how to care for her, explaining slowly and carefully that Lady was her responsibility.

With big and glowing eyes, she vowed always to care for Lady, and he told her gravely that he believed her. From that evening on, it was rare to find Amy indoors during daylight hours. She spent every waking hour with the pony and grew taller, tanner and fit, seemingly thriving on the late summer heat that caused others to languish.

Kyle gradually regained his strength and gladly left the bed to be reunited with his lonesome brother and take part in other adventures.

But Barbara no longer stayed around the family if at all possible, going upstairs, apparently to brood alone. No amount of sympathy or understanding would reach her. She also refused to see Ray. Stormy tried several times to talk to her but was rebuked so sharply she helplessly backed away.

Coming home one Saturday, after having shared an enjoyable lunch with Susan Miller from the new boutique, she recalled an earlier conversation that she had failed to mention to Barbara. Things began to click in her mind, and she could hardly wait to talk to her sister. Holding her tongue through supper proved irksome, but she managed. After supper, with a "leave the dishes for me, Mother," she followed Barbara up to her hideout.

"Barbara, I want to talk to you," she stated firmly, allowing no denial.

"I don't want to talk!" Barbara answered shortly, her eyes red and belligerent.

"You don't have to talk," Stormy coaxed. "I'll do all the talking. Just listen, please," she added, recognizing the stubborn look her sister had recently acquired.

"All right," Barbara snapped, walking over to the bed and flinging herself face down on it.

Stormy eyed her uncertainly, wishing she could assure her that everything would work out all right, but Barbara would not listen in her present frame of mind. Growing up and facing life was extremely hard at times, and something one must do on one's own — as she had found out the hard way for herself!

She sat on the edge of the bed and looked at the prone girl, then she said firmly, "I think you're being very selfish, Barbara," which got immediate results.

"What do you mean?" Barbara asked sharply, rolling over on her side and propping herself up on a shapely elbow. Stormy knew her sister did not have a consciously selfish bone in her body, but she had her attention.

"We're a family, and we've always shared our troubles," she said. "Mother and Dad — and me too for that matter — are hurt that you don't have enough confidence in us to talk to us." She stole a peek at her sister.

"It's not that way at all!" Barbara sat up in consternation. "I just hurt so badly, I don't feel as if I can talk to anyone. But I didn't want anyone else to be affected by my problems. I just figured if they didn't know, they wouldn't worry."

"Well, it doesn't work that way, as you should know from my example with Cliff."

"I'm sorry," tears filled her eyes, and Stormy's heart went out to her.

"Do you really want to go to college that badly?" she asked curiously.

"Yes!" the answer was quick and forceful.

"Why?"

Barbara studied for a moment, "Mother and Dad always wanted us to get as much education as we could, and they were so proud of your accomplishments."

"You know they're just as proud of you! Your going to college doesn't make an ounce of difference. You know that!"

"I guess so," she admitted reluctantly.

"Now, give me the real reason," Stormy demanded.

"Ray."

"Ray? He wants you to go to college? To me, he always acted as if he dreaded you going away for four years of college."

"I want to be the best wife I can possibly be for him!" Barbara cried, her anguish sounding in each word. "And I won't be, if I don't go."

"Says who?" Stormy snorted. "That's a bunch of silly nonsense. Who told you that?"

"Me!" her voice rose a degree. "And it's true. Ray has a college degree, and I would feel inadequate if I didn't have more education when we married. I could not come close to his level of knowledge, and I'm afraid he won't want to marry me if I don't go. Now that I can't afford to go this year, I'm afraid he'll get tired of waiting and find someone else!" With that, she flung herself back down and began to cry harder.

Stormy began to laugh. She laughed and laughed and laughed until her sides ached and tears rolled merrily down her cheeks.

"And this is what all the tears and moping have been about?" She went off into another gale of laughter as Barbara stared at her, angry and perplexed.

"Yes, it is!" she said defiantly. "And I wish you would stop laughing! I don't think it's funny at all!"

"Sorry, dear," Stormy went in search of a tissue to wipe her tears away, "but it does definitely have a funny side."

"Would you care to explain," Barbara said stiffly, hostility simmering in her eyes.

"All right, I will. First, Ray is in love with you, not your education. He has been plain crazy these last few weeks that you wouldn't see him. Do you realize what torture you have put him through?"

Barbara hung her head guiltily, "I have been wallowing around in self-pity, haven't I?"

"Aye, that you have!" her sister agreed with an affectionate smile.

"Ray doesn't want to marry you because of how much you know or even because you are beautiful. He wants to marry you because he loves you! He fell in love with the real you. Just be yourself! Be the warm and generous, lovely and loving girl that we all care about. If you think Ray's affections come from his head, you shouldn't even be considering marrying him. Love is for all eternity — make sure that's the way you feel about him, too! It's better to lose your love for someone — if it's not the lasting kind — before marriage than after!"

Barbara looked at her sympathetically, "You learned that from experience, didn't you?"

"Yes, I did. But there is no need for both of us to lose in love. You and Ray have a special kind of love, something that is solid and enduring, a love like Mama's and Daddy's. I'd give my eye teeth to have someone look at me the way Daddy looks at Mama and Ray looks at you. Count yourself very blessed, little sister."

"But now," she straightened up and spoke briskly, "back to the interrogation. Do *you* really want to go to college. Is it what you want most in life?"

"No, not really. I mean, not really what I want most. I have always enjoyed going to school, but," her cheeks colored prettily, "what I want most is to marry Ray."

Stormy chuckled, "That is just what I thought, and I don't see anything standing in your way now. Do you?"

"Nooo," the word was drawn out slowly with a great deal of thought behind it. Then the sweet, blue eyes began to sparkle with new hope. "No! No, I don't. Oh, thank you, Stormy." She gave her sister a big hug.

"I guess I thought God wanted me to go to college, and I was really confused because He had not seemed to make a way. But now I see that I had it all worked out in my own mind how *I* thought it would have to be. I really didn't give Him a chance to tell me differently. Now, I'm so glad He worked everything out in spite of me. So glad!"

She ran to the door, "I've got to go see Ray. I've missed him so much it's nearly made me sick. Oh, Stormy, I do love him so much. He's the best thing that ever happened to me, next to Jesus!"

"Whoa! Wait a minute," Stormy laughed in delight, "Slow down a minute. I have something else to tell you."

Barbara perched impatiently on a chair near the door, anxious to be off.

"I talked to Susan Miller the other day, and she told me her sister was interested in finding new dress designers. I had told her of you and your flair for designing your own clothes. She said for you to come by and see her some time." Stormy paused for breath, and Barbara's eyes grew starry with new dreams.

"Really?" she breathed ecstatically. "Do you suppose I might even be able to sell some of my designs?" she asked eagerly.

"I don't see why not," her sister said staunchly. "They're much prettier than a lot I've seen lately. It is certainly worth a try, isn't it?"

"Yes, oh, yes," Barbara clasped her hands together like a child. "I'll pick out my best ones and take them to her tomorrow. Will you help me?"

"I'd love to," warmth in the response reached out to the younger girl, who flew back to hug her sister again.

"I want to see Ray, but first I need to apologize to the family for acting like a sore bear," she said determinedly. "Poor little Amy. Why I nearly bit her head off the other night when she got on my nerves. Do you suppose she'll forgive me?"

Stormy laughed, "She's forgiven me for far worse! Let's go."

Barbara woke them up that evening when she returned from her date with Ray, demanding they must all come and see her engagement ring. It was gorgeous — a large, oval ruby encircled with dainty spirals of glistening diamonds in a heavy gold band of exquisite scroll work. It graciously adorned her slender finger, a promise of a lifetime of love.

The family rejoiced with her, staying up late and celebrating with cake and ice cream. Oh, how her exulting voice and happy face gladdened their hearts. Then she slipped into Stormy's room after everyone else had settled back down for the night to share with her all the wonderful things that had happened between her and Ray. He had taken her to the best restaurant in town and splurged wildly, after demanding an explanation of her recent coolness to him. She had revealed to him all of her heart, and things had been exactly as Stormy had told her.

Ray *had* been dreading the years that would separate them if she continued with her college plans, but he had kept silent. His love for her made him willing to suffer anything that would make her happy. When she had asked ever so hesitantly if he would be upset if she did not go, he had reached into his pocket and brought out the ring box. Could Stormy believe it? He had been carrying it around for a year, hoping and praying for the time when he could place it on her finger.

Stormy smiled and said yes she could believe it. Barbara was deliriously happy and Stormy was happy for her, but a little ache in her own heart betrayed an intense longing to experience the same bliss. How wonderful to possess the love of a good man, someone who would love her for herself, not for what she could be or could do. When Barbara at last left her room to get a few minutes sleep, the glow of life went with her. Stormy felt drained and lonely, the memories of her own unhappy love affair haunting her until the breaking of dawn.

Summer passed as the blaze of heat continued cooking gardens and burning crops to a crisp. But the long days were livened by occasional church get-togethers, watermelon feasts, and ice cream parties with the neighbors, as well as the once-a-month meetings of the women at the church. Vivian was the only unpleasantness at any of these affairs. She persisted in drawing attention to herself one way or another.

On one such occasion being held in her own home, Stormy found herself sneaking a look at the dark-haired beauty's ring finger. It was barren, but Vivian intercepted her glance, and her eyes narrowed balefully.

"Adrian and I looked at rings the other day," she said nonchalantly but quite loudly, then acted as if she had made a slip of the tongue. "Oops! I probably shouldn't have told that. You ladies will have to keep quiet about it. You know how men are, they like to be the first ones to tell when it's something important!"

"Oh! Isn't that wonderful!" Old Mrs. Bates' voice quavered in excitement as she rose to the bait. "That sweet Adrian's finally decided to marry — and a mighty pretty wife he's picked, too!" She nodded vigorously and beamed across the table at the sultry beauty.

Vivian looked around expecting more congratulations. But the other women were slow to respond, and Stormy's mother darted an anxious look at her daughter, whose suddenly bent head allowed her hair to shadow her face.

Vivian's mother hastily spoke up, "They surely do make a fine-looking couple, if I do say so!" She was a rather plain-featured woman, terribly proud of her comely daughter — perhaps too much so. She had hopelessly spoiled the girl, and in so doing, lost much of her love and respect. Vivian simply sent her a withering look for her compliment.

Gradually, one question led to another as the women followed their natural inclinations to talk about such things. Vivian guided them skillfully with hints and much pretty laughter, carefully avoiding any direct answers.

Stormy desperately wanted to excuse herself but felt obligated to help her mother serve. Her heart had experienced a severe jab of pain at Vivian's announcement, a pain she did not want to have and could not bring herself to investigate. She certainly cared nothing for Adrian. She disliked him tremendously most of the time! The jolt must have stemmed from Vivian's always getting anything she wanted.

Perhaps a subconscious feeling of envy had carried over from childhood days spent secretly watching another little girl obtain her heart's desire from everyone around her. If so, she would certainly have to deal with it before the Lord. But for now, it became a miserable effort to remain cool and sociable with the women. By the time they left, she was ready to explode.

She was angry at Vivian and Adrian and the whole world in general. Finally, she slipped upstairs to fling herself down on her bed and cry her heart out. Eventually, the storm ceased, and she sat up. Her eyes rested on the little figurine on her dresser. She walked over, picked it up, and stuffed it into the farthest corner of a bottom drawer.

Anna Winters had watched her daughter lose her pretty sparkle and grow quiet and despondent as the afternoon waned. She longed to take her in her arms and comfort her. Yet she sensed a withdrawal in the girl and wisely changed her mind. Instead, she sought the Lord in her prayer closet, laying the load down at His feet.

22
Burning Some Bridges

The first of September marked a significant change in Stormy's life and also marked a change in the weather. It was a cool day of clouds and welcome breezes. Also, it was the day she called Donald Adams at Eastland, Inc. and told him her final decision was to resign. She thanked him for the leave of absence and wished the company continued success. He expressed a genuine regret at her decision but wished her happiness. He also assured her that if she ever changed her mind, a position would always be open.

Slowly Stormy hung up the phone, one part of her sad and another part feeling free and excited. She had burned her bridges!

She was still working at Adrian's several hours each morning, but rarely saw him — partly because she worked hard at avoiding confrontations beyond the scope of necessity. She told herself he belonged to someone else and had never really shown her any special attention anyway. Certainly, he had never done anything to warrant the rapid increase in her pulse whenever he appeared or the pleasure that coursed through her body whenever he smiled that special smile and called her "little girl."

She and her mother spent hours discussing the new baby expected in November. They decorated the nursery and made tiny baby clothes. They made jams and jellies, canned soups and vegetables, and saved all they could from the dying garden which had slowly yielded to the unusual heat and to the hordes of grasshoppers that were sweeping the countryside, adding their own kind of misery to the frantic farmers.

The time for making the mortage payment had come and gone, and the Winters' were still praying and hoping for a way to be made to pay it, or to renew it, in spite of the impersonal bank notices.

Long summer evenings had been spent making music and singing or quietly sitting on the back porch, listening to the crickets and katydids harmonize with the bullfrogs, and watching the brilliant flashes of fireflies. The droning of electric fans began early in the morning and provided a soothing sound by which to fall asleep, unless the night proved to be cool enough to turn them off. There had been occasional storms bringing very little rain, but shaking the windows with thunderous voices and jarring the earth with a magnetic force. Jagged spears of lightning would hurtle toward the ground, seeking to wound some innocent victim. One did manage to demolish one of the huge trees in the backyard.

Stormy sighed. How could Cliff ever have thought farm life was dull and boring? More was going on each day than there was time to handle. Each new day brought its own set of problems and joys. But she loved it — yes, she dearly loved it. In spite of the cloud of disaster shadowing the little farm like a circling buzzard, there was always hope. They had survived before, maybe they could again.

October's slim late harvest brought a new dimension to the farm community as many began to talk of selling while they still could, counting themselves lucky to be getting out even at a loss. They were ready to give up rather than face another winter that could take everything they owned. Fear and uncertainty became a familiar expression, mirrors of despairing hearts and angry minds. There was a feeling of helplessness that broke spirits as many faced losing all they held dear. The ownership of land handed down for generations held them like anchors, and surrender would not come easy or without a struggle.

Farmers gathered in homes to talk for hours on end about measures that might be introduced and steps that might be taken to initiate security for their families. But in the end, the result was always the same. There was little they could do for those too weak to financially survive until spring arrived with its promise of hope.

One evening, when frost already had begun to nip the pumpkins, the twins burst into the house with the announcement that their youth group at church was going to have its annual old-fashioned hayride the next Monday evening. They were responsible for furnishing the wood for the bonfire at the end of the ride and for securing the company of two older couples as chaperones. Would Barbara and Stormy fulfill the latter obligation?

Barbara immediately accepted, saying she and Ray had been looking forward to it, but Stormy demurred.

"But why?" Keith asked, a shadow of hurt in his blue eyes.

"Well, uh," she fumbled for words, trying to think of a tactful way of telling him that she did not quite fill the bill for a "couple!"

"I think you could find another couple. It isn't that I do not want to go," she added hastily, feeling badly about the disappointment in his face, "It's just that I ...."

"Don't have anyone to go with," Kyle finished sympathetically.

"You could go with Adrian," Keith exclaimed innocently. "He said he'd like to go."

"He'll probably be taking Vivian," Stormy said dryly, refusing to give way to the annoying picture of the two of them sitting cozily in the hay. There was an irritable edge to her words that caused Barbara to look sharply at her.

"Are you kidding?" Keith snorted incredulously. "Can you imagine her sitting her fancy little self on dusty, old hay or drinking out of paper cups, not to mention roasting marshmallows on the end of a peeled stick? Oh, no — not her!" He started to say more but stopped as his twin shook his head at him.

"C'mon, Keith. We've got wood to gather," Kyle said. He smiled at his oldest sister, "You could come by yourself if you wanted to. You don't *have* to be with someone. Just think about it, and if you change your mind, you can let us know."

They disappeared out the back door, and Barbara spoke up curiously, her eyes on the dough she was rolling into a pie crust. "Would you go if you had someone to go with?"

"Sure!" There was no hesitation in her answer. Barbara's eyes glistened with sudden insight.

"Would you go with Adrian?" she reached for a knife to trim off the excess dough and caught a glimpse of scarlet in her sister's cheeks. "I mean, of course, if he asked you to."

"I … well, I guess so," the thought made Stormy feel uncomfortably warm. She ran a finger around the inside of her collar. "But I'm sure he wouldn't. He's engaged to Vivian."

"Oh, really?" Barbara dumped filling into the pan and began to roll out a top crust. "He never told us that!"

"That's what she said."

"She actually said that?"

300

Stormy thought back to Vivian's exact words, "Well, maybe she just implied they were. But she was congratulated, and she didn't deny it." Just thinking about it made her feel strangely depressed.

"I see," Barbara popped the pies into the oven and took off her apron, draping it over the back of a chair.

"Why don't we go upstairs and look at the magazines Susan gave me. She thought maybe they would give me some ideas." Barbara had taken Stormy's hint and gone by to talk with Susan and her sister about dress designing. They had been very encouraging.

Stormy followed her upstairs and looked at the magazines, but her mind frequently slipped away to dwell on a secret and growing hope.

Barbara noticed her absent-mindedness and speculated on what she was thinking about. Later, when Stormy left the room, she sent with her a silent wish that she would soon find the right man to love.

Sunday morning at church, Stormy felt no rest until she had once again viewed Vivian's ringless finger. But her budding hope was crushed when she overheard her mother talking to Adrian. She eavesdropped shamelessly.

"Adrian, we'd like you to go home with us today for lunch. We haven't seen very much of you lately."

"I'd love to, Anna," he said regretfully, "but I promised to eat dinner with Vivian and her parents."

"That's all right," she patted his arm. "I understand. I hear you'll be getting married soon."

Stormy was close enough to see the startled look in his eyes.

"Yes," he said slowly, searching Anna's face, and Stormy fled, rushing to the car in a very unladylike manner. What she had heard was to torment her day and night. Why it mattered so much she would not admit to herself. But deep down, she suspected she had a silly feeling of wanting Adrian to be a special friend — or maybe more than a friend!

Anna did not know Stormy overheard their conversation. So she had no idea of the cause of Stormy's despondency and preoccupied actions, but she did not worry about Stormy's mood, having just confirmed the truth of her ideas from a young man she already considered a son.

And so, the daughter wept bitterly, and the mother rejoiced.

23
An Old-Fashioned Hayride

Monday morning, Adrian strode into the office, pulled out a chair and sank down, as if he had nothing better to do than watch Stormy.

"Hi!" he said brightly, his eyes sweeping the thick braid coiled neatly atop her head. Wispy curls escaped it to trail down her neck and around her ears. He smiled at the confusion that colored her face before meeting her shy eyes, "Having a good morning?"

"Yes," she answered briefly, fastening her gaze on the desk between them.

He leaned forward, propping his elbows on the desk, and she drew back slightly from his nearness. She could smell the scent of his cologne, and it disturbed her senses.

"Have you got a date for the kids' hayride tonight?"

She drew in a sharp breath and said, "No."

"Care to go with me?" he asked impersonally.

She looked up to see his expression, finding only a look of friendship on his face, and answered, "Guess I could," in a nervous attempt to match his attitude.

"Great!" Warmth flooded his voice, and his smile drew a timid one from her own suddenly stiff lips. "Wear your hair like that tonight. I like it that way," he laughed and reached over to give her ear a tiny tweak. She quickly averted her pink face.

She could not concentrate the rest of the morning and finally left an hour earlier than usual, not daring to examine why she was so excited. She knew probably that she was second choice, and that he would not have bothered to ask her if the twins had not specified couples. Vivian must have refused to go.

Also, she was bothered about dating an "engaged man," even a "practically engaged man." But she soothed her conscience by deciding this was simply an innocent event in the company of a group of young people, and as he was such a good friend of her family, it was all right. After all, it was not a "real" date.

When the twins cautiously asked whether she had decided to go, she answered, "Yes," with a ring in her voice. Barbara and her mother looked at each other and shared a smile. Stormy was ready and waiting impatiently a few minutes before Adrian arrived. The twins had left with the truck, feeling important and grown up as they carefully maneuvered the wagon onto the main road.

Barbara looked fresh and lovely in a yellow and blue plaid long-sleeved shirt tucked neatly into a pair of yellow jeans with a light matching jacket tossed casually around her shoulders. Her blond hair swung freely around her face, and her eyes sparkled with life and excitement.

"Here he comes!" she cried as Ray turned into the lane, "See you later, Stormy," and she tripped lightly down the steps and across the lawn to greet her fiance. He greeted her with a kiss and led her back to the pickup with a possessive arm.

Stormy watched them with a lump in her throat. Would a man ever look at her the way Ray looked at Barbara? A look of passionate love and respect? A look that she had yet to receive from any man? Ray looked at Barbara with his heart shining in his eyes, and it was a sweet, precious thing to see. Cliff had never looked at her that way. She had seen admiration and desire in his eyes, but never a look such as she had seen given to her sister and her mother.

She wandered over to the long, oval mirror set in the front hall and critically studied herself. Her soft blue flannel shirt opening up at the base of her neck revealed a tiny pulse throbbing with life. The thick braid coiled on her head was laced with a blue satin ribbon. Soft, baby-fine hair escaped it to curl prettily around her face. Expressive eyes stared back at her above a short, stubby nose, now plentifully sprinkled with freckles. She sighed, and her eyes dropped farther, seeking some claim to beauty. She was well proportioned with a slender waist, shapely hips, and long legs which revealed a woman's figure beneath the faded blue jeans.

She *was* a woman with all the natural desires of a woman! But nowhere could she see beauty that might turn a man's head or win his heart. No, whoever fell in love with her, if anyone ever did, would have to definitely love her for herself. Suddenly she smiled mischievously at the girl in the mirror whose freckles began to dance, and the resemblance between her and Amy was startling.

"That's all right!" she said saucily. She could lay claim to brains that had won more than one man's heart! Looking herself honestly in the eyes, however, she knew she did want someone special. Her ill-fated affair with Cliff had given her only a hint of what could be, and she wanted it all. Her feelings of disillusionment disappeared. All her life she had seen true love in her parents' lives, and she wanted to experience the same thing for herself.

She was not going manhunting, she severely reminded the girl in the mirror. Neither would she shy away from a relationship that might bring unbelievable joys and delights. She would be herself, become more friendly and outgoing, take a greater part in community activities, and see what happened. She was not the kind of woman who could be happy living a solitary life, and she sent a quick prayer heavenward that God would help her know when the right one appeared on the scene.

As if in direct answer to her request, there was a knock at the door. Her prayer of supplication stopped, and her eyes looked up to the ceiling.

"Now, Lord," she whispered, "You know he's already taken. I'll just regard this as a coincidence!"

But her eyes were shining when she opened the door, and her heart gave a great leap when he placed his arm around her shoulders as they walked to the truck. She felt young and carefree, somehow certain that this was to be a very special night.

Her mother, watching from an upstairs window, smiled and nodded. This relationship was good and meant to be. She spent a few minutes with the Lord, asking Him to guide her children's lives and to bring them into a complete reliance on Him.

When they arrived at the farm where the ride was to start, everyone clambered on the hay wagon except Barbara and Ray and another couple, who were going to stay behind and get everything ready for the weiner roast to be held at the end of the ride. With much laughter and giggling, the young people scrambled into the hay. Stormy was pulling herself up when big hands reached down, caught her under the arms, and swung her effortlessly upward.

She landed on her feet with a gasp and was pulled down into a nest of hay as the truck began to move. She needed nothing more than the touch of his hands to identify her captor. Her skin tingled deliciously as she was tucked firmly into the crook of his arm.

"Comfortable?" he murmured softly.

"Y-yes," she stammered weakly, her body stiff with instinctive resistance.

"That's good," he leaned forward and covered their legs with a soft quilt, pulling it up around them, "can't have you getting chilled. Feels as if we are due for an early winter, maybe even snow in another week or so." White teeth flashed in a teasing smile. "Don't want the best thing that ever happened to me to catch a cold."

She said nothing. She couldn't. Her senses were reeling wildly at his heady nearness and the heavy weight of a muscular arm settling around her shoulders. Her mind churned with unanswered questions. Had he meant anything special with that last remark, or had he simply been talking about the work she did for him? Tonight, he was so different from the cool-mannered man for whom she worked. She was afraid of how she might respond if he....

"I hear you have a built-in radar when it comes to weather," she blurted out, trying hard to relax but growing nervous as he stroked her arm with the tips of his fingers, apparently unaware of what he was doing.

She shivered uncontrollably, unable to stifle the thrill that ran like hot oil over her body, making her melt against him in complete surprise. It was preposterous! Absolutely preposterous that this man's touch could erase the past and the future, making only the present seem real!

She had never felt this way with Cliff, even though he had sparked a physical response in her. But comparing him to Adrian was like comparing a spineless jellyfish to a great whale. This man fairly oozed masculinity, a masculinity that was gentle and loving, yet masterful. She felt giddy and wondered if her remark had sounded stupid.

"I don't think I'd call it radar," he mused thoughtfully. "I consider it a gift from God to be used to help people."

"Oh!" That sobered her. She turned to look up at him only to find his lean face dangerously close, thick, soft curls seductively framing it. She was hypnotized by the glittering darkness of his eyes that seemed to be saying something she was afraid to interpret. She swayed toward him as her eyes dropped to his mouth. His warm breath brushed her cool cheek. He smiled and drew her toward him, but she ducked her head, her heart racing as madly as the dark clouds scudding across the starry heavens. And a second later, her heart nearly stopped as she thought she felt the pressure of his lips against the top of her head.

Only when he began to laugh and tease Keith and his date did she draw a shaky breath. Her hand stole upward to quiet the tiny pulse jumping wildly at the base of her neck. Had she wanted him to kiss her so much that she had almost initiated it? "No!" her mind scoffed indignantly, but the echo of her heart rang louder. "Yes! Yes, she had!" Now, for the first time, she felt compassion and understanding for Denise, who loved someone so much she did not care that he was engaged to someone else! How self-righteous she must have sounded to that poor girl, whose love for Cliff had remained so steadfast all those years. She certainly did not approve or condone Denise's actions, but she was able to really forgive her for the first time.

She longed to know again the pleasure of being in Adrian's arms and of feeling the thrill of his lips against hers. She had never been able to forget their first kiss. Her heart had stored the memory like a precious treasure in a secret chamber and sealed it forever. Yes! This man did mean something to her, the woman within her cried. Love! A love that had begun on a cold, snowy day with frigid words, had survived hot summer days of heated tempers, and now called for a harvest of fulfilled dreams. She knew she loved him and accepted the fact with joy and honesty.

She was proud and glad to be at his side, no matter what tomorrow might bring. Perhaps he still was not committed to Vivian, or he might change his mind. Oh, how she prayed that it was not wrong to feel the way she did. She wished no harm to Vivian, but she knew her much too well — and she doubted Vivian had ever loved anyone but Vivian. Adrian was much too caring a man to be locked into a selfish marriage. Stormy realized that she loved this big man whose very strength filled her with confidence. He had been there when she needed someone ever since their first encounter in the snow.

If only she could be sure about what she thought she had read in his eyes just moments ago. She turned her head to look at the large hand resting heavily against her arm. Impulsively, she lifted her own hand and curled her fingers between his. Distinctive shock shook the frame of the man beside her, and she wondered at her own daring. Automatic flexing of his fingers as he cradled hers reassured her. Her heart rocketed skyward, as she shyly laid her head against his broad shoulder.

His arm tightened, drawing her closer, and her senses heightened quiveringly to the scent of his body, the warm hay, and the cool night air. She felt the warmth of his body through her clothes and the pressure against her head as he rested his own against it. Casting all doubts to the breeze whistling by, she allowed herself the pleasure of reverting back to a favorite pastime — dreaming. It was wonderful beyond words, this sweet rapture of love, more wonderful than she had ever dreamed! This love exposed the emotions she had felt for Cliff as being shallow and unfulfilling. Her feeling for Cliff had been that of an unawakened girl reaching for acceptance and reassurance.

So strong was the passion laying hold of her heart for Adrian that she was content to sit quietly and enjoy it. It felt so good just to be with the man she finally admitted that she loved and respected. It was thrilling! But also it was a little frightening to understand the desire within her for his touch and attention. Could anyone possibly have felt this way before? How could they have? It was so sweet and wonderful, so uniquely glorious. Surely if people had experienced these kinds of feelings, their lives would have been enriched and changed so much the world would be totally filled with love and goodness — just the way God intended it to be. She had never felt more alive in her life!

But she was given very little time to enjoy her new discovery as the wagon soon rattled back up to the side of the bonfire. She could not believe the long ride was over already! Certainly, it was a good thing all the youngsters along were so well-behaved. Their chaperones had been oblivious to their antics! Adrian rose to his feet pulling her up beside him as the youngsters eagerly jumped off all sides of the wagon.

Her skin prickled from the feel of his arm around her waist, and she thrilled to the sound of his voice as he called a teasing remark to Barbara and Ray, who sat cuddled together on a bale of hay near the fire. Then he jumped lightly off the opposite side of the wagon and held up his arms for her to jump. Her face glowed in the firelight, and her heart pounded against her rib cage.

She answered his grin with a shy smile, then jumped, trembling with excitement, into his waiting arms. His broad hands nearly spanned her waist, and her hands clutched at his shoulders as his hard body took the weight of hers without a flinch. She could not move, so hypnotized was she by the fire in his eyes. A shudder of anticipation shook her from head to toe.

"You're a beautiful woman, Stormy Leigh," he said huskily, his voice low and throbbing with passion.

No one was around to witness the next breathtaking moment, for everyone else had gathered around the fire. But the chilly night had no effect on the couple standing on the far side of the wagon, lost to the world, alive only to each other. Stormy's lips parted eagerly, her eyes closing instinctively as his dark head blotted out the moon. She had been waiting and hoping for this moment all evening. At his touch, she came alive with a passion that equaled his own. Her heart soared with rapture as her mind became drugged with the power of his kiss.

How long the kiss lasted, she never knew. She only knew she wanted it to go on forever. She clung to him, feeling his heart pounding against hers.

"Adrian?" The young voice penetrated the passion that burned like fire between them, and Adrian gently disengaged himself from her arms.

"Yes?" he answered. His voice was cool and calm, but Stormy was having trouble catching her breath. She doubted that she could have said a word if her life had depended on it.

"We're ready to eat!" Keith burst around the corner of the wagon, then stopped short. His face flamed with embarrassment. "Oh, I'm sorry," he mumbled, backing away at once.

"That's all right," Adrian chuckled, "We're coming." He slipped an arm around Stormy's waist, and she managed to steer her shaky legs in the right direction. He led her to a bale of hay next to Barbara and seated her before leaving to get them something to eat.

She hoped to have her voice back when he returned, and by the time he reappeared with two loaded plates, she was able to laugh and talk normally. He toasted her weiners and marshmallows, treating her with such special attention that her eyes sparkled with love and delight. It didn't take long for her sister to figure out that she was madly in love. She whispered to Ray, and he nodded. With smiles, they slipped away and left the spellbound couple to themselves.

Hours later, Stormy sat by the window, gazing dreamily at the big, gray house gleaming silver in the moonlight. She sat motionless, lost in thought. The evening had ended on a perfect note when Adrian left her at the door with a kiss of such tenderness that she had almost cried. He made her feel so desired and yet so honored. Floating on a cloud of wonder, she had longed to hear him say he loved her, but was content for the moment to just know the ecstacy of his lips. She had raised her arms, entwining them around his neck and tangling her fingers in his thick hair.

Then with a softly whispered, "Good night," he was gone. But as he paused to look back, she thought she heard him say, "I love you."

24
Foreclosure Threatened

When Stormy danced lightly up the steps of Westmoor Heights the next morning, the door was opened by Nora.

"Is Adrian around?" Stormy asked eagerly, her eyes searching the room.

"No, Miss Winters, he isn't," Nora smiled shyly. "He's going to be away for a couple of weeks. He left early, saying he had some important business to take care of."

"I see," Stormy immediately felt let down. "Thank you, Nora. Guess I'd better get to work."

"I baked some cinnamon rolls, like the ones you're so fond of," the housekeeper volunteered hesitantly. "Would you like some later?"

"That sounds wonderful!" Stormy exclaimed enthusiastically, her mouth watering at the thought. She had skipped breakfast in the hope of seeing Adrian before he left the house for the day. "Give me about an hour, and then bring them on."

"All right," Nora admiringly watched her walk away. Stormy Winters was a very special lady, and she secretly hoped she would someday be the mistress of Westmoor Heights. She would make a fine wife for Adrian and bear fine children too.

Stormy chaffed at the hours that separated her and Adrian, a lifetime of waiting would go by in the next two weeks! A little disquiet began to enter her heart again though. Why had he not told her last night that he would be gone? He must have known how she felt. Once again, a little thought of suspicion began to spoil her happiness, but she pushed it away.

At home, things began to happen that distracted her from an impatient counting of the days. That evening in their time of devotion, Charles Winters picked up the Bible and sat for a moment without speaking.

"Psalm 56:11," he said finally, without opening the Bible, his work-worn hands resting on its soft, cover. "In God have I put my trust: I will not be afraid what man can do unto me," he began, then paused and looked at each of them in turn as they sat quietly watching him.

"Psalm 57:1. Be merciful unto me, Oh God, be merciful unto me: for my soul trusteth in thee; yea, in the shadow of thy wings will I make my refuge, until these calamities be overpast," he quoted softly, tears shining in his grave eyes."

Stormy felt tears begin to trickle down her own cheeks. She had never seen her father cry except when touched by the presence of God or the pain of his wife or children.

"I am standing on the promises in those verses, making them my pledge to God," he said as he looked toward his faithful wife, and she nodded in agreement. We have just received the third and final notice from the bank. In two weeks, they will begin foreclosure proceedings. I see no possible escape from this thing, but our hope is in God, not in man.

"There is no way I can tell you how much your individual sacrifices have meant to me and to your mother. I appreciate the way in which you have joined with us in prayer. Our harvest is small, however, and the bills are growing every day. We don't have enough hay to last through the winter, and the cows are doing poorly already. In fact, as you know, we've already lost several head. We've paid our smaller bills, but we cannot pay the interest on the mortgage, much less the payment. And we are still facing the hospital bill for the baby. All I am asking is that you continue to help us pray."

He looked around at them and smiled sadly, "There are a lot of farmers across this nation with the same problems we have. Many will lose their families, health, and homes, but some will survive. It is not impossible for us to be among those who survive ... for God has not forsaken us. He still cares and watches over us. We will *anchor* our trust in Him until the storm passes by.

"He never promised that we would not have tribulations in this life, only that He would be with us through them," he continued. "If we must accept a change in our lifestyle, then we must. God will give us strength and courage to face whatever we have to face. He also said in His Word in Romans 8:28 that if our steps are ordered by Him, and we are called by Him, everything ultimately will work out for good. May He grant us peace of mind and heart through these events."

He bowed his head — and Stormy saw sorrowfully that his hair was showing much more gray — as he said, "Shall we kneel before God and ask His help and His blessings?"

Amy had patted Stormy on the shoulder when she saw her crying. Now she placed her little head against her in consolation before she knelt and began to earnestly talk to the Lord.

"Jesus," she said in a sweet little voice, "I know You'll take care of us. You always have. Please help Stormy know it too. I don't want her to cry or be 'fraid," she squeezed Stormy's hand reassuringly. "We want you to do something about our farm," she continued. "Daddy said You gave it to us. Please don't let anybody take it away, 'cause you know I love it, and I wanna grow up here just like Stormy. And who would take care of all the animals if we had to go away? You just gotta help us! Thank you, Lord. Amen.

"I feel much better now," she stated with satisfaction, peering at her sister who had not uttered a single word. "Don't you, Stormy?"

Her big sister hugged her tightly, not able to speak. Her heart was hurting too badly. Although the loss of the farm had been a possibility for some time, she had not really expected it to happen. She could not bear the thought of her parents losing all they had worked for through the years.

There were years when large payments had been made on the mortgage, and other years when times had been hard and no payment could be made. But the bank had always worked with them, allowing them to pay the interest and make up the payment later. Somehow, she had expected the same thing to happen when the new bank owners saw that the family really did not have the funds. She had expected the new owners to look back at their record over the years and understand that, sooner or later, her father always met his obligations.

Her mind spun without reason until she crept away to her bedroom like a wounded animal and fell limply across the bed. She was not able to remain for the other prayers or to attempt to console her parents. All their hard work and efforts had been in vain! It all amounted to one word — failure! It was not fair! It just was not fair! Bitter, angry thoughts welled up in her mind until she ran back downstairs, her face twisted with emotion.

"Daddy, why did this have to happen?" she cried bleakly, finding her father alone in the kitchen and not considering that she might be adding to his worry and stress. His face was drawn and weary, but his eyes still lit up at the sight of his daughter.

"I don't know, Honey," he poured her a glass of milk and slid the plate of cookies toward her. "Sit down and have a cookie. Maybe it will help you feel better."

She shook her head, "Nothing could make me feel better," she said dully. Not even her love for Adrian could comfort her. It seemed far away and unreal in the face of this new catastrophe.

"Isn't there anything else we can do?"

He set his glass down in consternation, knowing he was helpless to give her an answer she would accept in her present frame of mind.

"No, Stormy Leigh. We have done all we can do," he said gently, as if talking to Amy. "It's in the hands of God now. But He's never failed us yet. He will see us through this thing."

"No! No, He won't!" she shouted, tears breaking through the frozen dam of her emotions. Anger raged hotly in her soul. "You keep saying that, but it's not true! We've worked and worked and worked — and all for nothing! God isn't *going* to help us! It's too late! If He was going to do something, He would have done it long ago!"

"Stormy Leigh!" her father jumped to his feet, his face stern. "I can't let you say that. It's not true!"

"Yes, it *is* true!" she sobbed brokenly. "It is true, and you know it," she turned and ran back up to her bedroom to weep herself to sleep.

Shamefacedly, she apologized to her father the next morning for her outburst. She had realized how selfish she was in pouring all her emotions and doubts out on him. She had only added to his burden. But the clammy chill remained around her heart. Her prayers, when she could bring herself to pray, went no higher than her head because she was still angry at God. She wanted to flee back to Kingston to get away from it all. But she knew she could not leave her family. She did begin to wonder, however, whether she should go back to her old job in order to help support them wherever they had to move.

25
Loss of a Good Friend

A week later when the first cold, blustery storm of winter hit, the family was plunged into a nightmarish experience, one that shook them to the depths of their souls.

At supper one evening, they discovered that Amy was missing. Further investigation showed that Lady also was gone. Their concern mounted immediately. The little mare was heavy with foal, and it could prove fatal for her to be caught out in such wet, icy conditions. Knowing that Amy was probably with her, Charles, the twins, and Stormy hurriedly donned heavy clothing, rounded up several blankets, and headed the old farm truck out across the fields. Barbara stayed with her mother in case she should need her help. The baby was due in a couple of weeks.

Anxious minutes rushed by as the truck lumbered slowly across the first field adjacent to the now-swollen creek. The rain that had been missing during the summer had recently made up for lost time. The headlights seemed weak and ineffective against the encroaching darkness. Four sets of eyes strained in every direction for a glimpse of the child and her pony. Three more fields were scrutinized without results. Stormy began to panic.

"Oh, God," she prayed frantically, chewing on her bottom lip, "Where can she be? She's too little to be out here alone! Please let her be all right. Help us find her!" Again and again, she repeated the phrases, while fear kept its painful grip on her heart. What would happen if they did not find her soon? Were they even now too late? There was no way of knowing how long she had been out in the freezing rain.

"Daddy! What are we going to do?" she cried, tormented to the point of hysterics.

"Keep looking and praying," he said quietly, his eyes moving constantly. The dash lights revealed his tense features to his daughter and she turned to look wildly out her window. "She has to be out here somewhere. We've just got to keep looking until we find her."

"Dad," Kyle spoke up slowly, just remembering something. "When Keith and I were small, we made a little fort to play cowboys and Indians in. Remember? There's not much of it left, but Amy always loved it. Do you think she might have remembered it?" He peered toward his father.

"Yeah! That's right," Keith exclaimed excitedly. "It's down close to the creek! Down there!" He pointed, and his father swung the truck in that direction.

Nothing further was said, but their hearts beat faster with hope as the truck lurched across the fields. The headlights at one point struck rolling, black waters, and Stormy gasped, her hand fluttering to her frightened heart. Was there any chance the shelter was standing? Or had it been swept away, and Amy along with it? She felt she could not bear the anguish of not knowing for another minute.

"Daddy!" she cried feverishly. "Hurry!"

"There she is!" Kyle's voice rang out suddenly. He pointed to where his keen eyes had distinguished a faint movement.

"Thank You, God!" the father breathed, and loud "Amens" echoed his sentiment. As they drove toward her, they could see her little arms waving wildly as she tried to attract their attention. The tiny shelter still stood, although very rickety, and she and the pony were huddled under its dripping roof.

"Oh, Amy! Baby!" her father smothered her in one of the blankets they had brought and clutched her to his heart. Her lips were blue and quivering in the light of the truck, and she shook with cold and shock. Ice had frozen solid in the long, brown braids, and her eyes were red and swollen from crying.

"I couldn't leave her, Daddy!" she cried, her teeth chattering loudly. Her numb little hands sought to hold fast to his coat. "She fell down and couldn't get up."

"Boys, see if you can get her up," Charles instructed tersely, handing Amy to Stormy. "We have to get Amy back to the house."

The mare struggled valiantly to get to her feet, but she was too heavy and weak. Charles quietly examined her and then stood up. His eyes were bleak as he shook his head and said, "Let's go! We've got to get out of this weather."

"But what about Lady?" the child cried fearfully. "We have to take her home too. We can't just leave her here."

"We have to, Honey," he said, surging to his feet after one last, sad pat on the pony's sagging head. He knew she would soon be gone. There was nothing he could do, even if he could get her to the barn. But his father's heart would not let him tell the little girl the harsh truth so soon after she had given her all to save the pony she loved.

"No!" Amy screamed in terror, struggling madly to free herself from her sister's arms. "No! We can't leave her! She'll die! And her baby will die!"

There was nothing that could be done to soothe her, and her fears were true. They all knew the pony was old and unlikely to survive the storm. Her will to live was gone. Amy fought and scratched like a wild kitten. No amount of sternness could subdue or silence her, until Stormy spoke up desperately, "Amy! Amy! I'll stay here with Lady."

As her father shook his head, she said, "It's all right, Daddy. We have another blanket with us. I'll keep it, and the twins can come back for me.

"Well, okay," he reluctantly agreed, his concern for Amy forcing him to agree. Stormy watched them leave. As Keith held Amy in his arms, she plastered her cold little nose against the back window in an effort to see Lady as long as she could.

The darkness swallowed them up, and Stormy shivered. It was agonizingly cold. She wrapped the blanket around her and scooted up close to the pony for added warmth for both of them. Throwing part of the blanket over the little mare's head and back, she began to talk to her.

"Oh, Lady, I'm so sorry this happened. You should be home in a safe, warm barn. Why did you have to leave the cow lot and wander off?"

Fondly, she stroked the cold ears that twitched as the pony listened to the soft voice, and ruffled the thick, wet mane. "Amy loves you so much. We all do."

Lady's neck drooped lower. Stormy placed an arm around her and lifted her head. "Please don't die," she pleaded, looking into the huge, sad eyes. "Please don't die! If you die, your baby will die with you! You have to live. For Amy's sake, you have to live!"

Tears choked her as she swung the woolly, brown head onto her lap. Sliding her cold fingers down the slender nose, she caressed the velvety nostrils. The short spasmodic breaths of the exhausted creature warmed her fingers, reassuring her of life. Pity welled up inside her for the courageous little animal. She began to pray again, begging God to spare its life. Tears streamed down her stinging cheeks and fell onto Lady's head.

But the pony did not respond to her loving attention. With a long quivering sigh, Lady closed her eyes and rested her head in the human hands she had trusted. Alarmed, Stormy reached to stroke her nose again, but no breath of life warmed her fingers. With a groan of defeat, she bowed her head and wept bitterly.

When she saw the headlights of the truck coming, she stood up, took the blanket from around her shoulders and spread it over the little mare. She knew the pony couldn't feel its warmth, but it gave her a small measure of comfort to do it. Her family had just lost a good friend. For the gentle ways and sweet nature of Lady had left each of them with precious memories. She turned to meet the truck.

The twins understood the blanketed pony and wisely refrained from questioning Stormy when they saw her teary eyes. She spoke not a word until she reached home, when Amy had to be told the dreadful truth. Hours later, she wept herself to sleep, almost inconsolable.

26
Plain Talk From Mother

Charles Winters was very concerned about his daughters. His youngest was facing the possibility of pneumonia from her extensive stay in the raw, cutting wind and rain, and his eldest was unreachable. He feared she would turn her back on God, unable to trust Him in these trying circumstances. She had been numb with grief when the twins brought her back. He doubted his wisdom in allowing her to stay with the pony when he had known death was certain. Her eyes were bleak and vacant when she answered his questions.

The condition of his daughters drove him to his knees seeking wisdom, guidance, and strength from his Source in order to continue in the face of all this adversity. Then with his heart at ease and his mind at peace, having committed all to the Lord, he climbed into bed. Gathering his beloved wife in his arms, he was able to immediately fall asleep.

A few days later, Stormy returned home from Adrian's to find his truck parked in front of her house. Her heart leaped with joy. He was back! She flew into the house in search of him. Coming up short at the kitchen table, she looked around.

"Mother, is Adrian here?" she asked eagerly, her tone reflecting her adoration of the man she was seeking and her state of mind about him. Her mother leaned heavily on a mop.

"Yes, dear, he's in the office with your father — talking business," she added as her daughter started back down the hall. Stormy stopped and came back.

"Do you think maybe I shouldn't bother them?" she asked curiously, studying the carefully blank expression on her mother's face.

"They'll be out in a few minutes, I'm sure," she said evasively. "They've been in there for quite some time."

"Oh," Stormy said, seeing the mop in her mother's hand for the first time. "Here, let me do that," she scolded, pushing a chair into the hall. "You sit down out here and rest." She fell to mopping the floor vigorously, her mind groping for answers. Finally, she gave in to curiosity.

"Mother? What are they talking about?" she burst out, her eyes bright and inquisitive as they probed the serene face.

"The farm," her mother said simply, returning her gaze.

"But what ... ?" she listened for a second, then laid the mop aside as she heard the front door close. "Never mind. I'll ask him." But by the time she reached the door, the motor was purring in his truck. He drove off without a backwards look.

Dismayed, she fought back a tear and swallowed hard on her disappointment. She followed her father back into the kitchen, carefully avoiding the wet area. He drew up a chair to the table. His wife placed a cup of hot coffee within his reach and sat down cross from him. He took her small slender hand in his big, rough one and smiled in resignation, yet with a certain air of relief.

"It's done," he said simply.

"What's done?" his daughter demanded sharply from the doorway, her attitude fearful and aggressive.

"Come sit down, Stormy Leigh," he welcomed. She

slid into a chair across from them, ignoring her freshly mopped floor.

"Adrian just told me he would buy the farm," Charles said, as he looked down at the hand held firmly in his own. He missed the expressions on the faces of the women facing him. One relaxed in great relief, but the other registered disbelief, shock, and growing anger.

"How could he?" Stormy ground out, all her old suspicions flooding back into her consciousness. "How could he!" She rose in agitation and paced back and forth.

"What do you mean, dear?" her mother asked in perplexity. "Suspecting how you feel about him, we hated to even broach the subject. But we've been praying for deliverance, and this is much better than we had dared to hope for."

"What!" Stormy glared at the paper in her father's hands. "Can't you see he has had this planned all along? He's been using us, all of us! Snooping around all the time, pretending to be so nice and helpful and just waiting for a chance to get his hands on our farm!"

"Stormy!" Her parents' voices rang out in shocked unison.

"He's our friend," her mother said sternly. "And he's as dear to our hearts as our own children. He didn't know we were in so great a financial bind, or he would have offered help before. And he certainly didn't have to buy this farm — but he did. And we're grateful!"

"No! No!" Stormy cried shrilly, her searing anger burning away any love for Adrian. "He didn't have to — he wanted to! We fell into his waiting hands like ripe plums!"

"Stormy Leigh! Settle down," her father said in the most severe tone he had used to her since she had grown up. Brooking no disobedience, he said sternly, "Sit down and listen! Stop jumping to such foolish conclusions and pointing an accusing finger when you don't know the whole story. I heard Cliff make the same accusations that time, but it never entered my mind you really believed Adrian wanted our farm!"

With a red, mutinous face, Stormy sank into her chair and stared holes in the table.

"Now," her father continued more gently, "Adrian is willing to let us stay in the house as long as we like. He didn't want to accept any rent, but I insisted. So he named a very reasonable sum, much less than the mortgage payments had been. Wait!" he held up a cautioning hand as she started to protest. "Or he's willing to pay me good wages, including the rent, if I want to work for him and keep up the farm."

"Oh, Daddy! How can you?" she began to sob, her heart breaking at the thought. "How can you just become a hired hand on a farm that once was yours? How can you bear the thought of paying rent to stay in a house that once was your own home?"

He sighed deeply, his eyes sad and troubled, "It will not be easy, Stormy Leigh." His wife squeezed his hand comfortingly. "But Barbara, Keith, and Kyle are practically grown and very soon will be paying their own way in life. And you have been on your own for years. We'll only have Amy and the new baby to provide for. If we can stay in the house we have loved over the years and make a living farming the land we love, we can survive. In fact, we'll be doing better than we're doing right now. The worry of whether the farm pays or not will be Adrian's, not ours."

If he had hoped to instill some enthusiasm into his daughter, he failed, for she was barely listening as he continued. "We can always raise a big garden, and in time, we'll adjust to the change. We need to thank God for making a way of escape for us. Many of our neighbors will not be so fortunate."

But Stormy's mind was made up. She and Cliff had been right! Adrian McAllister had tended his innocent flock very carefully only to steal their wool and throw them to the wolves. If her parents wanted to still blindly believe in him, they could, but not she! She abruptly pushed away from the table and stalked outside, boiling with so much anger she could not politely excuse herself.

The idea that the farm might be more of a burden financially to Adrian with the way things were in agriculture never occurred to her. Without her realizing it, all of the anger at Cliff's betrayal had gotten intermingled with all of the anger she had released at Adrian during the past year — and now all of it was being justified in her mind and focused on Adrian. The fact that none of it made good sense was beside the point. She was being driven by judgmentalism and a root of bitterness, forgetting that in Hebrews 12:15 the Bible warns against letting any root of bitterness spring up.

She drew in deep breaths of cold, crisp air and kicked furiously at everything in her path. Oh! He had duped her too! She actually had begun to imagine herself in love with him, even to the extent of trying to draw words of love out of thin air! Of course, she would not put it past him to say he loved her if it would suit his purpose! Oooh! Men!

She kicked a big rock, which made her howl in pain and even more anger. She limped over to the old cistern in the back yard. Plopping down on it in disgust, she gingerly nursed her throbbing toe with a shaking hand. Stupidity ought to be her middle name. She seemed forever doomed to repeat her mistakes. And God! Where was He in all this mess? Where was the love, protection, and help she prayed for so earnestly each night?

How they had all united together seeking deliverance from the oppressor! Her father felt Adrian had been instrumental in bringing about that deliverance. Well, she did not see it that way. Adrian had done nothing more than enlarge his own empire by snatching up a choice piece of adjoining property and throwing out a handful of promises in return.

She hurt all over, from head to toe, heart and soul. She had just had too much lately! She glanced up at Amy's window. The child had slept most of the day, still fighting a fever and a hacking cough. She was tired — tired of the endless chores, endless problems, endless heartache. Never stopping to consider that her parents had lived victoriously through more than a quarter of a century of this kind of life, or that, once again, she was not helping but adding to their worries, she considered more seriously the idea of returning to Kingston to work.

She was pretty sure she could even have her old job back. It was doubtful she would be happy working there now, but it might be worth a try. What she would really like to do was wipe out the memory in Adrian's computer. She grinned vindictively! That should put him in a real bind for a while. Or maybe she should make a small bonfire out of his floppy disks. She licked her lips in malicious anticipation. Teach him to hire a whiz to run his computer! Why she could do so much damage his records would be fouled up for months! Maybe years!

She swung her foot back down to the ground. No wonder he had not stayed to talk to her! There was no way he could have missed seeing her car parked in the drive. He had not wanted to see her. Well, Vivian could have him — and good riddance! Angry tears danced in her eyes making Ol' Tom look like two cats as he purred his way up to her. Vivian and Adrian would make a dandy couple! She reached for the cat and drew him close, finding comfort in his undemanding attention. But why did it have to hurt so much! She gulped, and the cat patted her face softly.

"Dear old Tom," she crooned, ruffling his fur the wrong way, as he pretended to attack her hand. "Are you as fickle as the other men in my life?" He purred even louder, and she nodded sadly, "I'm sure you are. You probably have every female cat in the county on your calling list." She deposited him gently on the ground and stood up. "Guess it's time to go and apologize for my sharp tongue," she told him ruefully. "One of these days maybe I'll learn to go through life without making so many waves."

Apologize she did and forgiven she was, but her heart remained cold toward Adrian. The new flame flickered weakly under pressure intended to completely snuff it out. And she did not change her opinion of him or of the circumstances, in spite of the apology.

Amy's fever continued to rage, and finally, they took her to the hospital. Stormy called Westmoor Heights, and stiffly informed Adrian she would not be able to come back. Briefly she explained the situation to him and longed heartily to hang up on him when he kindly offered to help in any way he could. But for the sake of her parents, she remained polite but cool until he had hung up.

Then she snapped, "No thanks, buster!" giving way to the pleasure of slamming down the phone. "You've done enough already!"

She drove her mother to the hospital to spend the day with Amy, who was still fighting pneumonia. The roads were so icy and treacherous, she was a bundle of raw nerves before they reached town. Part of the strain was caused by her mother's condition. She fussed and worried over her. It would never do to get stranded in this kind of weather.

Her father had gone in earlier to meet Adrian and finalize the sale of the farm and had not yet returned when they had to leave for the hospital. Returning home, she spent the rest of the day cleaning house and baking. She was tired and grumpy when she made the return trip to the hospital. But her spirits lifted when she heard Amy was doing much better. She saw her mother safely into the house, then ran back to park her car in the old garage behind the house. When she walked into the warmth of the kitchen, her father was showing her mother the bank lien papers with "Paid in full," marked across them.

"I guess it's final then," Stormy said in a small voice.

"Yes, Honey," her mother smiled sympathetically. "Adrian has taken the deed to record at the county courthouse as soon as possible. Everything is going to be all right."

"I don't feel as if things will ever be all right again," she whispered to herself, tying an apron around herself and moving toward the potato bin. Her parents went back to the living room.

She was totally unprepared for the back door to fly open a few minutes later. A sharp blast of piercing cold air hit her, and she frowned at the twins' tempestuousness. A reprimand rose to her lips, and she said, "Shut that door!"

"Yes, Ma'am," a voice answered meekly. She whirled around to see Adrian standing there grinning, cap in hand, and blue eyes dancing with mischief.

"Oh, it's you." She turned her back, certainly in no mood whatsoever to be polite. "Mother and Daddy are in the living room."

Suddenly she felt his warm breath stirring her curls a second before he lifted them and planted a soft kiss on her neck.

"Sorry I've been too busy to talk since I got back," he started to explain, thinking that was the cause of her unfriendliness. "But I had a number of loose ends to tie up. Did you miss me?"

"No!" She shoved past him, trembling inside at his touch but covering her weakness with a quick spurt of anger, "I didn't!"

She did not see the disappointment on his handsome face or the hurt that crinkled his brow at her harsh tone.

"Is anything wrong?" he asked quietly, watching her angry movements with puzzled eyes.

"Yes!" she finally exploded, spinning around to glare at him. "Yes, there is! How could you have led Mother and Daddy on, pretending to be such a good friend, so you could grab the farm if it went under?"

"I didn't …," he began, his lips growing stern at her withering accusation.

"Yes, you did!" she cried wildly. "Cliff was right!" Conveniently forgetting she had given Cliff the idea, she threw her harsh accusations at him. "You're just out for your own profit, out to pad your own fat bank account. You knew all along how good Daddy's land is. Why couldn't you have been honest enough to say so from the start, instead of worming your way into their affections? They still can't see you for what you are."

"Stormy Leigh!" his voice cracked with pain. "How could you think such a thing? Do you hate me so much you believe me to be without honor?"

"Yes!" she screamed. All the agony and tension of the past months erupted like a volcanic force. Hot waves of anger flowed through her, loosening her control over her tongue.

"Yes! I do hate you! I do! Get out! Get out of here right now!" she yelled and stomped her foot, pointing a shaking finger toward the door.

Then he moved — not toward the door, but toward her. He swiftly swept her up in his arms and placed a tender but possessive kiss upon her surprised lips. Her mouth fell open in shock, and she began to tremble anew as he released her.

"At least I shall have one more kiss to remember," he said huskily. "Goodbye, Stormy Leigh," and he walked briskly down the hall to join her parents.

Stormy threw herself into a chair, sobbing wildly ... but only for a moment. Then she lifted her head and wrinkled her nose defiantly. Was she crying over a man again? Feeling upset and empty, she moved over to finish peeling the potatoes. A few minutes later, she heard the front door close and an engine roar into life. She did not need to look to know it was Adrian leaving.

Slow, heavy steps neared the kitchen, and she turned to see her mother. One hand rested on her abdomen, and she gazed at her daughter with a troubled expression.

"Stormy Leigh, what was all that about?" she asked with concern.

Stormy flushed guiltily and bit her lip. "Oh, Mama," she flew across the room and fell on her knees in front of her mother, who eased herself into a chair. "I lost all control of myself and my tongue."

"So I heard," her mother remarked dryly. "You could have been heard all the way to the road."

Stormy had the grace to blush. "I'm sorry, Mother," she whispered miserably. "I just couldn't stand it anymore."

"Did you mean what you said?" Her mother's tone was kind, and a loving hand smoothed the thick red curls away from the fair forehead.

"I don't know!" she wailed. "I did when I said it, but now I really don't know."

"Well, I have a few things to say," her mother tipped her chin up and looked gravely into her eyes, "and I want you to listen carefully."

Mutely the girl nodded, her eyes curious.

"And don't interrupt until I'm through, even if you disagree with me. Understood?"

She nodded again, and her mother said, "Adrian McAllister is very much in love with you."

Stormy thought her heart had left her body, so great was the surge of joy that shook her.

Anna continued, "He as much as told me that one Sunday at church when I mentioned having heard he was getting married. He looked at me rather oddly, then said, yes, he was, if the girl he loved would have him. And I knew he was talking about you."

Stormy gasped, remembering how she had felt at the time, and how she had held it against him later that he was engaged but would go around kissing other girls.

"Just now I asked him straightforwardly if he loved you? Do you know what he said?"

Stormy barely moved her head, her heart wavering between hope and fear.

"He looked at me with tears in his eyes and said, 'You know I love her, Anna. But she hates me. I think she always has. I've been through a lot of hard things in my life. But this is by far the worst. I'd give anything in the world to have her love me, but it looks as if that is an impossibility.'

"Then I asked him about the little figurine he gave you Christmas, because its resemblance to you had always puzzled me. He said he found some school pictures in his house when he began to remodel, and fell in love with the girl who looked so much like a princess and who could write such honest and heartfelt remarks on the back to her 'Prince Charming.' Did you take those pictures to Westmoor Heights?" she asked curiously.

Stormy nodded again. Each year since she was old enough to dream of a husband, she had taken a picture and left it for the prince of her dreams. She remembered the childish letters she had written on the backs of them and colored furiously. Adrian must not have recognized her the first time he saw her in the snow because she acted so differently from the kind of girl he had envisioned from her pictures and notes — and of course, because she gave him the wrong name.

"I have just one more thing to say, Stormy. You have lost a lifetime of happiness if you have lost that man's love. He has loved you for months, going out of his way to go to Kingston and check on you. That's right," she nodded firmly as Stormy's eyes searched hers. "We didn't ask him to every time. He went on his own because he was afraid you might need someone. He wanted you to know you could always count on him."

Stormy bowed her head. She had needed him — so much. He had been a lifesaver on more than one occasion. She felt even more awful, remembering his thoughtful actions.

"Think about it, Child," her mother patted her comfortingly on the shoulder and rose to her feet. "True love comes only once to many people. Be wise in your decision and thoroughly examine your heart before you irretrievably throw away the love of a man like Adrian."

And with that final admonishment, she left her daughter to her own thoughts and walked away praying Stormy would heed her advice.

27
Making Peace With God

Stormy slept very little that night. She made several trips to the window to stare at the big, dark house sitting silently in the moonlight like a huge, silver cube. Torn between her own beliefs which she was reluctant to turn loose of and her desire to accept her mother's words as truth, she paced the floor for hours.

A gray morning with heavy, blinding snow brought a hard-won decision. She had not really given Adrian a chance to explain nor had the courtesy of giving him the benefit of the doubt in his relationship with her family. She was not even sure anymore that she had anything for which to forgive him. Perhaps he had not intentionally done anything to hurt her. Her love for him began to grow steadily, choking out the doubts and disillusionments, until at last she got up, dressed in the dim light and hurried downstairs.

As soon as she was sure he was up, she would call him and apologize. She wanted his love more than anything! And she could not — would not — lose it, if there were some way to recapture it. She found her parents fully clothed in the family room. Her father looked at her gravely. "The hospital just called to say that Amy had a bad night. But she's resting easier now," he said quickly, reading the alarm in her eyes. "Your mother wants to go into town to be with her. She's also starting to have a few pains."

He nodded toward the suitcase by the door. "She's packed and ready to go. Can you take her? I need to haul some hay to the north pasture. If you can take your mother into town, I'll have the twins help me load the truck before school. Adrian thinks we are in for a bad storm, and I agree. Maybe you should come back here to help me feed the cattle, then we'll return to town together."

He put his arm around Anna, "Little Mother, will you promise to wait to deliver this one until we get there?"

Anna smiled, "I'm willing, but I'm not too sure this little one is."

Stormy felt a fresh surge of love at the mention of Adrian's name, but her world came tumbling down around her ears at his next words.

"Adrian stopped by this morning and said you wouldn't need to come to work today, Stormy Leigh," he stooped to pick up the suitcase, then started for the door with his arm encircling her mother's waist.

"He already came by?" she asked pitifully.

"Yes. He said he had extra work to do getting ready for the snow and wanted to get an early start. He offered to take Anna in, but I thought you'd be able to do it and not hinder his chores."

She followed him to the car and helped tuck a thick quilt around her mother.

"I'm sure the baby is coming today," her mother announced cheerfully, studying Stormy's unhappy face.

"Oh, I hope so!" Stormy roused herself to talk about the baby. She could not stand the thought that Adrian might not want to accept her apology. What if he really had loved her and she had killed that precious love with her cruel and unjust accusations? She had to keep her mind on other things or she would burst into tears.

So she chattered away about a number of things until they arrived safely at the hospital. Her mother kissed her fondly and told her to make sure her father did not stay out in the cold too long. Stormy agreed and hurried back to the car. She could barely see to drive home and was relieved when she finally pulled into the lane. She told the twins to have the bus driver let them off at Hutchens' store after school. Barbara would make sure they got home or take them over to the hospital to wait on their father.

After they ran through the thickly falling snow toward the blinking lights on the bus, she bundled up well and hurried out to the barn. Her father was tossing a last bale of hay onto the truck.

"Thought I'd better take an extra one or two," he greeted her with a warm smile, his nose and cheeks red and shiny from the cold. "Did you get your mother to the hospital?"

"Yes," she grinned at him and opened the truck door, "and I think our little surprise definitely is going to arrive sometime today."

"Good," he nodded in satisfaction. "I've been rather worried about your mother."

"She'll be all right, Daddy," she reached across the seat to pat his arm. He started the old truck with difficulty, and they moved slowly toward the first gate. Stormy jumped out to open it and ran shivering back to the warm cab.

"A storm like this could be dangerous," her father squinted through the mushy flakes that splashed against the windshield, making it hard to see. "Especially with the wind chill factor so low. A person could freeze to death in no time, if he got stranded."

Stormy left the warm security of the truck several times to open the gates. The lowing of the cattle was their only guide when they switched the engine off to listen.

"There they are, Daddy!" Stormy pointed to a large group of snow-encrusted, hump-backed creatures bunched together under the scant protection of a huge, bare-limbed tree.

"I knew I should have moved them closer to the barn," her father said ruefully. "But there was still grass here, and I wanted to keep them on it as long as I could to save the hay."

"Is that all of them?" she asked anxiously.

"It should be most of them. You drive the truck while I throw out the bales." He rolled up his coat collar, opened the door, and disappeared into the dense whiteness. She scooted across the seat, rolled the window down and listened. As soon as she heard him yell, she put the truck into gear. Leaning forward, she peered through the small hole the defroster managed to keep thawed. After moving slowly for several minutes, she glanced into the rear view mirror and saw her father toss off the last bales.

"Thank goodness!" she sighed, and shifting gears she began to move on more quickly in order to turn the truck, pick up her father, and head back. Then she yelped sharply as the truck struck something, bucked violently, and the engine died. "Well, for goodness sake," she muttered, "must have hit the only stump still left in the whole field!"

Turning around in the seat, she looked anxiously through the back glass, but her father had vanished. She waited for him to come to the door, but when he did not, she opened it and stepped out. Stinging little balls of ice pelted her cheeks, and large flakes clung to her lashes as she pulled her stocking cap lower over her ears. Hardly able to hold her eyes open in the wind, she felt her way along the truck bed on the driver's side, calling as she went, "Daddy? Daddy, where are you?"

The wind snatched the words from her lips with a roar so loud she could scarcely hear herself. She stubbed her toe and fell heavily onto her hands and knees. Then she saw him.

"Daddy!" she screamed in horror. "Daddy!" She crawled under the truck bed and over to the other side where Charles lay quiet and unconscious. His thighs were marked by the tread of the truck tires. He must have climbed out of the truck to walk back up to the cab, then stumbled and slid underneath just as she started off. The back tires had run over his thighs.

"Oh, God," she sobbed in her fright. "Oh, Jesus! Please let him be all right. Please let him be all right!"

She was scared worse than she had ever been in her life. Panic suffocated her.

"Daddy," she put her face down next to his, trying to see his eyes in the dim light. Her tears fell on his cold, still face. She stroked his face with her ungloved hand as if to wipe away the gray, sickly pallor. His eyelids flickered, and she cried, "Oh, thank you, Jesus. Thank you, Jesus."

His mind began to function, and he turned his head toward her. "Stormy Leigh," his voice was weak and shaking! "You've got to go and get help!"

"I can't leave you, Daddy!" she exclaimed.

"You must!" he insisted as his body jerked in pain, his voice trailed off with a groan. "You can't get me in the truck. I'm too heavy. Go start the truck, then come back, and I'll tell you what to do. Go!" he pleaded, as she stared at him in shock.

She couldn't move fast enough as she scrambled out from under the end of the truck, felt her way back to the door, and wrenched it open. She climbed up into the seat and cranked the engine, but it only clicked.

"God, make this truck start, please!" Fear gnawed at her as she pumped the accelerator and tried again. For what seemed like an eternity, she tried to start it. At last in defeat and frustration, she made her way back to her father's side.

"Daddy, I'm sorry! I couldn't get it to start!" she cried, the sight of his pained face breaking her heart. "What'll I do now?" Her desperation reached him, and he stirred, groping for her hand, "It'll be all right, Child."

"But Daddy! I'm so scared," she wailed, chafing his hands with hers, their coldness chilling her heart. She knew he must be in a state of shock, yet he was trying to soothe her. "Daddy, I've got to do *something*. Nobody will look for us for hours. Maybe I can find my way back on foot."

"No!" he weakly shook his head. "I don't want you trying to do that. You could freeze to death if you lost your way. Better to stay here. At least we're partially protected from the weather. Do you think you could find the last bale or two I tossed off the truck? They might block off part of the wind."

"Yes! I'll try," she said, eager to do anything to help them survive. "I'll be right back," she promised. As he nodded his head and closed his eyes, she scurried like a rabbit into the storm.

She found the first bale by falling over it and dragged it back to the truck. She placed it by her father's head, and with a sob, inched away again from the safety of the truck. She found another bale and placed it on the other side of her father. But on the third trip, she nearly got

344

lost. It was long minutes before she gained the safety of the truck, weak and trembling. She placed it across the other two bales to try to block the wind off the upper part of her father's body.

Then she tried to start the truck again without results, finally crawling back under the truck and across to Charles. She was glad for the small amount of heat still radiating from its engine. But it was not long before she began to shiver in earnest. Her father's body also shook from time to time with long, painful shudders. She lay next to him, opening her coat and shielding him as best she could from the whistling wind and drifting snow that continued to seek them out.

Her father opened his eyes again, "Stormy Leigh, I want you to go get in the truck. You'll stay warm in there longer."

In her frenzied state of mind, it seemed his instructions were spoken with finality. She began to sob. "I won't leave you, Daddy!" she cried in a childish voice, "I won't leave you! If you die, I'll die with you!"

"We're not going to die," he said softly. "God will take care of us."

"But Daddy, I've been so mad at God lately 'cause bad things keep happening to us. I'm not sure I'd go to Heaven if I did die!"

"Why have you been mad at Him?" he asked, twisting his head to look at her. His eyes were glazed with pain, "He's always taken care of us, provided for us, healed us when we were sick, and blessed us."

"I know He has, but," she sighed heavily. "I was angry at first because Barbara didn't get her scholarship. She wanted it so badly, and we all prayed about it for so long."

"But it all worked out for the best, didn't it?" he questioned with a sharp gasp of pain.

"Yes, it did," she admitted. "But then I got mad over Kyle being bitten by the snake."

"But during that time, Kyle turned his mind to more serious matters and decided to become a doctor. Besides, his leg healed without permanent injury, didn't it?"

"That's true too," she said thoughtfully, as he searched her face for confirmation before closing his eyes wearily.

"But what about Lady dying? What good did that bring? We all loved her, especially Amy."

"Lady was old when Adrian bought her. He was sorry she was pregnant, knowing it might shorten her life. But he felt she would be good for Amy, and she was." He rested a moment before continuing. She scooped the snow back away from his head. "It would have been much more painful for Amy, if she had watched Lady die. As it is, Adrian has promised her that she can pick out a little foal from his herd as soon as she is well. Lady's absence will not be felt so much."

"And what about the fire that destroyed the hay field?" she asked.

"'Many are the afflictions of the righteous: but the Lord delivereth him out of them all,' Psalm 34:19," he quoted slowly. "As long as we live in the natural world, bad things will happen from time to time. I don't have all the answers, Stormy, only God does. But I've found that He always delivers me out of my troubles. His Word is true, of that you may be sure."

He grimaced, and her heart pounded with concern. She wondered if the pain would be intolerable now that the shock was wearing off.

"How do you feel about the farm now?" he suddenly asked, opening his eyes again and focusing on her face.

"I don't know, Daddy. How do you feel?" she countered.

"I can't say it doesn't hurt to lose ownership of it. It does. But I know of no man I admire more and would rather have it than Adrian. He gave us a good price. The bank lien on the place was paid off, plus we had a nice little sum to put in the savings account. He didn't have to buy it, and he certainly didn't have to pay us what he did. Are you still mad at him and God over it?"

"No," she shook her head sorrowfully. "I'm ashamed of what I've said and done, and especially of what I thought. It seems I get mad when things don't go the way I think they should, and I don't wait to see what the end results will be. If I trusted God as you and Mother do — I mean *really* trusted Him — I wouldn't have had so many worries and fears. But you know what?" her face lighted with determination. "From now on, I *am* going to trust Him for everything. His ways are better than mine even if I don't understand them. If He had the wisdom and knowledge to create the heavens and earth and keep them functioning perfectly, He certainly can take care of me."

"That's good," the whisper came so low she had to lean close to catch it.

"Daddy?"

He opened his eyes once more and smiled. "I love you, Stormy Leigh, and God does too. He'll see us through this thing ... just trust Him!"

Stormy knew Jesus was there, right under the truck with them. She found herself talking to Him as freely and easily as she had with her father, whose head had sagged to one side once he was certain she had accepted his direction to "trust God." She leaned over to look at him and felt only the faintest whisper of breath touch her face. Fear tried to grip her mind. In horror, she cupped his face, begging him to speak to her. But his lips remained closed. With a shock, she realized he could not hear her.

"Oh, Jesus! Help me! You've got to help me! I'm so scared I can't even think what to do. Please help me. I *do* trust you, Lord — please show me what to do."

Gradually a sweet peace flooded her soul, and she said, "I'm not angry anymore, Lord, and I'm really sorry I haven't trusted you. I know it must have grieved You, because I am Your child. Please forgive me. I *know* You can do anything. Forgive me for being so childish in my way of thinking and help me to be more childlike ... like Amy. She has all the faith in the world in You — and God, I do too!

"Father, I feel so terrible about what happened to Daddy! It was all my fault. I should have been more careful and waited for him to climb back inside before trying to turn around and head back. But You know I wouldn't have had it happen for anything!" A tear trickled down her cheek and fell into the snow without a sound. "Oh, Lord, please don't take him home just yet. We need him — what with Mama and the little one and the twins being the age they are. And Amy would be deprived of the joy of growing up under his leadership! I don't mean to be selfish," she brushed away the snow that encircled his head and tugged at her coat to cover him more.

"I know he would be very happy to be with You, but Father, we need him so much! I don't know what else to say except that I put it all in Your hands, and I ask You to take control of this terrible situation. I don't know what to do. Please, please help me!"

Her toes had grown numb, and she was too weary to wiggle them. But when she became aware that the storm had let up slightly, she crawled out from under the truck and looked anxiously around. Squinting her eyes, she saw the dim outline of the first gate not too far away. Standing on wooden feet while the world swayed dizzily around her, and the snow fell at a crazy angle, she began to pray again.

"Lord," she whispered, her teeth chattering loudly, "If you'll go with me, I'll go get help. But I can't make it on my own." In answer to her plea, a solitary ray from the sun burst gloriously through the clouds pointing toward home. She knew she had her answer. "I'll be right back, Jesus," she promised.

It was torture to force her stiff legs to crawl back under the truck, and she slid down beside her father's still form in exhaustion. She had lost her gloves and could not feel her fingers. They refused to operate right, and it took some time for her to unbutton her coat and shrug out of it. Once she had it off, she quickly spread it over her father, praying it would help keep him warm. She placed a loving, reverent kiss on his cold forehead with tears streaming freely down her face and her heart nearly bursting with pain.

"God be with you, Daddy," she whispered. "God be with you!"

She drew the coat up over his face, tucked it around him as best she could, and with one last reluctant look, she wriggled out again into the cold, open air. The raw, whipping wind cut through her clothes like a sharp knife, pierced her lungs and stole her breath, but the ray of sunlight was still there, beckoning her onward. She stumbled toward the first gate. Reaching it, she pulled herself up and over and plodded on. Her mind grew fuzzy, her sight hazy, and at times she heard herself praying out loud as if her spirit involuntarily called out to its Maker for strength and courage.

She stopped counting the times she fell, but ruthlessly set her face toward home, heaving to her feet and staggering drunkenly on. Her path became marked by bright drops of blood that ran from her torn flesh, saturating her shirt and jeans and falling unheeded to lie like costly jewels in the snow.

Vaguely, as she struggled to climb yet another fence, she sensed the snow had stopped beating her. The wind did not burn as badly, and it seemed all creation waited in hushed silence, as if to see if the young girl would have the stamina, courage, and faith to survive.

Her eyes were unseeing as she reached the last gate. She was led totally by the warmth of the sun on her eyelids. Her face was as white as the snow that lay around her. Her warm woolen cap had been lost during one of her many falls, and the sun sought out the melted flakes that clung to her curls like sparkling diamonds caught in a fiery web. A long scratch marred one smooth cheek with a crimson finger, and her clothes were heavy with water.

She topped the gate with a tremendous effort and slipped, falling heavily to the ground on the other side. Her eyes closed in futility and her body sought a haven of merciful darkness from the pain that gripped it. Her fingers relaxed, one hand outstretched toward home in touching appeal.

"God," she whispered, "I trust you."

The breath that had come in ragged gasps as she had groped for the gate stilled. A small whimper parted her lips, and she moved no more.

28
An Answer to Prayer

Adrian McAllister was worried, very worried. He had called the hospital to check on Amy and been informed that she was doing much better, and that her mother was in the delivery room. Could he contact Charles Winters and ask him to come into the hospital? There had been no answer at the Winters' home.

Promptly, he had placed his own call to the house but received no answer. The phone rang hollowly in his ear. Thinking he had not allowed enough time for Charles to finish feeding the cattle, he decided to complete his own chores and then drive over to the house.

His work took longer than he had intended as the fury of the storm mounted. It was some time later that he and Ray, who had stopped by to check on a sick cow, decided to drive over to the Winters' house. When they arrived, they found no one there. They went separate ways to check the barn and outbuildings before meeting again at the truck.

"I don't like it," Adrian said worriedly, shaking his head. "Charles knew Anna would have the baby soon. He would have been in a hurry to get the chores done. Do you suppose he came in and left for the hospital before we got here?"

"We could go on into town, I suppose," Ray said thoughtfully, "or better yet, if the door's unlocked, we could go in and call to see if he's there."

"Good idea," Adrian confirmed, "The door would be locked if he's gone into town."

But the back door opened easily, and they entered the quiet house. The answer from the hospital was negative. The nurse once again asked him to please get Mr. Winters to the hospital. The doctor was now expecting trouble with the delivery.

"No luck?" Ray asked, his eyes disturbed.

"No," Adrian's face was grave. "I think we had better do some more looking around. I wonder which way we should go." He stepped back outside and scanned the fields.

"What's that?" Ray pointed to the gate farthest from the house. "Something reddish and shining, probably something of Amy's."

"I think we'd better check it out," Adrian strained his eyes in that direction. Then his heart leaped within him.

"Bring the truck!" he shouted to Ray and began to run as fast as he could toward the odd-looking object.

"Hurry man," he yelled, as he glanced back over his shoulder and saw Ray staring after him in mystification.

"It's Stormy!" his voice broke and cracked.

Ray jumped into action, running toward the truck as if his very life depended on it. A million thoughts raced through Adrian's mind as he raced on foot toward the still figure on the ground. It had been a glimmer of her red hair against the snow that had drawn his attention, for she was heavily coated with snow. She lay like a broken angel in the snow, and he could not bear the thought of her precious body lying against the cold, hard ground.

He fell on his knees beside her and lifted her to his breast, crooning her name sobbingly, his heart breaking at the pallor of her soft skin and the faintness of her breathing.

"Stormy! Oh, my poor, sweet angel!" He unbuttoned the great overcoat he was wearing, slipped out of it, and wrapped her poor frozen body in it. He held her tightly to himself, waiting for Ray to bring the truck, and was rewarded by a slight moan from the still figure. He could have shouted for joy! She was alive! She would be all right — and unashamedly he wept, great tears falling freely to melt the snow at his knees.

Following the crimson trail of blood with his sharp eyesight, he easily read the direction from whence she came. Thank God the snow had not yet drifted to cover the trail! He lifted her into the cab of the truck and ran to open the gate, nearly tearing it off its frozen hinges. Then he ran back to the truck and lifted the girl back into his arms.

"I think maybe Charles is in the back field," he said, trying to rub more life into the girl's numb arms that hung limply at her sides.

Ray nodded and set off at a terrific speed, sharing his friend's anxiety about the older man. In a few minutes, they could see the stalled truck. Adrian gritted his teeth, shaking his head.

"Something's wrong!" he exclaimed. "Badly wrong!" He stretched the girl's body across the seat before he got out. He could see the bales of hay piled beside the truck, and he headed in their direction, yanking off the one on top as soon as he reached it.

"Oh, no," he cried in horror, "Oh, God, no!"

Ray appeared instantly at his side, and they ever so gently slipped the man out from under the truck. His head lolled lifelessly to one side. His body felt cold. With great love and tenderness, they carried him to the truck — very carefully in case his legs were broken.

"Can you ... tell how bad they are?" Adrian asked anxiously, his eyes darting to the girl and the man. Ray was a veterinarian, but he should have medical knowledge that could help some.

"No, I can't," came the terse reply. "I think Stormy's probably suffering from exposure and exhaustion, seeing how far she got, but I'm afraid Charles may be more seriously hurt. We need to lay him flat in the back and keep his legs straight. Can you ride with him? I'll drive and hold Stormy on the seat."

"But the main thing we have to do is pray, Ray! Pray God will keep them alive! Pray with everything that's within you! Only God can help them now."

Riding in the back with Charles, he placed his warm hands against the man's cold cheeks, and the bluish eyelids flickered. His stiff lips moved with obvious effort.

"Stormy?" There was no sound, only movement. Adrian was not sure the man could even see him.

"She's all right, Charles. She's all right." He repeated it several times, trying to reach the man's worried mind. Finally his eyes lighted with hope. He slowly nodded.

"Thank God!" he whispered and sank once more into unconsciousness, his head nodding slowly forward.

The night was terribly long for the rest of the little family. Barbara and the twins rotated from room to room, constantly checking on the three loved ones whose very lives hung in the balance. Ray was a strong shoulder for them to lean upon, and his presence gave Barbara the courage she needed.

Adrian never stirred from Stormy's side the long night through. He never slept and constantly prayed. His only source of hope was his knowledge of the promises of God. He used them, quoting them softly hour by hour to the girl who had won his heart. He stroked the hair he loved so much and touched her face with the lightest touch, unwilling to irritate its softness with the roughness of his big fingers. He caressed the long, slender fingers, often pressing the cold hands to his warm lips, his dark eyes eloquent with unshed tears.

All night long he kept watch, and none could shoo him away. The dawn erupted into spontaneous life, spraying his beloved's hair with fiery gold strands and kissing her softly with lips of warmth. At their touch, he was rewarded for his vigilance by seeing the soft, full lips tremble into a deep sigh. As her eyelids shot upwards, bewilderment flooded their rich, brown depths.

"It's all right, my love," he said, his heart soaring with thankfulness. Her head turned toward him, and her eyes filled with anxious questions.

"He's all right, Stormy Leigh." As he reached to touch her cheek, she caught his hand and pressed it against her face. His heart swelled within him, and he rose to sit on the bed, pulling her into his arms. His tears dampened her tousled curls.

"My little girl," he cried brokenly. "My precious angel, so brave and so wonderful. I love you! Oh, I love you!" He felt her body stiffen, and he settled her back against the pillow, looking at her apprehensively.

"What's wrong, Angel," he asked, feverishly searching her face.

"Even though I said I hated you?" she croaked, her voice hoarse and splintered.

"Yes," he said simply. "It makes no difference whether you love me or not. I love you, and I always will."

To her, it was rapture, pure and divine, for his eyes shone with truth and adoration. Her joy was immeasurable.

"Praise God!" she whispered, reaching for him. "I love you, too, Adrian McAllister."

"Will you marry me, Stormy Leigh?" he asked huskily, his eyes shining with hope, and she nodded.

"Yes," she whispered with a radiant smile, "with all my heart, yes!"

He would not let her talk long but lovingly insisted she sleep. The nurse slipped into the room and administered a sedative, which worked immediately. Her eyelids drooped, and as her grasp on his hand loosened, he slipped away to check up on the other members of his promised, new family.

He found Anna proud and beaming from ear to ear, plump little daughter resting drowsily in her possessive arms. Worry about her husband and oldest daughter had not made her delivery any easier, but at least the problem the doctor anticipated had not materialized. He shared the good news about Stormy with her, then squeezed the twins' shoulders as he left the room in teasing consolation.

But his delight was even greater when he asked to see his prospective father-in-law and found him wide awake and demanding to be wheeled in to see his newest offspring.

"Charles!" he exclaimed joyfully, eagerly clasping the warm hands offered to him, and seating himself beside the man's bed.

"You don't know how good it is to see you looking so well! How are your legs?" he asked frankly, and the older man smiled in wonder.

"It was a miracle, Adrian. A miracle! The doctor says he does not understand how it can be, but my legs were not broken, only badly bruised. It is a miracle."

"It is indeed," Adrian agreed gravely, "in more ways than one!"

"Have you seen Stormy Leigh?" the father asked urgently. "Is she all right?"

"She's just great!" Adrian exulted happily. "She needs a lot of rest. Time for cuts and bruises to heal, and time to get her strength back. But she looks great. It's another miracle that neither of you were badly frostbitten!"

"She saved my life, you know," Charles said soberly. "I'd have frozen to death before anyone found me, if she hadn't gone for help. I wish I knew what happened during the time I was unconscious."

"I know what happened, Charles," Adrian squeezed his hand, his eyes glowing with love. "She told me that she asked God to help her, and He did. She said she would never have left the safety of the truck, if she had not believed she could trust Him to take her home. She became so blinded by the wind and snow that she had to close her eyes. He led her safely home by the light and warmth of a single ray of sun. She gives Him all the credit, Charles."

"She's a great little girl," the father said huskily.

"She sure is," Adrian echoed. "But I'm afraid you're about to lose her."

He quieted the sudden look of alarm that arose in the other man's eyes with a happy laugh. "She's going to be mine, Charles. She promised to marry me!" He said the words slowly, as if relishing them and marveling at the fact, his happiness radiating toward the man who watched and smiling his benediction. "She loves me!"

A few days later, Stormy was up and moving slowly around, impatient to be out of the hospital gown and into something pretty for the man who came to see her every day. A knock on the door announced the entrance of her sister, who carried a dress box and a smile.

"Hi! How are you feeling?" she asked brightly.

"Impatient to see what the rest of the world is up to," Stormy retorted throatily.

"Well, this should cheer you up considerably," Barbara laughed, pulling a bright blue mound of material out of the box and laying it on the bed. "Compliments of Susan Miller's dress boutique!"

"Oh, Barbara! It's beautiful!" Stormy squeaked, pouncing upon it with glee, "but it must have cost a fortune!"

"No, not a fortune. Just one dress design," her sister said proudly, "I bought it to celebrate the signing of a contract."

"That's marvelous! Simply marvelous!" Stormy said, shaking her head in wonder, "A dream come true for you."

"Yes," Barbara held up the dress. "But come on. Let's see how it fits. Adrian will be here any minute," she added wickedly, spurring her sister into action. "I saw him down by Dad's room a while ago. Probably asking for your hand in marriage," she teased, watching the pale face pulse with new color.

"Why didn't you give in sooner?" she asked, helping Stormy dress. "We all knew you were perfect for each other. We could see that when you came home for Christmas last year." She laughed merrily, "You got so flustered every time you were around him and reacted so seriously to everything he did and said, and he couldn't keep his eyes off you."

"I guess we did go the long way around," Stormy chuckled ruefully, standing still so Barbara could zip up the back of the dress. "But they say half the fun is getting there. Only now I'm ready for a different, calmer type of fun … like that of old married folks. How do I look?" she asked anxiously, relying on her sister to act as a mirror.

"Gorgeous!" Barbara said. "Here, let me slip this in your hair." She slipped a blue comb into the mass of burnished curls, lifting them away from the unscratched cheek and letting them fall softly over the other one. "Very elegant, I'd say."

"I'm still not sure why Adrian chose me. Especially when he could have had someone as beautiful as Vivian Langley," Stormy meditated.

"Because Vivian can't light a candle next to you. Why you've got more class, more beauty, more brains…."

"And you've just lost *your* brains, if you expect me to believe all of that!" she snorted in a very undignified manner.

"Well, it's true," her sister insisted. "Just ask Adrian."

"Ask me what?" Adrian's black, curly head appeared around the edge of the door. He whistled admiringly at the tall, slender girl who eyed him a mite uncertainly. "That dress is fantastic! What say we go get married right now?"

"And mess up a childhood dream of having a double wedding?" Barbara cried in mock fear, pretending to hold Stormy back. "No way."

"Well …," he acted extremely disappointed. "Perhaps you would care to be escorted to your mother's room. Your father and Amy are there, and our presence is desired also."

He gallantly offered his arm, and Stormy moved readily toward him, loving his dancing eyes and the way he slipped his arm protectively around her waist.

"Do you suppose they wish to give me their blessing or run me off?" he asked anxiously of his bride-to-be.

"I haven't the slightest idea," she shrugged her shoulders. "Guess we'll just have to wait and see."

"I can see you're going to be a very encouraging wife," he mused dryly, loving the pert sparkle in her mellow eyes.

"The best," she answered sweetly, and he had to stop and steal a kiss from the tempting lips that were for him only.

Their arrival created a great flurry of hugs and kisses, their happy chatter filling the room until a nurse knocked on the door. Smiling like a mother herself, she entered, carrying a precious bundle in her arms. Carefully, she placed it in its mother's arms and left the room.

"Stormy," Anna smiled lovingly at her oldest daughter, "your father and I would like for you to have the privilege of naming our little girl, because," she lifted the blanket away from the tiny face, "she looks so much like you."

"Oh! She's beautiful!" Stormy breathed ecstatically. And she was — fair flawless skin, plump rosy cheeks, and a thick, curly thatch of red curls. "Could I hold her?" she asked, and immediately found herself in possession of the baby.

Her mind was made up the instant she touched the baby, and the baby's eyes opened to look into hers. A tiny mouth puckered into a huge yawn and tiny fingers curled trustingly around Adrian's big finger as he touched her hand.

"Elizabeth," she said softly. "Elizabeth Ann. The name I loved and wanted for years, until you," she smiled into the eyes of her husband-to-be, "made me love my own name more. 'Elizabeth Ann,' if it's all right with you, Mother."

Her parents nodded, smilingly. "Somehow we thought you'd choose that name," her father said. "It was our choice, too. Elizabeth Ann Winters it shall be."

29
A Double Wedding

One week before Christmas, on a bright Saturday afternoon with the world glistening in a fresh overnight coat of new snow, something of tremendous importance took place in the old Westmoor Heights manor.

Two lovely young ladies in satin and lace were the center of attention. Their father waited to kiss his daughters a last goodbye before giving them away. Their mother was busy giving last minute instructions to fluttering bridesmaids. And a very excited, very pretty little flower girl kept insisting she needed practice throwing her rose petals.

One young woman was tall and slender. Her long, satin gown flowed graciously behind her as she moved about in the small circle allotted her. Her gorgeous red hair, lifted high and cascading down her back, was adorned with flowers and pearls. A misty veil fell from her tall headdress, draping her face in mystery and solitude. In her white gloved hands, she carried a white Bible and a single, long-stemmed red rose.

The other young lady, much more talkative, was fitted in frothy layers of lace that started at a fitted bodice and fell in layers to her tiny satin shoes. Her golden hair fell silkily around her shoulders, and her veil was lifted so that she could converse with her mother. In her arms, she carried a small sheaf of mixed flowers, their colors vivid and beautiful.

They could hear the arrival of the guests downstairs and knew the ceremony would soon start. There had been too many guests invited to allow the ceremony to take place in the small church, so another of Stormy's childhood dreams had materialized, for she had often visualized herself stepping down the broad sweep of the curved front stairs dressed as she was today.

A flash of light, reflecting from her ring as she moved her hand, caught her eyes. She smiled, remembering how Adrian had said Vivian certainly *had not* helped him pick out a ring. She had dragged him into the local jeweler's on a pretext of advising her on a purchase. He had bought Stormy's ring in Kingston on the business trip he made before buying the farm. He had felt sorry for Vivian and tried to help her adjust to widowhood. But most of their encounters had been initiated by Vivian. Stormy had seen how insinuations and suggestions interwoven with imagination had made that which was not seem as though it were where Vivian was concerned.

Stormy's ring was stunning — a huge oval sapphire encircled with many beautiful, full-cut diamonds.

"A ring fit for an angel," Adrian had declared as he placed it on her finger. "The best I could find for my angel."

A knock sounded on the door and brought an immediate hush of expectancy. Amy began to snatch up the few petals she had dropped. A young man entered the door, attractive in a dark blue suit with a matching ruffled shirt. And an identical young man followed him, resplendent in a dark, burgundy suit with a matching pink ruffled shirt. Both tugged uncomfortably at their ties.

Keith bowed low before them with dancing eyes.

"We, the two lowly brothers, most mournfully now outnumbered in our family," he sent a saucy look toward his mother, "bear gifts for the beautiful brides from the waiting grooms."

He offered his token to Stormy, and Kyle gave his to Barbara. Then with youthful snickers, they bowed their way out of the room to return downstairs and take their places by the sides of their heroes.

"Ooooh!" Barbara exclaimed and everyone rushed to crowd around her and admire the sparkling gems that lay in white velvet. "It matches my ring!" she said, her eyes marveling at the exquisite necklace of rubies and diamonds. "Isn't it fantastic? Ray must've been saving his money for this since he began practicing as a vet!"

They lifted her hair, so she could clasp it around her slender neck and stood back to admire its perfection as it nestled amidst the pureness of white lace.

But Stormy was staring at the small white card she had pulled from the long, legal-looking envelope, its bold, black lettering sprawled across the whiteness in a manly fashion.

"Dearest Angel,

"I thought long and hard about what to give you as a token of my love on our wedding day, and many things came to mind ... things that I felt would give you great pleasure, and many things which I shall give you later. But I wanted to give you something very special today. I could think of only one thing that would do. I had planned to give it to you later when I could have the joy of watching your lovely face and share your delight as you give it away. I shall miss that now. But I can see your sweet face in my mind. I wait for you lovingly and impatiently.

"Forever yours, Adrian"

"What could he give me that I could possibly want to give away?" she mused curiously, her long fingers once again delving into the white envelope. She laid the envelope atop her Bible which she had placed on a small, glass-topped table, and unfolded the long document she had withdrawn from it.

Her eyes widened as she recognized what it was, and her heart leaped with joy.

"Oh, my!" she exclaimed. "Oh, my!"

The name on the old deed had never been changed. The change of ownership had never been recorded at the courthouse. The man who waited eagerly for her downstairs had never intended the land to change ownership. He had always meant for her family to have it forever. She could see it so clearly now. Her heart was momentarily filled with a great sadness that she had ever doubted his love for her family.

She clasped the paper to her breast in sheer happiness. And as she did so, her eyes fell upon the white Bible that had become so infinitely precious to her since she had personally met its Author and learned that in Him rested all her happiness and hope.

In a flash, she recognized that what Adrian had done for her family, Jesus had done for her. He had loved her in spite of her rejection, and loved her when she carelessly turned her back on him during the years she had lived in Kingston and sought after other things. He had been there all the time, patiently waiting and longing for her to return to Him.

Yet it had been her sins and sorrows He had borne upon His precious back when He went to Calvary, taking upon Himself the weight of her debt to God that she might go free. He had made it possible for her to lay down at His feet all her worries and problems and walk away with a joyful heart, a peaceful mind, and a brand-new beginning. He had taken away her old desires that had caused her to stumble and presented her heart back to her, fresh and debt-free.

Her heart soared with love for her Redeemer and a solitary tear escaped her blurred eyes to splash unheeded upon her satin gown. A tear of joy and wonder that He could love her and care about her so much after she had neglected Him for so long. Oh, it felt so good to be back home, forgiven and blessed, free to forever enjoy His blessings with the wonderful man He had given her.

She looked again at the deed in her hands, her heart rejoicing at the love of a man who had made it possible for her to present to her parents the best possible symbol of their love. Excitement coursed through her as she visualized their faces when she handed it to them, and her face was lit with the light of unspeakable joy.

"Mother, Daddy! Come and see!" she cried, her voice ringing clear and joyful.

Heads turned toward her, and more than one person gasped at her magnificent beauty as the sun crowned her head with a shimmering, fiery halo, and her eyes blazed with glory.

"Everyone! Come see what God and Adrian have given to me!"

30
Living Happily Ever After

Early Christmas morning, Stormy awoke to feelings of wonder and excitement, remembering many happy Christmases and knowing this one would be the best yet.

She turned to awaken her husband and found herself alone in the huge canopied bed. Gazing through the misty drapes that secluded it in intimate privacy, she saw Adrian standing by the window. She slipped out of bed and padded softly over to him, wrapping her arms lovingly around his waist.

"Merry Christmas, Darling," she whispered huskily.

"Merry Christmas, Angel," he drew her in front of him and wrapped his arms around her, resting his chin lightly on the top of her head.

"Oh, it snowed again last night!" she exclaimed with childish delight.

"It looks like about six more inches. It's beautiful, isn't it?"

"Yes, it is."

A full white moon shone brightly on the crisp new snow and painted a picture of Christmas-card beauty for the lovers to behold. They could see the little Winters' farm nestled snugly in the hollow with its big weather-beaten house waiting quietly and patiently for the sounds of love and laughter that would soon fill it.

"I wonder if Amy's awake yet," Stormy laughed merrily.

"If she is, we'll soon see lights on all over the house. She thinks she has to be the first one up on Christmas morning. I think she stays awake most of the night just so she will be. But she looked so sweet when she woke me up last year, just like an excited little angel in her white flannel gown, and her long, dark hair streaming down her back.

"I stood here last year, too," her husband confided, "waiting impatiently for the first sign of life in that house. I was so eager to get another glimpse of you that I could scarcely keep from rushing right over when I saw the first light come on."

"You did?" Stormy tilted her face up to him, receiving a kiss that caused an excitement far greater than Christmas to course through her veins. She pulled him down onto the broad, padded windowseat and curled up beside him where she could watch his handsome face in the moonlight.

"I used to stare out my window every night and dream about this place," she mused looking about her in wonder. "And I can still hardly believe my dreams have come true. Oh, Adrian!" impulsively, she reached for his big hand and clasped it to her heart.

"God has been so good to me! I could just cry when I think of how He must care about the dreams of children! He knew how much I loved this grand old place, and He knew all about you, the man of my dreams. The man who found all the little pictures I left and read all the little love letters I had written him. I'm so glad God opened my eyes and helped me to see that I was going in the wrong direction, because there's no place I'd rather be than right where I am this morning."

She smiled dreamily, "I opened my eyes a while ago and realized that another little dream had come true. I've always dearly loved Christmas, and I've always imagined how wonderful it would be to decorate this house for Christmas."

She turned loving eyes upon her husband. "It was sweet of you to give Amy all the decorations you used last year and let me have the pleasure of choosing new ones. Amy was speechless with joy, and I know just how she felt, because I felt like a little girl too when we went and bought all those lovely new decorations."

"And you looked like a little girl," Adrian chuckled, "with your pretty eyes all starry and your cheeks rosy with excitement. I enjoyed watching you more than I enjoyed the shopping."

Stormy gazed at the farmhouse below them in the valley. "You always have treated my family as though they were your own, and I love you for it."

"I suppose I adopted them," he said thoughtfully. "I was raised in an orphanage and placed in several foster homes while growing up — until the age of sixteen, when I ran away and tried to make it on my own. None of the people I lived with loved or wanted me," his beautiful, dark eyes filled with remembered pain, and Stormy caught her breath.

"I never knew that!" she cried, her heart and hands reaching for him.

"I never told anyone," he said huskily. "It was a very painful period in my life that I don't dwell on. Nevertheless," his eyes cleared as he chased the memories away, "I always wanted a family of my own, people that I could love, and who would love me in return. Constantly, I would think about all the nice things I would do for my family. Perhaps it was God's way of helping me survive without becoming too hard or embittered until I could find Him and learn of His great love for me. I had a lot of love in my heart to give away. I simply had to find someone to give it to who would not reject it. The people I found were your family."

Tears filled her great, brown eyes, and one escaped to trickle down her cheek. "I'm so sorry for the terrible way I treated you, and all the mean things I said and thought about you! Please forgive me."

He cupped her face in his big, rough hands and kissed the tear away.

"Don't cry, my little angel. You are the one who made my life complete. I just look forward to all the wonderful things ahead of us and marvel that you love me."

He was silent for a minute, then asked shyly, "Would you like to know why I call you my angel?"

"Yes, I would," she said eagerly, sensing an interesting story.

"When I was a little boy, probably about five years old, I lived with some people who had a son of their own who was twelve years old. His name was Willis. He was good to me when his parents were around, but when he caught me by myself, he would always think of something mean to do to me."

"How awful!" she exclaimed, enraged that someone should have mistreated her beloved when he was a little boy. And what a beautiful child he must have been, she thought, studying his dear face. He would have been a child with soft, silky curls the color of ebony and deep, lustrous blue eyes set in a dark, serious little face. "Didn't you ever tell them?"

"No. They wouldn't have believed me. They thought the sun rose and set in their son and often accused me of lying."

Seeing her rising indignation, he smiled and patted her hand reassuringly, "It's all right, Angel. It all happened a long time ago."

"Anyway, there was a very nice lady next door who sometimes gave me a cookie or a bit of pocket change, and she gave me a little Christmas angel a few days before Christmas. It was the most beautiful thing I had ever seen or owned. She was dressed in a long white dress and had little wispy wings as fine as silk on her back, tiny silver slippers on her feet, and a silver halo on her head.

"But instead of the usual golden hair, she had beautiful, flaming red hair. I realize now that the color was rather unusual, but I thought nothing of it at the time. I only knew she was mine, and I loved her. I took her to my room and hid her in a shoe box that had clean white tissue paper in it. Every morning and evening I would take her out and sit and look at her. I didn't dare let Willis see her, but he found her anyway.

"When I went to get her on Christmas Eve, she was gone. I searched everywhere I could think of, but I couldn't find her. I begged him to tell me what he'd done with her, but he only laughed. He said she was ugly and had funny red hair, so he had gotten rid of her."

Stormy's heart began to break for the little boy, and a hot tear splashed on the hand she lifted silently to her lips, a large, calloused hand that had once known the childish agony of loss.

"She had become my reason for living," he said, his voice cracking at the memory.

"I thought I could take anything life had to dish out as long as I could go to my room and look at her. I cried myself to sleep that night, but it was the last time I cried for many years — until God in His mercy once again softened my heart. My foster parents gave me no presents Christmas morning, saying I had been a bad boy and didn't deserve anything.

"So, rather than sit and watch Willis play with his toys, I went outside to play in the snow. And there I found my angel. She was all broken and twisted and covered with snow, and I wouldn't have found her had it not been for her hair that shone like fire against the snow," he choked in remembrance and drew Stormy into his arms, holding her tightly against his heart.

"And that's how I found you the day of the terrible snow storm. I couldn't keep from crying when I picked you up in my arms. It was as if I had once again lost the one precious thing that I treasured above all. Oh, how I thanked God when you began to move, and I knew that He had kept you alive by His great power. I had waited so many years for the woman of my childhood dreams, and when I saw you the very first time, standing knee deep in snow with your red hair gleaming in the sunshine, I knew down deep that you were the one."

"Many a night since then I have stood at this window, hoping and praying that some day you would love me too. I was devastated when you came back from Kingston with an engagement ring on your finger. I could barely stand the thought that my angel belonged to another, and I rejoiced when you walked away from him. I knew, then, that if necessary, I would spend the rest of my life proving to you how much I loved you."

"Oh, Adrian! I *love* you!" She could say no more, but her kiss told it all.

"My beautiful, beautiful Christmas Angel," he said softly, with great reverence. "How I adore you!"

And as they sat marveling at the sweet, wonderful love God had blessed them with, a window in the Winters' house suddenly blazed with golden light. They looked at each other and smiled. Another precious little angel had awakened to excitedly greet the dawning of the birthday of the Savior.

Scripture quotations are taken from the *King James Version*.

Sharon Foster grew up on a farm in southern Missouri. Born into a Christian family, she accepted Jesus as her personal Savior at a very early age.

She met her husband when she was sixteen. She says, "God brought a very special person into my life at that time, a young man named Steve, who was destined to become my best friend as well as my husband. We were married in September, 1974. We make our home in the country, and the distinctive beauty of the Ozarks has been a source of joy to us all our lives."

Mrs. Foster recently resigned from her position as loan teller at a local bank where she had been employed for the previous fourteen years. She plans now to spend most of her time writing and working with her husband.

Concerning the writing of *Stormy*, which is her first published book, she says:

"In July of 1984, the Holy Spirit led me to pick up a pen and begin writing. I was amazed and delighted to find that His inspiration blessed and thrilled me, giving me a lovely feeling of fulfillment in the work to which He had called me. About that time, I asked Him to be my agent, to go before me and open the right doors. In return, He gave me a promise that has proven to be a blessing and a reality. That promise is found in Psalms 37:4,5.

"I am so glad God is willing to use ordinary people to reach others with the extraordinary Gospel of Jesus Christ. May the gift He has entrusted to me inspire and motivate others to walk the exciting and rewarding walk of faith."

Additional copies of
Stormy Leigh
are available from your local bookstore, or from:

Virtue Books
P.O. Box 35035
Tulsa, Oklahoma 74153

To contact Sharon Foster,
write:

Sharon Foster
Route 2, Box 363
West Plains, Missouri 65775